THE
Remember Box

✻

Books by Patricia Sprinkle

Fiction

The MacLaren Yarbrough series
When Did We Lose Harriet?
But Why Shoot the Magistrate?

Nonfiction

Women Who Do Too Much
Children Who Do Too Little

T H E

Remember Box

PATRICIA
SPRINKLE

ZondervanPublishingHouse

Grand Rapids, Michigan

A Division of HarperCollinsPublishers

Acknowledgments

Any book of this size and scope owes a debt to many people. Clary Holt, attorney, pointed me in the right direction in matters of North Carolina law in the middle part of the twentieth century. Betty Carr and Betty Pulkingham steered me to Clary. The North Carolina Division of Archives and History and the Statesville Public Library provided invaluable assistance with the background information I needed about this particular year. Chester (Bud) and Maxine Middlesworth provided a bed, good conversation, and years of encouragement from the time this book was first conceived. Dorothy Cowling, Lois Graessle, Priscilla Apodaca, and my dad, Sam Houck, read and sometimes reread various drafts, making excellent suggestions for revisions, and my mother Eddis improved the stories. Hali Earwood, 14, drew Carley's map for the front of the book to help keep readers straight and Ann Bass read the final page proofs.

I greatly appreciate my editor, Dave Lambert, who never lets me get away with telling instead of showing and who worked very hard to help me shape this story into a book, and his associate Lori VandenBosch, who polished the final product.

Most of all, thanks to Aunt Miriam and Uncle Jim, for providing the inspiration, and to Bob, my faithful Patron of the Arts, who cooked, did laundry, put up with a rocky move, and humorously kept my nose to the grindstone for years until I was done. If he'd had his way, I'd have called this book War and Peace in North Carolina.

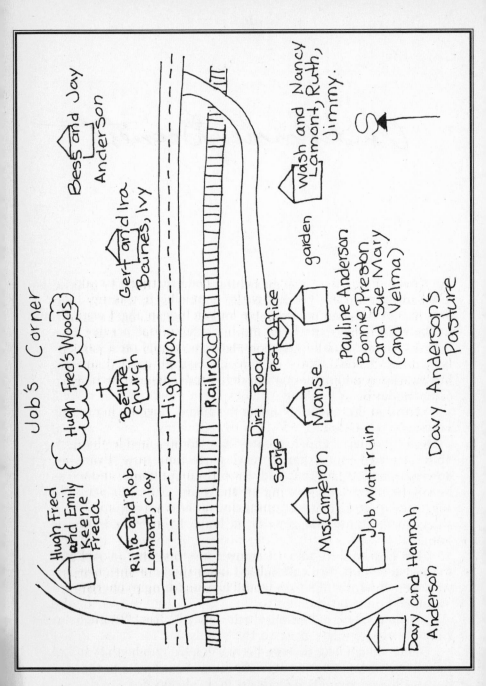

Carley's Map of Job's Corner

Unwelcome Bequest

Maybe it was the sunlight behind her, creating a twinkling aureole around her red curls, or maybe it was my own delight, but Abby on my doorstep looked like an angel visitant. I hadn't seen her since her mother's memorial service two months before, and I'd just completed revisions on a particularly difficult book. With my sons grown and married and my husband away on business, I was delighted to have somebody to celebrate with.

"To what do I owe this honor?" I asked, hugging her. "Can you stay a few days?"

She set down a small tapestry suitcase just inside the hall. "No, just tonight. I have to leave early tomorrow. I've been down helping Daddy move into the retirement home, and when he and John left this morning for an Alaska cruise, he *strongly* suggested that I run something by on my way home." We shared a grin. My house is a six-hour detour "on her way home."

"I'm glad to have you," I assured her, meaning it. Abby is more sister than cousin. Besides, I felt a tingle of anticipation. Any memento of Aunt Kate would be something to cherish.

Or so I thought, then.

I looked pointedly at the little tapestry bag. "It must be small. Jewelry, perhaps?"

Abby's laugh has always been a happy gurgle that is far more imp than angel. "You greedy thing! Your box is in the car. But you'll have to help me carry it in. It's heavy."

Together we wrestled a large cardboard box out of her trunk

and carried it in awkward tandem through the front door. "Do you know what this is?" I asked.

"Yes . . ." For an instant her gray eyes lost their light, looked puzzled and hurt—an expression so like Mama's that my breath stopped. It has never seemed fair to me that Abby should look more like Mama than I do.

"Do you want it?" I offered, concerned. "After all, she was your mother . . ."

"No." She spoke quickly, as if convincing herself, but I couldn't miss her wistfulness. "He specifically wants you to have it." Was it her mother's possession, or her father's giving it away, that she regretted? I couldn't tell. She added, "Daddy says you have to read Isaiah thirty-eight before you open it."

We left the box in the middle of the front hall, and I fetched my Bible. Abby perched on the edge of the couch, shuffled off her shoes, and confessed, "I already looked it up, but it makes no sense. It's about King Hezekiah begging God for fifteen more years. Do you think Daddy's asking God for fifteen more years? He'd live to be nearly a hundred."

I quickly scanned the chapter (in case Uncle Stephen ever asked if I read it), then set down the Bible. "I don't know. Let's see what he sent."

"I know what he sent." Again her voice was small and puzzled.

"Don't tell me," I warned as I went for a knife. Kneeling, I carefully sliced all four corners of the carton. Cardboard fell like rose petals to reveal its heart: an old rowan-wood box two feet long, one foot deep, and eighteen inches high.

"The Remember Box!" I stroked the satin wood in delight and confusion. Why should Uncle Stephen send it to *me*? No wonder Abby was hurt. The box was not only one of Aunt Kate's favorite possessions, it is possibly the oldest thing in the family.

Gently I traced thistles carved on the top and front. "I remember when she got this. A woman in West Virginia brought it by the house the day we moved. She said her great-great-great-grandmother brought it from Scotland, and since she and her husband had no children, she wanted Aunt Kate and Uncle Stephen to have it to remember them by." My voice wobbled. As much as I wanted the box, I knew Abby should have it, to pass on to little Katie.

"Its lock is missing," Abby said carelessly, as if she didn't care. "John tied it shut."

I managed a smile. "I knew it wasn't Uncle Stephen. He'd have nailed it down."

"If he hadn't been a preacher, he'd have been a carpenter." It was a favorite family joke. As we laughed together, the small wound between us healed. She came to kneel with me, and I felt like we were four and eleven, about to say bedtime prayers.

She must have felt the same, for she urged with childish eagerness, using her old pet name, "Let's see what's inside, Carley cousin."

The Remember Box was Aunt Kate's private place, the one we were sternly forbidden to open. I never did but once, when I shoved something down inside. From the way Abby now avoided my eyes, though, I suspected she had occasionally peeked.

In a ray of sunlight streaming through the front door panels, golden dust motes swirled around us like little lost worlds. Suddenly I was reluctant, even fearful—a modern Pandora, about to let out our own lost world. Whether Uncle Stephen was asking God for fifteen more years or not, that box held one year I'd spent a lifetime trying to forget.

Abby sneezed. "Pshew! You need to dust. Are you going to open the box?"

Slowly I raised the lid.

Abby pounced on a small red book. "Your old diary!"

"*My* diary," I reminded her firmly, grabbing it and putting it behind my back.

"Come on, Carley. What did you write about? When you were at school, I used to get the key from your mattress and try to read it, but—"

"You didn't!" My indignation surprised even me.

Abby stuck out her tongue. "Did so. But I couldn't read cursive. Look! Here's an old Nancy Drew that's practically falling apart. And my first shoes!" She held up white high-tops.

"Those were John's. See the red mud stains? Yours would have been gray with coal dust. Now here is a treasure." I read a penciled letter aloud: *Dear Big Mama. Thank you for my Easter dress but I got chicken pox. I love it. Your fiend, Abby.* "Did you love the dress or the chicken pox, fiend Abby? At least you got that part right."

She swatted me lightly. "I loved that dress! Big Mama sent gloves with it—my first."

"Here they are." Mere wisps of yellowed organdy, but Aunt Kate saved everything.

Abby perched the gloves fondly on two fingers. "Were we ever really that small?"

"You were. I wasn't—not by the time Aunt Kate got this box." I was rifling through a stack of photographs. "Bethel Church, Job's Corner manse, and—oh, look! Mrs. Cameron's store! It looks even smaller and more decrepit than I remember it."

Abby peered over my shoulder. "I don't remember that at all."

"That's why your daddy took the picture." I showed her the back, where Uncle Stephen had scrawled, *Taken the day it was bulldozed, April 1951, to prove it once existed.*

She studied a snapshot of two tall people on their front steps. The tall, stout woman was caught midsentence, as usual. "Aunt Hannah and Uncle Davy never changed, did they?"

Only two months removed from losing her mother, she didn't need to be grieving Aunt Hannah and Uncle Davy again, as well. "Look at this!" I held out a snapshot of children sitting on steps. Two were kissing. The third, with cropped red curls, was visibly annoyed.

Abby tried to snatch it, but I held it. "Throw that one away," she ordered.

"Not on your life. I'll enlarge it and frame it for your den."

She was already lifting out other small pieces of our lives: a letter of call to Uncle Stephen from Bethel Church, Aunt Kate's North Carolina teaching certificate, and letters. Burrowing near the bottom of the box, under Abby's favorite pink sunsuit and some of John's infant clothes, I found three small items. As I lifted them out, each started a small earthquake of memories that threatened to bury me.

An ugly beaded coin purse—"ugly as sin," Abby dubbed it. I had to agree. She just didn't know how ugly that particular sin had been.

A small granite rock shaped like a heart, that made my own turn over.

A molting green rabbit's foot key chain. Abby chortled when I unearthed it. "I bought Daddy that for Christmas with my very own money!"

I remembered a dark and rainy night when it nearly cost my life.

"Oh!" Abby gave a short grunt of pain. She held a handful of clippings from a manila envelope, her eyes shocked. "Did you know about this?"

"Of course. It was one of the primary things that happened that dreadful spring."

Abby, climbing to her feet, paused midway up. "What dreadful spring?"

"Our first one in Job's Corner—remember? The one you had chicken pox."

She was bending to stretch out her joints, so her voice was muffled as she objected, "Everybody gets chicken pox. That's not dreadful. And we *loved* Job's Corner. It was a perfect place to raise children, with Sue Mary, Aunt Hannah, Grace . . ."

"Miss Pauline, Miss Nancy—"

She stood erect and put both hands on her hips, like she used to do at four when she demanded "Why?" This time she demanded, "Why do you say their names like that? And whatever was the matter between Mama and Miss Pauline? They didn't like each other the whole time we lived there, did they? Yet Miss Pauline was such a jolly, friendly woman, I don't see how anybody could help liking her. Remember how she used to leave food on a plate beside her back door in case we children got hungry? And she taught me to draw rabbits and cats. But even the last week of Mama's life, when I said one of her nurses had hair as bushy as Miss Pauline's, Mama's lips tightened up. I wonder why they never got along?"

It takes a lot to make me speechless, but Abby succeeded. Could a child grow up utterly ignorant about forces so powerful they changed her family forever? I fumbled in the very bottom of the box to find what I knew must be there, because Aunt Kate saved everything. I handed her a second manila envelope of clippings without a word.

Abby spread both sets of clippings around her. Jay Anderson's face and her father's stared up from the floor. She read the headlines, bewildered. "Murder? Church trial? It can't be! Job's Corner was such a *nice* place to live." She pushed the clippings away in distaste, waiting for me to reassure her.

"It was at first," I agreed. But those clippings had drenched me in a wave of anger and resentment as fresh as it was years ago. And under those two envelopes I'd found a third—a blue one—holding clippings from the year I was born. I hadn't seen them since Big Mama spread them out on her quilt, and their headlines still had the power to chill my soul. I tucked them under me before Abby noticed.

"It was a *nice* place," she repeated stubbornly. Then, as if determined I should not have time to disagree, she scanned a fresh-looking sheet of paper that had slipped to the back of the box. "Oh. This is from Daddy to you."

> *Carley,*
> *Leaving next week for Alaska with John. Moving into Knox Retirement Home tomorrow. Sending Kate's old Remember Box to you via Abby. Before you open it, read Isaiah 30:8. Then do what it says—for all our sakes.*
>
> *Much love, Uncle Stephen*

I climbed stiffly to my feet. "It was Isaiah thirty-colon-eight, not Isaiah thirty-eight."

Abby beat me to the Bible. She found the verse and intoned in a voice very like her father's when he was young and strong. How that man loved to read Scripture aloud!

"Go, now, write it before them on a tablet and inscribe it in a book,

so that it may be for the time to come as a witness forever."

She set down the Bible, puzzled again. "What do you think he means?"

I sank to the couch and stared unhappily at the jumble on my hall floor. "I think he means I'm to finally tell the story of Job's Corner."

I reached out to close the box, but spotted something deep in one corner, carefully wrapped in tissue paper. A small doll with a hand-carved head.

"Maggie!" Abby snatched it and cradled the small brown head to her chest. "Oh, I do remember Maggie!"

I stood. "Do you realize how late it has gotten? Let's go find a very special dinner. Then first thing tomorrow, after you leave, I'll begin on this. But it may take a while to sort it out. There's so much to tell . . ."

Abby was exhausted from helping her daddy move. As soon as we got home from dinner she went upstairs, bearing Maggie with her. I stayed downstairs and spent over an hour culling everything in the Remember Box from our first year in Job's Corner. I arranged the artifacts around me on the floor like a sacred circle. I remembered another sacred circle, one I made against the dark.

As I looked at the new circle, I breathed a silent prayer that this one would let in light.

I, like Aunt Kate, had carried bitterness too long.

❀

Restless, I knew I wouldn't sleep. Finally I bore five items to my desk and began to type. When Abby padded down in search of coffee, the sky was turning pink and I was making my third pot. "Why did you leave all those things spread out in the front hall?" she asked sleepily. "Do you want me to repack them?"

"No! I don't want them touched or moved an inch until I'm through. I've got them in order. I'll just step over them."

"Writers are weird." She swallowed a yawn. "What's all this around my place mat?" I had arranged a rainbow for her of the items I'd chosen the night before. She picked up a letter with a puzzled frown. "Who was Raifa? Her spelling is atrocious."

I handed her a steaming mug. "I once said the exact same thing. Your daddy asked, 'If you'd had to quit school in third grade to look after little brothers and sisters so your mama could work, could you spell?' But I'm surprised you don't remember Raifa. Not at all?"

Abby shook curls that gleamed as soft as an old penny in the morning sun.

"So much for the permanent effects of unpleasant early childhood experiences." I poured myself some more coffee and joined her. Beyond the window, our yard was a fairyland of dogwoods and redbuds, but after writing all night I felt disoriented in time and space. The present and my own yard seemed far less real than North Carolina in 1949.

Abby picked up a small red shovel. "I sure remember this. How many hours do you reckon Sue Mary and I spent in her sandbox?"

"Thousands, at least. You, Sue Mary, and Velma."

"Oh, Velma! How could I have forgotten Velma?"

"How could you indeed?"

"But I got to thinking about Job's Corner before I went to sleep, and I think I remember the old store. Was it always dim and mysterious, and did it smell wonderful?"

"Sometimes it smelled wonderful. On cold, rainy days it smelled like the mud beneath the cracks in its floorboards."

Abby got up and made us each a piece of toast. As she rummaged for jelly and butter, she said, "I don't remember any Baineses, though. Wasn't he the one who got murdered?"

"Eventually. He was the kind of man most people wanted to throttle." I gave her a suspicious look. "You don't remember Miz Baines—and what you did to her?"

She turned in surprise, handing me a paper napkin in lieu of a plate—like her dad, she's apt to take charge in my kitchen. "Why do you look like that when you say her name?"

I turned away, pretending to look out the window. "Like what?"

Abby didn't answer.

"She was part of—what happened. You really don't remember her? White hair screwed up in a bun? Chin that almost met her nose? Glasses that made her eyes enormous?" Just thinking of the Baines family made my stomach lurch.

Abby slid into her chair and cupped her chin in one hand to think. "Maybe I remember her a little, but it's vague. Did she keep John and me for a while?"

"For a while, until you got her fired." I sipped coffee to settle my butterflies.

"How could I get her fired? I was only four years old. But I didn't like her. I think I remember that much." She narrowed her eyes, then shook her head. "There is something else, but I don't know what it is." She bent her head and asked a blessing, then gave me a confident nod. "Write it all down, Carley cousin. The world needs to know."

Part 1

As It Was in the Beginning...

On my desk I arrange a rainbow of memories: a penciled letter,
a moving receipt, a small red shovel, the snapshot of Aunt
Hannah and Uncle Davy and the one of old Mrs. Cameron's store.
These were all part of our introduction to Job's Corner, but when
I sit down to write, my first memory is of Preston...

Chapter 1

I clearly remember the hot summer minute when I decided if the alternative was to forgive Preston Scott Anderson, I'd rather go to hell.

Still, I followed that thought with an anxious glance toward Uncle Stephen's open upstairs window. Was he still typing? He'd been too engrossed in the next day's sermon to stop Preston and me from fighting, but sometimes he seemed to know my very thoughts.

It was a beautiful afternoon, the kind with puffy white clouds, dark blue sky, robins chirping in a tree, and Abby clearly audible through the open bathroom window, telling a story to her rubber turtle in an after-nap bath. Much too lovely a day for the feelings roiling inside me. My stomach ached so bad, I was afraid I'd give Preston the pleasure of watching me throw up all over the soft cool grass.

"Go home!" I commanded, feet apart and a fist on each hip.

Preston still hadn't had that growth spurt he'd been promising all year, so at almost eleven he was still shorter than I at almost twelve. Under the blooming pear tree he was pale and sweating, rusty freckles standing out on his face like dried hen dookey on a very white egg.

Dookey was a new word I'd picked up from Ruth Lamont, and it seemed exactly right for Preston. I could imagine him standing under his Uncle Davy's hen roost while Biddy, the meanest of Miss Hannah's hens, dripped on his face.

Nothing a hen could drip, though, was as nasty as what was coming out of Preston's wet pink mouth. "Just you wait, Carley

Marshall! Your Uncle Stephen's a Commie and a nigger lover. He'd have lied like a rug to get Jay off—"

Hot blood rushed to my head. "Jay didn't kill anybody, and you know it. And Uncle Stephen would never have lied. But he'll whip you good if he hears you calling Jay that. Now get off our property!"

"Ain't your propity, it's church propity," Preston reminded me with odious superiority, "and you don't know anything, smarty pants. If you knew everything there is to know—what old Stevie boy's really been doin'?—well, all I gotta say is, when we get through with him, he'll be lucky if he don't get tarred, feathered, and run out of town. Just you wait!"

I wasn't smart enough to know he was just quoting his elders.

I rushed him, fists flailing the air. "Don't you call him Stevie!" One punch grazed his round soft jaw. "You call him Mister Whitfield!" A second brushed his right ear. "And if you don't get out of this yard this minute, I'll kill you!" My third punch hit solid, burying my arm almost to the elbow in Preston's pillowy midriff. He reeled and fell with a satisfactory "Oof!"

I straddled him, still punching. Nothing had felt so good in a long time.

"Carley!"

I jerked my head upward. Uncle Stephen stood framed at the screen, cradling his pipe in one hand and shoving back his hair with the other. "Time for your piano practice," he said mildly. "Go on home, Preston, and do your arithmetic exercises. If you need help, come over later. Okay?" He turned and disappeared into the darkness beyond the screen.

I glared at Preston. He glared back, his blue eyes like hard little marbles. "You don't know what I know, Carley," he rasped. "It's big as God! And people're gonna do everything they can to make sure your precious Uncle Stephen gets 'zactly what he deserves." He limped toward the road and his own house next door. His limp was always worse when he knew somebody was watching.

"You're fat and ugly and your mama dresses you funny!" I yelled after him. But I yelled softly. I didn't want Uncle Stephen wasting a perfectly good suppertime talking about turning the other cheek.

That afternoon I abandoned my new sonata, dug out an old

book I'd finished years before, and found "The Happy Farmer," which I could bang out fast without thinking. "I'll never forgive him," I vowed again, pounding away at the chords. "Never! If I have to go to hell—okay, I will."

Determination must have poured through my fingertips, for Uncle Stephen called down the stairs, "Sounds like the happy farmer's taking a beating from his angry wife."

How could I know, that hot, still afternoon, that of all the people in Job's Corner, only Preston Anderson—with a face full of freckles and hair like a rusty toilet brush, with eyes so weak he had to hold a paper almost to his nose to read it—only Preston saw clearly what was going on?

⁂

That happened in June 1950, but if I'm to tell this story correctly I must begin in July 1949, when I turned eleven. I wanted a weenie roast. Mama gave me a pink party—pink cake, pink ice cream, and eleven little girls in pink dresses bringing presents wrapped in pink. Not by a single flicker did the eleven pink candles on my cake warn me what was coming my way in the next twelve months. If they had, I'd have gone to bed and pulled Big Mama's quilt over my head.

In those days I lived with Mama and her mother, Big Mama, in a little town perched on the North/South Carolina border just under the Blue Ridge mountains. We lived in a big white house with a wide front porch, where I loved to sprawl on the cool gray floorboards to read. Aunt Sukie—brown, gnarled, and so bent with arthritis she wasn't taller than me—came in every day to cook and clean. Even though Pop, Mama's daddy, had been dead two years, his name—Henry Marshall's—in big white letters on a red brick store in Shelby still insured that everybody in our little town knew who we were.

I always think of that town in terms of big trees, cool grass, and sleepy summer afternoons. It also had frosty winter dawns and autumn mornings so ablaze that my heart went flinging into the bright sapphire sky, but it's summer I chiefly remember. Windows wide open at First Baptist, where we went three times a week. Eating watermelon under our mulberry tree. Carrying dirty clothes down the dirt road behind our house to the neat swept yard and small unpainted house where Pearl, the woman who did Big Mama's washing, lived. Those were days without plastic, microwaves, or computers, a time without air-conditioning or television, a time when clocks ticked comfortingly in the night and a cool breeze was a gift.

I turned eleven on July 2. Two days later, at the First Baptist Fourth of July picnic, Mama picked up a pretty little boy to calm him down while his mama set out deviled eggs and potato salad. When one of the women saw Mama's copper curls bent over his blond ringlets, she cooed, "I swan, don't they look like two angels?" I knew right then Mama would never put that crybaby down. She always did have more poetry than common sense.

It was poetry that named me Carolina Rose—too pretty a name for a scrawny baby who grew into a plain child with fine tan hair that wouldn't hold a curl, bookworm-rounded shoulders, and glasses that hid the only good feature I had: dark blue eyes with long lashes. Thank goodness Big Mama started people calling me Carley before I could walk. Only Mama called me by my full name—as in "Carolina Rose, stand up straight. With those eyes, you're going to be a beauty." See? More poetry than common sense.

That afternoon at the picnic, I begged her to come wade with me in the creek. "It's too cold to wade," she said, flat-out ignoring the fact that wading season always began on Memorial Day. Wading season never began for Mama. She hated mud between her toes.

She reached down beside her chair and picked up a granite rock. "Look! This rock is shaped just like a little heart! Carry it with you while you wade, and you'll carry my heart." I shoved it angrily down in the pocket of my terry-cloth jacket. Something deep and mean inside me snarled—and still occasionally whispers—that Mama would have put that child down and gone to the creek with me if he'd been ugly.

Instead, she rocked and kissed that pretty little boy through the entire hot afternoon while he sniffled and whimpered, "I doesn't feel good."

The next day his granny called Big Mama. I heard Big Mama's shocked whisper from where I sprawled on the speckled sitting room linoleum reading *Life*. "Polio?"

The little boy lived in an iron lung for several days before he died and was buried beneath a marble angel. Mama died before they ever got her into an iron lung.

❈

All I remember about her funeral is a ladybug crawling around a yellow daisy on the coffin wreath—and the new preacher (who everybody excused later as too young to know better) coming down the row of Big Mama's sisters at the graveside, patting their old wrinkled hands and murmuring, "Weep not, you'll be with her soon."

Aunt Cleo, Big Mama's youngest sister, rared back and said tartly, "Young man, I sincerely hope not!"

I've been told I went to visit Mama's grave every day for a month, taking a quart jar of iced tea and a book to read. "Wouldn't tote a bite to eat," Aunt Sukie grumbled, "and you already skin and bones. I never saw a child grieve so."

I don't remember. Does grief leave a hole in your memory? It must, for how else could a year so long have an entire month missing?

❊

Summer stretched out hot and thick with thunderheads. *Life* magazine reported that St. Louis was having race riots over the desegregation of city pools. We didn't have race riots. We didn't even have a city pool. What we had was polio, a word everybody was afraid to whisper lest we attract the attention of a passing germ. *Life* called it "this uncontrollable disease." It began to reach national epidemic proportions in sultry, drought-ridden August.

One morning Big Mama came out to the porch where I was rereading old *Reader's Digest* jokes. Slowly she lowered herself into the white wicker chair that had widened and curved to hold her bulk. She rested a minute, then spoke in the soft wheeze she always got after doing something as strenuous as walk from the kitchen to the porch. "Carley, I have a surprise for you. You know Stephen and Kate?"

Of course I did. Aunt Kate was Mama's only sister. She was married to Uncle Stephen and had Abby, who was three. For five years Uncle Stephen had pastored three small mountain churches in the West Virginia coalfields, and Big Mama was proud as a banty rooster that Aunt Kate had married a preacher. It just grieved her that he was a Presbyterian.

"Well," she went on, "Stephen has received a call from a church in Job's Corner, right here in North Carolina. They're moving next week, when little John turns two weeks old."

That wasn't a surprise. For a month Big Mama had been telling the same thing to any perfect stranger willing to listen. But what she said next would have knocked my socks off if I hadn't been barefoot. "Kate has her hands full with moving, Abby, and the baby. You could be a big help, so I'm fixing to send you up there."

I pictured myself with stamps all over my forehead, and wondered how many it took to mail a child. However, I had no intention of going. "No, ma'am. I don't want to go way up there. I hardly know them. I haven't seen Uncle Stephen since Pop's funeral, and Abby won't even remember me. She hasn't seen me for a year."

Big Mama tightened her mouth in the way that meant she'd made up her mind and didn't want any sass. Fire and ice flickered over me in twin ripples. I flung myself at her, burying my face in the flour and bacon smells that collected in her thick white apron between washings. "Please don't make me go— please, ma'am? I don't want to leave you."

"I have to, honey." Her voice was sad, but final. As her big hand patted the top of my head, her thick wedding ring thumped my skull like doom. Go! Go! Go! Go!

Wildly I searched my mind for an argument she might listen to. "What if Jesus comes back while I'm up there? He'll never find me."

She ruffled my hair gently. "I don't think the Lord will come while you're away, but if he does, we'll both know where to find you." She sighed again—a sound like when she sat me down to tell me Mama had died. "I hate to send you, but I can't have you down here with all this polio." I knew then how scared Big Mama was of polio. It was worse than Presbyterians.

Before I left, she gave me Mama's locket. Instead of my baby picture, it now held a tiny one of Mama. That locket was a heavy weight around my neck in more ways than one.

Big Mama was much too stout to make the trip, so she asked two sisters from First Baptist to drop me off in Bluefield on their way to Washington. All you need to know about them is, if their dispositions had been as sweet as their face powder, I'd have had a better trip.

Chapter 2

That whole week in West Virginia with Uncle Stephen and
Aunt Kate my stomach ached something fierce. I was
prone to stomachaches in those days, although no doctor ever
found a thing wrong with me. I felt dizzy, too, like somebody
had spun me around fast and let me go. Nothing was familiar.
Outside, everything looked like somebody went out each
morning to give it a fresh dusting of coal powder. I nearly
washed the skin off my hands and face trying to stay clean, and
my new socks would never be white again. Their house—a
dingy box in the third tier of houses clinging to a mountainside
for dear life—was full of packing boxes. My slender, pretty
Aunt Kate was puffy and fat, her auburn hair lank and
unstyled. My face must have shown my shock, because as soon
as she hugged me she said fiercely, "I won't be fat forever. I
promise."

Every time she looked at me, her eyes filled with tears. I
kept being afraid she'd want to talk about Mama, but she stayed
too busy with baby John and moving.

"How can I help you?" I asked over and over that first day.

"Play with Abby. That will be the most help," she told me
distractedly.

Abby wasn't a baby anymore, but a magpie who followed
me constantly. Her favorite game—crossing the street in front
of their house and rolling down the mountainside to the back
fence of the house below—terrified me. Not the rolling, but the
long-horned skinny cows that roamed loose up and down the
streets grazing on what little grass they could find. When Abby

found out I was terrified of cows, she giggled. "Cows doesn't hurt you, Carley cousin. Dey gives us milk."

"They can kill you quicker than you can spit," I assured her, keeping careful watch over my shoulder for another one of the beasts. "Big Mama told me so."

The worst beast, however, was Raifa, the maid.

Raifa and I detested each other from the night I arrived. Plumb worn out after the hot, all-day drive, I asked politely for a glass of milk. "Get it yourself, smarty pants," Raifa snapped. "I ain't here to wait on you." She kept washing pots.

I poured my milk and told her, between sips, "Where I come from, maids are polite."

She shrugged and wrung out her dishrag like she wished it was my neck. "Things is diff'rent up here."

"Then no wonder nobody likes Yankees." I set my glass in the sink and left.

Raifa didn't act like any maid I'd ever known. For one thing she ate with the family, and sat there glowering as if I didn't have a right to be there. Worse, she wiped her wet hands on the family's kitchen towel. Aunt Sukie would no more use our towel than our toothbrush. And Raifa not only used the towel, she tossed it onto the counter in a damp wad. I could count germs breeding in its folds. Those first two days I changed the kitchen towel so often, I finally had to explain to Aunt Kate why.

Raifa was mean and sly, too. When she wiped Abby's bottom, she did it so roughly that Abby whimpered. When Aunt Kate wasn't looking, Raifa made terrifying faces, wrinkling her nose and scrunching her eyes until Abby hid her face. But when Aunt Kate or Uncle Stephen was around, she was sweet as smoke. "Yes, Miss Kate, no, Mr. Stephen." So if Abby whined that she didn't want Raifa putting her to bed or helping her in the bathroom, Aunt Kate fussed at Abby. The best I knew to do was keep Abby close to me and explain to Aunt Kate after we'd left Raifa behind.

As it turned out, I explained to Uncle Stephen before that. He came out on the porch my fourth afternoon, while Abby was napping and I was reading *Life*.

"Anything good happen this week?" He settled into the other sooty rocker and lit his pipe, surrounding us with a lovely sweet cloud.

I adjusted my glasses. "Not much. You want this? I'll read the new *Reader's Digest*."

"No, I want to talk to you. Kate tells me you're having prob-lems with Raifa."

I appreciated his calling her "Kate" instead of "your Aunt Kate," but his tone warned me we weren't about to talk grown-up to grown-up. "What exactly did she say?"

He gave me a sideways look as he relit his pipe. Uncle Stephen never could keep a conversation and a pipe going at the same time. "She said you don't like drying your hands on tow-els Raifa has used." Another cloud of smoke rose between us. "Now I know that at your grandmother's, you have two sets of kitchen towels . . ."

"And we hang them up, too." That's all I said, for two rea-sons. First, I didn't want to hurt his feelings. Big Mama had warned me I'd need to make allowances for Uncle Stephen. He grew up on a farm and didn't learn the same manners we did. But the other reason I stopped was more complicated. For sev-eral years I'd been walking a tightrope between things I knew were right, because Mama and Big Mama did them, and things that didn't quite make sense. Having two kitchen towels was one of them. It was a lot easier to do than think about.

Uncle Stephen gave his pipe two quick puffs. "Aunt Sukie even has her own dishes, which she washes after she's finished the white people's pots and pans." It wasn't a question. He'd been there. He knew.

"I wash them, too. It's not like Aunt Sukie's a slave or any-thing. Big Mama cooks some, and Saturdays I help clean and carry dirty clothes down the road to Pearl's—"

"I know. But this towel and dishes thing—it's not necessar-ily right. It's just something you've been taught."

I swung wildly on that tightrope. "I wasn't taught. It's the way things are." He didn't say anything, just looked at me . . .

I was four years old, standing on a chair with a dish-towel around my waist, helping Mama wash dishes. I put Aunt Sukie's plate in the dishpan with the others. Gently Mama took it out, rinsed it, and put it back on the drain board with the dirty dishes. She poured out the water, shook in more soap powder, and turned on fresh water. Then, softly, so only I could hear, "That's Aunt Sukie's plate, honey. We'll wash it with her silverware later."

"Why?" Looking over my shoulder, I saw Aunt Sukie put-ting the mayonnaise back in the Kelvinator.

"We just will." Mama leaned so close I could smell lilac perfume. "They're dirty."

"They're all dirty," I pointed out. Mama gave a little puff of frustration. "Yes, honey, but these are dirtier. You aren't old enough to understand yet. Someday you will."

Now I was eleven, and doing the best I knew how.

After that day at the dishpan I'd watched Aunt Sukie furtively. I saw her use her bent brown fingers to push leftover chicken together on the platter so it would fit under a bowl. I saw her knead dough for biscuits or put a pinch of salt in our scrambled eggs. For a time, Mama's and Big Mama's acceptance filled me with astonishment and revulsion. If Aunt Sukie was dirty, she shouldn't be touching our food! Finally I concluded Aunt Sukie's hands must be clean from dishwater. Only her spit was dirty. My own spit was dirty, too, but—

Since I had no map for finishing that sentence, I let it dangle. A lot of sentences dangled by then. I hoped they'd get tied into bows by the time I was grown.

Uncle Stephen sucked his pipe. "If you had a sister, would you wash her dishes in cold greasy water after the pots? Would you treat her like she was dirty, or make her use a different towel?"

"Of course not."

"When you read your Bible, does it tell you all people are brothers and sisters?"

I wasn't going to answer that question. I could see where he was going. He was about to make me step right into a pit. That was the trouble with grown-ups: some of them dug pits, and others pushed you in.

As I suspected, Uncle Stephen didn't want an answer. He assumed I already knew the right one. He stretched his legs out and sprawled in his chair, getting comfortable for the sermon he'd come out to preach. "In this house, we treat everybody— no matter what color they are—like brothers or sisters. Do you understand?"

I glowered at him. "If I had a sister as mean as Raifa, I'd beat her to a pulp."

He chuckled as he tapped his pipe on the porch railing to empty it. "I know you and Raifa don't always see eye to eye."

"Eye to eye nothing. She's mean as mud! She pinches Abby, scares her to death—"

"Now, Carley—"

I jumped up and blazed at him. "If you love some mean old colored girl more than your own flesh and blood—"

"That's enough." Uncle Stephen's voice was stern. I could tell he didn't believe a word I said. "In this house, we use the word *Negro*, not *colored*. And if you catch Raifa hurting Abby, you come and tell me about it. Otherwise, treat her like you would a sister. You understand?"

"Yessir." But I wouldn't. I wouldn't treat her like a sister, and I wouldn't tell. If I told on her, Raifa would get back at me. He might not believe that, but to Raifa and me both it was clear as spit.

I couldn't wait to head back to North Carolina and home.

Chapter 3

We traveled all night through West Virginia's mountains to the North Carolina Piedmont. Uncle Stephen drove through the hot August darkness hoping the children would sleep. Abby obliged, but John wailed in his mama's arms, refusing to eat. Their car was a '43 Chevy two-door coupe, preacher black. We rode with the windows down, but once we left the mountains, the hot wind was as rough and unwelcome as a fat boy's kiss. Rowdy, Aunt Kate's cocker spaniel, panted on the shelf under the back window, emitting waves of what Uncle Stephen called "l'aire du dog."

Between the curves, the dog, and the smells of John, I rode with my nose stuck out the little triangle window at the back and felt sick to my stomach the whole way. I couldn't sleep, scrunched at one end of the cramped backseat while Abby shared a pillow at the other end with Raifa. Yes, Raifa. They were bringing her "to help with the children." "You'd do better to take a snake," I muttered—but not so's Uncle Stephen could hear.

Her bony knees poked me all night.

In the soft light that heralds dawn, I heard a sharp, excited whisper. "North Carolina!"

Uncle Stephen chuckled softly. "Home, Kate. Feel better?"

"Immensely."

I put on my glasses and peered out the backseat window, expecting something I could recognize. All I saw were shadow trees against a gray sky. It didn't look like North Carolina to me. But Aunt Kate leaned far out the open window to breath deeply of the hot pine-scented air, then reached over to stroke

Uncle Stephen's neck below the dark hairline. "Thank you," she whispered.

"Bless you, Kate, for these last five years. I know it hasn't been easy." As he turned to her, something shimmered between them in the dimness.

She gave a soft little laugh. "It wasn't so much hard as—different. It'll be good to get back where things are familiar . . ." She trailed off with a contented sigh, then asked anxiously, "Do you think they'll like us down here?"

He chuckled again. "You, they'll love. Maybe they'll tolerate me for your sake."

She smiled at him. When he smiled back, a glow of happiness lit the car. *If Big Mama could see them now,* I thought drowsily, almost asleep, *she wouldn't wonder why Aunt Kate married such a homely man.*

"Look!" Aunt Kate pointed, then began to sing softly, "Nothin' could be finer than to be in Carolina . . ." Out to the east I saw the first pink feathers of dawn.

"North Carolina," I whispered in satisfaction.

The last thing I heard before I slept was her soft, happy crow: "Home. We're back home!"

❧

When I woke, the sun was high and the dawn magic gone. Raifa took up so much room I was curled in my corner like a pill bug. Abby's foot was in my face. My left arm was asleep. Rowdy's chin was on my head. John was making pitiful little mewling noises. And my clothes felt like they'd been damped for ironing and tied around me in odd places.

Aunt Kate was once again trying to get the bottle in John's mouth, but he turned away, screaming. "Stephen, we've got to get this baby dry pants and a new can of milk. I think his bottle went sour in the heat."

"We've got to get that baby a distant room." Wet patches dotted the back of Uncle Stephen's white shirt between his red suspenders as he hunched over the wheel. All his life he was so skinny, he had to wear suspenders to keep his pants up.

He raked one hand through his straight thick hair. I knew what that meant. I'd overheard Aunt Kate tell Mama once, "Stephen's got the evenest temper in the world, but I can always tell when he's upset or worried. He starts shoving back that hair."

When I put on my glasses, the first thing I saw was Raifa looking across the car through half-closed eyes. Big-boned and the color of caramel, she had large dark marks under her eyes that she called beauty spots. I called them ugly as sin. With a sly smile, she moved her legs so her knees poked me harder. I swung around and put my feet on the floor, out of her reach. She patted the twelve crisp braids that snaked around her head and said softly with a smirk, "Your hair's like a rat's nest, girl."

I glowered. "You stink. You need a bath."

She reached over and gave my arm a sharp, quick pinch. I yelped and rubbed the smarting red spot. Aunt Kate spoke crossly over her shoulder. "You girls stop fussing."

"Yessum." Raifa's voice was like a cat's purr.

Rowdy stretched behind our heads, emitting fresh stench. Abby squirmed. "Fix me, Carley. My clothes are all which-away." Her curls were tousled and sweat beads dotted the light freckles on her nose. I held her between my knees to tug her dress around. I couldn't tug my own skirt around straight, but I tugged down my blouse and pulled up my socks.

Raifa pulled a comb through Abby's curls, hit a snarl, and yanked. Abby roared. John screamed louder. Aunt Kate gave an odd little strangled sound, like a sob.

"Good Lord!" Uncle Stephen exclaimed under his breath, driving faster.

"You cussin', Preacher?" Raifa demanded.

Uncle Stephen's neck turned pink. "No, Raifa, praying."

He finally brought the Chevy to a stop, skidding its tires. "Job's Corner. Everybody out." He climbed out and flexed his hands and shoulders. Before Raifa, Abby, or I could escape the steamy stinking car, Rowdy tumbled onto us, pushed ahead, and waddled toward the nearest tree. It was the only time in my life I ever wished I was a dog.

I climbed over Raifa as soon as I could shove my feet into my saddle oxfords. I was astonished to see Uncle Stephen breathing so hard his shoulders rose and fell. Intrigued, I lifted my face and sniffed, but couldn't smell a thing except new-mown hay. Abby sniffed, too, then wrinkled her nose. "Smells funny, Daddy. What is it?"

"Fresh air. Something we haven't had much of in your lifetime." Uncle Stephen faced the sky, breathing like he was afraid any minute somebody would pass a law against it.

Abby tiptoed toward the grass and winced as pebbles bit her

bare feet. "Funny coal." As she bent and picked up two small chunks of granite with black, white, and diamond speckles, I felt tears smart my eyes. That granite was just like the gravel in Big Mama's drive, and it was lying in a bed of chickweed, just like grew in our yard. People can waste a lot of words saying what home is and isn't. It all boils down to this: home is where you know the weeds by name.

Uncle Stephen knelt down and hugged Abby hard. "Those're rocks, Punkin. They don't have coal down here."

"Got lots of dust, though." Raifa thrust a long brown leg out the door and joined us.

Uncle Stephen looked at the reddish haze that still mapped our arrival. "It is a bit dusty," he admitted, wiping his forehead with one arm, "but the houses are far enough back from the road, they shouldn't get the worst of it." He picked Abby up and called through the open window. "Kate, aren't you coming?"

"In a minute. John has finally decided to eat."

"What do you think of our new home?"

That was the first I'd thought to look at the house. It was enormous, a two-story mountain painted white, with four brick chimneys rising above a steep green roof. A wide porch circled three sides, and both the porch and the house bulged on the front left corner. The whole thing perched on thick brick pillars firmly planted in hard red clay.

Five maples marched like sentinels across the broad yard that blurred softly into the dust of the road. No sidewalks. No fences, either, except across the back. On the left the yard ended in a row of scraggly forsythia Abby would soon call "the switch bushes." On the right, a tall althea hedge almost hid a small field planted in cotton. Beyond the cotton field sat an unpainted building with a porch so saggy it might fall off any minute.

Abby took one look around and said firmly, "Dis is not home."

"It's our new home," Uncle Stephen explained. "We live here now."

That's when Abby first realized what moving meant. "No!" She pounded her daddy on top of his head. "Dis is not home! Dis is not it!"

I was glad it wasn't *my* home, that I'd soon be back at Big Mama's cheerful house and sunny porch. This house watched with window shades like half-open eyelids, its bulge pregnant with secrets. Suddenly I saw us as the house must see us: rumpled, tired, and very small. In spite of the sunshine, I shivered.

※

I'll let Raifa describe Job's Corner. I was supposed to mail her letter the day after we arrived. Instead, in a fit of pique, I shoved it under my mattress. Months later I hid it in Aunt Kate's Remember Box. I copy it here in public expiation for my sins:

Dear Mama,
I promis Id writ soon, but dont spec much. Im plum wore out from the trip, and so homsik I cant stan it. Jobs Corner isnt more than a corner, and thats a fack. Reel cuntry. We got a coton feld next door. Can you emagen that? Theys a reel purty house down a side rode. We ate there rite after we cum. But theys no stop lites and no stores. Cep an old wommin next door sells stuf in a bilding looks like it will fall down if you blo hard. Theys a dirt road with 3 houses an ours lind up on 1 side, all bilt far apart. Acrost the dirt rode is a ralrode trak, reel close to us, then a hiway. Other side the hiway is 2 more houses, with Mr. Stephens church plonked smak in the midle. Big brik church looking rite at our house, with whit steps, whit colums, and a baryin groun on each side. They's a manshun up the hill behind all that, and they cum to Mr. Stephen's church, too. Evrybody does roun here.
I maybe can get ust to wirkin acrost from ded peeple, but what I cant get ust to is the skie. Its so big feels like it will mash me.
Got sompin makin me sad, Mama, but wont tell you that now. Mr. Stephen says mabee he can fix it. Dont wory.
Well I got to go to bed. Tomorow me and Miz Kate got a lot to do. Carley is a pane. I pray shel be sent paking to her granny soon. She needs a not jerkt in her and Im the one to do it! Just want you to know we get here alrite.

Yours truly, Raifa

※

Aunt Kate finally climbed out, holding John in one arm and rubbing her shoulder with the other. He had spit up on her again. Her blue blouse was wrinkled and stained. Her navy skirt had a dark circle at the lap. "I sure hope I can change before I see anybody."

"You look fine, honey."

"I don't look fine." Both Abby and I stared. Tears streamed down Aunt Kate's cheeks, and we weren't used to grown-ups crying. "I'm fat, and filthy—"

Uncle Stephen reached one long arm to encircle her. "We'll get cleaned up soon, and you aren't exactly fat—" He whispered something in her ear that made her laugh in a little hiccup, then he gently jerked one of her curls. "What do you think of the house?"

She gave it a long, doubtful look. "It's enormous. And you didn't tell me it was so close to the tracks and the highway. What about the children—and Rowdy?"

"Lotsa work to clean, too." Raifa took John and jiggled him on her hip.

Abby squirmed in her daddy's arms. "I gotta potty."

Aunt Kate sighed. "Is the house open, Stephen?"

He pulled out his pocket watch. "Ought to be. The van should get here soon, and I don't think they lock up much around here. Davy Anderson said—"

Just as Uncle Stephen said the name, a dusty old blue pickup growled to a stop behind our Chevy. Uncle Stephen lifted his hand in delight. "Here's Davy now!"

It didn't occur to me he'd watched for the car while he milked and come up as soon as he saw our dust. For me, Davy Anderson would forever retain a whiff of the miraculous.

Uncle Stephen had stayed with the Andersons when he came down to preach for the congregation, and he must have told us a hundred times, "Those Andersons are the nicest people I ever met. And Davy has lived in the same house since he was two!" I kept wondering, if Uncle Stephen thought that was so all-fired wonderful, why was he moving?

At fifty-six Davy Anderson looked exactly like he would at ninety: long, thin, and loosely hinged, with a circle of white hair, a wisp on top, and eyes the same blue as Big Mama's tea pitcher. "You got here all right, then," he said slowly, swinging legs even longer than Uncle Stephen's down from the cab. He walked as slowly as he talked. Mr. Davy never hurried. No matter how busy he was, he always gave the impression that what he was saying or doing at that moment was all he had to do in the world.

A musty odor of oil and field dust followed him from the truck as he bent to stroke Rowdy's muzzle, then extended a work-gnarled hand to Aunt Kate. "Davy Anderson, ma'am. I know you're worn out. My wife, Hannah, says for you all to come on down to breakfast and have a little nap before the truck comes. She's got everything mostly ready."

"Oh, we couldn't—" Aunt Kate began.

Uncle Stephen pulled out his watch again. "The van ought to be here soon."

Mr. Davy shook his head. "They called down to the house just a few minutes ago. Had a tire blow out coming over the mountains, so they'll be a mite late. You all come eat and freshen up. They ought to get your things here 'bout the time we finish."

In spite of how grubby I felt, I was hungry. My spirits rose as we piled back in the car and headed down a dirt side road where the Anderson's high green roof rose among towering black walnuts and cedars. The house, two gleaming white stories with dark green shutters and soft red chimneys, sat surrounded by a soft emerald lawn they had wrested from the hard red clay and dotted with pastel flowerbeds. Big hydrangeas made soft blobs of blue and pink in front of a wide front porch and a deep side porch along the long back wing.

"It's prettier 'n a calendar!" Raifa exclaimed.

"Hannah used to be a florist," Uncle Stephen said proudly, as if their having met once made them kinfolks. "Now she shows flowers all over the state. Wins prizes, too."

Aunt Kate broke out in short, angry sentences. "Oh, Stephen! It's exquisite! You should have told me!" She scrubbed her face and hands with a handkerchief, held John high to rub at her wrinkled wet skirt, and sniffed her shoulder where he had thrown up last. "Phew! You should have told me! I'd never have come! I can't go in there looking like this!"

"Slow down, Daddy!" Abby ordered. "I'm countin' cows. Fifty-leven, seventeen . . ."

With horror, I saw thick red cows with white faces grazing on both sides of the road. "Big Mama knew a woman who got gored by a cow and died," I warned.

Aunt Kate made a puff of exasperation. "She would."

"There's nothing but three strands of barbed wire between us and them," I pointed out. "They could break that down in a minute."

Uncle Stephen called over his shoulder, "Look beyond the cows. Mountains!" Far across the western pasture rose the same purply humps I saw from Big Mama's side yard. If I could leap high enough, they would pull me like giant magnets. I could dash down the dim cool hall, fling myself onto Big Mama's white aproned chest . . .

"Ssst!" Raifa hissed in my ear. "Straighten up your face. We goin' to meet Mister Stephen's bossfolks."

Chapter 4

As we pulled to a stop beneath an enormous black walnut, Davy Anderson came toward the car carrying a full water bucket. "That looks to me like one thirsty dog." When he set the bucket down and Uncle Stephen opened the door, Rowdy wiggled down from the car and lurched toward the water at the closest that dog ever came to a run. Davy Anderson deftly looped a long rope around his collar and tied the other end to the garage door. "That ought to keep him. He can stay here while you're moving in."

Raifa shoved Abby out and followed her. Aunt Kate got out, too, clutching screaming John. "Come on, Carley."

"No thank you, ma'am. I'm not getting out with those cows. I'll wait right here."

"Get out of that car this minute." One second she was glaring at me, the next she was giving Mr. Davy the sweetest smile in the world. You could tell Big Mama raised her.

I climbed out, keeping a wary eye on the pasture. We stood in a clump on the drive, "Like a band of filthy gypsies," Aunt Kate muttered, her lips tight.

Through our car's dusty haze we saw more purple and blue hydrangeas, a rosebush thick with pink blossoms climbing a trellis at one end of the side porch, and purple sage surrounding a white birdbath to one side of the circular drive. "Look! Ducks!" Abby darted to pat four white concrete ducklings with bright yellow beaks, following their plump mother across the lawn toward the birdbath.

They never reached it. In coming months, no matter how

often Abby and I moved those ducks to water, on our next visit they'd be ten feet away. I wonder now if Aunt Hannah used those ducks to say something about her own life.

A big woman hurried down the walk, grizzled black curls carefully confined under a net. Words poured from her like water from a faucet. "I declare, look at those tired little faces! Are you plumb worn out? Riding all night in this heat . . ." Her own face was flushed and damp and she sounded plumb out of breath.

"Hannah always sounds breathless, because she never stops for breath," Uncle Stephen would say later. "I never knew a person could talk so much."

Without waiting for introductions, she leaned down and held out her arms. Abby left the ducks, went straight to her, and laid her head on that shelf-wide bosom as if she'd done it every day of her life. The woman circled her with one arm and held out the other to pull me close, almost smothering me. "Come here, old dear. Let me give you a hug, too. I hope you'll both call me Aunt Hannah."

"Aunt Hannah," Abby repeated. I didn't plan on being around long enough to call anybody Aunt. Besides, when she hugged me, she smelled like face powder and lavender soap, but felt like wood. "Corsets," Aunt Kate would tell me when I got up my courage to ask.

She released us and turned toward Aunt Kate. What a contrast they made—the large woman with her purple flowered Sunday voile, polished black lace-up shoes, and netted grizzled hair, and my small, baby-rumpled aunt. Yet the cleaner woman acted like she was the one receiving the honor. Her plump hands fumbled with the belt that encircled her stout waist, and she spoke humbly, "I'm Hannah. We're so glad you got here, Mrs. Whitfield."

Hannah Anderson was always shy and a little awkward around Aunt Kate. Although Aunt Kate soon called her "Hannah," the older woman always said "Mrs. Whitfield" with grave respect. I remember one evening as we all rocked on her porch, she turned and asked, "What do you think of that sunset, Mrs. Whitfield?"—as if Aunt Kate's opinion would determine her own.

That morning, however, Aunt Kate clutched John to cover her shoulder. "We're such a mess, ma'am, I'm ashamed to have you see us like this."

Miss Hannah reached for John and drew him, sticky and squalling, to her own chest. "Poor dear!" It was John she clasped, but Aunt Kate to whom she spoke. "You must be plumb worn out. Davy, take Mrs. Whitfield's suitcase to our room so she can freshen up before breakfast. I laid out towels on the bed." She propped John on her shoulder and rubbed her chin against the top of his fuzzy head. He gave a whimper, a hiccup, and grew still.

Over his head, Miss Hannah nodded to Raifa. "I know you've been a big help to Mrs. Whitfield on the trip. Janey Lou's in the kitchen. She'll look after you. Come in, come in, all of you." Still talking without taking a breath, she led us like ducklings toward the cool side porch, through the musky smell of boxwoods. The porch was full of rockers, for the Andersons kept the comfortable rockers on the side porch for company, reserving the swing and two small rockers on the front porch for children at play.

A grizzled Negro woman in a starched navy blue dress and a white apron held the kitchen door wide. She was as skinny as Miss Hannah was stout. "This is Janey Lou," Miss Hannah said in her breathless way. "I couldn't get along without Janey Lou."

Inside, the house was a lot like Big Mama's—polished mahogany furniture, polished silver, polished mirrors, and Oriental rugs. Once Aunt Kate had washed, changed into a clean yellow sundress shaped like a tent, and brushed her hair until it lay in soft auburn waves around her face, she came out sparkling and talking like she felt right at home—when she could get a word in edgewise.

Our doctor used to tell Mama he'd made a mistake and vaccinated me with a phonograph needle, but Miss Hannah talked more than me. Over heaping bowls and platters of fried country ham, grits with redeye gravy, scrambled eggs, and fluffy biscuits with homemade muscadine jam, she kept up a blue streak about how glad they were we'd come, how much they hoped we'd like Job's Corner, how much the church needed a young preacher like Uncle Stephen—then she started all over again. Mr. Davy ate placidly, giving occasional nods of agreement and shoving bowls our way when we ran out of food.

We were nearly finished when we heard a bicycle slide to a stop just outside and somebody yelled, "The van is here! The van is here!"

Mr. Davy waved toward the screened door. "That's my

nephew Preston. He said he'd let us know when the truck arrived."

"Van's here." A boy flung open the screen and burst importantly inside. He had a fat freckled face topped by a bristle of rusty brown hair. As he stuck his thumbs in the bib of faded overalls (which seemed to be the only garment on his pink round body), rolls of flesh showed under his arms. He stank of dirty little boy.

He ignored me and I ignored him, until Miss Hannah said breathlessly, "Preston, these are the Whitfields and Carley, Mrs. Whitfield's niece. She's eleven, going into sixth grade. Preston is ten, going into fifth grade."

If that last bit was for my benefit, she'd wasted her breath. I didn't care what grade he was going into. I'd be shaking Job's Corner off my sandals as soon as I could get on a bus. Why didn't Aunt Kate tell her I was only there to help them move?

Maybe because Miss Hannah didn't give her a chance.

Miss Hannah pushed back her chair and asked Preston anxiously, "Do you want something to eat?"

"Just a biscuit." He grazed my ear with one hand as he reached for the plate. Every one of those stubby fingers had warts. And he stood there dribbling crumbs on Hannah Anderson's fine dining room rug as nonchalant as if he owned the place.

Did he know, even then, that one day he would?

※

Uncle Stephen and Davy Anderson left in Davy's truck. Preston rode in glory in the back, gloating that we girls had to stay behind. Aunt Kate and John stretched out on Miss Hannah's mahogany four-poster while Miss Hannah took Abby and me out back to see her kittens—wild leaping things that led Abby a merry dance around a huge blue hydrangea.

Miss Hannah's back porch—actually the far side of the back wing, nearest the chicken house and pigpen—was a homely place of dented feed buckets, barn shoes, and two rump-sprung chairs for shucking corn and stringing beans. Janey Lou brought out iced tea in lovely aluminum glasses—robin's egg blue for Abby, apple green for Miss Hannah, and rose pink for me. Abby gulped hers and ran back to the kittens, but I could have sat forever on that porch while condensation dripped through my fingers like the patter of our talk.

Miss Hannah and I enjoyed talking together. We could talk as much as we wanted to, and nobody ever interrupted either one of us to say, "Let somebody else talk, now." She was the first person I ever talked to about Mama. If sometimes I had to stop and clear my throat or wipe my glasses, she didn't seem to mind. She just leaned closer, encouraging me to go on. "Daddy died before I was born," I finished, "so I don't really miss him, but I miss Mama terribly sometimes."

She leaned down and kneaded my shoulder with her strong big hand. "I know how you feel. My daddy died when I was seventeen."

After that, neither of us said another word—or wanted to.

Finally Aunt Kate came to the screened door. "I had a wonderful nap, but I guess we'd better be getting up the road. This day has just begun."

Chapter 5

The following April at Ira Baines's funeral—desperate, I guess, to say something nice and take our minds off murder—Uncle Stephen would recall, "Our first day in Job's Corner, Ira came to help us move in."

"Yeah," Abby would pipe from the balcony, "and he smelt sumpin' terrible."

"We all smelled terrible." Uncle Stephen craned his neck and peered up to admonish her. "We were moving in."

"Yeah, but—"

I covered her mouth with my hand, but I knew what she meant. Ira Baines always smelled like he hadn't bathed since Noah left the ark.

That night after the funeral, listening at their bedroom door, I overheard Aunt Kate. "I'd forgotten Ira came over on moving day, but once you mentioned it, I could just see him. He tottered to the car on those bandy legs and pumped my hand like he was looking for water." Her voice mimicked his nasal whine exactly. "'Good to meet you, Miz Preacher. If they's anything me and my misses can do—anything atall—you jest let us know.' Did we actually get a lick of work out of him all day?"

"I doubt it." Uncle Stephen turned over and added drowsily, "If we'd had any notion of the trouble he'd cause, would we have had the good sense to repack and leave?"

❀

On moving day, the manse was a mess. Furniture and boxes sprawled everywhere. Movers and church men swarmed in and

out while Uncle Stephen stood on the porch popping his red
suspenders and directing them. He was so dirty, sweaty, and
unlike his usual starched-white-shirt self that Abby ran and
clutched his legs to be sure it was him.

Something in me wished I had a daddy to hang onto, too.
Instead, I struggled up the walk with a slippery gallon jar of iced
lemonade Miss Hannah had sent. "Get the cups, Abby," I called
crossly. "You were supposed to carry them."

She scampered down the walk for a box of Dixie cups while
Uncle Stephen wiped his forehead with one arm and waved me
to a tall dish barrel still standing on the porch. "Pour some for
everybody, Carley, while I round up the men."

It was hot, with scarcely a breeze. I had my work cut out to
keep flies off the cups. As the men arrived, Abby handed out
lemonade so solemnly you'd have thought she was passing
communion. Uncle Stephen looked around. "Where's Raifa and
Jay?"

One man jerked his head toward the screened door. "Jay's
settin' up your bedroom."

Another added, in a nasal whine, "He's okay. He kin git
water if he wants it."

Aunt Kate had gone inside with Raifa. Now she came out
carrying squalling John. "Stephen, when you're done, would
you move the living room couch and chair and the Philco from
the front room to the second one? I'd rather have them back
there."

"Sure, honey." Uncle Stephen turned to me. "Carley, run
tell Jay and Raifa to come have some lemonade with us."

The men shifted uneasily.

Aunt Kate gave Uncle Stephen a warning frown. Quickly,
before he could say another word, she plopped John in my arms,
reached for the jar, and filled two cups so fast she sloshed all
over the barrel top. "Abby, carry these to Raifa in the kitchen,
please. She's busy unpacking and doesn't need to bother with
coming out." She didn't look at Uncle Stephen.

Abby stood on tiptoe to reach for the cups but Uncle
Stephen gently caught both her hands in one of his and pushed
her back. "Go tell Raifa and the other man to come out here,
Abbikins." His voice was soft, but he meant business.

"They're okay inside," one of the men said, like he was
explaining something Uncle Stephen must not understand.

Uncle Stephen shoved his free hand through his hair. The

porch grew so still I heard for the first time a cardinal perched on the telephone pole. "Cheer! Cheer! Cheer!" it urged, but nobody paid any attention.

Over on the far corner of the porch, a stocky man with black hair muttered something behind his cup. Another nudged him and said, "Now, wash." I didn't understand—I didn't know yet that "Wash" was his name. Preston opened his mouth, but Davy Anderson laid a hand on his shoulder. Preston snickered instead, waving a fly from his cup with warty fingers.

Abby, knowing something was wrong, looked anxiously from her mama to Uncle Stephen. He looked at Aunt Kate. She turned away from him with a careless little laugh. "Carley, come give me the baby and you and Abby take these cups on in."

Abby had no idea what was going on, but she squirmed and drew back against Uncle Stephen's long legs. "I doesn't wanna go in there."

Standing with her back to the men, Aunt Kate nodded slightly toward the cups and gave me a look straight from Big Mama. I handed her John, grabbed those cups before Uncle Stephen knew what was coming, and headed for the screened door. He might not know what was proper, but Aunt Kate and I did. And I'd seen those men watching what was going on. They were with Aunt Kate all the way.

The long cool hall through the middle of the house smelled of men's sweat and the lingering clamminess of old people. At the far end was a door with a large crackled glass window— probably the bathroom. "Anybody could see your shadow," I muttered, vowing never to use it if people were in the house.

Three doors opened to my right, two to my left. I heard Raifa singing at the end of the hall on my right, so I hurried that way. In passing, I saw at once why Aunt Kate wanted the living room furniture moved. The dining room was big and bright, but the living room was a poky little place with dark gray walls. Any light that headed its way was strangled by the porch and those five maple trees.

I found Raifa in a big dismal kitchen, elbow-deep in excelsior.

"Is somebody named Jay out here?" I asked.

"He's working 'cross the hall. Set it down. I'll give it to him."

Rude as she was, I still felt sorry and strangely embarrassed that she had to drink lemonade in that gloomy, messy kitchen while the rest of us were on the porch. Atoning for a sin I couldn't name and didn't feel was my fault, I picked up Jay's cup and sipped. "I'll stay back here, too," I said casually. "It's cooler."

"Suit yourself." She leaned against the cabinet, glaring. We drank in silence. I didn't know if she wanted me or not. When I finished first and started to go, she said, "Don't forget to bring Jay some lemonade." Her eyes were dark and hard like my old teddy bear's.

"Why even try to be nice to her?" I muttered as I headed up the dim hall. I also shuddered. Big Mama knew lots of stories about maids who went berserk and hurt people.

I carried another cup inside, looking for the man named Jay. Abby tagged at my heels.

In the room across the hall from the dining room, a man was setting up Aunt Kate's bed. His skin was the exact shade of the mahogany.

"Don't scratch that headboard, now," I warned.

"Mama'll kill you dead." Abby wandered over to inspect John's crib in the corner.

"Then I'll sure be careful. It's a pretty bed." He stroked one pineapple post.

"Dat's a pretty box, too." Abby pointed to the rowan box that had been set on top of the chest. "A wummin gived it to Mama yesterday. It's a remember box, but it hasn't got a remember in it. Not yet." That's when it was first named.

"We brought you some lemonade." I held it out.

"That's mighty nice of you." He reached for the cup, careful not to touch my fingers.

"I'm Abigail Marshall Whitfield," Abby informed him. "Who are you?"

He grinned down at her. "I'm Jay Anderson."

"How do you do?" Just learning to shake hands, Abby stuck out one grubby paw. He hesitated, then solemnly shook it.

Uneasy, I stuck out my own. "I'm Carley Marshall." His hand was dry and smooth, the palm as pink as ours. I had never touched a colored man before. Should I go wash my hand? I couldn't think of any way to do it without hurting his feelings, since the bathroom was right next door. Anyway, his hand looked a lot cleaner than Abby's.

Abby had noticed something I'd missed. "Is Uncle Davy Anderson your daddy?"

I was scandalized, but Jay laughed and shook his head. "No, but my aunt works for Miss Hannah." He set his cup in the windowsill and started settling the springs onto the slats.

"What's a *ahnt?*" Abby asked, pronouncing it the way he did.

"He means *aunt,*" I whispered, saying "ant."

Abby was entranced with his way of saying it. "What's your ahnt's name?"

Jay wrestled the mattress onto the springs. "Janey Lou."

She gave a happy hop. "I knows Janey Lou! She gived me iced tea. I likes her."

"I like her, too." He gave the mattress a twitch to settle it in place. "Now I've got a bed to set up in the next room. A pink one."

"Dat's mine!" Abby told him importantly.

The front room had three doors—one into the hall, one into Aunt Kate's room, and one with glass panes opening onto the west side porch. Dark brown bookshelves lined the two straight walls. One corner of the room curved where the house bulged, and the bulge was filled by five curved windows overlooking the front porch. "I likes dis room," Abby decided.

Before we could examine it further, Uncle Stephen called from the porch, "Abbikins, come see what I see."

❄

Abby ran to the end of the porch and peered between two banisters shaped like a fat woman's legs. I hung over the rail and looked, too. Past the forsythia bushes sat a small square house with blotchy sycamores reaching over its steep tin roof. Beneath one sycamore, in a sandbox, sat a little girl with white hair, a yellow sunsuit, and a red shovel.

"Hi! Hi!" Abby shouted, waving.

She never looked up, just sat letting sand slowly dribble off the tip of her shovel in a stream as white as her hair.

"Come on." Uncle Stephen grabbed us each by the hand.

"We don't know her," I protested, pulling away.

"You will in a minute," he promised. "She knows who you are, I'll bet. She's probably sitting out there waiting for you all to come over."

"How's she know me?" Abby demanded.

"Because you're her new preacher's little girl." From the edge of the yard he called, "Good morning! I'm Mr. Whitfield, and these are my girls, Carley and Abby."

I was startled by the offhand way he claimed me, not sure whether I was glad or mad. As he led us across the grass, the girl watched gravely. Her irises were such a light blue they blended into the whites of her eyes. "What's your name?" he asked.

She slowly lifted shovelfuls of sand and dribbled them back into her sandbox, a dainty elf child with a pointed chin and delicate arched brows that made her face look like a heart. Her hair really was as white and soft as the sand, cut perfectly straight across her forehead and beneath her ears. When she finally spoke, her voice was high and tinkly, like the sound of cut crystal. "Sue Mary Anderson. It was supposed to be Mary Sue, but the stupid nurse at the hospital got it backwards. Mama didn't notice till it was too late." She bent her head, intent on letting another shovelful of sand stream precisely off her shovel.

We would learn that Sue Mary talked slowly, walked slowly, dressed slowly, and took twice as long to eat as any living child. And always, before she ever said a word, she took time to think out exactly what she planned to say. That first morning, Abby was captivated. She went on tiptoe across the yard to the sandbox and stood, silent and shy, one finger in her mouth.

Uncle Stephen was nonplussed. "How old are you, Sue Mary?"

Long pause. "Four. Last month."

"You must be Preston's sister." He spoke in the voice grown-ups use when trying to forge instant friendships with children. Sue Mary gave no sign that Preston meant a thing to her. Uncle Stephen tried again. "Abby will soon be four."

Abby finally took the lead that would become habitual with them. Swinging one leg over the sandbox, she plopped down in another corner. "I wants to play wif you."

The girl shifted her feet slightly to make room. "Okay." Uncle Stephen turned and went back to the house, leaving us in the timeless, thoughtless manner of grown-ups to get acquainted as best we could. I waited a few seconds, then climbed into a third corner. There was space, if no welcome.

We played in an awkward silence under the sycamore. Sue Mary continued to dribble sand off her shovel. Abby and I, shovelless, burrowed our bare feet in the chilly sand, heaped them with slithering, formless hills, and wiggled our toes to free them. After a while Sue Mary began to burrow her own feet too, in her serious, intent way. Suddenly Abby seized her shovel, dumped a scoop of sand into the grass, and gurgled with laughter.

"Don't!" Sue Mary cried. "That's my shovel, and Uncle Gil brought this sand from White Lake. He'll whip you good!"

Abby chuckled wickedly and heaved another load over the side.

Sue Mary grabbed for the shovel. I opened my mouth to warn her, but I was too late. Abby sank an even row of teeth into her forearm.

When I pried her off, Abby had left a small red semicircle as identifiable as any fingerprint. She'd bitten most of the children in Uncle Stephen's old churches at least once. She'd even bitten me. She didn't bite because she disliked you; it was her instinct when attacked. As an adult, she would mark a mugger by tooth prints on his wrist.

Sue Mary hadn't made a sound when she was bitten, but watched in horror as two small drops of blood rose in the groove. Then she opened her prim little mouth and screamed.

"Whatsa matter? Whatsa matter?" A woman tall as Pop and fat as Big Mama dashed out their front door, a bush of brown hair flopping around her big pink face. She grabbed Sue Mary and rubbed the wound with a corner of her green flowered apron, glaring at me above big red cheeks.

"I didn't bite her!" I jumped up, mortified, and tried to tug Abby home. She'd gone limp as rags. I was glad to see Aunt Kate running our way, John bobbing on her shoulder.

She knew at once what had happened. She thrust John into my arms, jerked Abby out of the sandbox, and smacked her on the bottom, then looked toward Sue Mary and her mother. The big woman was already halfway to her porch, dragging the child like a sack behind her. "Please wait until Abby apologizes," Aunt Kate called after them.

"Need to get Mercurochrome on that bite," the woman bawled over one shoulder. "Don't want her dyin' of rabies."

"My child doesn't have rabies!"

"Can't ever tell." The woman slammed the screen behind her.

Aunt Kate watched the door for a few seconds, as if hoping it would pop open again. When it didn't, she hurried us home. On our way she broke a branch off the forsythia and switched Abby good. Then she confined us both to the yard.

"I wonder," she would tell Big Mama later, "if Pauline and I would have had so much trouble if Abby hadn't bitten Sue Mary right off the bat."

❊

I was furious at being grounded. I hadn't bitten anybody. But when I begged Uncle Stephen to take me to the bus station, he said shortly, "I can't take you anywhere right now."

Preston bustled up. "What can I do now?"

Uncle Stephen peered down at him. "Are you strong?"

Preston flexed a flabby biceps. "Sure."

"Then shove all the boxes in my study against one wall, so we can bring up my desk."

Preston lumbered importantly toward the steps. I figured I might as well see the upstairs, too, so I stomped after him, followed by a tearstained, snuffling shadow.

Uncle Stephen's study was just across from the head of the stairs. When I glanced out the window, my heart lurched in my chest. Over a pear tree and Preston's roof I could see the mountains, as clear as anything. I went over and pressed my forehead against the big pane, wishing I could fly. "What you doin'?" Preston demanded. "You gonna jump?"

"'Course not." I turned away. "Come on, Abby, let's see what else is up here."

In the room behind Uncle Stephen's study, Raifa's clothes sat in paper bags atop a single bed. The only other furniture was a small chest, on which she had set up three treasures: her radio, a picture of Nat King Cole framed from a magazine, and a picture in a silver frame. I looked doubtfully at it. Raifa claimed it was her granny, but that woman looked white to me.

Next to Raifa, at the end of the hall, was a second bathroom, with a deep claw-footed tub, a large pedestal lavatory, and—I noted with satisfaction—a thick solid door. Over the kitchen was an empty attic. Above the dining room and living room were two more bedrooms, empty of all but dust motes dancing in sunlight. In the huge room stretching across the downstairs hall and Abby's room, I found my own suitcase on Aunt Kate's guest room bed. Five curved windows looked straight into the maple tops, making it like a high castle tower. If I had to, I wouldn't mind sleeping there for one night.

Reluctantly I returned to the study. Preston was piling

boxes right next to the door. "You can't leave them there, stupid. The men can't get the desk in."

He rubbed one forearm over his sweaty forehead, smearing both with red dust that matched his freckles. "The preacher said against the wall. He didn't say which wall."

He stunk so bad I went to raise the window high. "He figured you'd know not to block the door." I shoved the nearest box of books, but couldn't budge it. Uncle Stephen had built them himself, out of pine. I bent and put all my weight against it, but it only moved an inch.

"Get out of the way." Preston bumped his hip against me and shoved the box. It went right across the room. "I'm strong," he boasted. "I'm fixin' to have a growth spurt."

"Then move 'em by yourself," I said haughtily. "I need to make my bed."

Sheets lay in a heap on the double bed. I made it with hospital corners tight enough to please even Big Mama, and it looked so good that Abby and I curled up and slept an hour.

I woke to see sleep-tousled copper curls and two deep gray eyes in a small oval face, watching me. I peered nearsightedly, unable to breathe. For a second it was Mama in miniature. Then she gave a happy gurgle to see me awake. "Good mornin', Sunshine!" She caught my face between her hands and deposited a kiss on my nose. She snuggled against me and slid both arms around my neck. "I's *so* glad you's here, Carley cousin."

Since Mama's death I'd felt cold inside all the time. Abby was a golden fountain, splashing me inside and out with warm shining love.

Chapter 6

Sleeping in a tower is good preparation for meeting a princess. Abby and I got downstairs to find one on our porch, standing between a man in a crisp blue seersucker suit and a woman who looked like a skeleton in nice clothes. Aunt Kate seemed flustered. I thought it was because of the way she looked. She'd brushed her hair and put on fresh lipstick, but the yellow dress she'd put on earlier was streaked with dirt and damp under both arms. It only took one look at the woman's creamy linen dress dribbled with tiny stripes of butterscotch that exactly matched her camel pumps to know Aunt Kate wished she'd had time to change. Pop would have said this woman cost a lot to dress, and he ought to know.

Abby bent down and gingerly touched the woman's leg. "You got de littl'st ankles I ebber did see!"

"Abby, Carley." Aunt Kate hastily reached to encircle us both. "This is Mr. Hugh Fred Keene, the Clerk of Session . . ."

No wonder she looked flustered. For Southern Presbyterians, the Clerk of Session was right up next to God, and this one looked like a movie star, with wavy black hair, broad shoulders, and a beautiful smile.

"And this is Mrs. Keene and their daughter—"

"Freda," the man finished for her. "Named for her daddy, Hugh Fred." *Fredda*. I rolled the name around in my mind. Like me, Uncle Stephen would spell it like it sounded when he typed his first Sunday's bulletin. After Mr. Hugh Fred corrected the spelling during announcements, Aunt Kate would doodle in her margin, *"If they wanted to call her Fredda, why did they spell it Freda?"*

That day on the porch, though, when he looked at Freda, I felt physical pain. Big Mama said God would give back one hundredfold anything he took from us, but nothing I could get would make up for never getting looked at like that by my daddy.

Freda handed Aunt Kate a blue bowl like it was an offering to the Lord—if anybody offered the Lord potato salad. "We've brought you a bite to eat."

I stared in astonishment. She wasn't much older than me, and she had *pale pink polish on her nails!* As Aunt Kate took the bowl, Freda curtsied slightly, setting black ringlets bobbing below a pink velvet bow. If her eyes bulged slightly, they were at least a lovely brown. And if her upper lip was short, at least it showed teeth as white as her organdy dress. She had ruffles instead of sleeves, edged with pink embroidery. What seemed to me almost as wonderful as her nail polish, her socks had pink lace sewed around each dainty ankle.

Abby and I had taken a bath when we woke up and put on the least wrinkled things I could find, but next to her I felt like a hick.

Mr. Keene adjusted the knot of his red tie. "Stephen around?"

"He's gone to the church, but he should be back soon." Aunt Kate sounded more hopeful than certain.

He waved toward his car. "As Freda said, we've brought you a bite for dinner. Shall we bring it in?"

They'd brought far more than a bite. The trunk of their new gray Hudson held enough fried chicken, green beans, creamed corn, sliced tomatoes, and cloverleaf yeast rolls to feed us a week. I personally carried in a fuzzy white coconut cake and a gallon of tea with lemon rounds floating on top. When the dining room table was full, Aunt Kate said faintly, "I can't thank you enough. You must have cooked all morning."

Mrs. Keene gave one of those little laughs that meant she was lying to be polite. "It was nothing, really."

Uncle Stephen always claimed Emily Keene had beautiful bones, but it seemed to me God ran out of skin before he finished her face. It stretched much too tightly across her wide cheekbones and was always shiny, like she creamed it hourly.

Beneath pale blond hair, she wore her lipstick and rouge very bright. Only her eyes were beautiful. The first time I saw sherry, I thought of Emily Keene's eyes. Except sherry doesn't look forever anxious.

"You all might as well go ahead and start," Mr. Keene decided. "Stephen might be a while." He spoke rapidly. "Lord, for what they are about to receive, make them truly thankful, Amen." I didn't have time to bow my head or even close my eyes. I hoped the food was truly blessed. Awkwardly, we filled plates and followed our guests out to the porch.

Mrs. Keene hesitated before one of the rockers. "Here, honey, let's put my handkerchief on that," Mr. Keene offered. Aunt Kate and I would watch later, mortified, as he retrieved it, neatly patterned with coal dust.

Raifa appeared at the screen door, bringing her own plate to join us. "Would you keep John inside out of the heat?" Aunt Kate asked quickly. Raifa glowered, but carried John and her plate back inside.

Aunt Kate sat in a porch rocker with Rowdy at her feet, taking occasional bites and saying over and over, "I hate to eat when you all aren't eating, too. Won't you have something? There's so much."

"No, you go right ahead," Mrs. Keene kept replying. It was like a duet.

Abby and I ate on the front steps while Freda told us, "I'm going into seventh grade, and I like to ride horses and play the piano. I play for church. What do you like to do?"

"Read, mostly." I felt like a boring clod. "I took piano lessons back home."

"I take lessons from my Aunt Rilla. She lives over there, next to the cemetery. And we live way up there, on the hill." She pointed to a white house so distant I hadn't noticed it before. It had four two-story columns holding up the porch roof, a white gazebo, and a large white fenced pasture where three horses grazed. Graceful and huge, the house overlooked the entire valley—a mansion fit for a princess.

"Abby," Mrs. Keene asked, "do you think you're going to like it here?"

Abby, her mouth full of chicken and her chin all greasy, heaved a dramatic sigh. "I dist hope to goodness Daddy can keep all dese peoples straight."

She sounded so like her mother that Aunt Kate gasped with

embarrassment, but Mr. Keene laughed so hard I could see fillings in his back teeth. "Nobody's ever kept the folks in Job's
Corner straight, honey. But if anybody could, I bet it'd be your
daddy."

He stood and jingled change in his pocket. "I think I'll run
over and see if Stephen's finding everything to his satisfaction.
Can you ladies take care of yourselves?" As soon as his wife
nodded, he headed for a well-worn path through the weeds and
over the tracks.

Mrs. Keene smiled brightly at Aunt Kate. "Did you bring
the girl with you?" She jerked her head daintily toward the
house.

"Yes. I don't know what we'd do without her. She's an angel
with the children."

I nearly choked on my green beans.

Mrs. Keene lowered her voice. "Have you found her a place
to stay?"

Aunt Kate looked embarrassed. "We're putting her upstairs
at the back for now."

"Oh, I don't think you—" Mrs. Keene stopped abruptly and
cocked her head, listening to John's screams. "Is that baby sick?
I'm a trained nurse. I'd be glad to look at him."

"Would you?" Aunt Kate hurried in and carried him out.

Mrs. Keene sat in a rocker and laid him on her lap. Carefully
she poked and prodded his scrawny body, then shook her head.
"He doesn't look good. Is he eating well?"

Seemed to me like she had no business asking that, skinny
as she was, but Aunt Kate sighed and shook her head. "He's not
eating at all. Or, rather, he throws up anything he gets down.
I've tried everything I can think of, but—" She sighed again,
sounding very sad. "I hope it's just the move—that when we're
all settled down—"

She stopped for a train whistle in the distance.

Mrs. Keene pinched John's skin between two long fingers
and let it go. It stayed pinched. "He needs to see a doctor soon.
Let me give you a number." She took a little pad out of her
purse and wrote from memory with a little gold pencil. As she
was handing the paper to Aunt Kate, we heard the train whistle
again, nearer.

A woman called from the walk, "Hey, there! My husband
says you're all moved in." She bounced up our walk, ruddy and
damp in a homemade green sundress and sturdy brown lace-up

shoes. Her black hair, frizzy on the ends from an old perm, was held off her pink face with a bobby pin.

Just as she reached our steps we heard a thundering as if the train had jumped its tracks and was heading straight for our porch. Abby yelled. I leaped up and whirled around, heart thudding in rhythm with the thuckety-thuckety-thuckety of wheels eating up track. Rowdy lurched to his feet and would have hurled himself at the engine if I hadn't grabbed his collar. Instead, he barked himself hoarse. As the engine slowed, the noise was deafening. Our whole house shook.

In the yard next door we saw Sue Mary run from her sandbox to the edge of the grass and wave like mad. Preston dashed out of their house and across the lawn to slide to a stop on the gravel verge, holding out his arms. A man in blue overalls and matching cap held on to an empty boxcar with one hand and swung a bag with the other. Preston caught it and waved. The little engine whistled again for the upper crossing, picked up speed, and clattered away. The man in blue hung out his door waving as long as we could see him. Preston and Sue Mary waved and Rowdy barked while the train disappeared. Pauline Anderson lumbered out her door shouting something I could not hear.

As if nothing had happened, the newcomer thrust a work-reddened hand at Aunt Kate. "I'm Nancy Lamont, Sunday school superintendent. We live just up the road." She turned to Abby and me. "Don't you girls ever go on those train tracks without a grown-up. That train has no set schedule, and it can come up on you out of the blue." Her words were short and sharp, like a hatchet. "The man next door was killed by a train. He never heard it coming."

Abby was fascinated. "Was he all mushed 'n' bloody?"

"He certainly was." She turned back to Aunt Kate as if she hadn't just been scaring us to death. "We're glad you got here. I'll be bringing your dinner tomorrow—not that I can cook as good as Emily's Miranda." She laughed, sounding jolly but not happy.

There was an awkward silence. I wondered if Aunt Kate was remembering, as I was, Mrs. Keene's little laugh when she'd said all that cooking was "nothing."

Miss Nancy broke the silence by heading for the front door. "I'd like to run inside a minute, to make sure everything's in order. We had a girl who was supposed to clean, but—" She left the sentence dangling. Mrs. Keene and Freda both followed her into our house.

"Going to see what we brought," Aunt Kate told me softly, biting a chicken leg.

We heard them in the hall, in the back rooms, then tromping up the stairs. After a while they trooped back through the screened door. "Why on earth have you put that baby's crib in your room? There are two perfectly good empty bedrooms upstairs!" Miss Nancy asked as soon as she reached the porch.

Aunt Kate hastily swallowed her last bite of roll. "I'd rather have him near me. It's easier to get up with him in the night."

"You shouldn't get up with children," she said firmly. "Just let them cry."

Abby stared at her in horror. Aunt Kate gave a strained little laugh. "Oh, I'd rather have them downstairs, anyway. What if there's a fire?"

Now *I* stared in horror. She hadn't minded putting Raifa and me up there.

"You haven't put anything in the parlor yet," Freda pointed out. "Mrs. Grant had the prettiest rose velvet sofa."

"I'm going to let the girls play in there. The middle room is so much lighter. Oh, look!" She sounded relieved. "Here's Stephen!" Beyond the dirt road, railroad, and paved road, I saw Uncle Stephen and Mr. Keene waiting for a truck to pass so they could cross.

Miss Nancy went right on as if Aunt Kate hadn't spoken. "And those movers mistook Mrs. Grant's best guest room for the minister's study. The study's right here with its own door, where people can find him if they need him. They've put a pink bed in there!" She couldn't have sounded more scandalized if she'd caught us hiding bodies.

"That's my room," Abby told her importantly. "It's got shelves for my toys 'n' books 'n' *stuff*." As if reminded of all that stuff, she trotted inside to play.

Miss Nancy rared back like a banty hen. "Those shelves are a memorial! My husband built them in memory of my father."

Her lips looked like a drawstring marble bag and her voice had carried. Uncle Stephen hurried up the walk with his widest smile. "Sorry I wasn't here to greet you folks. Everything all right, Kate?" He climbed the steps two at a time and went to lay a hand on her shoulder. I had the odd sense he was protecting her.

Miss Nancy stuck out her hand. "Hello, Mr. Whitfield. I'm Nancy Lamont, Sunday school superintendent. I was just pointing out that the pastor's study is the room right off the porch, here, with its own outside door. It has the Tom Macallester memorial bookshelves, given in memory of my father." Indignation rose from her with the smell of baby powder.

Uncle Stephen gave her the smile Big Mama said could charm a turtle into trying to fly. "If your father raised children as nice as you, I know he wouldn't mind if his shelves were used for a little girl's toys until she's old enough to sleep upstairs. I was so delighted, you see, to get a study upstairs. Remember what the Psalmist said, 'I will lift up mine eyes to the hills'? I look forward to working with those lovely mountains out my window. I've never had such an inspirational view."

Miss Nancy looked like she had more to say, but Mr. Keene shoved up his sleeve and looked at his gold watch. "I need to get back to work. Want a lift up the road, Nancy?"

"No, I need to stop by Pauline's." She gave us a wave and trotted away.

He offered his elbow to help his wife up. "Goodbye for now. Be sure to call if you need anything."

Freda reached out and shook my hand. "It's been *real* good to meet you, Carley. I *do* hope I'll see you Sunday. I just *know* we'll be friends." Her daddy beamed with approval. For an instant I regretted that I was going home. I'd never been friends with a princess before.

As they started down the steps, Mrs. Keene turned to Aunt Kate and said graciously, "Don't worry about getting the dishes back right away. Bring them to church, if you like."

When the Hudson rolled off in a cloud of dust, Uncle Stephen went in and filled a plate. When he came back, Aunt Kate gave a laugh that wasn't the least bit funny. "Bring the dishes to church, nothing! We'll take them before that."

"What's your hurry?" he asked, taking the rocker Mr. Hugh Fred had dusted.

"How can I carry dishes across a highway along with a baby, a diaper bag, and a Bible? Carley will have her hands full with Abby, and I doubt you'll be around to help."

"Carley won't be here," I reminded them. "I'll already be back at Big Mama's."

They didn't say a word. I got to my feet and went to stand

where they had to look at me. "When am I going? I thought it would be as soon as you moved. Will it be tomorrow?"

Aunt Kate looked troubled. "Not tomorrow, Carley. I can't think about anything else right now, except moving and John—" Her voice trembled.

How could I fuss after that? What if I bothered Aunt Kate and John died? Everybody would blame me. I'd already let Mama die. I should have made her come watch me wade.

"I'll stay as long as you need me," I promised reluctantly, making amends in the only coin I had. "Shall I go arrange Abby's things on the Macallester memorial?"

Uncle Stephen chuckled appreciatively. "That would be great." He bent his head over creamed corn, green beans, and chicken.

I slammed the screened door loudly behind me, but stayed just out of sight. I wanted to hear what they'd say after I was gone. And if you think I ought not to have listened to private conversations, you never got raised by Big Mama. I'd never have known a thing growing up if I hadn't learned to listen at doors and lie so still reading on the floor that she forgot I was there.

Aunt Kate sighed. "I don't know what to do. If Mama had just *told* her! But since she didn't, *we* certainly can't. Not yet, anyway."

I heard him forking up food. "Does Mrs. Marshall know yet when it will be?"

"Nobody does. Mama's simply petrified."

Petrified? Big Mama? I'd seen her kill a rattler with a hoe and talk a drunk off our front porch. I couldn't imagine her scared of anything. And what was the "it" Uncle Stephen was talking about? When he spoke again, though, it was about something entirely different. "Did everything go all right while I was gone?" He sounded anxious.

Again Aunt Kate gave that odd, not-funny laugh. "Except that we've got a Negro living here, Abby's sleeping in the preacher's study, and you're studying in Mrs. Grant's best guest room. I never met Mrs. Grant, but I'm beginning to dislike her intensely."

"You'd have disliked her if you *had* met her. I did years ago, and she was a tartar. But remember, honey, the Grants were here for thirty years. People got used to their ways. We'll have to be tolerant and patient, make changes slowly."

"You're a fine one to talk. I thought you'd have a fit this

morning when the men didn't want Jay and Raifa drinking lemonade out here with them."

"That was different. After Jay was kind enough to offer to help us move in—"

"You can't change everything overnight. We'll *both* have to be tolerant and patient and make changes slowly. But what business is it of anybody's where we put our furniture?"

"Absolutely none. But they *were* kind to bring the food." He set his plate on the floor for Rowdy to lick. "How about if we take a look around our new estate? There's a little barn out back where I thought about fixing a dog pen. Shall we go see? I haven't had five minutes alone with you all day."

They wandered off holding hands, and I went to shelve Abby's toys—and worry myself into a stomachache about what might be making Big Mama so scared when I wasn't there.

Chapter 7

L ate that afternoon we met a witch.
　　She was wide and dumpy, with skin like raw biscuit dough and hair like white thread skinned up to a little bun on top of her head. Her nose curved down over lips so thin they were just pink lines cut across wrinkles. Her eyebrows were white caterpillars, her eyes huge and gray behind rimless glasses. Their glance was as impersonal as a snake's.

She came late, when the sun had crossed the house and left the dining room dim and cool. All afternoon Uncle Stephen had been unpacking books and making bookshelves out of the wooden boxes. While Raifa unpacked in the kitchen—singing along with her radio—Abby and I colored under the dining room table. Aunt Kate played with John in his black rubber tub set on the table over our heads, and Rowdy thumped his stubby tail on the floor at her feet.

After dinner Aunt Kate had taken a bath and put on a clean aqua sundress. It wasn't as pretty as the dresses Mama wore—Big Mama often said it was a shame Aunt Kate spent so little on herself since she got married—but as she stood smiling down at John, even plump and worn out with no lipstick on, she looked pretty. Uncle Stephen must have thought so, too, because he came in for a minute, stood very close to her, and buried his face in her neck.

After he went back upstairs, she powdered and dressed John—who started screaming at once. With a big sigh, she sat on the sofa and tried to give him another bottle. As always, the milk no sooner got down than it came right back up. He started squalling. Aunt Kate stood and began walking him. That's when the witch appeared.

Rowdy gave one sharp bark, then we heard, "What's the matter with that youngun?" Her voice was scratchy and soft with a high whine. As soon as I heard it, I became aware that Abby, Aunt Kate, John, and I were alone. Maybe it sounds funny: four of us alone. But "alone" has more to do with feeling safe than with numbers.

I pushed Abby into a far corner under the table and crouched in front of her, peering out. The woman was broad of hip and shoulder, with long, powerful arms. Her feet—which I could see best—bulged in her brown shoes like they wanted to rip the leather wide open and let her toes spring free. The shoes rolled to the outside, like she often walked along a ridge. Between her ankles, which were covered with white socks, and her draggy black skirt, her calves were fish-belly white.

I hoped Aunt Kate would slam the door in her face and call Uncle Stephen. Instead, she answered like the witch was an ordinary woman. "Poor baby, he's had a rough trip and can't seem to keep down his milk."

"From the look of 'im, he ain' kep' nothin' down since he 'uz born." She stomped across the room and poked his chest with one thick finger.

Aunt Kate drew him back slightly, but managed to smile. "I'm Kate Whitfield."

"'N' I'm Gert Baines. My husband Ira 'uz helpin' out earlier. We live across the road, and I wondered if you'd be needin' he'p with your house and younguns. I got lots of experience with younguns. Got one of my own." She paused and said almost reverently: "Ivy. 'N' I usta he'p out Miz Grant." She stopped and stood there, a pure lump of ugliness.

How long had she watched the house before she decided it was time to force her sore feet into tight shoes, cover her wide buttocks with hope and her second-best black skirt, and hobble across two roads and a railroad track to offer her services? At the time, I figured she'd zoomed over by broomstick.

Raifa stuck her head in. "Mrs. Whitfield, you wanting—oh, pardon me. I didn't know you had comp'ny." Raifa always popped in when somebody came, always begged pardon, and always told the same lie: "I didn't know you had comp'ny." Aunt Kate introduced the two witches, then sent Raifa back to the kitchen.

Raifa wasn't gone good before the witch demanded, "You brung her with you?"

Aunt Kate nodded. "We hope she'll like it here and stay. She's real good with the children. Girls," she called, bending down a little to catch my eye, "come meet Mrs. Baines."

I reluctantly dragged Abby out and we climbed to our feet, but I clasped my hands behind my back while Aunt Kate said our names. Abby usually did what I did, and I didn't want Abby shaking her hand. The witch shook her head and pursed her lips. "Funny names," she said, looking down at us through steel-rimmed glasses. I could see myself in her lenses and wondered if she could see herself in mine.

She looked back at Abby and bent to stroke her hair. "Abigail's a Bible name," I said loudly to turn her attention.

"A queen." Abby stuck a finger in her mouth, lifted her eyes, and smiled. I wished she were as plain as I. Witches always preferred pretty children. Sure enough—

"Yon one's bonnie." She looked back at Aunt Kate. "Two girls 'n' one boy. That all you got?"

"Actually, Carley's my niece, staying here while we get settled. We just have the two."

"Grants had ten, all born whilst they lived here." Mrs. Baines's eyes darted from Abby to John as if urging them to multiply. "Mrs. Grant's buried right over there." She jerked her head toward the front of the house and paused for Aunt Kate to reply.

In her journal, Aunt Kate would later write: *Mrs. Grant had herself buried near enough to rise up and haunt me when necessary.*

The pause grew long before Aunt Kate said, with a nervous little laugh, "Two children are plenty for me."

"Well, if you're not needin' he'p, I'll be gettin' on home. I'll be glad to come over when your girl hightails it off. Never can tell when they'll up and go."

I looked at Aunt Kate, expecting fireworks. Instead, she pressed her lips hard together.

Before she left, Mrs. Baines stumped over to the couch to pick up the cloth Aunt Kate used to wipe John's mouth after he spat up. When she put it to her nose, I held my breath. What spell was she casting on our baby? She sniffed once, then dropped it. "If that baby cain't keep nothing else down, git him milk straight from the cow. They's some babies cain't take nothin' else. Smells like he's one of 'em." Without a word of farewell she trudged out. The screened door slammed behind her.

"Witch!" I hissed.

"Witch!" Abby echoed, crawling back under the table.

"Carley! If you can't say something nice about somebody, say nothing at all. You know how Abby copies you." Aunt Kate's temper cooled as fast as it rose. She put an arm around me and pulled me over to the couch. "I'm sorry, honey," she said softly, "but you need to understand something. Stephen has come here to preach God's love. If we're rude, they'll think he can't even teach his family. Do you want to shame him?" I shook my head, but something welled up inside me—something so big I had to blow out through my nose and so dark I expected black smoke to come from my nostrils.

Aunt Kate gave me a squeeze. "I know what you mean, though. I was glad you were here when she came. I might have been scared, if I'd been by myself." I preened to think I had protected her from anything. She gave me a harder squeeze. "I love you, Carolina Rose, but remember: from now on, that woman is Miz Baines." Aunt Kate was a wonderful mimic. She said the name just like the witch said it.

"Miz Baines," I repeated. "May I call her Miz Baines?" We both knew it was sassy. Special women were honorary aunts. Others were "Miss-plus-a-first-name" or given the full, respectful "Mizziz."

Aunt Kate winked. "Miz Baines will be fine."

Late that afternoon, Mrs. Keene came back. "I had to see that baby again." When Aunt Kate handed John to her, she gave him a kiss that left a bright pink flower on his forehead, then clasped him to her flat bosom. "Bless your heart, I've been thinking about you all afternoon. Did your mommy call the doctor?"

"We have an appointment tomorrow morning." Aunt Kate hesitated, then asked in a quick, anxious voice, "Have you ever heard of giving a baby fresh cow's milk? Mrs. Baines was here earlier and suggested it."

"Gert might know," Mrs. Keene said thoughtfully. "She's helped raise a lot of children. If she said try it, I'd try it. Let's call Hannah and see if she has any left." She headed for the telephone in the hall. "She'll bring it right up," she reported in just a minute.

Years later, when my own children were babies, I read an article saying cow's milk is not suitable for infants. I mailed it to John, then six-foot-four. He mailed it on to Aunt Kate, scribbling in the margin, "NOW they tell us!" Because when Hannah Anderson brought up a fresh bottle of milk, the cream thick on top, and Aunt Kate warmed it and fed it to John, he drank greedily, gave a healthy burp, laid his head on Aunt Kate's shoulder, and went fast asleep.

Aunt Kate swears he wore his first smile.

From then on, every morning Davy Anderson deposited two quarts of fresh milk on our doorstep before we were up. John thrived.

❋

That evening we had a leftovers picnic on the front porch. The sun wasn't down yet, but the day had that sleepy, golden look it gets just before the sun slips over the edge of the world. Uncle Stephen took his plate to the swing. "Come sit by me, Kate. After supper we can smooch." She blushed happily and went to join him.

Raifa filled a plate and dragged a rocking chair over to where John lay in a cardboard box Aunt Kate had padded with a quilt to make him a porch bed. He lay contented, staring up at nothing. Abby and I took our plates and perched on the top step, using the porch floor as a table between us. Rowdy stayed close to Aunt Kate, where he most loved to be.

"Look, Abby, see how pretty our new church looks?" Uncle Stephen sounded as proud as if he'd built it himself. No wonder. The miners' churches he'd served were all small and dingy, but Bethel's red brick sanctuary sat high atop a daylight basement in a large grassy lawn. Its roof was shaded by a grove of maples, oaks, and one enormous magnolia. Fifteen white steps led up to a white columned porch, and double white doors led inside.

Raifa voiced what we were all thinking. "It's a real pretty church."

While we ate, several cars drove slowly by, raising clouds of dust. Everybody waved, but nobody stopped. Next door, Sue Mary sat in her sandbox with her back to us. When we'd finally eaten our coconut cake down to crumbs, Aunt Kate waved away the flies and said, distressed, "I used all our waxed paper after lunch and we've still got tons of leftovers."

"Put bowls over them," Uncle Stephen said lazily. "That's what Mama always did."

"Your mama had eight boys to eat leftovers fast. We're going to be eating them for days. I'll have to refrigerate a lot of stuff, and I don't have that many bowls. You can't imagine how much food is in that kitchen."

"Send Carley and Abby to the store. Davy said it stays open until dark and has a bit of anything people are apt to run out of. I'd say waxed paper is something people run out of." He fumbled in his pocket and brought out a silver half-dollar. "Here, Carley. Get yourselves each a piece of candy, too, and bring back the change."

It was far enough to feel adventurous and close enough to feel safe. Barefoot and holding hands, Abby and I skipped down the warm cement walk and picked our way gingerly along the soft edge of the dirt road, avoiding sharp gravel. As we passed the cotton field next to our yard, dusk settled around us with a smell of honeysuckle and sweet hay.

The journey from the manse to Mrs. Cameron's store was no mere skip next door. It was an excursion back in time.

"Dis isn't no store," Abby objected when I led her off the dusty road onto the foot-worn path through Mrs. Cameron's broad lawn. It wasn't like any store I'd ever seen, either. No bigger than a good-sized room perched high on six brick pillars, it had been hammered out in hand-hewn boards and painted with time and red dust by the brush of the wind. The setting sun drew from its weathered boards a soft glow of silver, brown, and pearl pink.

The narrow dirt path, cool beneath our soles, meandered crookedly through the rough-cut grass to four wooden steps leading to a bowed porch. The building did not look so much derelict as ancient, sinking wearily into the earth.

Whatever it contained, it guarded well. There were no windows on the front, just two wide wooden doors held back by rump-sprung straight chairs. Any view of the dim interior was blocked by the bulge of rusty screened doors decorated with faded Cheerwine signs. A small woman dressed in black was planted on a third chair in front of the screens.

Mrs. Cameron was bent by age into the same crook as the black cane on which she rested her chin. Her hair was yellow-white, pulled back to a knot on top of her head, and secured with enormous gray hairpins. Between the scanty strands I could see her scalp. She didn't say a word until we reached the steps, then raised her head and peered at us from under bushy eyebrows thicker than her hair, and just as white. "What you younguns want?"

"We're from next door—"

"I know where you're from and what you're doing there. Your mama send you?"

"She's not my mama—" I began, but Abby interrupted importantly.

"Wax paper. We wants wax paper."

It was the first time I was ever sent to a store," Abby *would write later in my margin. "I felt as big as you."*

The old woman waved one arm toward the left side of the store. "Next to the bottom shelf near the front. Blue box. Don't touch anything else."

Abby skipped to the door, looked in, then shook her curls. "I'm not going in dere. It's dark!" She backed to the top step and sat down, her lower lip a sulky perch. When I got to the screened doors, I wished I were three. I didn't want to go in, either. The single window at the back was caked with dust. The only light in the whole place was the patch of sun slanting sideways through the screened doors, making my shadow enormous.

I turned back to the old woman. "I don't think I can find it."

She jerked her head toward the door. "Go on in there. Ain't nothing gonna bite a big girl like you." Our gazes held until she won.

My fear turned to anger. I was mad at Uncle Stephen for sending us when he could have come himself and madder at the old woman who couldn't be bothered to wait on us. Scraping open one screened door, I stomped onto the gritty floorboards. Then my bare toes curled. Wide cracks lay between the boards. Rats as big as cats probably lurked under there.

While my eyes were adjusting, I forgot where the old woman kept the waxed paper. Not brave enough to go back out and come in again, I peered desperately around the gloom.

Strange, unidentifiable shapes hung from the ceiling and high on the wall. Lumpy piles lay on the floor. On nearly empty shelves a few loaves of bread sat next to toilet paper, spools of thread next to sugar. Cans of chicken noodle soup were mixed in with matches, wax candles, and a galvanized bucket of nails. It smelled of tobacco, coolness, red dirt, and bread. Just like I'd feared, something rustled in a far corner. Clenching my fist to keep from running back out and disgracing myself, I looked harder. There! Two blue boxes on a bottom shelf.

"What you doing in there?" her cracked old voice called from the porch.

I grabbed a box and headed toward the door at a trot. In my haste, I blundered into a long strip of flypaper dangling from the ceiling. Rough with dried victims, it caught my hair.

"Don't you touch nothing 'cept what you came for," she warned. "You hear me?"

I flailed at the flypaper with the waxed paper box and yanked out several hairs to get free. "Don't you worry. I won't!" Pelting through the front doors I came to a stop before her and scrubbed my fingers furiously through my hair. "I'll probably be combing out dead flies for days. It's filthy in there," I told her hotly.

"Folks get what they pay for," she replied.

"I'm not paying for dirt." I swiped the waxed paper with one hand and got a thick red smear on my hand. "Just look at that! If we use this to wrap our food, we'll probably get ptomaine poison." I blew a cloud of dust into the evening air. "Phew!"

"Phew!" repeated my faithful echo from the top step.

"Don't get sassy, Missy. You bring any money?"

I dug in my pocket and pulled out the half-dollar. She jerked her head toward a yellow cigar box sitting on a table just by the door. "Take it for a quarter and make change."

The box held a dollar, five quarters, and a nickel. I held a quarter on my palm to show I wasn't cheating her. "My granddaddy kept a store, but he kept his *clean*."

She stared me down. "My husband kept this store nigh on sixty years afore he died. I don't 'spect your granddaddy had that kind of record."

Abby remembered what we'd been told at lunch. "Did your daddy get runned over by a train? Was he all mushed?"

Abby's bad manners shocked me as my own had not. "Don't mind her, ma'am. Somebody told us the tracks are kindly dangerous."

The crone leaned so far forward on her chair that I thought she'd fall on top of Abby. "He was right smart mushed, Missy. You stay off those tracks, 'less you got your sister with you. You hear me?"

Not the least abashed, Abby shook her head. "I don't got a

sister. I gots a baby brudder. He cried all de time, but den he drunk milk—"

Abby was capable of talking all night. I grabbed her by the hand and jerked her down the steps. "We gotta go now. Bye."

Abby called over her shoulder, "You can come see my baby if you wants. He's cute when he isn't crying." I jerked her hand again.

"You're hurting me!" she protested. "And dis road has rocks. Carry me."

With a sigh I bent and hauled her up onto one hip. Facing back toward the store, she remembered something. "Stop! Right dis minute!" She squeezed her arms around my neck so tight she cut off my air. "Daddy said we could get candy."

I tugged her arms to loosen them. "I am not going into that dark filthy place again tonight. Besides, the candy would probably be so dirty it'd kill us."

She opened her mouth and took a deep breath. An Abby Roar would wake the dead in the cemetery and bring every living soul in Job's Corner to their yards. "Look!" I cried, desperate, "Fairies! In our yard. See?" The first fireflies were beginning to test their batteries.

She squirmed down and ran toward them, chortling.

Relieved, I walked slowly past the cotton field through the deepening dusk, watching the soft cold lights come and go and feeling sadness well up inside me like water in a fountain. I stopped, lifted my face to the first star, and exhaled wishes from my open mouth. They fell all round me in a spray of invisible light.

I wished I was at Big Mama's about to take my bath in her big claw-foot tub. I wished I could rock on her porch to watch the sun set over the mountains. I wished I could climb into my own bed and pull up a sheet still smelling of Pearl's hot iron. I wished I could go somewhere and cry. I wished Mama hadn't died.

❧

Parked in front of our house was a dilapidated black Chevy even older than Uncle Stephen's. The porch light was on, showing two strangers standing on the steps with their backs to us. I ambled up the walk slower and slower, not wanting to meet anybody else.

As I got closer, however, I recognized the woman: Janey

Lou, still in her navy cotton dress but without the apron. The man's skin shone darker, almost black in the light. He wore ironed work pants and a work shirt as gray as his tight curls. Both stood awkwardly, saying nothing.

Uncle Stephen leaned up against one porch pillar like he was relaxed as could be, but he shoved back his hair as I came up the steps. Aunt Kate, burping John in a rocker, darted him a quick anxious look, then looked back at John. Her hair gleamed in the dimness, but her face was white as a moth circling the porch light. When Abby—hanging on her chair arm—tried to tell her about the fireflies, Aunt Kate shushed her impatiently.

"You remember Carley, don't you, Janey Lou?" Uncle Stephen sounded too friendly, too bright. He said her name like he thought I'd forgotten it, like no white person but him could remember a Negro's name.

"Of course we remember each other, Uncle Stephen. We just met this morning. How you doin', Janey Lou?"

Before she could reply, Uncle Stephen went on talking about me like I wasn't even there. "Carley's been over to Mrs. Cameron's to get us some waxed paper."

"And I need to get food wrapped, if you'll excuse me." Aunt Kate got up, laid the box of waxed paper on top of sleepy John, and hurried inside. Abby chattered at her heels.

Uncle Stephen started talking again right away. "Carley, this is Janey Lou's husband, Meek. They've come to invite Raifa to stay with her sister."

"She's got an extra room," Janey Lou explained.

If they thought I'd protest that Raifa already had a room, they had another think coming. I didn't want to sleep on the same floor with her. Big Mama's Aunt Helen had her throat slit by a Negro woman who worked in her house. Big Mama had told me that story several times. And not long ago the Charlotte paper told about a Negro butler who stabbed his mistress to death. I'd already figured out how to jam my door so Raifa couldn't creep into my room and slit my throat.

Before anybody could say anything else, Raifa came down carrying a cardboard box, her radio tucked under one arm. "This is all I'll need for tonight. I can get the rest tomorrow." She went down the steps, got in the car, and slammed the door without another word.

Janey Lou gave me a smile that made a gold tooth gleam.

"Come back to see Miss Hannah sometime, Carley. She really enjoyed you girls this morning."

"I will," I promised.

Uncle Stephen walked them to the car. I went to sit in the porch swing outside the circle of light and pushed off with one bare toe.

As I slowly swung back and forth, Uncle Stephen stood on the front walk watching Meek's taillights cross the railroad tracks and turn onto the highway. Then he came slowly up the steps. "There wasn't a blessed thing I could do."

Was he apologizing to me, Raifa, or God?

Part 2

Early in the Morning Our Song Shall Rise . . .

From the circle around the Remember Box, I select Uncle Stephen's favorite briar pipe, a yellowed bulletin with words penciled in the margin, and a snapshot of two little girls in the sandbox. On the back Aunt Kate has written "Sue Mary, Abby, and Velma." How could Abby forget Velma? I add the map I made of Job's Corner and left on Uncle Stephen's desk, touched to find he kept it. Finally I choose a small granite stone shaped like a heart. As I hold it in my palm, it warms up like love.

Chapter 8

When I woke our first morning in Job's Corner, my room was the same soft pearly gray as the sky, for I had left my shades up to catch the breeze. I'd gone to sleep hearing an owl in the pasture and frogs down at some creek. Now I heard several roosters. Out the curved east window, pink glimmered where the day was just opening its eyes. I woke thinking about Big Mama, Pop, and Mama. When I couldn't stand it, I reached for my glasses and got up.

I put on a blue shorts set and crept downstairs with a Nancy Drew I'd only read once.

Uncle Stephen and Rowdy stood in the front hall. "You're up early," he said softly, picking up his summer hat—a gray straw with a navy band. "Want to take a walk?"

"Yessir!" I felt as privileged as royalty.

Uncle Stephen always rose at dawn, put on his hat, took a long stick, and went for a walk. He claimed getting up early becomes a habit if you grow up milking cows. By the time Aunt Kate got up he was always in the kitchen cooking breakfast, singing, "Holy, Holy, Holy, Lord God Almighty, early in the morning our song shall rise to thee." Uncle Stephen's own song rose a little off-key.

I tiptoed out ahead, and he closed the screened door behind us. "I don't know why we're so quiet," he said. "Kate and Abby sleep through anything, and John's making up for lost time." But we still spoke in hushed voices. The newborn day seemed holy as church.

The cement walk was cool and rough beneath my bare feet,

the air fresh and sweet with growing things. Uncle Stephen cocked his head. "Does it seem to you that colors are brighter and birds louder at dawn? At this hour, Nature shows her hand. Most of the time she pretends to be subdued by us, but early every morning she comes out and roars."

Seemed to me Uncle Stephen was almost as poetical as Mama.

We turned toward Preston's. Rowdy snuffled happily beside us, getting to know the neighborhood in a doggy way. The dust was soft and squishy between my toes, but some rocks were sharp. "Can you walk barefoot?" Uncle Stephen asked when I winced.

"Yessir," I assured him. "My soles are tough." I'd have walked over spikes for the privilege of walking with him. I hadn't had a man to talk to since Pop died.

I still missed Pop a lot. Slender and dapper, smelling of Old Spice, he talked to me about baseball, the store, and current events—very superior to my friends' daddies, who smelled of hair oil and just asked if they'd done their homework. I'd never missed having a daddy until I started school. When I asked Mama about him, her face got a look like a wadded Kleenex and her voice wobbled when she said, "He came to a tragic end just before you were born."

I threw my arms around her neck. "Don't cry, Mama. We don't need a daddy. We got Pop." After that, we never brought the subject up again.

But it was nice to walk beside Uncle Stephen, especially when he lit his pipe. The spicy aroma enclosed the magic of the morning. And if you are wondering why a preacher was smoking, remember: North Carolina is the tobacco capital of the world, and in 1949, nobody was talking about health hazards. Most men in the state smoked and many women, too—the difference was, most women sneaked.

"How about if we talk about each family as we go along?" he proposed around his pipe stem. "That will help fix them in our minds. This first house"—he gestured with his pipe—"belongs to Miss Pauline Anderson and her three children: Preston, Sue Mary, and Bonnie—who's going to eighth grade. Bailey Anderson was Davy's brother, but he died of a heart attack soon after Sue Mary was born. You and Preston have that in common—you both understand what it's like to lose a parent."

I'd lost *two*, but losing a hundred wouldn't give me one thing in common with Preston. When I didn't say any of the nice things he expected, Uncle Stephen sucked his pipe. "Think Sue Mary will ever forgive Abby and become friends?"

"I don't know. I'm not sure Sue Mary would be much of a friend, anyhow."

He pointed toward an unpainted building half the size of Mrs. Cameron's store, but a whole lot sturdier, perched on pillars at the front of the Anderson yard. "Know what that is?"

As Rowdy lifted one leg to mark its pillars, I guessed. "A chicken house?"

"He can't wet on that! It's gov'mint propity!" Preston dashed up gasping for breath. He'd run so hard, his eyes looked like blue marbles stuck in bright pink bubblegum with orange dots. To his overalls from the day before he'd added a disreputable straw hat and a hoe.

Rowdy lowered his leg and snuffled on around the corner. Like me, he didn't think Preston worth noticing. Uncle Stephen, however, lifted his hat. "Mornin', Preston. Out early?"

"No, sir. I mean, yessir." Preston pulled off his own hat to wipe sweat from his forehead. I'd have been ashamed to put that hat on a mule, but Preston smelled worse than a mule. I stepped back as he panted, "Me 'n' Bonnie was weeding." He jerked his head toward the back of a huge garden between his house and the next, where a tall skinny girl was hoeing vigorously. "But I told her I'd come show you around a bit." He settled his hat back on his head. "Mama makes me wear this to keep off the sun. I freckle."

"You aren't telling us anything we don't know," I informed him.

Uncle Stephen laid a warning hand on my shoulder. "Then you certainly need to wear a hat. Tell us about this interesting little building."

"That's the United States post office. Mama's the postmistress."

"When can we expect the mail each day?"

"Whenever the train comes up track on its way to Mr. Keene's chair facktry. When she's got it put out, Mama hauls up the flag. Afternoon paper comes then, too," he added proudly, "The *Staichville Daily Record*."

"It isn't Staichville, it's Statesville," I corrected him.

"That's just how it's spelled. We say Staichville." He started hoeing long grass beside the post office steps. "Get a few snakes here from time to time." He slid a sideways look at me. I didn't flinch. He was just fooling and we both knew it.

Uncle Stephen looked at the railroad tracks like they'd changed in the last five minutes. "I knew that spur went up to Hugh Fred's factory, but I didn't realize the post office used it."

"Yessir." Preston leaned on his hoe like an old farmer. "They throw off the bag when they come up, and Mama throws it back on when they go down."

"We'll watch for the flag. And we'll leave you to your weeding."

Preston shook his head. "I told Bonnie I'd show you 'round some. She won't mind if I'm gone a little while." He propped the hoe confidently against the post office.

Uncle Stephen puffed his pipe. "Looks like a big garden for one person to weed."

"We just got the back. The front is Miss Nancy's." He pointed toward someone working near the road. I couldn't see her face for a big straw hat, but the shape was familiar.

"Neither Preston nor Pauline ever do a lick of work they can help," Aunt Kate would tell Big Mama, "but they both work poor Bonnie to death."

"Mornin', Miss Nancy," Preston called cheerfully as we reached the garden. It gave out a musty smell of leaves, dirt, and growing things.

She wore a flowered wash dress, a straw hat, an apron, and house shoes. She looked up and laid one hand on the bib of her apron. "Oh, Mr. Whitfield, I hate to have you see me looking like this. I was picking beans for your dinner. Would you like a tomato for your breakfast?"

She turned to a tomato row behind her and wrenched off a big red one. She handed it in my direction, so I started toward her through the tall grass between the road and garden.

A sound like dried beans in a gourd came from somewhere between us. Her eyes grew big. I felt like I'd turned to ice.

"Stop, Carley," Uncle Stephen commanded—as if he needed to!

At the sound of his voice the noise stopped, then rattled again.

Uncle Stephen raised his stick and stepped cautiously past me. "Can you tell where it is, Miss Nancy?" he murmured, moving stealthily forward.

"Under that first tomato. I see it!" She only moved one finger to point.

"Don't move." He needn't have warned her, either. She stood like a concrete duck.

Rowdy plunged after Uncle Stephen, nose to the ground. "Hold Rowdy back," Uncle Stephen said softly.

Did he expect me to wade into weeds after a dog with a rattler loose? I was frozen in the high grass, scarcely able to breathe.

Preston charged past me and dragged Rowdy back by the collar. "Come out of there! Come out!" Rowdy barked in protest and strained against him. Preston hung on.

The snake rattled again. Uncle Stephen crept slowly forward, stick raised.

"Hush that dog," Miss Nancy begged. Her black eyes were big as checkers. Sweat poured off her face in spite of her hat.

I felt so faint I thought I'd slide to the ground. But ashamed that Preston had been braver than me, I reached behind me to pet Rowdy. "Hush!" He leaned against my leg, hot, quivering, but still.

We all stood like statues.

Uncle Stephen's stick sliced the air with one fierce blow. "Got him," he said in satisfaction.

Miss Nancy sank to her knees with a long "whoosh," like she was a balloon somebody had stuck a pin in. "You saved my life, Mr. Whitfield. You plumb saved my life." Her hands were shaking, her face white. "We've never had a rattlesnake in this garden before."

Uncle Stephen prodded around with his stick, then lifted the heavy body. It was well over three feet long. Miss Nancy looked at it, shuddered, and stepped backwards—right into her bucket. It turned over and she fell. "Oh, my beans!" She started scrabbling around on her hands and knees in the dirt.

Uncle Stephen dropped the snake and bent to take her elbow. "You know, we have vegetables left from yesterday. Why don't you leave those beans and go rest a while? You deserve to sit down a minute."

When he helped her to her feet, she fanned herself with one hand. "I kinda think I might. Thank you. Thank you." She stomped across the field and up a well-worn path from her garden to a side porch cluttered with baskets, more buckets, and boots.

"That's where Lamonts live," Preston announced unnecessarily. "His dad, Mr. Rob, lives over there." He pointed across the road to the house past the church. "They're builders."

Washington Lamont must have used his leftover shingles on his own roof. It was a hodgepodge of brown, green, and black. The big old house was built like Davy Anderson's, but very severe. No shutters or porch rockers softened the house; no trees or even bushes softened the sparse hard lawn. Red geraniums in a white three-legged pot made the only splash of color—that and a dusty green tractor in the open door of an unpainted barn at the back.

Uncle Stephen brought the rattlesnake toward us and stopped with it five inches from me. I jumped back. Rowdy barked. Preston stood there whistling like he killed snakes daily. "Go drop this on the other side of the tracks, Preston."

Preston gingerly carried the stick over the tracks, dumped the snake quickly, and hurried back. Uncle Stephen asked him in spurts around the process of relighting his pipe, "Don't I remember that the Lamonts have children?"

"Yessir. Ruthie's ten and Jimmy's four."

Uncle Stephen laid a warm hand on my shoulder. "Sounds like a friend for you."

Before I could point out I wouldn't be around long enough to need a friend, Preston warned, "Ruthie and Jimmy don't play with other kids. Lamonts keep to themselves."

"I see." Uncle Stephen blew a cloud of smoke. "Well, let's mosey on." It didn't occur to him that anybody else might need to rest after that snake.

I trudged along behind, thinking how fine this ruined morning had promised to be and keeping a wary eye out in case that snake had kinfolk. When I finally let go of Rowdy, Preston picked up a stick and threw it. Rowdy obligingly dashed after it and brought it back. Preston threw it again.

"You're gonna wear him out," I objected. "He'll get all hot and tired."

"It's good for him. He's too fat."

"*You're* a fine one to talk!"

"I ain't fat, I'm fixing to have a growth spurt. In a year you'll come up to my chest."

"Dream on, Fatso."

Beyond the Lamont's and a cotton field the road curved

back across the tracks to the highway. Uncle Stephen paused. "Shall we make like chickens and cross the road?"

Preston hung back. "I ain't 'lowed across the road. 'Sides, ain't nothing over there 'cept the Baineses and Rob Lamont's. They're all a bit peculiar."

"The church is over there," Uncle Stephen reminded him.

"It ain't Sunday." He stood first on one leg and then the other, trying to decide between disobeying and hoeing. When we heard his mother bellow up the road, his relief was obvious. "Breakfast. Gotta go." He turned and galloped as fast as a fat boy could run in the direction of more food.

❧

Uncle Stephen took my elbow and bent to hold Rowdy firmly by the collar. "I don't ever want you crossing this road without permission, and always cross down at the house. That curve makes it hard to see what's coming, and cars just fly along here." As if to prove his point, a black-and-orange truck whizzed by so close that Rowdy and I both trembled.

On the other side we faced a field of new-mown hay. Uncle Stephen took a deep breath, and as I started up the broad stony verge he called from behind me, "Don't you think smelling hay on a summer morning is fine living? When a day is this new and fresh, I feel like we're given the privilege, just for a moment, to glimpse the very bottom of things."

"The bottom of things?" I was far more interested in black-berry briars trying to snatch me to the snakes who lived inside them.

"You know, like in the poem by Gerard Manley Hopkins, 'There lives the dearest freshness deep down things.' When a day looks and smells this good, I feel like we've finally gotten down near the very bottom, where everything is perennially new and fresh."

My mind sank to the dark blank well of unshed tears where I'd spent the summer. "Some bottoms aren't so pleasant."

As if he knew what I was thinking, Uncle Stephen dropped a warm hand onto my shoulder. "Painful places aren't the bottom, Carley, they're just on the way. To reach the very bottom sometimes we have to go through a lot of heartache." He squeezed my shoulder, then dropped his hand and added, "Even evil."

"Evil?" I spoke scornfully, swerving around a huge thistle. "You sound like you think we get to heaven by going to hell."

"Not *to* hell—but often through it. Hell's the place where people get stopped on their way to good—or what they perceive is good."

Another truck flew past, and I heard him mutter "Bother!" as he sidestepped right into an enormous blackberry bush.

"Hell is a lake of living fire," I reminded him, waiting for him to disentangle himself.

"Sure it is. Fire that burns the people there and anybody else they touch. But even wickedness recognizes the superiority of goodness. Every wicked thing in the world is done in the name of good. Hitler himself claimed he was building a better world. It's because our notion of good isn't always God's that people start toward the bottom and wind up stuck halfway down—like I'm stuck on this briar. Can you get my back?"

As I disengaged the grasping little hooks, he took a deep breath again. "Even with briars, life's good, Carley. And deep down at the bottom it is good and fresh. On days like this"— freed, he stepped onto the verge and waved one hand grandly— "we get a glimpse of it."

All I could glimpse was a little white house sitting next to the church cemetery. It wasn't much of a house, cowering beneath black walnuts and sycamores down a rutted drive, but a huge black dog guarded it like it was a castle, stiff-legged and barking threats that he'd eat us alive if he could only get free. I backed closer to Uncle Stephen, who seemed oblivious to our danger. "That dog's chain could snap any minute. Big Mama knows dogs who've killed people."

He looked like he was going to say one thing but decided to say something else. "That's where Gert and Ira Baines live, with their daughter, Ivy. See that white rocker under the tree? Hannah says Ivy sits in that chair hour after hour. She's apparently a little slow."

"Maybe she's enchanted. Her mama's a witch."

He stopped to relight his pipe. "You seem to know a lot about Mrs. Baines on slight acquaintance. Maybe she'll grow on you when you know her better."

"I don't want to know her better. Not her *or* her man-eating dog."

He laughed. "We need to improve your acquaintance with the animal kingdom." I was afraid he meant to begin right away, but he just waved his pipe toward the drive curving past the house into a piney wood. "Down that bend is another house we can't see, belonging to Janey Lou's sister Bess, and her son, Jay. He helped us move in, remember?"

"Yessir. Is that where Raifa is staying?" They might as well name it Witch Lane.

"No, she's another of Janey Lou's sisters, up in a community called Pleasantdale. That's where most Negroes live, so they can work at the chair factory. Janey Lou will bring Raifa down each day and take her back at night." He puffed hard to get the pipe going.

"Why didn't Raifa stay with Jay's mother? Then she could walk to work."

"They don't have room. Besides, Janey Lou and Meek thought Raifa would be happier up there. Bess and Jay Anderson are the only Negroes in Job's Corner proper."

That seemed odd to me. Where I came from, Negroes and whites lived all mixed together. Lots of driveways ended like Big Mama's, in a Negro family's swept yard. Pop's three farms had white and Negro sharecroppers, living just up the road from each other.

"Isn't it funny," I said, just to make conversation as I bent down to tug up a grass stalk to chew, "that they're Andersons, too—just like Preston and Mister Davy?"

"Probably descendants of Anderson slaves. Slaves were often given their master's surname—like Aunt Sukie's a Marshall, for instance."

I was so shocked, I swallowed wrong and choked. He slapped my back while tears ran down my cheeks. Finally I wiped my glasses and gasped, *My relatives didn't own slaves!*"

"Sure they did. Anybody down here who had money and land to farm owned slaves. It was a way of life. And it dies hard."

I no longer noticed sharp rocks underfoot. "How long ago was that? Were Big Mama and Pop alive?" Big Mama bossed Aunt Sukie a lot, and Pop used to fuss sometimes at the men on his farms, but I could no more imagine them buying and selling people than I could imagine them getting drunk. Just the thought made my stomach ache.

"Oh, no. Their *parents* were children during the war."

I felt a little better, but not much. Until then I'd thought Aunt Sukie was a Marshall because she lived in our house.

When I read about race riots in other places, I'd felt smug that our town had *good* race relations. Now . . .?

We'd finally reached the cemetery. Bending down, I picked up a clod of red dirt and flung it as hard as I could over the wall. It shattered against a granite tombstone with a satisfactory "thunk."

The church sat on a large grassy lawn broken by a circular drive and surrounded in back and on each side by the cemetery. The eastern half of the cemetery had a proper granite wall, but this western end was enclosed by only a low row of piled rocks. Rowdy climbed clumsily over to chase something only he could see in the tall cemetery grass. Uncle Stephen propped one foot on the rocks, puffed his pipe, and contemplated the cemetery's fuzzy short-leaf pines. I should have known he wasn't through talking about slaves. No matter how bad it made a body feel to think about her relatives owning some. I wondered miserably if Aunt Sukie knew, and how I'd ever face her again.

Uncle Stephen sucked his pipe some more, then waved it toward a dark tree in the distance. "These days there's a Negro church and cemetery up the road, but past that big holly tree you'll find a slaves' burial ground from days when everybody attended Bethel."

I had no intention of looking for slaves' graves, and I couldn't believe what he'd just said. "*Colored* people came to this church?"

"Negroes, Carley. As long as you live at our house, that's what we expect you to call them. And sure they did. The church balcony was built for slaves and free Negroes. One day we'll all worship together again, and sit wherever we like. Maybe even in our lifetime."

Uncle Stephen is plumb crazy, I thought. He proved it by bending down and patting that little old piled-rocks wall like it was a puppy. "Know what this is?"

I surveyed it with disdain. "A memorial to when they ran out of money for cement?"

He chuckled. "No, it's a dry stane dike—a dry stone wall built without mortar. You'll find walls like this all over Scotland. Job Watts built this one when he came here after the Battle of Culloden in Scotland. He built a house right over there." He pointed to the big vacant corner just beyond Mrs. Cameron's tiny white house. It was an odd lot, with big trees around the edges but only short trees and blackberry bushes in the middle. "The old stone house actually stood until a few years ago. When it was finally abandoned, people took it apart for their own uses."

"They *stole*?"

"They probably didn't think of it that way. Almost everybody around here is descended from Job Watts one way or another. Scratch two people deep enough and you'll find cousins."

"But nobody is a Watts."

"No, his only surviving daughter married an Anderson. We can explore the ruins someday, but we'll have to watch out for poison ivy and snakes." Just how I wanted to spend my visit: wading through poison ivy and snakes looking for old house foundations. Uncle Stephen was definitely nuts.

He bent to pat that wall again. "At the end of January we'll celebrate the two hundredth anniversary of Bethel Church. There aren't many churches that old around here—Thyatira over at China Grove and Concord at Loray are the only two I can name. But this wall was here way back then. What do you think of that?"

I looked at the wall with reluctant respect. Two hundred years is a long time, even for a straggly pile of rocks. He took his pipe out of his mouth and gestured toward the placid, sleeping houses of Job's Corner. "I wish these people would realize that the very same thing that brought their ancestors from Scotland to Job's Corner—a dream of something better for their children—is what's motivating Negroes in this country today." He whistled for Rowdy. It's a good thing he didn't expect an answer, because I had none to give.

We ambled toward the church drive and reached it just as Mr. Keene's Hudson turned in. He climbed out, handsomer than the day before in a light blue suit and white shirt with a striped tie. "Good morning, Stephen. How-de-do, little lady? You're both up early."

Uncle Stephen took off his hat and held it aloft. "Who could sleep when the lark's on the wing—"

"—and the snail's on the thorn?" I finished, delighted I knew what came next.

Mr. Keene looked puzzled. He must not read much poetry. "Did your girl get settled up the road?"

From the look in Uncle Stephen's eye, I was afraid we'd get another sermon if I let him answer, so I answered first. "Janey

Lou and Meek took her up. We haven't heard yet how she likes it."

Mr. Hugh Fred stepped closer to Uncle Stephen and put an arm around him. "Bear with us, Stephen," he said so softly I had to move closer to hear. "Bear with us. These are good people, but you can't rush things. You've been living with Yankees so long, you've forgotten how slow things move down here."

Uncle Stephen shoved back his hair. "It's not a matter of Yankees and Southerners, it's a matter of justice and brotherhood."

"I know how you feel. You were real straight when you came to meet us, and I'm with you all the way. But I'll remind you of what I said then: lead gently and they'll follow you anywhere, but if you get their backs up—well, they can be stubborner than Balaam's ass."

"Balaam's ass wasn't stubborn, he was blocked by an angel of the Lord."

Mr. Hugh Fred beamed at me. "Don't you like a preacher who knows his Bible?"

It was such a weird thing to say, I was glad he didn't wait for an answer.

Uncle Stephen watched him pull out of the drive, then pointed his pipe toward the granite wall that ambled downhill behind it and surrounded a second cemetery. "That's what we're up against, Carley—they still call that the *new* cemetery, even though it has graves dating from the Civil War. To some folks, that war ended just last year."

I didn't want to talk about history any more. There was something else I was suddenly desperate to ask. "You said Aunt Sukie is a Marshall because—you know. But why am *I* a Marshall? Didn't Mama change her name when she got married? Shouldn't I be Carley something else?"

Oddly enough, it was the first time that question had ever occurred to me. Living with Mama, Big Mama and Pop, I was so proud to be Carley Marshall of the Henry Marshalls, I never questioned it. Now, however, I knew something was wrong. Half afraid to find out what, I still needed to know.

Uncle Stephen started walking like I hadn't said a word.

"Wait a minute!" I yelled, hurrying after him. "Did you know my daddy?"

By now his long legs had carried him well away from me. "No," he called over one shoulder. "I didn't meet Kate until she was teaching and I was in seminary. By then you were two and he was gone."

I struggled to catch up, wincing as granite chunks bruised my feet. "Didn't Aunt Kate ever tell you anything about him? Wait a minute, can't you?"

He slowed until I caught up. Then he held up one hand to stop questions. "Before you came, Kate made me promise not to talk about your daddy. That's how she and her mother want it. I don't know enough to matter, anyhow."

I stamped my foot, coming down hard on a rock and grimacing with pain. "You have to know more than I do! I don't know a dadgum thing except he died before I was born." Angry tears stung my eyes. "I don't know what he looked like or what his last name was, I don't even know what his *first* name was!" A tear spilled over. I was clever enough not to wipe it away.

Uncle Stephen put out a finger and wiped it himself. "Roy. I'll give you that much. But it's all I *can* give. I can't break my word. You hear me?" Numbly I nodded.

I trudged along beside him in silence. Roy. My daddy's name was Roy. It ought to mean something, be something I could hug to myself. Instead, it was a short sound made by three letters. "Roy what, Uncle Stephen? Was he a Marshall? Or Roy *what?*"

"Not a Marshall. But I cannot break a promise. Please don't ask me to."

Angry, hungry for breakfast and feeling my glasses slipping with the rising heat, I was glad when Uncle Stephen whistled again for Rowdy and jerked his head toward the house east of the church, a big white one hidden behind the only screened porch in Job's Corner. "There's nothing else over here except Rob Lamont's, hay fields, and the road up to Keenes's."

Between the two crossings at each end of the dirt road, the only path across the tracks was the one in front of the manse, a narrow strip of red bordered by high grass and weeds. "I guess the whole congregation must use this way to get to church," he said.

"Then the women ruin their stockings on burrs and thistles. You sure there aren't snakes in those weeds?" I listened carefully before I set my feet.

He gave the weeds thoughtful consideration. "Rowdy hasn't roused any, but they could be lying low. I'll bring a scythe out later today and cut this back. Look, there's Mrs. Cameron in her garden. Isn't she amazing? Eighty-two, and just look at her!"

The old crone was harvesting tomatoes from a little patch near her back door, putting them in a bucket so old it was black. Uncle Stephen strode down the road and across her yard, calling loudly, "Good morning. Can I help you with that?"

I scampered gingerly after him, arriving in time to hear her reply. "Been carrying my own tomatoes since your daddy was in diapers, young man." But she handed him the bucket and took the arm he held out to help her up her back steps.

"Not my daddy, ma'am. My daddy's eighty. I'm his seventh son, and he started late. Those are mighty nice-looking tomatoes. But you'd better dust for worms."

She peered up at him through her eyebrows. "What you know 'bout gardens?"

"I grew up on a farm. Shall I come over late this afternoon and dust those for you?"

She jerked her head toward me. "Send that 'un. 'Bout time she made herself useful."

He smiled. "I'll do that."

Which is why at five o'clock that afternoon, I wore Aunt Kate's rubber boots knee-deep in weeds in a garden patch that probably harbored a hundred snakes, shaking dust over poor little green worms who didn't have the sense to run.

❋

Uncle Stephen needn't have worried about Sue Mary forgiving Abby. When we got home, we found her perched on our top step looking like a marble angel in faded blue gingham awaiting Judgment Day. Bare toes together, heels apart, sunlight making a halo on her white hair, she placidly picked at a scab on her arm the shape and size of Abby's teeth.

"Good morning." Uncle Stephen tipped his hat politely. Rowdy woofed a greeting, too.

"Stop!" she piped in her tinkly voice as I started up the steps. She held up one hand like a policeman. "Come up t'other side!"

I looked from one empty end of the steps to the other. "What's the difference?"

We waited while Sue Mary composed her answer. Finally, "Velma's there. You can't see her, but if you step on her, it hurts."

Uncle Stephen—as crazy as Sue Mary—gave the empty steps a solemn little bow. "Good morning, Velma. Have you girls come to play with Abby?"

Sue Mary thought that over, then nodded. "Yes. Bonnie said she may come to our yard. But Mama said if she bites, she'll get a whipping."

"Shall we go see if Abby's up yet?" He held out one hand to each ghost—the invisible one and the pale little girl you could almost see through.

I sat in the swing and tried to think about a daddy named Roy, but he wasn't any realer to me than Velma.

Chapter 9

Raifa stomped in, ate her breakfast without a word, and washed dishes with her lower lip stuck out like a buzzard perch. When Abby came in from the sandbox begging for a drink, Raifa jerked her hair. "Don't you hurt her!" I stormed.

Aunt Kate hurried in. "Raifa's got ironing to do. You girls go play in the sandbox."

"I'm not going to play in the sandbox with an invisible girl," I protested.

"Then go read in the swing. You can watch Abby from there. Don't let her bite."

Which just went to show how little she knew me. When I was reading, I wouldn't notice if Abby ate Sue Mary whole.

I did hear the train, though. Again it sounded like it was headed straight for the porch. Sue Mary and Abby ran from the sandbox waving like mad. Preston dashed across the road holding out his arms, and the man in overalls threw the mailbag straight to them. Preston staggered, but didn't fall. Sue Mary and Abby—and, I suppose, Velma—waved until the train disappeared around the curve.

As I was about to sit back in the swing, I noticed a short heavy person in a white dress across the road. Even after the train was long gone, she still waved her arm after it in great wallops over her head. She must have been sitting in the rocker under the oaks when it came. As she sat back down, she noticed me, and waved some more. I waved back, but she wouldn't stop. Finally I turned my back to her.

I couldn't concentrate on my book, though. Preston had carried that mailbag like treasure while Miss Pauline bellowed, "Bring it on in, I ain't got all day!" Could there be a letter for me? I ought to write Big Mama. . . .

I covered a page and sealed the envelope, fetched three cents from my new red wallet, and called that I was going for the mail. Raifa came from the kitchen pulling an envelope from her apron pocket. That's when I ran back upstairs pretending to get money for another stamp, but shoved her letter between my mattress and springs. I didn't feel guilty, just avenged.

The post office had a counter with pigeonholes behind and a small aisle in front. No fan, no stove. Except for a gray postal scale, the whole place was unpainted wood. Even with the door and single window wide open, it felt like a large oven and still smelled like Preston.

Miss Nancy and Miz Baines leaned against the counter gossiping with Miss Pauline. As soon as I appeared, they hushed.

"You want the Whitfield mail?" Miss Pauline's sundress was soaked under the arms and in little scallops under her immense bosom.

"Yes, ma'am, and one stamp, please." Miss Nancy and Miz Baines pressed back against the wall, as if waiting for something. I laid my three pennies on the counter.

Miss Pauline lifted several sheets of stamps, licked her finger, and fumbled for a loose one. Laboriously she handed it over, put the money tray back on top, added my pennies to others, and closed the box—making a bigger production out of selling one stamp than Marshall's did out of selling a dress. The stamp was pretty, though: George Washington in one corner, Robert E. Lee in the other. Big Mama would like that combination.

When I'd licked my stamp and stuck it on, Miss Pauline tossed my letter carelessly into the empty mailbag on the counter. I hoped the bag didn't have to be full before she sent it.

"If you need stamps when I'm not out here, you can get them at the house anytime," she wheezed, "but if you need a parcel weighed and stamped, bring it when the flag's flying. I can't keep running back and forth. My heart won't stand it."

Preston popped up from behind the counter and chimed in. "You want your mail when we're closed, they's a key hanging inside our screen door." He shook his stubby forefinger at me. "But don't you go reading other people's mail while you're here."

I lifted my chin and gave him a withering look, but he was hard to wither.

Miss Pauline handed me three letters—all addressed to "The Pastor, Bethel Church." I hadn't known how much I wanted a letter until I didn't get one.

"That ain't all." Fumbling beneath the counter she produced a large box. No wonder Preston staggered when he caught the bag. I felt the women behind me stir as she shoved it across the counter. She planted one fat finger on a Marshall's store label addressed to Aunt Kate in a script as round and neat as Big Mama herself. "Your name's Marshall too, ain't it?"

The other women moved a little closer. "Yes, ma'am. That's from my pop's store."

Preston wrinkled his stubby nose. "Your daddy don't own no store."

"My granddaddy did, when he was alive. Now it's my Big Mama's—Aunt Kate's mama." Seemed to me it might help Aunt Kate and Uncle Stephen if their congregation knew she came from a good family.

"Her mother owns Henry Marshall's?" Miss Nancy asked behind me.

I turned. "Yes, ma'am."

"Oh, la, la!" Miss Pauline twirled one finger in the air. "Must be nice."

"It is," I assured her earnestly.

Big Mama's parcel had new Sunday outfits for everybody, including me. She'd even sent a new white shirt for Uncle Stephen. Aunt Kate lifted wet eyes to the west. "Oh, Mama, you shouldn't have, but I'm so glad you did!" Her new dress was smart: brown with white polka dots with a big white collar and a yellow silk rose at the front.

My dress was yellow dotted swiss and real pretty, but I had two Sunday dresses with me already. Why would she send another—unless she meant for me to stay in Job's Corner until school started? I tried to hide my disappointment as I picked up Nancy Drew and wandered back to the swing. The woman across the road waved and waved. Feeling foolish, since I didn't know her, I waved back.

I tried to concentrate on reading, but every now and then I'd lay down the book and look over at her. She sat there like a thick white statue, rocking in her chair under the oaks. Resolutely I turned my eyes instead to the silver highway heading west. If I walked far enough, would it take me home? Would it take three weeks to walk it?

❋

I thought about my daddy a lot those next few days. Maybe it was watching Uncle Stephen rock Abby and nuzzle John's fuzzy little head under his chin. I pretended Daddy hadn't really died, just developed amnesia. He'd be back any day. I spun long conversations, accompanied him to baseball games where the Dodgers always won, and one day gave him a complete tour of Job's Corner, telling him about everybody who lived there. I also made up conversations about his work. He was a lawyer, like Nancy Drew's dad, and glad to talk his cases over with me, because I could help him figure out who was really guilty.

For the first time in my life, I missed him almost as much as I missed Mama.

Thursday evening, after John and Abby were in bed, Aunt Kate came out to the porch to take tucks in the hem of Abby's new dress because Big Mama had sent it one size too big. Aunt Kate said she'd grow into it, but I thought poor Abby was the only child I'd ever known who'd have to wear her own hand-me-downs.

I was hurrying to finish a new book before it got dark, feeling particularly charitable with Aunt Kate. She'd taken us to the library that day and let me check out four Nancy Drews on her card. But when Carson Drew walked into the story, a question just popped out. "Did you know my daddy?"

She knotted her thread and didn't meet my eyes. "Not well. I was in their wedding, but I was away at graduate school by then, so I only saw him that once. Why?"

"What happened to him? How did he die?"

She pulled off another piece of thread and snipped it. "What did Lila tell you?"

"She said he came to a tragic end, but that doesn't tell me a blessed thing."

"It about sums it up." I'd heard her sound more interested in Rowdy's dinner.

"*How* did he die? Did he get sick suddenly, like Mama? Or did he have a long wasting disease? Or"—my throat nearly closed up at the thought—"did he get hit by a train?"

"No, he . . . I wasn't there."

"But they must've written you. Didn't you go home for his funeral?"

"No, I didn't. I'm sorry, Carley, you'll have to ask Mama." She licked one end of the thread and squinted at the eye of the needle. The light was beginning to fade.

"How can I ask Big Mama when I'm here? I can't write that kind of thing in a letter! What if it got lost and circulated around the entire United States? What would people think about a family who lets a girl get to be eleven without telling her about her own daddy?"

What Would People Think was the biggest cannon in our family arsenal.

Aunt Kate gave me an expression straight from Big Mama.

I backpedaled quickly. "At least tell me what he looked like. Please? I've never seen a single picture." I trembled to think she had actually seen him, maybe hugged him after the wedding. She sat there biting her lip, then got up and left the porch without a word.

My stomach ached with cold fear. Had I made her mad? Worse, had I made her cry?

No. In a few minutes she flipped on the porch light and handed me a framed sepia studio portrait. Mama, younger than I ever knew her, with her head on a man's shoulder. "They sent that after the wedding. You can keep it." Aunt Kate's voice sounded thick.

My breath and all time stopped. I held that picture so close to my glasses, it blurred. Mama looked so young and real I wanted to inhale her, keep her inside me forever. But when I looked at the man, I was disappointed. He looked *ordinary*—straight light hair slicked to one side, a thin face only slightly handsome. I wasn't skilled enough to trace my own face in his.

"Roy," I murmured—trying to connect the name to the face and both to me. Nothing happened. "How tall was he? What color was his hair?"

She lifted her hand not far above her own head. "Oh, about—not too tall. And he had brown hair and eyes, I think."

"Brown eyes?" I peered closer. "But we learned in science that brown eyes are dominant. How come I don't have brown eyes?"

"I don't know, honey. His mother has blue eyes. Maybe that's why."

"You knew his *mother?*" I couldn't take it all in. Then my mind pounced on one word. "You said 'has.' Is she still alive? Where does she live? What's her name?"

I'd never imagined I might have other grandparents, maybe even cousins. If you think that's odd, you have to remember how happy I was with Mama, Big Mama, and Pop. The subject of another family just never came up.

Or maybe that should read *the subject of another family deliberately never came up.*

I knew from the way Aunt Kate clutched Abby's dress to her chest that she was going to hold on to what she knew unless I pressed her. "Tell me, Aunt Kate! *Do* I have another grandmother? Another granddaddy, too?"

"Just a grandmother. And I can't tell you any more. Mama wouldn't like it."

"Why didn't anybody tell me before?" No answer. I leaped to my feet. "Nobody ever tells me anything!" I stamped my foot against the warm porch floor.

I had Gone Too Far.

"That's no way to speak to an adult." Once she'd said that, in that tone of voice, we both knew the conversation was over. Aunt Kate had been raised by Big Mama, too.

Uncle Stephen came out jingling his car keys. "Janey Lou went home early today with a headache, so I'm going to run Raifa home. Wanna come, Carley?"

I climbed into the front seat and Raifa slid into the back. We were equally sullen and steaming. Uncle Stephen called over his shoulder, "You're mighty quiet back there, Raifa."

Her eyes flickered in the dimness. "Enjoying the peace. It's all I'll get till morning."

When we arrived, I saw what she meant. Pleasantdale wasn't at all pleasant, just a few hot run-down houses around a packed dirt circle, without even a store. Every house seemed to have a radio in the window blaring music. Children squealed and cried. Grown-ups shouted from house to house. Dogs barked. One crazy rooster was crowing, even though it was night.

Uncle Stephen and I went in to meet Raifa's landlady, and she wasn't at all like Janey Lou. A huge sloppy woman with run-over house shoes and her slip hanging down, she didn't stop talking to breathe. Raifa took me to see her "room," and it was just a curtained alcove off the front room, big enough for a single bed. There were two hooks for dresses. She had to keep everything else in boxes under her bed. She didn't even have a window or a fan.

I felt real sorry she had to live there—and so glad I was white and didn't.

Raifa walked us out to the car like she wished she could get back in. Uncle Stephen gave her a sympathetic pat. "I'm working on it."

She lowered her eyelids and pursed her lips. "Huh!" Then she stomped inside, slamming the screened door behind her.

Chapter 10

Uncle Stephen was wrong about the congregation using our path across the tracks. Everybody drove to church except us. After waiting for two huge trucks to whiz by in a blast of hot air, Aunt Kate, Abby, and I arrived with pink faces, blown hair, burrs at our hemlines, and red dust on our white shoes and gloves. Briars had pulled Aunt Kate's stocking seams crooked. Everybody else looked cool and pretty in pastel dresses and clean shoes.

Uncle Stephen was right, though, about people being friendly. We'd barely gotten into the crowded back hall before women crowded around us cooing like pigeons. "Are these the Whitfields? What a darlin' baby—and so good! We're so glad you all got here safely. Are you gettin' moved in? What a pretty little girl! Is there anything you all need? Please let us know. What a darling baby—and so good!" Aunt Kate shifted John to hide where he'd wrinkled her collar, tugged her straw hat straight, and shook each hand as she came to it.

Nobody paid any attention to me, so I closed my eyes and pretended I was home. The hall had that same musty holy smell they could bottle and call "church."

Miss Nancy came in looking like a well-fed canary in a yellow homemade dress trimmed in brown rickrack. With her were two children, a boy and a girl. "Ruthie and Jimmy," a woman called, "come show the Whitfield children where to go."

"Don't want to." The girl was plump and sullen, with stubby black braids, a red flowered dress, and thick black brows that met over huge gray eyes. Her nose was a dab, but she had nostrils like caverns. Her mouth hung slightly open, for she breathed through it, and her teeth were big. To make up for breathing through her mouth, she talked through her nose.

The little boy, who looked just like her, echoed venomously, "Don't *want* to."

Startled, Abby and I drew closer to Aunt Kate. Another lady bent over John. "Is that sweet boy going to the nursery? Yes, he is, and I get to take care of him."

Aunt Kate drew him back. "I'll keep him with me today. He's so young—"

Miss Nancy pursed her lips. "Oh, no. Babies can be so disruptive in a Bible class, don't you think?" She took John and plopped him in the other woman's arms. Then she stood back and looked Aunt Kate's dress up and down. "Is that from Henry Marshall's? It's nice!"

"Ooh—Henry Marshall's!" chirped several other women. "It's so pretty!"

I hoped they didn't notice where it gapped at the bosom if Aunt Kate wasn't careful. I also hoped she wouldn't die from holding her breath because the belt was too tight.

Miss Nancy tugged Aunt Kate's elbow. "Bible class is down the hall here." She paused to call over her shoulder, "Toddlers and juniors in the basement. Second door to the right."

Abby stuck out her lower lip. "I doesn't like basements. I wants my mama."

"You can have your mama after Sunday school. Come on." I jerked her hand. She fell to the corrugated rubber mat and roared. "You aren't hurt!" I hissed, shaking her. "Hush!"

She stopped roaring, but looked down and saw a tiny ruby drop. "Look! I bwoke my knee!" Her lower lip quivered.

"Bless your heart, are you hurt?" Miss Emily Keene knelt beside Abby with no regard for her white linen suit. A cloud of perfume enveloped us all. She took a tissue from her pocketbook and dabbed the wound gently, then kissed it, leaving Abby with a red flower on her knee. "You are such a brave girl." She stood and held out her hand. "Shall I take you to class? I'm one of your teachers."

Abby's lashes were as spiky from tears as Miss Emily's were from mascara. "I likes you to be my teacher." The little traitor took the proffered hand and happily abandoned me.

I felt very alone until someone spoke behind me. "Can I help you? I'm Bonnie Anderson." The tall, soft-voiced girl was nothing like Preston or Sue Mary. She was very thin, for one thing, and had thick brown hair not only pulled to the nape of her neck, but in a soft fuzz on her arms. Her green dress looked like it was made for a woman, not a girl, but her dark eyes were kind. "I'm going down to Sunday school. Let me show you the way. I'd sit with you, but I help in the kindergarten class."

She led me to a noisy room full of girls and boys. Yes, girls *and* boys—which was only one way this Sunday school was different from mine back home. Baptist children got points for attendance, reading our lesson, bringing a Bible, learning a memory verse, and bringing a visitor. We swarmed all over a new child, wanting visitor points. At Bethel the children stared but barely said hello. Not even Freda, at the piano. But when I saw her blue organdy dress, I was real glad I'd worn my new yellow-and-white dotted swiss.

That was the one thing I found to be glad about. After I'd gone to all the trouble of lugging my Bible across the highway, reading my lesson, and relearning a memory verse, the only thing they gave credit for was showing up. Accustomed to thinking of myself as a soldier in God's army, I considered standards in the Bethel regiment pretty lax.

We sat on hard chairs in rows. Freda played, missing a lot of notes, and Mr. Mayhew led singing. He was short and not quite plump, with wavy brown hair and lips that pooched out like he wanted to kiss if somebody would volunteer. But he had a beautiful tenor voice.

He could teach, too. I hated to admit it, but he made our lesson a lot more interesting than my teacher back home. He said Jericho was like the Russians, and God knew the only way to deal with people like that was by tricking them. That's why Joshua marched around the city seven days without saying a word—to spook them. By the time the trumpets sounded, those city walls fell down from shock. "We have to be real clever when dealing with folks like that," he told us, "and you can't ever tell when a Russian might be in our midst. There could be one here right now." Everybody looked at me, the only stranger in the room.

❊

Miss Nancy took it on herself to show us where to sit in church—down on the second pew. "This is where the Grants always sat." She bustled off.

Bethel had three hundred members. Every one of them and all their kinfolk had watched Aunt Kate and me come down that aisle. "Shouldn't I go to the nursery?" I pleaded. "John and Abby might need me."

"I need you worse," Aunt Kate said out of one corner of her mouth. "I've never sat so far up front in my life." The three pews right behind us were empty and stayed that way.

Still skittish about being in a Presbyterian church, I peered around at creamy walls, mahogany pews, long clear glass windows, and maroon aisle carpet. Back home our pews were set in a semicircle, so you could see other people, the baptistry, and a window showing Jesus the Good Shepherd. At Bethel all pews faced a purple curtain with a gold cross hanging high above the choir. "Don't Presbyterians baptize people?" I whispered.

"Shhh. They use that." Aunt Kate nodded toward a little pedestal with a lid.

"Not even John could fit in there," I protested.

She touched one finger to her lips and bowed her head.

After hearing Freda's prelude, I decided to pray for better music. If I missed that many notes in a recital piece, my teacher would never permit me to play in public again. Also, our church back home had a piano, organ, and a choir of forty who sang their hearts out in blue robes. This church had a piano and a choir of eight who wore regular clothes and sang like they were afraid somebody might hear them. The only one I *could* hear was my Sunday school teacher, who directed them. He sang a lovely offertory solo.

Even with the windows open, the sanctuary was so hot that all during the sermon I could hear people waving paper fans behind us. Our pew didn't have fans. Sweat trickled down my back and made my glasses slip down my nose, but I hated to lift my hand to push them back. Everybody could see me. I wondered how Mr. Davy could look so cool in a navy suit and white long-sleeved shirt. Most men had on shirts with open collars.

I didn't know how Uncle Stephen could stand his long black robe, either. He wiped his forehead several times with a handkerchief, and I suspected he was secretly wishing he was Baptist and could preach in a white suit.

I might have known he would preach on God and history. He read one of the Deuteronomy passages about remembering, and talked about all the people who had gone to that church for nearly two hundred years. Then he shocked me to my socks.

newfangled Bibles. Saint James is good enough for me." I opened my mouth to tell her it was King James, and he was no saint, but Aunt Kate shook her head at me just like I'd shaken mine at Abby.

Last in line, the witch came by with the skinny little man who'd hung around on moving day. He didn't stink quite so bad, and in honor of the day his thin gray hair was wetted down and he wore a dirty navy blue suit.

"Good mornin', Ira, Miss Gert." Uncle Stephen greeted them as nicely as if he'd been able to breathe normally.

I held my breath as Mr. Ira stuck out a claw to Uncle Stephen and jutted his lower lip. "Well, Preacher, as sermons go, that was certainly one." He laughed at his own joke, spraying me with spit brown with snuff.

The witch's magnified gray eyes peered up into Uncle Stephen's. "Good sermon, Preacher, even if it did run over a mite." Though I knew to expect it, her raspy voice still chilled me. She pulled the arm of the girl by her side. "This here's Ivy, our pride and joy."

The old man cackled. "Eighteen years old, and a delight every one of them."

Now that I saw Ivy up close, I saw she was just a very big girl, but I couldn't see how she could be anybody's pride and joy. Her brown hair was thin and flat. It had obviously been rolled in pin curls for church, but they were crooked and stuck out in odd places. Her skin was a soft flabby white. Her lips were thick and slack, and beneath her blue cotton dress, her bosoms were so heavy they sagged and rounded her shoulders. What made me most uneasy was the expression in her pale eyes. It made her look younger than Abby.

"Good to meet you," she said on one note with no inflection. Then she reached up and touched Abby's penny-red hair. "Pretty. You pretty," she said in her strange, flat voice.

Abby drew back. "Don't touch me! I doesn't like to be touched."

Ivy withdrew her hand, but her eyes were hungry as they fastened on Abby's face. "Pretty," she said again. "Pretty."

"She is pretty," her mother agreed. "You're pretty, too, baby. Now, let's get home to our dinner."

Mr. Ira turned at the bottom step. "Miz Preacher, if you need anything—anything a'tall—you just call on me. I'm real handy."

"Don't believe him," Uncle Stephen murmured to Aunt Kate as he turned back to lock up the church. "Davy says Ira seldom does a lick of work."

Aunt Kate set Abby down and motioned us to go out to the yard. I heard her joke behind us, "If we ran a contest for laziness, who would win—Pauline or Ira?"

Uncle Stephen didn't even need to think. "Ira, hands down. Pauline bathes."

Chapter 11

That first month Uncle Stephen wrote sermons, mimeographed bulletins, went to meetings, and visited people. He also got some of the bigger boys to help him paint all the Sunday school rooms in the church basement one afternoon. When he got home, Aunt Kate laughed so hard she had to sit down. "You look like you've got yellow spotted fever."

Generally, though, she and Raifa were working too hard to laugh. Every woman in the church seemed to think we'd starve if she didn't bring us something. After our third bushel of beans, Aunt Kate confessed to Miss Hannah, "I don't know what to do with all this food. I don't want to hurt their feelings, but we can't possibly eat it all."

"Law, honey, you'll want to can most of it."

"I don't know how to can!"

"You and Raifa come down, and Janey Lou and I'll teach you."

Our kitchen became a steamy place of boiling water, drying jars, and rows of colorful vegetables cooling after being processed. Every night before supper we all had to admire the jewel jars proudly displayed on the countertop. I offered to help, but after I nearly pulled a pot of boiling water over on myself, she suggested I just watch Abby instead.

Abby didn't want watching. "Dis is private," she'd object if I joined them in the sandbox. She permitted me to tie enormous string houses between five sycamores in Miss Pauline's yard, but didn't want me to play in them. She did invite me to slide under Mr. Davy's fence each morning when she and Sue

Mary ran across the pasture to one of the big salt blocks he'd set on posts for the cows, but only because she knew I wouldn't. They'd lick one side of the salt while a cow licked the other. To this day Abby claims that pink, yellow, and white salt blocks all taste the same.

"If a cow gores you, I'm not coming to save you," I warned. They laughed.

I spent hours in the swing with Nancy Drew. I waved back and forth to Ivy until my arm got tired. I kept hoping to get to know Bonnie Anderson, but she was too busy. She dusted, swept, mopped, and baked all morning, then canned until suppertime. Miss Pauline put out mail, then sat on her porch fanning flies. Sometimes she snapped beans. Aunt Kate said that was one job you could do sitting down. Preston sat beside her, putting together an endless stream of model airplanes.

Except at church, I only saw Freda riding a brown horse or entering the Lamonts' house across the highway. I kept hoping she'd call, but she never did.

One afternoon when the canning was done for that day, I heard Raifa singing along with the radio in the kitchen while she ironed. I was bored and Aunt Kate and the children were napping, so I moseyed to the kitchen. Beyond the windows the world was hidden behind silver curtains of rain. Lit by one overhead bulb dangling from an eleven-foot ceiling, the kitchen felt like a steamy tropical island on which Raifa and I were marooned.

"You sing real good," I told her, sliding into a straight chair to listen.

By the way she slapped the iron down on the pillowcase, I could tell she was pleased. "You ain't heard nothin' yet. If I had a real backup band and could open out, I could blast this whole state apart. This child's gonna make it big someday. Just you wait."

"You think you'll ever go back to West Virginia?" I tried not to sound hopeful.

"No reason to go back now. Had a boyfriend. We was gonna get married, but Mama thought seventeen was too young, so she made me go work for Miss Kate. Heck, I can't see the difference. If I'da got married I'da been doin' the very same things, 'cept for my own self." She picked up the pillowcase, shook it, put it back on the board, and ironed it again.

Seventeen? I'd thought Raifa was a woman, when all the

time she was just a very big girl. But girls didn't get married—or did they? I crooked one knee around the table leg and leaned on my elbows. "Would you get married if you went back?"

She licked her lips and shook her head. "He done got married. He was *ready*, child."

"Oh, Raifa, I'm sorry!" No wonder she was mean. Her heart was broken. Vowing I'd be nicer, I reached for laundry to fold, then drew back, furious. "You starched my pajamas!"

For just an instant, she looked sorry. Then she tossed her head. "You can do your own wash if you don't like the way I do it."

Uncle Stephen spoke from the door. "Still ironing, Raifa? Don't forget you need to mop this floor. Kate's got Circle meeting at the house tonight."

Raifa ironed that pillowcase like she was getting paid by the stroke. "They's too much ironing to do. Maybe Princess Carley could put down her book and he'p once in a while."

I knew for a fact she'd ironed that pillowcase three times. Nevertheless, to my utter lack of surprise, Uncle Stephen assigned me to become the family sweeper and mopper. Between Abby, Rowdy, and all the church people tromping in and out to use the telephone, that house took a lot of sweeping and mopping.

❋

Job's Corner had only three telephones: Keene's, Davy Anderson's, and ours, which sat in a niche in the front hall. "Ours," however, actually belonged to the church, which meant it belonged to everybody.

Whenever there was no mail, the post office called Miss Pauline to tell her not to look for a bag. Uncle Stephen sent me with the message.

When the bread truck had a flat, the bakery called Mrs. Cameron to tell her they'd be a day late. Aunt Kate sent me with the message.

When Miss Pauline's sister in Hickory decided to come down for an afternoon, she called the manse. Uncle Stephen sent me with the message.

When Jimmy Lamont had a fever, Nancy came down to phone the doctor. Later, when the drugstore called that her prescription was ready, I had to carry the message.

After three trips one day, I knew why the Grants had ten children: to carry messages.

Not only did we have to deliver messages, we were constantly unhooking the screened door to let people in—until Miss Pauline informed us, "Mrs. Grant never locked her door. That way we never had to bother her." But that meant that almost any time of day or evening, we could find somebody in our front hall using the phone.

One morning I was wakened by shouting. My clock said seven, so Uncle Stephen had already left on his walk. I grabbed my robe and hurried downstairs.

A short man with a beet-red face stood by the phone waving his fist in the air. "You gotta give people what they want, and what we want is lower taxes!" His voice rasped like a file on steel. Barely pausing to listen he went right on. "That's hogwash and you know it. I didn't come all this way to call you— yessir, all the way across town. And I'm sorry I woke you up, but some folks go to work this early. As governor of this state, you oughta be at your desk by now. There's work to do, sir!"

Aunt Kate's door opened, then shut softly. She wouldn't want to be caught in her gown. I, however, stayed to get a good look at anybody who'd wake up the governor.

I remembered him from moving day: Rob Lamont. He looked like a chubby dwarf, with thick white hair growing back from his face. His hands were black in the creases and his fingernails and shoes were stained with tar, but his baggy gray pants and shirt were freshly starched and ironed. He took no notice as I tiptoed past toward the porch and the book I'd left in the swing.

An old white bulldog sprawled at the doorsill, fat as its master and nearly as grizzled. When I pushed against the screened door, it opened one eye and rumbled.

"Nice doggy." I opened the screened door a crack.

It clambered to bow legs and its growl inched a gear lower. When it looked at me with both eyes, the second was pure white. Hastily I backed up, ready to bolt. It rumbled like an engine, low and constant.

"Good day to you, too, sir. Good to talk to you." The man hung up and turned his attention to me. "Old Patch'd kill you in a minute if you tried to get past him. He's my bodyguard. If the President'd get a bulldog, he wouldn't need secret service. But you think he'll listen?"

In the glare of that one bulging eye, all I could manage was a weak shake of my head. He didn't seem to expect an answer.

"No more'n the governor listens when I tell him he's gotta lower taxes. What's the matter with those people? Give 'em a little power and it goes to their heads. But at least they're honest Democrats. You a honest Democrat?" I nodded, mesmerized. I'd agree with anything he said. Patch, still growling, guaranteed it.

He went right on as if I'd added something to the conversation. "My son Wash, now, he's a dadburned Republican. Anybody knows we don't have Republicans in North Carolina, but he claims to be one. We don't agree on a thing, hardly—'cept when we're on a roof. You can't be disagreeing with a man on a second-story roof. You keep that in mind."

I gulped and nodded. "Yessir. I will." At the moment, I was keeping his dog in mind. If it leaned much harder on our screened door, it would tumble through.

"Got to get to work now. Good talking to you. I like a child speaks up for herself." Mr. Lamont opened the door and rolled across the porch. Patch waddled after him, meek as a mouse. But when it reached the sidewalk, that old dog turned and gave one sharp "woof"—to remind me what a bloodthirsty monster it was.

❊

After two weeks in Job's Corner, I decided if I didn't get back home, I would die.

I found Aunt Kate canning tomatoes. Taking a deep breath, I said, "I think it's time I got on back home, don't you? I need to get ready for school." It sounded as good as I'd practiced.

Aunt Kate turned toward the Kelvinator. "I just made some cherry Kool-Aid. Let's go on the porch while these tomatoes process. I need to sit down."

On the porch, thunder grumbled on the edge of hearing while the air held its breath. Aunt Kate wiped sweat off her forehead. "It's sure missin' a great chance to rain."

For a few minutes we rocked companionably, sipping icy Kool-Aid and watching John stare at a red tomato almost as big as his head, a green cucumber as long as his arm, several squash as softly yellow as his hair. I've always wondered if John's grown-up love of gardening stemmed from looking at seed catalogue pictures his first six months.

Finally Aunt Kate set down her glass. "Honey—" She stopped.

"Yes, ma'am?" I asked, trying to help her along.

Words tumbled out like she'd been practicing, too. "Your Uncle Stephen and I want you to stay with us this next year."

I was so startled, I sputtered. "*All year?* No, *ma'am!* You all are real nice, but this isn't *home*. I need to be getting back. Big Mama needs me. We belong together."

"Mama's getting too old to be thinking about school or PTA or clothes—"

"When Big Mama gets too old to think about clothes, she'll be dead."

She laughed unsteadily. "You're right about that. But, honey, you can't live with her this coming winter. We want you to stay with us here."

I stuck out my lower lip and her mouth tightened exactly like Mama's used to. When tears stung my eyes, she misunderstood. "Crying isn't going to change anything."

I leaped to my feet in a flash of temper. "You just want a free baby-sitter! I'm not going to stay here and sleep in that fire-trappy upstairs with all those ghosts. I won't! I won't! I won't!" I only stopped when sobs choked me.

Uncle Stephen clattered downstairs and through the screened door and stood looking from one of us to the other. "I see you've told her."

"I had to. She made me." Big tears now rolled down Aunt Kate's cheeks, and her mouth was all twisted up. She looked up at me and spoke in the saddest voice. "Sweetie, I'd send you home in a minute if I could. Not because I don't want you, but because I know how bad you want to go. And if you want us all to sleep upstairs, we will. But you have to stay. You just have to. Someday you'll understand."

"I won't understand! And I won't stay. You can't make me. I'll run away!"

I lunged toward the front door—the wrong direction for running away. Uncle Stephen shot out one arm and held me fast, but spoke to her. "Why don't I talk to Carley while you go fix your face?" She jumped up and fled.

Uncle Stephen steered me to the swing, then sat beside me and set it moving gently. "I don't know exactly what Kate told you, and I'm sorry we haven't said something sooner, but we just talked to Mrs. Marshall last night."

My heart thudded so loud I could hear it. "Did she call you?"

"No, we called her."

I let out a big sigh of relief. Big Mama wouldn't call long distance unless she was dying. "She didn't say she wants me to stay here. I know she didn't. She wants me home."

"Yes, generally, but—" He stopped. "I'll be hornswoggled if I'll do this for her. She's going to have to tell you herself." He fumbled in his pocket for change. "Go get me some pipe tobacco and let me talk to Kate."

I walked across the grass avoiding bees on pink clover and hoping I'd make it back before lightning struck me dead. It already flickered over Statesville, five miles away.

Mrs. Cameron sat on the porch, as usual. In spite of the heat, she was dressed in a black blouse with long sleeves, a black cardigan over her shoulders, and a black skirt to the tips of her lace-up shoes. Looked like a crow and cawed like one, too. "What you needin'?"

"Pipe tobacco."

"Don't carry it. He'll have to get it in town." Thunder rolled in the distance.

I turned, but she called me back. "I heard yellin'. What was all that ruckus about?"

I hesitated. I wasn't raised to tell old women to mind their own business, but on the other hand, old women shouldn't ask about what didn't concern them. "It was just me. I, uh—" I stuck out one grubby bare foot. "I stubbed my toe. Nearly broke it, but it's better now."

She reached behind her into the cigar box and brought out a dime. "I didn't pay you for dustin' them 'maters t'other day. Here." She thrust the coin over her black lap.

I hobbled—hoping people with broken toes had to hobble—toward her, but didn't put out my hand. "Thank you, ma'am, but I couldn't take money for helping you."

"Nonsense, girl. Here! Take it!" Lightning sparked across the sky and thunder rumbled closer.

"No, ma'am. I can't take money. Uncle Stephen wouldn't let me."

Her hooded black eyes bored into mine. "Can you take candy?"

"Yes, ma'am. That would be fine." I nearly jigged.

"No more than a dime's worth, mind. Go get it."

In the daytime the store's dimness was cool and pleasant, smelling of fresh bread. I chose ten Mary Janes and carefully displayed them on my palm when I came out. She counted them and nodded sourly. "More 'n the work was worth, but take 'em." Lightning flashed again as she spoke. "Better hurry, now. And don't forget to limp."

The clouds emptied like a pitcher as I reached our steps. I dashed to the swing and sat chewing a mouthful of peanut butter taffy while streams cascaded off our roof. There's something mighty comforting about a Mary Jane.

Uncle Stephen joined me with his pipe. "Kate and I have decided she will drive you and the children to Mrs. Marshall's on Thursday while I take a bus to see my daddy. Raifa will stay at the house to feed Rowdy, finish unpacking, and give the house a good cleaning."

"Aren't you scared to sleep in this big place all by yourself?" I asked Raifa later. "That cemetery has ghosts. I see them some nights."

She jutted out her square jaw. "At least they's quiet."

Nobody promised I could stay at Big Mama's once I got there, but I figured I could hide until Aunt Kate headed back. The way she and Uncle Stephen smooched when they thought nobody was looking, she wouldn't want to be away too long.

They didn't hug much in the next few days, however. Several times I caught her giving him a worried, angry look. The night before we left, I got up to go to the bathroom and heard them arguing in the kitchen.

". . . borrow my brother's car, that's how."

"Mama will be furious."

"Furious or not, I'm going. Somebody should have long ago."

"You can't judge that. You don't know—" Her voice broke. "What'll I tell Mama?"

He gave a short, not-funny laugh. "Tell her I'm making a pastoral call."

❋

When we got there, home didn't feel much like home. Mama's room was now green, not blue, and had organdy curtains and a new flowered bedspread. "She just couldn't stand looking at it, and that's the truth," Aunt Sukie told me when I complained. "This summer has nearly worn her to the bone."

Nowhere close to the bone—Big Mama was much too stout for that. But she looked older. Her long dark hair, which she rolled at her neck, had a thick white wing at each side. Also, she kept stroking our arms like she wanted to be sure we were really there.

We ate Aunt Sukie's good cooking and talked like we couldn't get enough of it. Big Mama laughed till she cried when Aunt Kate mimicked Miz Baines and Mr. Ira, and Aunt Kate giggled like a girl when Big Mama told her how fat and ugly her old boyfriend had gotten. Aunt Sukie refilled my milk glass with iced tea and nobody fussed.

But as we carried dishes to the sink, Aunt Kate sighed. "You'd die, Mama, if you saw my kitchen. It looks like an institution. Gray walls, white cabinets, black linoleum countertops, black-and-white floor, and a old wringer washer where I spend hours wringing diapers. The cabinets are so high I can scarcely reach the bottom shelves. For the others I have to climb on a chair. Abby climbs the counters like a monkey, leaving a trail of red footprints."

Big Mama set the leftover chocolate meringue pie on top of the Kelvinator. "Why don't you get a few cans of paint and smarten it up?"

"I'd like to at least paint the cabinets. But Stephen says if the Session objected to Raifa living with us, they'd probably object to anything. He is so bullheaded, Mama—"

"Shhht." Big Mama looked at Abby and me, and Aunt Kate hushed like a child.

We all stretched out for a while after dinner, with dark green shades pulled to the sills against the afternoon sun. Abby slept with me so her mother could rest better. I told her about both our mamas getting born in Big Mama's bed, but she was scornful. "Mommies don't get born, Carley. Babies get born." She turned her back, stuck her thumb in her mouth, and slept.

I looked at her soft neck where the red curls parted and realized how much I'd miss her. Another word for love is hurting. Unless all the people you care about are in one place, even when you're enjoying the ones you have, you're regretting the ones you don't.

At supper Aunt Kate and Big Mama still talked like they would never catch up.

"Did you wear your new dress to church?" Big Mama wanted to know. "Did it fit?"

"It's a little tight, but I held my breath. And it's beautiful, Mama, but you mustn't send any more. We're in the country.

Most of the women make their clothes—or get them made. Only Emily Keene and Hannah Anderson wear nice ones. I don't want to look like I'm showing off."

"Surely they won't mind if you look nice!"

Aunt Kate laughed, but it wasn't funny. "They mind about a lot of things. Old Mrs. Cameron criticized my wash on the line." Aunt Kate turned down her mouth and made her voice crackly. "Don't you have any white clothes, Mrs. Whitfield? All I ever see are colored clothes. And you don't even hang the same colors together."

Big Mama laid a big hand over Aunt Kate's and rubbed it gently. "What did you tell her, Daught?"

Tears filled Aunt Kate's eyes so swiftly, I knew they had been right behind her lids all the time. "It's been so *long* since I heard you call me that, Mama. Oh, it's good to be home!"

"It's good to have you." Big Mama patted her hand, her wide gold wedding ring gleaming in a shaft of light. For several minutes, nobody said a word.

I got the notion we were waiting for Pop and Mama to come take their seats. My throat swelled up with so much sadness I couldn't swallow. Suddenly Abby looked up through the dining room window and cried, pointing, "I sees de wishin' tar!" I didn't bother to make a wish. No star could fill those empty chairs.

While Big Mama helped Aunt Kate put the children to bed, I helped Aunt Sukie wash up the supper dishes. "You like your new place?" she asked, sliding me a sideways look.

"It's not my new place, I was just visiting. And I didn't like it much. There's nothing to do or girls my age, and Aunt Kate has the meanest cook you ever saw. So rude and sassy, I sometimes want to haul off and hit her." As soon as I said it, I wished I hadn't. I didn't want Aunt Sukie thinking I was as mean as slave owners. "I wouldn't really hit anybody," I added hastily, "but Raifa is mean as mud."

"You best not be studyin' hittin'," Aunt Sukie warned, finding a place in the Kelvinator for a bowl of cold green beans. "Mister Stephen will skin your hide. But it sounds like that gal's got thistles in her britches. You just stay out of her road."

I submerged the last pot in cooling dishwater. "I never plan to see her again."

In the back hall, we heard Big Mama saying, "Kate, I want you to go through Lila's things while you're here, to see if you can wear any of them."

"I'm too big for them," we heard Aunt Kate protest, "and I wouldn't have the heart."

"Looks like Big Mama's tryin' to get rid of Mama as fast as she can," I grumbled, "redecoratin' her room and givin' away all her clothes."

That's when Aunt Sukie said the summer had been hard on her.

"Well, it won't be hard on her any longer, because I'm *home*."

I reached for Aunt Sukie's dishes, but for the life of me I couldn't put them in that greasy water. I had to tip it out and fill the pan with fresh soapy water for one plate, one glass, and one fork. Even when you tried not to let him, Uncle Stephen could get to you.

Aunt Sukie wrapped the last of the chicken in waxed paper and didn't say a word. I wrung out the dishrag and flung myself into a chair. "Wanna finish the chocolate pie?"

Aunt Sukie was putting on her hat to go home, but she took it off again, cut us each a piece, and lowered herself arthritically into a chair across from me, "You still as much trouble as you used to be."

"But aren't you glad I'm home? I don't think I'll ever go anywhere again." I waved my fork toward the open double window, where fireflies flickered in the soft darkness. "There's nothing out there I'm needin'." That was what Aunt Sukie always said when we asked if she wanted to ride along on a day trip to the mountains.

She shot me another sideways look and bent her head over her pie. "Your grandmama's countin' on you goin' back for school. I wadn't s'posed to tell you, but I think you oughta know. And shut your mouth, 'less you're plannin' on catchin' flies."

"She can't make me go. I'll run away. Nobody will find me. I might starve to death."

"They's worse ways to die," she reminded me darkly.

For the first time in weeks, I remembered why I'd been sent away. "Is it polio Big Mama's scared of? I'll stay inside. I won't go out at all. I won't even breathe!"

Flinging down my fork, I ran into Big Mama's bedroom. She stood in her slip, hanging her dress in the closet. "It's okay, Big Mama! You don't have to worry anymore. I won't go near anybody who's got polio. I won't even go to *school* if you don't want me to. You can teach me everything I need to know."

She reached up, pulled out the pins, and let her hair cascade to her waist. I was relieved to see it was still thick and auburn except for those two white wings. "What on earth are you talking about, child? Of course you'll go to school. But right now, go on to bed. And remember, wash your feet."

❀

Friday morning Aunt Kate went to show Abby and John off to an old school friend.

"Come out under the mulberry," Big Mama invited. "Help me shell butter beans." That was family code for "Let's go have a private conversation."

I wasn't worried. After what Aunt Sukie had said, I'd already lined up my arguments against going back. I'd even practiced them in front of my mirror. Besides, it was too beautiful a day for disappointment. The air was fresh and a little breezy, the grass soft and cool underfoot. Fat puffy clouds sailed across the sun and back, and beyond the neighbor's yard the purple blur of the Blue Ridge Mountains melted into the sky.

Big Mama settled us in the shade of our huge mulberry tree with newspapers full of fat pods on our laps, a speckled dishpan between us on the grass for hulls, and a blue bowl for beans. Around the friendly patter of beans hitting the bowl, she told me things Aunt Kate wouldn't be interested in, like my principal was leaving and they hadn't replaced him, and she was president of the Women's Missionary Society again but would still have to put up with Elvira Jenkins as secretary. She never mentioned Job's Corner except once to ask how I liked it. I said it was fine for those who wanted to live there, but I didn't. She changed the subject.

Finally, when she'd shelled the last bean, she held the blue bowl in her lap anchored by her big hands, and her blue eyes looked enormous behind her glasses. "Do I understand, child, that you've been giving Kate grief about staying with them this next year?"

Giving Aunt Kate grief wasn't one of the things I had prepared to discuss. "I don't *want* to stay with them this next year. I'm planning on staying right here."

"I asked you a question. Have you been giving Kate grief?"

"Well—" At the look in her eye, I reluctantly nodded. "Yes, ma'am. I guess so—"

"That's got to stop. Kate and Stephen have kindly given

you a home, and you need to at least *act* grateful. You hear me?"

"But—"

"*Do you hear me?*"

In our family, that question had only one answer. "Yes, ma'am." But I also heard honeybees buzzing around overripe mulberries. I didn't intend to obey them, either. "But—"

"Don't 'but' me, Carley. And take that balky look off your face. Living with Kate and Stephen will broaden you, let you live in a real family for a change."

"*You're* my real family! You and Aunt Sukie. I don't need another one."

I thought from the look in her eyes that I'd won, but she tightened her lips. "Yes, you do. The age you are, you need a man around. Besides, I'm getting on, and Kate and Stephen are the only family you've got except me. You need to get to know them."

"I know them already. I know them real well. But I don't know anybody my age. I don't have a single friend in Job's Corner. Besides, Aunt Kate doesn't need me. She has Raifa. And my bedroom is way upstairs all by myself. I'm scared to death to sleep up there at night. What if there's a fire? I'd burn up before anybody knew it. And there are ghosts. We're right across from the cemetery—" All my good reasons gushed out like water from a hydrant, with no more effect. She didn't even blink.

I took a deep breath and hit her with the Big One. "You wouldn't believe their Sunday school. They don't even make us learn memory verses!"

A smile flickered on her lips, but disappeared at once. "You can learn memory verses on your own. What you can't do is stay here right now."

"You *need* me! Aunt Sukie said you rattle around in this old house without me."

"I won't rattle around much longer. I'm going to work at the store."

I couldn't have been more surprised if she'd said she was going to Mars. "The *store?* Ladies don't work at stores. Especially not—" I stopped, face flaming.

"Old ones? You're skating on thin ice, little lady." But she finally smiled.

She handed me a raw bean and munched another. Finally she sighed. "Since Pop died, honey, things have begun to slide at Marshall's. I haven't kept an eye on it like I should."

"But you can't *work.*" I still couldn't believe it. "You don't know how."

"That's all you know. I was women's buyer at that store the whole time Kate and Lila were coming up. I didn't stay at home until after you came."

I blinked at the stranger taking shape before me.

Oblivious, she went on, "That's going to take all my time and energy, so I need you to live with Kate and Stephen. I won't have time for you this fall."

"I could help you. I could sell, or put things on shelves—"

"I don't expect to be putting things on shelves, and I don't want you behind a counter. We haven't come to that."

I had a dreadful premonition. "Are we poor, Big Mama?"

"No, honey, but I need to be looking down the road—not just for you, but for John and Abby, too. Stephen's never going to make much. Besides, Marshall's is getting behind the times. I want to bring life and smartness back to it."

I wasn't old enough to suspect she could be looking forward to it. All I could see was my poor old Big Mama working hard, then dragging home to an empty house at the end of the day. "You'll need me here at night," I pleaded. "What if you get sick or something?"

"I'm not decrepit, child. Besides, Sukie and I are talking about her sleeping in."

"People wouldn't let Raifa sleep at Aunt Kate's."

"There's a world of difference between two old women sleeping in the same house and a colored girl sleeping in the house with a white man. Even a preacher."

"Why?"

She looked across the field to the mountains, but didn't answer. I racked my brain for another reason to stay. "What if a burglar comes? The way you snore, you'd never hear him. You need me, Big Mama. Please! Don't make me go." I didn't mind the tears in my throat. They might make her listen.

Her eyes redded up a bit. Did she almost tell the truth then, under the mulberry tree? Would it have made a difference? I will never know. She didn't budge an inch. Just went right on building a wall of careful plans between us. "I'm getting a dog. A man down the road has dalmatian pups, and he's offered me one. She'll scare away any burglars we're likely to get."

I flung the newspaper off my lap. "You'd replace your own flesh and blood with a dog? And an old s-s-s-store?" By now I was bawling in earnest. I stood there letting tears pour down my face. "If you don't want me, I'll bet my other grandmother does." I hadn't meant to say that, but sometimes my tongue has a will of its own.

Her eyes widened. Her jaw dropped. Then she hauled off and smacked me so fast I didn't see it coming. I couldn't hear the bees for the ringing in my ears.

We glared at one another in surprise and shock. Big Mama had often switched me, but not once in eleven years had she ever hit me.

How long did we stand like that, looking at each other across a chasm we didn't know how to bridge?

She drew both hands under her big bosom and clenched them tight. Each word was carved from rock as hard as the mountains. "Don't you ever speak to me like that again, girl. Do you understand? And you listen to me, because I don't aim to say this but once. You are going back with Kate this afternoon, and you're going to do as you're told. I don't want Kate writing me that you've been talking back and I don't want C's on your report card. You'll be back for Thanksgiving, and that's that! I have good reasons for this. Reasons you know nothing about. You just have to respect them."

She picked up the speckled dishpan and thrust it at me. "Now get those hulls down to Holly while I take the beans in to Sukie. We won't talk about this again." She moved ponderously toward the side steps, never looking back.

❦

Big Mama always said good training will tell. With my whole life falling apart, I shaped my face into happiness before I headed down the rutted road past the cornfield to Pearl's. Nobody could tell by looking that I wasn't the blithest eleven-year-old in the world.

But when I tipped the bean husks into Holly's trough and stood by her smelly pen, tears ran unbidden down my cheeks. I didn't see a huge black-and-white sow lying in the mud. I saw the pink piglet Pop and I picked out together for Pearl his last Christmas. We named her together, and I could still feel her squirm in my arms as I carefully carried her from Pop's truck to Pearl's empty pen.

I picked up a stick and scratched her back. If I closed my eyes, Pop seemed to be standing just down the fence. "If he were alive," I told Holly, swiping away tears on my shoulders, "he'd never stand for this." Holly grunted, but there wasn't a thing she could do.

"Stand for what?"

I turned to find Pearl's girl Geena behind me with a bucket of slops. We looked at each other awkwardly. I noticed she was taller than me now.

"Nothing," I mumbled, ashamed to be caught crying to a pig. Especially by Geena.

I could not have said what about that plump brown girl made me feel embarrassed and anxious, but from her too-tight tops to her worn-out shoes, Geena always made me wish I were somewhere else. Being with her started a prickle under my skin. We'd dart nervous glances at each other, but could never laugh and talk like normal people. I found myself chattering fast, brightly, about the dumbest things. I seemed to remember, a hundred years ago when we were children, squatting together in the dirt to play by her mother's wash pot, but I wasn't sure if that was real or I'd just imagined it.

"Here," I offered that morning, "let me throw those slops to Holly."

I hefted her bucket and poured the disgusting mess of table scraps and peelings into Holly's long wooden trough. The whole time they fell, I babbled like a maniac. "There, Holly, delicious cereal and carrot peelings and—" I couldn't recognize the rest. "Heavens, you'll eat like a queen today. All this, and bean pods too. What a lucky pig!"

Geena took back the bucket. "You come to stay?"

I shook my head. "No, just visiting and getting my things. I'm gonna live with Aunt Kate this fall, to help her with the baby. I'll go to school there."

"You like it?"

I shrugged. "It's all right. I'll come home Thanksgiving and Christmas, I guess."

"Mama said tell you to come by the house to say hello." She turned away.

Pearl loved to laugh, so we had a jolly time. I was funny. I was charming. If I was a liar, I had to be. Otherwise, what would people think? I even walked jauntily up the road, knowing Pearl could see me the whole way.

Not until I got to my own room did I let my shoulders slump. Then I repacked my suitcase. I got more brown bags from the kitchen and put in every single book and toy—even dolls I no longer played with. I added all my clothes without trying on the winter ones to see if they still fit. The only thing I left was the quilt Big Mama made from scraps of our favorite dresses. I hoped my leaving it would break her heart.

I toted my bags one by one to the backyard and set them in a circle near where Aunt Kate would park the car: my whole life in twelve brown paper sacks, and equally dreary.

Years later when I first saw Stonehenge, it was familiar. I once made my own sacred circle as a protection against the dark.

Chapter 12

Pop used to say, "Folks can't get your goat 'less you tell 'em where it's tied."

Riding back to Job's Corner, I vowed nobody was going to get *my* goat. Not one soul would know I was furious and brokenhearted. During the day, I pretended I was fine. But when Aunt Kate mentioned moving all their beds upstairs, I told her I'd gotten over being afraid. Ghosts and the threat of fire were a small price to pay for privacy in which to cry.

Big Mama never in my lifetime said "I'm sorry" to anybody, but the box that arrived a week later knocked Preston on his rear when the man threw it off the train. Those were the most school clothes I'd ever had, and the prettiest.

If she thought I was going to write and tell her so, though, she could think again.

In the middle of the clothes was the studio portrait of Mama in a gold frame that had always sat on Big Mama's dresser. She looked so real, I couldn't stand it. I shoved her down in my bottom drawer and covered her with sweaters, which I wouldn't need anytime soon. Then I went downstairs and did something truly, horribly wicked.

Sue Mary was scared of everything: bees, wasps, spiders, thunder, planes in the sky, cars on the road, Ira Baines, and Negroes. She wouldn't come in our kitchen if Raifa was there. She was especially terrified of trains. So long as she was in the yard when one came by, she would wave and wave, but if she was on the dirt road, she would dart into the nearest yard as soon as she heard the whistle. I guess she feared the train might jump its tracks.

Abby and I weren't afraid of trains, but we knew better than to play on the tracks. That afternoon, though, because I felt particularly, desperately wicked, I led them up past Lamont's to the far crossing. Brambles grew thick beside the rails up there, so nobody could see us except Ivy. Across the highway I saw her sitting in her rocking chair. She waved, and I waved back.

"Let's walk the tracks," I suggested daringly.

Sue Mary considered, then objected. "Velma 'n' me's not 'lowed to walk the tracks."

"If I'm taking care of you, you're allowed to do whatever I say." I balanced on one rail facing away from Job's Corner.

"I wants to do dat," Abby decided. She tried and promptly slid off.

"Take off your shoes. Here, Sue Mary, let me help you with your sandals." I pitched both pairs of little sandals over on the roadside by the crossing.

Arms held out, bare toes crimped against the hot rusty metal, we teetered along the narrow rails while the sun placed crowns of warmth on our heads. Abby and Sue Mary were better at staying up than I was. Their feet weren't any wider than the rails.

Sue Mary whimpered the whole time—"It's hot. I's scairt"—but I told her if she didn't walk, we wouldn't play with her anymore.

In my defense, let me say that I was careful. Even though normally we could hear the train half a mile away and feel its vibrations long before it roared through town, I firmly believed the grown-ups' warning that "on those tracks a train can come up behind you in a minute." I made sure we walked with somebody facing in each direction, lest a ghostly, silent train swoop down on us unawares.

We had been walking for some time when we heard the whoo-whooo at a distant crossing, coming down from the furniture factory. "De train!" Sue Mary flung herself at me, knocking me off the track. "We gonna get runned over!"

"It's miles away," I scoffed, climbing back on. "You can tell by how soft it sounds." I daringly held out my arms and walked slowly away from the crossing. Secretly, though, I was calculating to make sure we could run back before the train arrived.

The sides of the track were too overgrown with blackberry bushes for us to get off anywhere else.

In a minute we heard the whistle for the next crossing. The train was coming faster than I'd thought. "We's gonna get runned over! Runned over!" First Sue Mary, then Abby screamed, running down the track. That's when I saw that while I could make the crossing, they never could. They couldn't skip cross ties. They had to step on every one.

I seized them up under my arms and tried to run, but they were terrified, flailing, and awkward. Already the tracks vibrated beneath my feet. The engine grew louder every second. Because of the curve, the engineer would never see us until he was on top of us. "Help!" I screamed, trying to run without dropping either little girl.

Out of the corner of one eye I saw a battered green truck stop on the other side of the road. Jay Anderson jumped down, and it was like my eyes froze that moment for all time to come: him standing there in light tan pants, a tan shirt, and a green corduroy cap—the kind with its crown squished to the brim in front. I truly thought it was the last sight I'd ever see.

He pounded across the highway. Pressed his way through the waist-high blackberry bushes. Grabbed the little girls. "Run, Carley! Run!"

Breathless, I hared down that track. I could hardly breathe for a stitch in my side. I heard Jay pounding behind me, then beside me. He reached the crossing first.

He more threw than dropped those girls, yelling, "Get back, now!" Then he turned and reached one long brown arm in my direction. I grasped it gratefully. Felt my own arm pulled nearly out of the socket as I was slung toward the crossing and out of danger. I collapsed in a heap, gasping for breath, as Jay slid to a stop beside me. The train roared by four feet away. Sue Mary and Abby were still screaming.

"Hush, now. Hush up, now." His voice was quiet, soothing. He stood and put one hand on each of their shoulders. Slowly they subsided to gulps and hiccups. "Did your mamas know you were on that track?" He took off his cap to wipe his forehead with one arm. Sweat streamed down his face and beside his ears, leaving little runnels in sawdust. I realized his clothes weren't really tan, they were covered with sawdust, too.

Sue Mary said nothing. Velma, of course, said nothing either. But Abby always did have a big mouth. "Carley said not to tell." Her face was white, her eyes enormous. And the way her eyes accused me, I wondered if she'd ever trust me again.

Jay looked at me gravely. "I was listening for trains," I said defiantly.

"They come up faster than you ever expect." He brushed his pants, still breathing hard. Then he offered his hand to help me up. Reluctantly, I took it. My knees felt like rubber. I could hardly stand.

"I'm not gonna tell the grown-ups this time," he promised, "but don't you go on those tracks again. I wouldn't want y'all to get hurt. Run on home now."

"I can't run wifout shoes," Abby objected. "Dose rocks hurts my feets."

He considered her bare toes, wiggling in the dust. "Where are your shoes?"

"Over dere," Abby pointed. "Carley trew dem so de train couldn't run over dem."

He fetched them and helped put hers on. Sue Mary hung back, almost as terrified of Jay as she was of the train. "I'll do hers," I offered with as much dignity as I had left.

"I'll be off home, then. Mind what I said. Stay off the tracks."

I stumbled home with feelings chugging around inside like diapers in Aunt Kate's old washer—and equally unpleasant. Leftover terror. Deep relief. Embarrassment. Resentment. And a funny cringing that made me squirm. I'd never been reprimanded by a Negro before. I'd never had my life saved by one, either.

And I'd been living with Uncle Stephen just long enough to wonder: would most white men have saved three little Negro girls that quickly? I hoped so, but I still wondered.

❁

On Labor Day, the last day for bare feet, we went down to Anderson's creek for a swim and picnic. When we put on our bathing suits in an upstairs bedroom, mine seemed awfully skimpy. "It must have shrunk," I told Abby, pulling down the seat. I wrapped myself in my terry-cloth beach robe and felt something heavy against my thigh. A little rock, shaped like a heart. For a second, a giant rubber band tugged me back to Memorial Day, with none of the bad in between.

Tears stung my eyes, then rolled down my cheeks. "Don't

cry, Carley." Abby patted my hip gently. "Mama'll get you a new baving suit."

After supper, Abby noticed a picture in a silver frame on Miss Hannah's dresser: a smiling boy with dark eyes and smooth dark hair. "Is dat your boy?" she demanded.

"No," Miss Hannah said, "he was my sister's boy, but we loved him like our own. He had a bad heart, and died when he was twelve. That's been nearly fifteen years, but sometimes it seems like yesterday." She gently stroked his cheek with her fingertip.

"If I dies, will you puts my picture on your dresser and touch it?" Abby inquired.

Miss Hannah chuckled. "Give me your picture, dearie, and I'll put it there while you're still alive and kicking."

"I kicks good," Abby informed her. "Watch." She kicked me hard on the shin.

When I got home, I took Mama's picture out of my drawer and gently stroked her cheek. Then I set the picture in the middle of my dresser with the heart rock before it. Every morning for the rest of my life I have greeted Mama with a loving touch. That night, for the first time, my tower room began to feel a bit like home.

I had no inkling that in a week I'd be worried about getting bombed . . .

Part 3

Ere the Winter Storms Begin

Abby called me a couple of evenings after she got home. "I keep thinking about Job's Corner. Do you think Miss Pauline gave Sue Mary and me other people's junk mail? She always gave us at least one letter a day."

"She probably did. She wasn't exactly your orthodox post-mistress. When I remember how she hurled returning mailbags through the open door of a moving boxcar, I marvel that any of our letters ever reached their destination."

"Yeah, but think how practical that post office was. It let a single mother stay home with her children and still served a community with adequate postal service. Life could be easier today with a Miss Pauline post office every few miles. Well"—she yawned, ready for bed—"happy writing."

I was too busy thinking about Miss Pauline and her brother, Mr. Mayhew, to reply.

Chapter 13

Uncle Stephen could hardly believe we had a bomb drill our first day of school.

When I got off the bus, he was sitting in the swing reading *Life*. To my disgust, Preston followed me home. We were barely on the front walk when Aunt Kate came out with John in her arms and Abby at her skirt, so I knew they'd all been watching for me. "How'd it go?" they all called. Hope in unison.

I shrugged. "Okay, I guess. Nothing to get excited about."

Preston puffed, trying to keep up. "Yes, there was. They measured us, and I'm one quarter inch taller since I started my growth spurt. An' we had the bomb drill."

Uncle Stephen put down *Life* and stared as if doubting his hearing. "The *what*?"

I slumped into a rocker and explained. "You know, when you get under your desk and cover your head with your arms to protect it from atomic fallout."

Abby wrinkled her forehead. "What p'tects your arms?"

"They have a special soap to wash 'em off." Trust Preston to have an answer.

"Then why couldn't you just wash your face and head?" Aunt Kate took the other rocker and gave John a bottle, rocking gently while waiting for his answer. I waited, too. That question hadn't occurred to me before.

Preston's face got pink and earnest. "They *has* to be stuff to wash your arms. Otherwise, they'd all fall off and we'd be a nation of armless people."

"I likes my arms," Abby objected, flailing them about like small propellers.

Uncle Stephen's voice had an edge I'd never heard. "Who's making you go through this nonsense?" He looked sternly at me, like he thought it was all my idea.

"It's not nonsense," I told him coldly. "Mr. Mayhew says the communists are training all their children to fight. If we don't get prepared, they'll make communists of everybody."

"Is that Gilbert Mayhew?" Aunt Kate asked me. "The choir director?"

"Yes ma'am, my uncle Gil." Preston never minded answering questions addressed to somebody else. "Mama's brother. He teaches music at school, and this year he's also in charge of bomb drills. He told us all about it in chapel."

"Chapel?" Uncle Stephen's eyebrows rose above his glasses.

"That's when we all go to the auditorium each week for a program." Preston's freckles glowed, he was so proud to be explaining. "It's mostly on Fridays, but today we had a special one, since it was first day of school. We didn't do much, just dumb stuff like the Lord's Prayer and flag salute, welcomed new kids like Carley, got told who our teachers were—you know, just dumb stuff. But then Uncle Gil told us about the bomb drill."

"De Lord's Prayer isn't dumb," Abby informed him.

"They call it chapel." Uncle Stephen sounded a little dazed. "With a bomb drill—"

"No, that was in our classrooms," I began, but—surprise!— Preston jumped right in.

"—so we could get under our desks. We couldn't get under the seats in the auditorium. And even if we could, that floor is filthy and full of splinters."

"I'd hate for you to get splinters protecting your life," Uncle Stephen agreed.

If Preston was too dumb to recognize sarcasm, I wasn't. "We do have to protect ourselves, you know. Our whole nation is unprepared."

"Uncle Gil's having drills every week until we get fast." Preston's bristle of hair quivered with excitement. "Then, if they drop a bomb on Staichville—" He whistled as his thick hand swooped through the air like a missile, then flew straight down. "We'll be ready."

Uncle Stephen looked at Aunt Kate. "Have you ever heard the like?"

"Don't laugh about it!" I was too desperate to be polite. "Do you know how evil communists are? They're gonna take over the whole world if we don't look out!"

"We gotta be prepared," Preston repeated stubbornly.

"Mr. Mayhew said every family oughta be digging a nuclear shelter—"

"Preston? Get over here!" Miss Pauline stood on her porch and bellowed.

Preston clutched his books and headed down the steps. "Gotta go. Bye."

Uncle Stephen half-rose from the swing. "I'm going to call—"

"No, Stephen," Aunt Kate reached out a hand in warning.

"Please don't. Please?" My whole dreadful day came out in one long wail.

He gave me a level look and sat back down. "That bad a day, huh?"

I let my satchel fall to the floor with a *thunk*. "It started with Mr. Ira hanging around the bus stop stinking to high heaven and telling how he killed a white black snake right there. Ivy waved like she was sending us to war, and that's how I felt all day. I didn't have a nickel for a Moon Pie at recess, nobody talked to me, and *music* class? Mr. Mayhew treats us like morons who don't know one note from another. Do you know what our dumb homework is? Whole notes, half notes, and quarter notes. Draw twenty-five of each."

"That's pretty basic," Uncle Stephen agreed.

"There's Kool-Aid and cookies if you want them," Aunt Kate offered.

I gladly headed to the kitchen. Sixth grade in Mount Vernon Elementary, grades one to eight, looked like a mighty bleak prospect.

My going to school was hard on Abby, too. Later that afternoon she chopped off her curls above her ear on one side and below the ear on the other. When Aunt Kate tried to cut both sides to match, Abby looked in the mirror and roared, "You made me look like a boy!" She stomped into her room and slammed the door.

Miss Hannah came up later and took Abby out to rock on the porch. "I think your new haircut looks modern and smart," Miss Hannah murmured.

"I *is* smart." Abby sniffed. "I wouldn'tuv cut my hair if dey'd let me go to school."

❈

Uncle Stephen was reading on the porch when the bus brought me home the second day, too. Beside him in the swing was a package wrapped in brown paper. He held it out. "For brave and meritorious behavior." Inside were a blue fountain pen, a cherry red diary with a lock and a tiny gold key, and a bottle of Shaeffer's permanent blue ink with a well on the lip. When I carried them up to my room, I found a small pine desk and a dining room chair sitting in the curve of my windows. Uncle Stephen had made the desk by building two small bookshelves and nailing boards across them for a top. It wasn't fancy, but it was just my size. All year I poured out my heart into that little red book. When entries were too long for a page, I added sheets, until it was so fat I had to tie it shut with a scarf. I concluded my first entry:

Found a perfect hiding place for my diary key: the label on my mattress. I picked out one side and sewed on a snap. Will keep my locket there on school days, too. But the label says "Do not remove under penalty of law." I hope the police don't come checking on it.

Later entries from my dairy that would be important . . .

Saturday, September 9—Raifa asks all the time if she can move back in. Aunt Kate begs, "Be patient just a little longer." Late last night I overheard Uncle Stephen say, "Let's move her back in. I'll talk to anybody who complains." "You always think talking to people will make them do the right thing," Aunt Kate said. "It may not." She's right. Uncle Stephen can talk until he's blue in the face, but I'll never like Raifa or Preston.

Wednesday, September 21—Our class has chapel program next month, and our teacher wants us to sing songs from other countries. In a paper on hobbies, I said I play piano, so she asked if I play well enough to accompany them. Since I haven't touched a piano in months, I brought the music home and said I'd let her know. After school I went to church and tried them on the Sunday school piano. The songs are easy, so I'll say yes.

Thursday, September 22—Broke down and wrote Big Mama. Thanked her for my new clothes. Also asked her to send my music books. Uncle Stephen says I can play at the church if Abby doesn't cross the road. Raifa asked if I could play for her to sing. I won't go alone over there with her. She might slit my throat.

Chapter 14

One Saturday that month, Raifa came to work with her head tied up in a red scarf.

"Whatsa matter wif your hair?" Abby asked.

"It ain't my hair, it's my ear. It's killin' me." As Raifa pressed her palm against it, tears welled up and rolled down her cheeks. "Miss Kate, you know a doctor I could go to?"

Aunt Kate called Miss Emily for a doctor's name and sent me to fill the hot water bottle. In the hall, she spoke softly into the phone. "You treat Negroes?" She paused. "That's wonderful. Yes, I can bring her in right now. We were coming to the grocery store and library anyway."

Aunt Kate drove, because Uncle Stephen was over at the church polishing his sermon. "Catch the Greyhound back," Aunt Kate reminded Raifa for at least the fourth time as we let her off at the doctor's building. "The station is four blocks down that street. Tell the man to let you out at Bethel Church in Job's Corner."

"I know, Miss Kate." Clutching her hot water bottle, Raifa hurried inside.

We had barely gotten home and started putting away food when she stormed in. She slammed the screened door behind her, stomped down the hall, and steamed into the kitchen, muttering words none of us could understand. I thought she was talking African, until I recognized a few. I'd heard big boys yell them at one another when no grown-ups were around, but Big Mama washed my mouth out with soap when I tried them at home. Shocked, I waited to see if Aunt Kate recognized them, too.

Apparently not, for she turned with a can of tuna in one hand and a worried wrinkle between her eyes. "Didn't the doctor see you?"

"Sure, he seen me." Raifa slung the hot water bottle onto the counter. "Right away. Didn't make me wait or nothin', even though the waitin' room was plumb full." For an instant she looked gratified. "'N' he give me some medicine to help the pain, and a perscription. Got it filled on my way to the station." She got a glass of water and tossed down a pill.

"Do you feel any better?" No wonder Aunt Kate sounded anxious. Raifa didn't *act* like she felt better.

"Felt a lot better till I got on the bus. Dadblamed driver made me get up and walk to the back, when there were perfectly good seats all the way up 'n' down the aisle."

Aunt Kate turned pale as a peeled apple. One hand crept to her cheek like Raifa's earache had settled in her own tooth. "Oh, Raifa, I forgot to tell you!"

Raifa's lids half-closed over her eyes. "Forgot to tell me lotsa things 'bout livin' here." She flicked on her radio, but all it got was static. Abby must have been twirling the dial again. Raifa hit it so hard with her fist, she cracked the case.

I never expected Aunt Kate to put up with back talk, but she hurried to the refrigerator and poured a glass of Kool-Aid. She even put in extra sugar, the way Raifa liked it. "Here. Sit down. I'm so sorry. I can't imagine how awful that was—especially with your earache. It's a stupid custom, but I should have remembered to explain. I am so sorry!"

"Custom schmustom." Raifa ignored the Kool-Aid. "I'm sick and tired of white folks' customs. Sick and tired, you hear me?" She slammed her palm down on the countertop. A cup bounced to the floor. She stamped on it, ground it beneath her heel. Abby backed close to me. John started to wail in his kitchen box.

Aunt Kate's voice was getting exasperated. "I don't know what else to say. I can't help the way things are. But I could have prepared you better. I am truly sorry."

Raifa didn't say a word, just stood and glared.

Aunt Kate raised both palms, then dropped them beside her. "I need to change John. Then I'll fix dinner. Why don't you go out on the porch and rock a while until you feel better?" She scooped up John and headed for the bathroom.

Abby peered up at Raifa. "How come the dadblamed driver made you sit in the back?"

Raifa scowled. "'Cause just white folks get to sit up front." She snatched up her Kool-Aid and sat down at the table, draining half the glass in one gulp.

"Dat's Daddy's chair," Abby objected. "You 'posed to sit over dere." She pointed to where Raifa usually sat. Raifa set down her glass, drew back her arm, and hit Abby so hard she left four pink fingers and a palm imprinted on the cheek. Abby screamed.

"Don't you hit her!" I jumped in front of Raifa, sure she'd hit me, too. She'd been itching to for a long time. But before she could even think about it, Aunt Kate hurried back, carrying John with his bottom still bare.

She practically threw John at me and snatched up Abby, who was sobbing. "Did you hit her?" When she saw Abby's cheek, she spewed anger like lava. "I don't care how mad you get at a bus driver, you can't take it out on my child. Do you hear me?" She cradled Abby against her neck and glared at Raifa. Raifa glared sullenly back.

"You are not to hit my children, insult my children, or in any other way hurt them. I don't care what color you are or how bad you feel, you are *not to hit my children!*" She shrieked the last five words. Mrs. Cameron was getting an earful over at her store.

For a second, silence hung like a drop on the ceiling. Then the telephone rang.

I moved toward the door, but Aunt Kate shook her head. "I'll get it." Her voice was dead calm, but she was shaking. She carried Abby with her. I held on to John, even though he was holding out his arms to Raifa. She made a half-motion to him, then dropped her hand.

Because the kitchen was so quiet, we heard every word. Aunt Kate started in the bright "Everything is all right even if my world is falling apart" voice we both learned at Big Mama's knee. "Yes? Oh, hello! Yes, she said you did. I want to thank you for working her in. What?"

Her voice dropped. "Oh, dear. She didn't know. I didn't think—Of course. I understand. It won't happen again. Thank you for calling. And thank you again for working her in."

We heard a click, then nothing except Abby snuffling against her shoulder.

Finally Aunt Kate shuffled into the dining room next door, bent over like Abby was heavier than she could carry. She collapsed onto the couch and made soothing little noises, stroking the damp tangled curls. But tears streamed down her own cheeks, and she didn't even try to wipe them away. I went to sit beside her on the couch.

Raifa pushed back her chair and strode to the door. "Who was that? What did they want?" I stared at her in astonishment. She had never asked that before. It was none of her business who called our house.

When Aunt Kate didn't answer, Raifa persisted. "It was that doctor, wadn't it? What did he say? Tell me. What did he say?"

Aunt Kate's voice sounded like she was plumb worn out. "He said you went to the white waiting room by mistake. The Negro waiting room is at the back. He took you right away rather than embarrass you, but he asked me to tell you to please use the Negro one from now on."

She stopped. Raifa didn't say a word, just stood there. They looked at each other until Aunt Kate looked down. John crowed for me to play, but I ignored him.

Aunt Kate went on in that dead, sad voice. "I'm just sick, Raifa. Sick that a hurting person can be insulted this way. Sick that I have to explain it to you. There's no way I *can* explain it, really. It's just the way things are. If I could change them, I would. But I can't."

Raifa stood frozen for what seemed far more than a minute. Then she reached out to the counter beside the door. She grabbed a butcher knife lying there. In one second she raised it high above her head and slammed it so hard on the countertop that the blade snapped. I saw a chip of counter fly away.

Then she stood there with her shoulders heaving, nostrils flared, breathing hard.

I couldn't help it—a picture of Big Mama's Aunt Helen floated past my eyes, the one who had her throat slit by an angry field hand. I saw her lying in her own blood. And then I could see us all lying in our blood, too. It didn't occur to me that Aunt Kate and I were two against one. I fully expected Uncle Stephen to come home to find us all—Aunt Kate, me, Abby, and little John—dead on the floor.

Aunt Kate must have been thinking the very same thing because in the tone Big Mama used once when she said, "Carley, sit down, keep your feet up, and watch that rattler in the closet while I get a hoe," Aunt Kate said, "Carley, take John to my room."

I slid from the sofa like the seat was greased and reached her door at the same time she and Abby did. Quickly, without saying a word, we shoved the chest of drawers up against the hall door and propped a chair under the knob leading to Abby's room.

"What you doin', Mama?" Abby watched round-eyed from the bed, where Aunt Kate had dumped her. I'd dropped John beside her. Marshall women think alike in a crisis.

Instead of answering Abby, Aunt Kate looked at me. "Entertain her, Carley. I need to finish changing John." She was taking quick little breaths. Her face was pink, her eyes bright.

While she put a diaper on John, I sat on the bed telling Abby the story of Little Red Riding Hood. All the time, I was straining my ears toward the hall.

Oooh, grandma, what a big butcher knife you have!

"I doesn't want to stay in here." Abby wriggled off the bed when the story was done.

"Your daddy will be home soon," I promised, hoping it was true.

Aunt Kate was walking John, trying to make him forget he was hungry. "It may be awhile. Stephen was going up to help Wash work on his tractor when he finished his sermon."

Suddenly the bedroom didn't seem like a fortress. It felt like a jail.

What was it like for Raifa—seventeen, in pain, demeaned, far away from her mother—as her fury subsided and she realized she was cut off from us, as well? I can ask that now, but at the time, the question didn't occur to me—nor, I honestly believe, to Aunt Kate. The Bible says that perfect love casts out fear. The inverse is also true: perfect fear casts out love. Southern white women were taught from our cradles to be terrified of angry Negroes.

We all got hungry. Abby and John sobbed themselves to sleep. Aunt Kate and I were exhausted by indecision. Part of us said, "We could just walk out and pretend nothing happened." Another part asked, "But what if Raifa's waiting just outside to kill us?"

From time to time we crept to the door and pressed our ears against the wood. We heard nothing. Meanwhile, outside the window, Sue Mary piped away to Velma in the sandbox and Preston yelled to his mother. Normalcy was only a screen away.

"We could shout to Miss Pauline," I suggested.

"What would we tell her? We'll just wait for Stephen," Aunt Kate said grimly.

"How 'bout if I drop out the window and go get him?"

"It's too big a drop. If you were to break a leg—"

Abby woke suddenly, as she often did. "If I doesn't get to de bafroom, I'm gonna pop."

"You've been an angel to last this long," Aunt Kate told her. "Thank heavens we didn't get Rowdy in before Raifa got home. He'd have had to go out already, for sure."

"I has to go out, too." Abby squirmed off the bed and headed to the door. Aunt Kate picked up John and followed. I was right behind her. We listened. Heard nothing.

Desperate, Aunt Kate inched the chest away. "Okay," she whispered. "Only to the bathroom. We'll run together on the count of three. One, two, three!"

We dashed on tiptoe the five feet between doors. Aunt Kate slid the bolt. When we were done, we counted to three again and dashed back to the room, terrified we'd be caught.

I glimpsed Raifa's scarf above a rocker. "She's on the porch," I murmured when we were safe inside. "I could tiptoe to the kitchen for peanut butter and bread."

Aunt Kate considered, hunger battling safety. Finally she nodded. "Bring milk and cups, too." As I opened the door, she hissed, "And a table knife!"

First I peeped out. Raifa's red scarf still rocked on the porch. I wondered what Job's Corner thought, seeing her there all day. I turned back and whispered, "She's still on the porch. Why don't we grab some food and go to the yard?"

"I feel safer in here, with the children."

I moved about the kitchen like a daytime mouse, ears cocked for the slightest sound. Quickly I gathered up the food, adding three apples and a jar of baby food. I reached for a spoon and it clattered to the floor. I froze. Raifa's rocker stopped. I moved toward the back door. If she came for me, I'd run out the back door and get Uncle Stephen.

Then her rocker started to creak again. Back and forth. Back and forth. I collected everything into an awkward armful and tiptoed quickly across the hall. "It's just me," I whispered as I opened the door. We ate ravenously, heedless of crumbs on the bed.

Finally Uncle Stephen came home. We heard his voice on the

porch, Raifa answering. He came down the hall. "Kate? Where are you?" We heard him try the knob of the bedroom door.

Aunt Kate shoved back the chest with a screech. Just by standing in the doorway, he made our whole afternoon feel ridiculous. So did the expression on his face. "What in the world?"

We confronted him, rumpled, sweaty, and defiant. Our indignant story poured out in three simultaneous streams. ". . . pulled a butcher knife . . . hit me hard, right dere! . . . had to ride in the back . . . then the doctor called . . ."

Uncle Stephen held up one hand. "Whoa! Why don't you all come out here on the porch with Raifa and me, and let's all talk this over together?"

Aunt Kate shook her head. "I will not bring these children out until Raifa has gone. Go get her things and put her on a bus tonight for West Virginia. I will not live in fear for myself and my children."

Uncle Stephen got mad, of course. He sent Abby and me to Abby's room, and said a lot of things to Aunt Kate about bus drivers and doctors. She agreed with everything he said until he got to, "Negroes have a lot to put up with, Kate. We have to make allowances."

"I know that. But I also know people have to learn to control the ugly streak that comes out in all of us when we get angry. I will not live with someone who slaps my children and picks up a knife when she's mad. Put her on a bus, or I won't come out. I mean it."

Hair standing on end, he finally turned angrily and went to Raifa on the porch. As we heard the Chevy drive off, Aunt Kate muttered, "I can't be a good preacher's wife. I don't possess enough charity."

I was on the porch when Uncle Stephen got home. I couldn't seem to get enough fresh air and sky. Was that how people in jail felt when they finally got out?

He came heavily up the steps and handed me a brown paper bag. "Raifa left this for you."

It was her radio, with a note: "To rember me by, Raifa."

I went to my room feeling like dirt. I sat on the side of my bed and prayed God would forgive me for all the bad things I ever said and thought about her. I even promised to listen to her station as a memorial. Maybe someday I would hear the announcer say, "And now, Raifa Brown!"

Then I plugged in the radio. No matter where I turned the dial, all I got was static. And when I got ready for bed, I discovered that Mama's locket, which I always took from my mattress label at night to look at for a minute, was missing.

"Call the police!" I yelled, running down to Uncle Stephen, who was smoking his pipe in the swing. "Raifa stole my locket!"

"You don't know that," he said curtly. He wasn't happy with anybody that evening.

"It was there last night and now it's gone. Who else could have taken it?"

"The house stays unlocked. Anybody could have come in while you all were barricaded behind that chest. And even if Raifa did take it, surely you can forgive her. She's been through some pretty awful things recently."

"I've been through some pretty awful things, too, and that locket is my greatest treasure. I want it back!"

He puffed on his pipe for a minute or two before he spoke. "Maybe Raifa's jealous of all the good things you've got. Had you ever thought of that?"

"If she's jealous of an orphan with no friends, she's crazy. She's got a mother."

"Other people's lives often look better than our own. There's an Indian proverb that before you judge somebody, you should walk a mile in her shoes."

"If I walked a mile in Raifa's shoes," I replied grimly, "I'd find my locket."

Chapter 15

Not one soul asked about Raifa leaving. I didn't know if that was because they'd all believed, like Miz Baines, that she would eventually "hightail it up the road" to West Virginia or if old Mrs. Cameron had gotten an earful and spread the news.

Or maybe people were too busy thinking up other people to call on the phone. That fall Statesville put in the telephone dial system so we could make calls without using the operator. Aunt Kate claimed people sat up at night thinking of relatives to call. We were also assigned five-digit numbers. Miss Hannah grumbled playfully, "I'll never remember all that."

As we moved into October, the North Carolina sky was clear blue without summer's haze, but it was so dry that everything was covered with orange dust. The trees still hadn't turned, but looked limp and weary like they were thinking about it. Aunt Kate looked limp and weary, too, from keeping that enormous house clean, visiting the whole congregation with Uncle Stephen, and caring for her children.

For several weeks Uncle Stephen's sermons were so full of baseball illustrations, Aunt Kate said she could tell he and I'd been listening to the World Series when he should have been preparing them. But nobody else complained. People were still falling all over themselves saying how glad they were he was there, how much they enjoyed his preaching, what darlings his children were, and (except for Miss Nancy and Miss Pauline) how much they admired "that nice Mrs. Whitfield." Uncle Stephen said they were in a "honeymoon period." We ate every Sunday dinner at somebody's house, and almost every day

somebody came by the manse with a cake, pie, jar of jam, or—
when farmers started to slaughter—package of meat.

Of course, Uncle Stephen hadn't started preaching about
politics yet—even though at home we talked so much about
Congress, civil rights, communism, and a coal miner's strike
that I started writing in my diary, *4 C's for supper again*. He and
Aunt Kate both worried that the miners they knew would suffer when winter came. They were mad at Congress for not giving President Truman money to help the poor and at governors
who wouldn't give Negroes rights the Constitution entitled
them to.

On the issue of communism, I felt trapped between Uncle
Stephen and Mr. Mayhew. I could not convince Uncle Stephen
what a threat the communists were, or persuade him that cen-
tral North Carolina was a likely bomb target. "Just talk to Mr.
Mayhew," I begged.

"I don't need to spend time listening to bigoted warmongers."

I looked up those words and returned to the battle. "That's
not a very Christian thing to say about a member of your
church."

"You're right, it wasn't. I repent. But let's just say I prefer
Drew Pearson, who claims it's not the Russian people who are
our enemies, but a handful of their leaders."

When I carried those words back to class, Mr. Mayhew
pooched up his lips. "Whoever you've been talking to is obviously poorly informed."

The next Sunday after church Mr. Mayhew lingered, fussing
around straightening choir chairs while Uncle Stephen and
Aunt Kate shook hands with people. I had a new job: collecting
bulletins people left in pews, but I'd bent over so he couldn't
see me. It was embarrassing to see a teacher at church. I wondered what he was waiting for.

As Uncle Stephen came back up the aisle on his way to the
closet where he took off his robe, Mr. Mayhew stepped up
behind the pulpit, like he was the preacher and Uncle Stephen
the congregation. "Mr. Whitfield, could I have a word with you?"

"Sure, Gilbert. The choir's sounding good. I particularly
liked the anthem this morning."

"Thank you, sir, but it's not music I want to talk about.
From what Carley tells me"—I scrunched farther down
between two pews—"you aren't taking the threat of communism to our nation very seriously."

From underneath the pews I saw Uncle Stephen's robe tail jerk, so I knew he'd taken it off. "I'd take it seriously if I believed there *was* a threat, but I don't—not from the majority of the Russian people. Most of them are just plain folks, like you and me. A lot of them are even Christians. We're in far greater danger, I think, from teaching our children to hate."

I heard a little puffy sound Mr. Mayhew always made when he got exasperated. "How can you say such a thing? Russians are the enemies of our Lord! We are bound to hate them!"

Uncle Stephen crossed his feet and propped himself up against the side of a pew. "The Bible teaches us to love our enemies, Gilbert. Doesn't that cover Russians, too?" He still sounded like they were just having a pleasant conversation.

Mr. Mayhew didn't say anything for a minute, then gave a hollow little laugh. "Sometimes we have to be practical, Mr. Whitfield. Your kind of thinking is dangerous!" He pounded the pulpit like a good Baptist preacher. "These people are menacing the very things our Constitution stands for!" He pounded the pulpit again. From his tone of voice, his eyes had probably begun to bulge out. His cheeks must be very red. In a minute he'd be talking about nuclear war and bombs in our peaceful skies.

Uncle Stephen's voice was still pleasant. "Loving instead of hating can always be dangerous, but that's one of the things that keeps Christianity from ever getting dull. Besides, hating people is a lot more dangerous to the person doing the hating. It can eat you up."

"What will it take to convince you, Preacher—nuclear war? Bombs in our peaceful skies? These people will destroy our nation while mealymouthed people are talking about peace and brotherhood!"

He pounded the pulpit once more, then he must have hurried out, because I heard Uncle Stephen call, "Wait! Gilbert?" and the door to the back hall slammed.

For a minute there wasn't a sound in the sanctuary. You'd have thought it was full of nothing except the quiet holiness of God. Then Uncle Stephen heaved a big sigh. "You can come out now, Carley. At least now I see what you're up against."

I climbed up out of my hideout very confused. Uncle Stephen had acted more Christian, but it still seemed to me like Mr. Mayhew made a lot more sense.

I tried not to let anybody see how homesick I was, but some days the sky was as dull and soft as Miss Hannah's blue damask tablecloth, and on the western horizon the periwinkle mountains looked so close I was sure three giant steps would take me home. I just couldn't step far enough. I wanted Mama so bad I could taste it. But I didn't talk about her to anybody. Instead I searched the Psalms and memorized the verse Uncle Stephen quoted to Miss Nancy that first day: "I will lift up mine eyes to the hills, whence cometh my help." I didn't know what kind of help could come from those mountains, but it was comforting to think it was up there if I needed it. I just hoped it could find me.

Most afternoons I practiced piano in the church basement. One day I'd been playing melancholy pieces that left me so sad and homesick, I decided to walk around the old cemetery before I went home. It was late, and Ivy had already gone inside. I was admiring a blaze of holly near a marble tombstone when Mr. Ira called from the wall that divided the cemetery from his yard. "Ever et a persimmon, girl?" He pointed to bright orange fruit on a tree.

"No, sir."

"Here." He twisted one off the tree and held it out.

I went over, holding my breath so I wouldn't have to smell him.

"Thanks." I took a bite from a place he hadn't touched. Before I could even swallow, my lips and cheeks felt like they were being sucked into my stomach. I couldn't open my mouth, hard as I tried. And all the while that horrid old man was cackling, slapping one grimy hand on the leg of his overalls. "Gotta wait till it ripens, girl. Anybody knows that."

I turned on my heel without a word and stomped home. If I told Uncle Stephen, he'd say God was giving me a chance to pray for one who despitefully used me. I knew what I would pray: *May Ira Baines rot in hell five years for every minute of agony he has caused me.*

Aunt Kate had reason in a few days to wish the same thing on Miss Nancy. We were eating supper Sunday night when somebody pounded on our door. We hurried out to find Miss Nancy with her face so red she looked like she'd been left out in the sun too long and Mr. Wash holding Rowdy by a rope around his neck. Rowdy's back was matted and bleeding.

"Rowdy!" Aunt Kate bent to hug him. "What happened?"

"That dog tore up my flowers!" Miss Nancy snapped. "So I beat him with a broom. First he chased our cat all over the yard, then he knocked over my pot of geraniums. They are simply ruined!" Her face crumpled like she was about to cry.

Mr. Wash reached over and patted her shoulder. "Now, Mother, don't get too upset. But you need to keep your dog penned, Preacher."

Uncle Stephen scratched his head. "I tied him. He must've worked out of his collar."

"He plumb ruined my flowers," Miss Nancy said angrily, blinking back tears. "If you won't keep him penned, he'll have to be put down. He just *ruined* my flowers."

"Those geraniums were the only beautiful thing in her life," Uncle Stephen explained after they'd gone.

Aunt Kate rubbed ointment gently into Rowdy's cuts and set her lips in a hard line. "That doesn't excuse her beating Rowdy with a broom until he bled."

Late that evening, Uncle Stephen pounded away in the barn making a pen Rowdy couldn't get out of. He'd tugged his collar plumb in two.

While he was working, Miss Hannah brought up some homemade black walnut ice cream. When Aunt Kate told her what happened, she promised, "I'll take her more geraniums. Don't you worry about this, old dear. It will all blow over. Don't worry. It will be all right."

As she drove away, still talking, Uncle Stephen asked Aunt Kate, "Is it possible for God to make an angel who talks too much?"

Mr. Wash must have felt bad about what happened, because he came by the next night after work. Uncle Stephen was reading the new *Life*, and I was doing arithmetic in the swing. Mr. Wash was grimy with roofing tar, so he wouldn't take a chair, but perched on the top step and offered Uncle Stephen a cigar. They smoked those filthy things in silence while I worked a problem and wondered why I needed to know about fence posts. The only fence posts I cared about were the ones that kept Davy Anderson's cows from killing me.

Finally Mr. Wash noticed what Uncle Stephen was reading. "I used to take *Life*," he allowed, "but I hate to lay out six dollars a year for something I throw away."

"How about if I pass mine on to you when I'm done with it?"

Mr. Wash thought a minute, then reached into his pocket and pulled out three dollars. "How about if I pay half? Then I'll feel good about you passing them on."

Uncle Stephen put the money in his pocket. "Done."

They smoked some more without saying anything, watching the sun go down and blowing filthy smoke my way. Finally Mr. Wash got up. "I'd better be getting home. Nancy'll have supper ready." Halfway down the sidewalk, he turned back. "Women get so worked up about little things, don't they?" I didn't know if he meant Miss Nancy or Aunt Kate.

Uncle Stephen took a long slow puff on his cigar. "Sometimes it takes work to keep them on an even keel." He blew smoke. "But I thank God he saw fit to give them to us."

"Me too," said Mr. Wash. "Well, good evenin'. Be seein' you."

"I'll send Carley up with the magazine as soon as I'm done."

For a second Mr. Wash looked like he'd plumb forgotten. "Right." He nodded. "I'll look forward to readin' it. Good evenin'."

"Good evening, Wash. Thanks for the cigar."

When he was out of earshot, Uncle Stephen murmured in the direction of the first star, "*Life* and a good cigar. You sure do work in mysterious ways."

Poor Aunt Kate had barely gotten back on speaking terms with Miss Nancy when she had a fight with Miss Pauline. The little girls had asked for canning jars, and Miss Pauline said "Yes" without asking what they were for. Sue Mary and Abby filled them with pokeberries and played like they were canning.

Abby had been warned a hundred times not to touch those permanent purple pokeberries, but when they got tired of canning, they took off their dresses, smushed berries against the chicken coop, and painted themselves purple all over—even their hair. Miss Pauline hauled Abby home. "It's all her fault. Sue Mary was never a speck of trouble till you all moved in."

Aunt Kate was furious. "When the girls play at my house, they get supervision!"

Uncle Stephen came out to see what was going on. "Your wife is insulting a member of your congregation!" Miss Pauline bellowed.

He took one look at Abby and laughed fit to split his pants. "If Indians come by looking for warpath volunteers, we've got one painted and ready to go."

Abby patted her mouth, whooped, and danced on the front walk in her underpants.

Miss Pauline threw back her head and laughed, too. "I got one over to my place, too. You send them to me if they come to you first." She wiped her eyes and moved closer to Uncle Stephen. Anybody who hadn't known might have thought she and he were the couple and Aunt Kate the neighbor. "Well, I better be gettin' back. Good night, now." She turned back to Aunt Kate. "It'll wear off, I guess, after a while. See you tomorrow."

When she'd gone, Aunt Kate was still fuming. Uncle Stephen put his arm around her and squeezed. "If you'll dip us both some of Hannah's ice cream, I'll take Pocahontas in and wash her hair."

Aunt Kate shook her head. "What next?"

It was a good thing she didn't know . . .

Chapter 16

The second Friday of October, my teacher told our class, "See you Halloween."

Startled, I blurted, "Where are you going?" The other kids snickered. "It's cotton picking vacation, stupid."

For days, bolls in the fields had swelled like oversized brown popcorn. Now they were bursting the seams of their pods, but I was as ignorant about what happened next in a cotton field as I was about other facts of life. My town school never closed for cotton. Uncle Stephen, however, remembered cotton vacations from his own school days. "They can close school or face half-empty classrooms. Farmers need their children for picking."

Saturday morning we woke to find Negro adults and children working their way up and down the field by our house. I nearly didn't recognize Jay in a floppy hat, picking with his usual restless grace. When Abby saw that one picker was a girl her own size with a blue sack on one shoulder, she headed for the field. Later, she dashed in to Aunt Kate, who was ironing. "I wanna pick cotton." She stood with her legs apart and hands behind her, just like her daddy.

Aunt Kate didn't even look up. "You don't know what you're talking about."

"I do, too," Abby insisted. "Look out de dining room window."

Aunt Kate glanced out the window and went back to ironing. "You're too little."

"One girl's four like me," Abby argued. "I already went out

and talked to her. Her name's Maggie. She has her own sack, and when she fills it up she'll get paid. Real money!"

Aunt Kate shook her head. "Daddy and I don't want you girls picking cotton. Those children need the money. You all don't."

"Not Carley," Abby agreed. "Just me." Knowing a brick wall when she hit one, she scampered to find Uncle Stephen.

To our amazement, he thought it would be a good idea. "It will teach her what hard work's all about." He went to talk to the pickers, and came back to report. "The field belongs to Davy, and the pickers are Jay, his sister, her husband, and their children. I spoke with them, and if Abby stays out of the way of the adults, she can pick. Can you make her a sack?"

"I can make her a sack," Aunt Kate said shortly, "but I won't help her fill it. And I won't send her into that field without somebody watching out for her."

"Carley can read in the swing," Uncle Stephen suggested.

"When Carley reads, she might as well be on Mars. But we can all take turns doing something on the porch, if you are determined to let her do this."

"It will be hard, dirty, and not much fun," Uncle Stephen told Abby seriously. "You will have to work all morning, and not quit until dinnertime. Do you still want to try?"

"O' course," Abby replied indignantly.

Aunt Kate quickly sewed a sack while I helped Abby into her oldest overalls and found her a hat. Uncle Stephen handed her a brown paper bag. "What's dat?" she asked.

"Your snack. You've got a peanut butter sandwich, an apple, and a metal cup to dip water from a bucket."

"I doesn't like water."

"You can't be picky, Abby."

"I am picky. I'm a cotton picky." She hefted both sacks and skipped to the door.

Uncle Stephen poured iced tea for him and Aunt Kate and Kool-Aid for me, and we all went out on the porch to watch. "It'll be good for her," Uncle Stephen told us again. "She'll learn how hard some girls have to work. I told Cecile she has to stay all morning."

Aunt Kate looked across the side yard toward the tiny white child plodding down a cotton row beside a brown one. "It's your deal. I'm just the sack maker. But I'm not leaving my baby in a field of"—she hesitated—"people I don't know, without supervision. I've drawn up a schedule here, for the three of us. Which shift on the porch would you like?"

As it turned out, they were both busy, so I spent the morning on the porch. About eleven Mr. Hugh Fred came from the direction of his factory. He slowed at the post office, then kept on driving our way. He stopped beside the cotton field and got out, wearing shiny shoes and a gray suit. "Abby, come here a minute!" He sounded very stern.

She trudged to meet him. I left the swing, crossed our yard, and got there first. "Hey, Mr. Hugh Fred. What you doin'?"

He turned to me with a frown on his handsome face. "Does her daddy know this child is picking cotton?"

"Oh, yessir. He said it's good for her. She'll learn how some girls have to work."

"I's wukkin' very hard." Abby set down her half-filled bag with a soft thud. Sweat glistened on her lightly freckled nose. Her cheeks were bright pink. "I's powerful tired." I'd heard one of Maggie's older brothers whining that all morning. He looked about my age.

Mr. Hugh Fred squatted down to her height. "It's time for you to quit. You've picked enough, and it's mighty hot out here."

Abby sighed. "I has to fill my bag two more times. Den I gets a quarter."

He stood, jingled his change, and brought out two shiny quarters. "How about if I pay you right now? Then you can go play."

"Okey-dokey."

Before she could take them, her daddy called. "Abby?" She paused, hand out, as he came down the steps, shoving back his hair.

"Hey, Stephen," Mr. Hugh Fred greeted him. "You needin' extra income, that you've put this baby to work?" He sounded friendly as usual, but he was frowning again.

"I's not a baby!" Abby said indignantly, still eyeing the quarters.

"I didn't send her, she asked to go. But we thought it would be good for her to learn the value of hard work." Uncle Stephen laid one hand on Abby's shoulder. She squirmed.

"That's what I told him," I volunteered, shoving my glasses up my nose.

"Plenty of time yet for her to learn about hard work. And

those folks need every penny of cotton money they can earn. You don't want to be takin' it away from them."

I could tell Uncle Stephen hadn't thought about that. Mr. Hugh Fred stepped closer and said angrily, "You've no call to get folks' backs up! They won't like seein' your little girl workin' side by side with field hands." He bent down. "Here's your pay, Abby. Now go play." He clapped Uncle Stephen on the shoulder and walked quickly to his car.

Uncle Stephen hadn't gotten a chance to say a word.

Abby looked at her two quarters in glee. Picking up the limp sack, she ran toward the field. "Maggie? Maggie!" We watched as she poured her cotton into Maggie's sack. After just a second's hesitation, she handed over one quarter, too. "Dere's your pay. Now come play."

"Can I, Mama?" Maggie begged.

Cecile cocked her head uncertainly toward Uncle Stephen. He nodded. "It's all right."

As we turned toward the house, he muttered angrily, "Might as well get hung for a sheep as a lamb."

❋

I leave my computer and go call Abby. Cradling a small white sack in my lap, I ask, "Do you remember picking cotton?"

"I sure do! All day in the broiling sun for two quarters. These days—"

I head her off before she can begin a familiar diatribe about how little her children work and how much they expect to be paid. "Actually, you only worked a couple of hours. What else do you remember?"

She considers. "A few scenes, like snapshots. Maggie's mama—was her name Seal?"

"Cecile."

"Oh! I always thought Seal was a funny name for a mother, but kind of nice. Anyway, I can see her big blue bottom as she moved down the row ahead of us. And you, sitting on the porch drinking Kool-Aid when I just had water. I can see the man with scales, who weighed the cotton and wrote in a book. When I took my first sackful, I asked, 'Do I get money?' 'Fill it two more times and you get a quarter,' he promised. 'Now hustle.'

"'I'm gonna hustle,' I promised. I ran all the way back to my row." Abby's gurgle bubbles over the line, full of mischief. "Oh, and Maggie! Remember Maggie?"

"Do I ever. After that day, anytime Cecile helped Janey Lou at Aunt Hannah's parties, I had to baby-sit Maggie along with you and Sue Mary."

"And Velma. Don't forget Velma."

"Never. I once wrote Big Mama asking if she knew she'd sent me to Job's Corner to baby-sit a colored child and a ghost."

Abby clears her throat, like she's trying to decide whether or not to tell me something. Finally she confesses, "I also remember that Maggie and I went to the bathroom together."

I could tell there was more to it than that. "What happened?"

"I told Maggie I was going home to potty and she said, 'We doesn't go home, we goes to the bottom of the field.' She took my hand and led me. When we got there and she pulled down her pants, her bottom was brown. I was dumbfounded! I'd assumed black people were white under their clothes. 'Are you brown all over?' I asked. 'Yep. Is you pink all over?' she asked. I pulled down my pants and we each turned around while the other had a good look. I poked her bottom and said, 'You're just like a soft Hushey bar.' She poked my bottom and said, 'You're just like a baby pig!' We giggled, then squatted facing each another. We were astonished that the water came out the very same color. I couldn't have put it into words, but that was when I first knew race was a matter of skin."

"What happened next?" I was surprised at how vividly she remembered when pressed.

She gurgled again. "Seal caught us and said it was time to stop playing and get back to work. Playing! We were having a life-changing experience. And that's all I remember—except Mr. Hugh Fred came and paid me two quarters. I decided right then I'd rather be paid not to work than paid to work."

I'd remembered something else—something that makes me blush to remember it, something I would never remind her of: I remembered that when she and Maggie started inside to play, I suggested they play outside instead. "Negro children don't go into white houses," I whispered to Abby.

"Why not?" she demanded.

"They just don't," I told her. "You'll understand when you get bigger."

I didn't understand myself, but it was what I had been taught and felt compelled to pass on to the next generation for its own good.

Chapter 17

My debut on the Mount Vernon Elementary piano was an unexpected success. I used a few tricks Pop showed me to jazz up songs, and Mr. Mayhew bustled right up to declare, "I didn't realize you were so musical. How about if you become my assistant?" While gratifying, however, that was nowhere nearly as exciting as Freda saying on the bus, "You play almost as well as I did at your age. Maybe we can do a duet sometime."

That spurred me to practice even harder, though I had no hope of taking lessons all year. Then one afternoon during cotton vacation I got so bored I went over to read tombstones in the new cemetery. By then, leaves hung on trees like living was getting to be too much for them. Whenever I got to thinking about Mama, I felt like living was too much for me, too. That day, though, I gradually heard a Chopin polonaise played so beautifully I couldn't help following it straight to Lamonts' front door. I waited until the last note died, then twisted the bell. Bells in those days were round, with handles to twist.

A woman came to peer through the screen. She was medium tall and wore a faded gray calico. Her hair waved in soft gray waterfalls on each side of her face and was pulled back to an untidy bun. Even her eyes were gray, and she seemed so timid I couldn't believe she'd played with such power—until I saw her hands. They were big and strong.

"Hello," I said. "I'm Carley Marshall, and my uncle is the new preacher. Are you Miss Rilla?" She nodded. "That's one of my favorite pieces, and you played it beautifully."

"It's one of my favorites, too." Her voice was low, scarcely more than a whisper.

"You must have a very good piano," I hinted.

She hesitated, then stepped back from the door and motioned to the hall. "Won't you . . .?" Although she didn't finish the sentence, I hurried in. She showed me into the living room and whispered, "I'll fetch you some lemonade."

"I hate to put you to so much trouble," I said politely.

"It's no trouble at all." She sounded shyly pleased I was there.

The room was dreary and stuffy, a gray couch in front of a cold fireplace and gray drapes pulled tight against the sun. She'd been playing by only one little lamp, without music.

Once I saw her piano, I didn't notice another thing. It was a gleaming black Steinway concert grand, the most wonderful instrument I'd ever seen. I bent over the keyboard playing silent scales and wanting to play just one or two chords so bad I could taste it.

But somehow, I felt I was being watched. Turning, I saw four sepia infants hanging over the fireplace in oval frames. Was one of them Mr. Wash? Before I could cross to look good at them, I heard her square-heeled old-woman shoes coming back. I met her by the door.

As we drank lemonade, she scarcely said a word. I chattered desperately. When I told her about Abby picking cotton, her laugh sounded as rusty as her doorbell. Finally I blurted, "Mrs. Lamont, would you give me piano lessons? My grandmother will pay whatever you ask, and I would love to study with you."

She picked at the skirt of her dress. "No," she murmured, "I can't. I'm terribly sorry, but . . ." After a second or two, she whispered, "I don't give lessons."

"You teach Freda," I reminded her.

"Yes . . . well . . . she's my great-niece. Her father's mother was my sister."

"Then I wish I were your great-niece. The thing I miss most about not being home, next to my grandmother, is taking piano lessons. I would practice every day. I really would. My old teacher said I showed promise, but I have to have a teacher. I can't learn by myself."

She looked at me, making a little drawstring of her lips like she was thinking. "Play something for me, child. Anything."

I decided to play Grieg's "Elfin Dance." That house could do with some life and light. Her piano was so marvelous, it charmed me into playing more. I played Chopin's fourth prelude, then Bach's "Solfeggietto" before I stopped, embarrassed at having gone on so long.

She gave me a shadowy smile. "You show real talent. I would like . . . but I don't know. It's difficult . . ." Most of her sentences didn't really end, just trailed off into nothing.

"Please, Mrs. Lamont, I am desperate! I will do anything you ask. Please?"

Just then there was another knock. "Oh, my goodness!" Mrs. Lamont sounded as if two visitors in one day was unheard of. She ought to live in the manse for one day.

I heard Uncle Stephen's voice. "Is Carley here? Abby said she saw her come in."

I went into the hall to find Mrs. Lamont hovering inside the screened door like she didn't know what to do with him. "Yes, she's here. Would you like . . .?"

"I appreciate it, ma'am, but I can't come in right now. Kate's got our supper ready."

I decided to make one more pitch before I left. "I asked if Miss Rilla would give me piano lessons, but she won't." I gave her a pitiful look.

"I . . . I don't . . ." She fumbled at her waist with her hands.

Uncle Stephen looked from her to me. "Carley sure has been lonesome since we moved here," he told her. "If you could see your way clear, we'd be very grateful."

She looked from him to me and struggled like a close-held bird. Finally she whispered, "Tuesday afternoons? A dollar a week?"

I didn't walk home that night, I floated. And as soon as we finished supper, I went to see Mrs. Cameron. If anybody knew about those baby pictures, she would.

I found her sitting in the circle of light made by one of the naked bulbs dangling overhead. "Got in some school paper and ink, girl, like you suggested." She jerked her head toward a parcel sitting unopened on the counter. "I doubt it'll sell, though."

"It will sell," I assured her stoutly. "I almost need a new bottle of ink myself."

I dawdled a bit, then told her about Mrs. Lamont and how well she played. Mrs. Cameron said the oddest thing. "Rilla Lamont gave up her life to that family of hers."

"That's a very Christian thing to do."

Mrs. Cameron sniffed. "Not the way Rilla did it. Buried herself in that house and gave up every single thing that ever mattered to her."

"How many children does she have?"

"Two now. Had four little girls, but they all died." I stared at her, shocked. "The ones she has pictures of in the living room?"

"Yep. Had the two boys later. Both fine and strong, but Rilla like to worried herself to death over both of 'em. Least little sniffle and she'd send Rob for a remedy."

"Now that they're grown up, looks like she could get out more," I said boldly.

"Got her husband to look after. Rilla lives with more than anybody ought to bear."

"She doesn't have to look after him. He's building houses all day."

She clicked her false teeth. "He won't build all winter, child. Just you wait."

Chapter 18

Only a preacher would need permission to build a barbecue grill in his own yard. Uncle Stephen persuaded the Session he needed one to throw parties for the whole church.

Janey Lou's husband, Meek—who worked for Mr. Rob and Mr. Wash—came with Jay to lay the bricks one afternoon after they got off work. I perched on the picnic table Uncle Stephen had already built, to watch. When Jay laid a paper bag beside me, I figured it was a snack.

Uncle Stephen soon came out, too. He was constitutionally incapable of staying inside when any kind of building was going on. Meek leveled the space with sticks and string, then placed a row of bricks, slapped on cement, placed another row of bricks, and scraped off the extra mortar. Jay and Uncle Stephen mixed cement. I handed bricks.

"What are your plans for the future?" Uncle Stephen asked Jay.

Jay's answer surprised me so much I nearly dropped a brick. "College, sir, if I can get in."

Meek grunted as if in sudden pain. "You ain't be goin' to no college, boy. College takes money. Get them notions out of your head and be happy with the good job you've got."

"I don't want to make chairs all my life," Jay protested.

"Know what you want to be?" Uncle Stephen asked him.

"Yessir. A doctor. Surgeon, maybe."

"He's good with his hands. I'll give him that," Meek admitted grudgingly. "But talk sense into him, Mr. Whitfield. Tell him it's too hard a row for a poor boy to hoe."

"Might not be, Meek, if he's got determination. I went to college on a scholarship."

Jay's head jerked around like somebody had pulled a string. "You did? No kidding?"

"No kidding. My daddy was a farmer with seven boys. How are your grades?"

"They *were* real good," Jay said earnestly, "but I've been out of school five years."

"Then you'll need to review a bit before you take an entrance exam. If you want help reviewing and applying for a scholarship, let me know."

Jay's eyes shone. "Thank you, sir! If you mean it, I'd be proud of your help."

"I'd be proud to help you." Uncle Stephen wiped brick dust off his palms and stuck out one hand. Jay hesitated only a second before he shook it. Meek turned his back, but not before I noticed that his eyes were watering. Brick dust, I figured.

About the time we finished, Janey Lou drove up in their Chevy. "Maggie!" Abby ran toward them in glee.

Maggie leaned out the window. "Did you bring my dolly's head, Uncle Jay?"

"Sure did." Jay reached into his paper bag. "Has Auntie got a body ready?"

Janey Lou reached across Maggie to hand him another bag. "Ready, stuffed, and dressed. This child has deviled the life out of me to get that dolly finished before her birthday."

Abby reached for the thing Maggie held. "Oh, looky! I wants one, too!" It was a little head carved out of wood and painted with brown eyes and black hair. For its neck it had a long shaft.

"Did you make that?" I asked in amazement.

Jay nodded. "It's just a scrap of leftover wood. It's not hard. Auntie makes the bodies."

A few days later he came over with a finished doll for Abby. The head was carved from dark brown wood, but it had blue eyes, red painted curls, and a pink body firm with sawdust. "Tell your mama to make her some clothes, now."

Abby named it Maggie. "When I grows up," she told us seriously at supper, "I'm gonna have chocolate babies. They are prettier than vanilla ones."

❋

The last Saturday of October we had a church-wide picnic. Uncle Stephen announced in church, "I'll throw hot dogs on the grill, and you bring whatever you like to eat with them. Knowing this congregation, nobody will go away hungry." They gave a Presbyterian titter.

Unless I missed somebody, we had sixty-six adults and forty-two children—including Mr. Ira, who hadn't thought the occasion warranted a bath. He arrived announcing, "Does ev'r'-body know the county's offering a mass evacuation of dogs against rabies?"

"What happened to your cheek?" I asked.

He rubbed a line of dried blood. "Got caught on a bramble, Missy. Caught on a bramble." He lied and we both knew it. He just didn't know I knew.

That morning, after I'd mopped the whole downstairs and gotten our old kitchen floor as shiny as those black-and-white squares were ever going to get, I'd gone to the swing to hide before Aunt Kate thought of anything else for me to do. It was chilly, but crisp and very pleasant with a jacket. Across the road, I saw Mr. Hugh Fred riding an enormous black horse at the edge of the woods behind the cemetery. From the way he weaved in and out of trees, you'd have thought he was making a pattern—unless you knew that's where the path went. In a minute he came out at the edge of the Baines yard. Ivy waved from her chair. When Mr. Hugh Fred rode over near her, that big black dog strained its chain trying to get him. Although I could only hear it faintly, I could see it barking like it would eat that horse up if somebody would let it loose.

Ivy got up and went over to pet the horse. Mr. Hugh Fred leaned down talking to her. From where I was sitting, they were like people in a silent play.

Mr. Ira came storming out, waving his arms. The dog pulled harder at its chain, leaping up and falling back. Ivy stumbled back to her chair and hunched over. Mr. Ira stomped over to the horse, looking like a midget beside it. Mr. Hugh Fred leaned down to talk to him. Mr. Ira waved his arms and stomped his feet. Mr. Hugh Fred sat up and started to ride away. Mr. Ira picked up something to throw. Mr. Hugh Fred turned back and lashed at him with his whip. Mr. Ira clapped one hand to his cheek and sat flat on the ground, still waving one arm. Mr. Hugh Fred rode away. I expected "The End" to float over the railroad track.

Mr. Ira's presence at the party just went to show that in real life stories never really end, they just keep going. Fortunately, I didn't know at that time how far some stories can go.

Miz Baines didn't bring food, but other women brought enough baked beans, potato salad, homemade pickles, and pies to feed a small town. Miss Hannah brought baked ham and chess pies. Miss Emily's cook sent her famous coconut cake. Nancy Lamont brought fried chicken because, "My children won't eat hot dogs." I personally saw Ruthie eat three.

Uncle Stephen, Mr. Wash, and Mr. Davy had laid boards across sawhorses to make tables, but it was a good thing Aunt Kate spent the whole week cleaning. "Those women are going to look under every bed and in every cabinet before they're through," she told us. Sure enough, the women took their plates and headed inside. All evening, shadows moved and lights flashed on in various upstairs rooms.

Although it was nippy, we children preferred being out with the men. Tag kept us warm away from the fire. After dinner I got tired of tag, but Freda and Bonnie had gone to Bonnie's without asking me. Lonely, I went to the galvanized washtub of drinks behind the grill to get a second Cheerwine before they were gone. I found Mr. Hugh Fred fishing around in the ice for one, too. He popped off both caps with his pocketknife and nodded toward a couple of empty chairs. "Tastes better sitting down." Savoring the cherry cinnamon on my tongue and feeling grown-up, I followed. "What you been doing with yourself during vacation?"

"Nothing much. Miss Rilla's gonna give me piano lessons, though."

"I don't know how you persuaded her, but she's a great teacher if you'll work hard."

"I'll work hard," I promised.

He leaned back and gave a little burp. "Hard work never hurt anybody. Remember that, and keep up your ambitions. I had big ambitions as a boy and worked hard to achieve them. Worked hard as a boy, work hard as a man. God's blessed me for it."

"He's blessed you real good," I agreed, thinking about his mansion, new Hudson, and the big black horse. "I saw you riding this morning."

"You'll have to come over sometime and ride Emily's mare. She doesn't get enough exercise." That was the kind of invitation the Keenes always extended—sounding like they were going to call you tomorrow to invite you over for something delightful, but they never did.

"Do you know Jay Anderson?" I asked. "He lives back in those woods and helped build our grill."

"Sure, Jay works for me. Good worker."

From a nearby chair, Mr. Wash butted in. "Got ideas too big for him."

"That right, Wash? What kind of ideas?"

Disregarding Big Mama's good teaching about letting grown-ups talk first, I jumped in to impress Mr. Hugh Fred. "Ambitious ideas, like you used to have when you were young."

Mr. Wash leaned over and slapped him on the back. "Yeah, Hugh Fred, back when you were young." Several other men laughed. I could have died.

"Jay wants to go to college," I blurted, trying to give them something to chew on besides me. My words fell into one of those silences that occur in the largest and rowdiest of crowds.

Somebody muttered just beyond the rim of darkness. Guffaws flew out and were stifled. Then the conversation exploded like hot little firecrackers popping all around me in the darkness. Just about the time I got one tuned in, another erupted somewhere else.

". . . enough intelligence to go to college?"

"Give 'em an inch, they'll take . . ."

". . . and your daughters, too." More laughter.

". . . but I fought beside some of 'em in the Pacific . . ."

"Sure—just reg'lar fellows, like you and me. I mean I wouldn't . . ."

". . . if God had intended people to mix . . ."

". . . but it ain't right that . . ."

"Gettin' too big for their britches, if you ask me." Mr. Ira's whine rose above them all.

Mr. Hugh Fred finished his drink and wiped his mouth with the back of his hand. "Well," he spoke loud enough to stop all the little conversations, "you don't need a college education to work in a factory. But Jay shows promise. I'll grant him that. Might make foreman one day."

"Don't write off college too soon." Uncle Stephen forked the last hot dogs onto a plate. "Jay's smart. He could get a scholarship."

Again I heard mutterings around me in the darkness. Then Davy Anderson said, "I'd like you to tell us something about your plans for the two-hundredth anniversary, Mr. Whitfield. What did you have in mind?"

I went to see if the women were talking about anything more interesting than church. The ones who weren't taking the Grand Manse Tour were spread out through the dining room and kitchen, sitting on or leaning against every piece of furniture we owned. I went to the kitchen, hoping for a second piece of devil's food cake. We'd run out of paper plates, but Miss Hannah obligingly moved away from the cabinet where our everyday ones were kept.

Miss Gert pointed my way. "I swan, who in this family walks on walls?"

Everybody in the room turned to look. "I scrubbed those counter fronts this very afternoon!" Aunt Kate apologized. A trail of smudged pink footprints showed where Abby had followed Benjamin Franklin's advice sometime later and helped herself.

"Nothing leaves a good clear print like North Carolina clay," one woman consoled her.

"I used to have a light gray floor, and it was a mess," another added. "But you know what I did? I smeared mud on a piece of paper, took it to the store, and told the man, 'That's the color of new floor I want.' Now it's great—mud blends right in." Everybody laughed.

"I keep wishing we could paint those cabinets," Aunt Kate admitted. "Maybe a real dark green that wouldn't show dirt. Do you think the Session would mind?"

"It isn't long since we did this kitchen," Miss Nancy objected from near the stove. "My daddy built the cabinets."

"Your daddy's been gone twelve years," somebody reminded her, "and we did the kitchen at least a couple of years before that. It could use some paint and more light." She looked up at the gloomy ceiling with its one dangling bulb.

Miz Baines bent down and knocked on the linoleum like she was testing a watermelon. "Floor's good for years yet, 'n' floors are expensive. This one'd look real good if it was clean."

"I mopped and waxed it this morning!" I blazed indignantly. "But it never stays clean more than a minute."

Miss Hannah walked over and lightly touched the hole where Raifa knifed that chunk out of the countertop. "These counters are getting rotten. Dark green or rust would be pretty, wouldn't it, with the green cabinets? And maybe a soft yellow for the walls?" Immediately we could see what a cheerful place that drab old kitchen could be.

"While we're at it, we might as well get a nice rust floor that wouldn't show the dirt." That was the woman who'd already gotten one and liked it. The women started buzzing happily.

"Sure would be nice if the Session voted to fix it up." One by one Miss Hannah looked around at the wives of all the elders.

I saw them later, out with their husbands at the edges of the darkness where nobody could overhear. Then the men drifted together like cows heading for a barn at sunset.

At the end of the picnic, Mr. Hugh Fred made an announcement. "We want to give our new preacher and his family a belated welcome present. We've had a jackleg Session meeting tonight, and voted to redo the kitchen!" The women applauded like it was the elders' own idea, and the elders expanded two inches through the chest. Southern women were real good at expanding their menfolk back then.

That was, possibly, one of the last times everybody in Bethel Church agreed on anything.

Chapter 19

The way most people loved Aunt Kate, I would never have imagined she'd be the first to get the whole church's back up—although she wasn't exactly easy to live with at home. She could get downright ornery between keeping that big house clean, taking care of the children, and "feeling a definite lack of kindred spirits"—whatever that meant. I think she'd hoped to become friends with Miss Emily, but the Keenes, like the Lamonts, kept to themselves.

She went to answer the phone one evening and came back to the supper table looking like somebody gave her a present. "That was Carley's principal." I choked mid-swallow, but she went right on, talking fast. "His fourth grade teacher's father had a stroke. She needs to be away until Christmas, and he wonders if I'd be interested in filling in. I know it's a lot sooner than we'd talked about, so I told him I'd have to talk to you, but oh, do you think I could?"

I knew Aunt Kate had a master's degree in education and had taught for years before Abby was born, but I assumed—along with a lot of other people—that women only worked until they could become mothers. I found her eagerness to leave home shocking.

Uncle Stephen frowned, but like he was thinking, not mad. "What do we do with—" He gestured from Abby, finishing her applesauce, to John propped in his high chair.

"Gert Baines offered to help when we first moved here. I could ask her."

"The witch?" I blurted, twirling grits around on my fork to cool them.

"Old witch," Abby said, sticking out her lower lip. "I doesn't like witches."

"She's not a witch, she's a nice woman." Aunt Kate gave me a look that reminded me how closely she was related to Big Mama. "Carley, tell Abby Mrs. Baines isn't a witch."

"Miz Baines isn't a witch," I said. "She just looks like one."

"We can't all be beautiful," Uncle Stephen teased, ruffling my hair.

Aunt Kate took several deep breaths, then her cheeks got pink and her lower lip trembled like she was about to cry. "You really don't mind?"

He laughed. "Carley, ask this woman where I first saw her and fell in love."

"Where did he first see you?" I obeyed. The second part was too embarrassing.

"At school."

She would have left it there, but Uncle Stephen never passed up a chance to make a short story longer. "I'd gone to visit my brother the teacher. On my way to his room, I passed a class where the most beautiful woman I ever saw was teaching the sun and its planets. Her hair was as red as Mars, her eyes as green as the seas of Venus, and she held that entire class of squirmy children in the palm of her hand. I stood at her door and prayed, 'Dear God, let me preach just half as well as that woman teaches. And please, God, make her my wife.'"

Aunt Kate gave a gentle snort, but her eyes sparkled like stars.

Abby held out her small palm. "How'd you hold all dose chilluns in your hand?"

Uncle Stephen ruffled her copper curls. "She didn't, really, Abbikins, I made that part up. But God gave your Mama a gift to teach. Don't you ever forget it."

The next Monday morning, Miz Baines trudged across the tracks early and Uncle Stephen took Aunt Kate to school. I rode the bus, as usual. I didn't want to be seen riding with a *teacher*. She rode the bus home, but sat up with the driver. I pretended I didn't know her.

Uncle Stephen had hot chocolate ready when we got back. "How'd it go?"

She sat down and propped her feet on an extra chair. "My

feet are killing me, but all day I kept having to remind myself, 'It's only until Christmas, Kate. Don't get too attached.'"

"No problems?"

"Ruthie Lamont acted up, but that's just because she knows me and wanted other kids to know it." She paused, then gave her little not-funny laugh. "And Gilbert Mayhew came into the teacher's lounge during morning recess and exclaimed, 'Why, it *is* you! I heard we had a Mrs. Whitfield taking poor Mary's place, but I was sure it couldn't be *our* Mrs. Whitfield. How can you teach and still take care of your children and the preacher?'"

Uncle Stephen set his cup down hard. "What business is it of his?"

"Absolutely none. How did Gert get along with the children?"

"Fine, apparently. Ira came by to walk her home just before you got here. He told me she plans to use her first week's wages to buy Ivy a tortoise blue bedspread."

When Uncle Stephen came home from Session that night, I was doing spelling in the corner of the couch. He was so upset, I think they forgot I was there. He shoved back his hair, which already stood on end, and informed Aunt Kate, "You can officially teach."

She looked up from grading papers. "What on earth do you mean?"

"Wash Lamont asked if it's true the preacher's wife is Ruth's new teacher. If so, he thought you already had enough to do between our children, the house, and the church. Before I could respond to that, Hugh Fred asked whether we need the money."

"Did you tell him we sure do?"

Uncle Stephen chuckled. "I thought about asking for a raise. But no, I told them that while extra money always comes in handy, you are teaching because you are needed, you love it, and"—he added proudly—"you're very good at it." He shrugged off his suit jacket and popped one suspender. "Then somebody asked whether your teaching would tie me down with Abby and John, so I explained that Gert is taking care of them and it's only until Christmas. Hugh Fred asked if you'll still be able to work on the choir's Christmas music. Somebody else wanted to know if you'd still be in the Circle . . ."

"Do they think teaching takes twenty-four hours a day?"

"I don't know what they think. I got to wondering at one point if somebody was going to call for a vote about whether the preacher's wife should be allowed to teach."

Aunt Kate looked mad enough to spit. "Would Hugh Fred's workers care if Emily took a job? Would Wash let anybody have a say about whether Nancy could work? Mama worked at the store my whole life and nobody asked whether Lila and I were being taken care of. No lawyer's wife or doctor's wife has to have anybody's permission to teach. Why is a preacher's wife any different? Besides, can't they believe I might be *called* to teach?"

Uncle Stephen shook his head. "God only knows. But be glad for Davy and Hugh Fred. Davy finally said, in his quiet way, 'If the preacher and his wife think she can handle it, I say let her try. It's not bothering us, and if I had a student in fourth grade, I'd be proud to have Mrs. Whitfield teaching her.' That brought it back to Wash. He shuffled his feet a bit until Hugh Fred said, 'I'll bet Ruthie will learn more these next six weeks than in the rest of the year put together. Now, don't we have to elect commissioners to Presbytery?' I could have kissed them both." He stood up and reached for her hand. "But before we go to bed, I need to throw things. Come on." They went for their coats.

Later, out the kitchen window, I saw them throwing pine cones at the barn, doubled over with laughter like Abby and Sue Mary. When he flung his arms around her, though, I went to bed. As long as I'd lived there, I still couldn't get used to all that hugging and kissing.

Mrs. Cameron couldn't, either. Next day when Uncle Stephen went by her store for some sugar, he said she told him, "I don't hold with folks carryin' on right out in front of God 'n' everybody."

❦

November was so generally balmy that leaves didn't turn color, just curled up and died. Our lives were much drearier than the weather. The men of the church were redoing our kitchen, but only evenings and weekends, so it was torn up for weeks. Sue Mary and Abby caught colds and left a trail of wet tissues everywhere they went. John was teething. Aunt Kate was busy with papers to grade and lessons to prepare. And then, as if things weren't bad enough, one night I got up for a drink and heard Aunt Kate and Uncle Stephen fighting.

I crept to the stairs to listen, and they were arguing about Big Mama.

"Your mama can't keep the whole world neat and tidy, Kate. There are messy parts out there. Even she's going to have to face them sooner or later."

"You don't have to drag them into *our* world."

"*She* put them in our world. I'm just dealing with them as I see fit."

"You went once. Isn't that enough?"

"I told you, I didn't get in. This time I have permission."

"You're laying a trail straight to this house, you know."

"But maybe I can head this thing off at the pass."

"What will people say when they hear where their preacher's been?"

"It's nobody's business where their preacher goes on his day off."

He was gone before I got up the next morning. Aunt Kate set corn flakes before us with a white, angry face. "I doesn't want corn flakes," Abby complained. "We gotta eat lots of Cheerios so Carley can send a dime and three boxtops to get me some comic books."

"Where's Uncle Stephen?" I asked quickly, not sure if Aunt Kate approved of comics.

"Away for the day," she answered shortly. We ate in stormy silence.

When we got home from school, he still wasn't back. As it got dark, Aunt Kate went often to the front door and peered into the night, as if she could drag him home with her eyes. She kept hugging herself and rubbing her arms, like she was cold in spite of her sweater.

He didn't return until after the workmen had gone. I got out of bed as soon as I heard his car and padded into the upstairs hall to peer over the banisters. I heard him murmur, ". . . to hell and back." As he took off his coat, he turned. His face looked pinched and pale.

As soon as I heard them in the kitchen, I tiptoed down. I heard Aunt Kate setting out his supper from the oven. Creeping to the kitchen door, I saw him bow his head, then eat like he hadn't eaten all day—looking at his plate instead of at her.

"So how was it?" She poured coffee with worried eyes.

"Grim. You were right about that."

I pushed open the door and joined them. "Where did you go, Uncle Stephen?"

"I had a meeting." He hunched so far over his plate I thought his hair would get in his creamed corn. As soon as he'd wolfed down his food he went upstairs. When I went back to bed, I heard him in his study, but even with my ear against my closet wall, I couldn't distinguish anything but groans.

❧

The one bright spot in my life was my weekly piano lesson, but I arrived one Tuesday to find Miss Rilla hovering near the front door. "I don't think . . . perhaps . . . We can't have a lesson today. Mr. Lamont is . . . ah . . . indisposed." I saw his feet, propped on the couch. The house smelled funny, too—not like medicine, but kind of sweet.

"Perhaps if I played softly," I suggested. I wanted to show her how far I had gotten on my new Strauss waltz.

"I don't know . . ." She looked uncertainly at the living room.

"Shut that damfool door!" her husband bellowed. "Can't a man take a damfool nap without somebody opening a door?" I was as shocked to hear a man swear as I would have been to see him at church in his undershirt. Nobody I ever knew talked like that.

"Come back tomorrow," Miss Rilla urged. "Mr. Lamont is not well."

The next day her house smelled of cinnamon rolls. Halfway through my lesson, he appeared in sock feet. Miss Rilla gasped and hurried toward him, but he pushed her aside and lurched into the room. "Good playing, Missy." He swayed, then weaved to the couch. Lowering himself carefully, he switched on the news. After only a couple of sentences, he shut it off with a click. "Don't know what the damfool president is thinkin' of. Better give him a call." He pulled himself unsteadily to his feet and started out.

Miss Rilla dashed after him. "Rob! Put on your shoes!"

She came back without meeting my eye. "Let me hear that waltz once more, slower."

As days passed, Mr. Rob showed up at our house at all hours to call the governor, state senators, and our congressmen. He always claimed to be mayor of Job's Corner, and he'd ramble on with advice about taxes, Russians, "darkies" (which is what a lot of old people still called Negroes), or the miner's strike.

One Saturday morning as I went to the post office, I saw him walking unsteadily just ahead of me. As he reached the steps, Miss Pauline shoved Mr. Ira through the door.

". . . and don't come bothering me again today!"

Mr. Ira staggered down, straight into Mr. Rob.

"Get outta my way, damfool!" Mr. Rob waved him away like he was a particularly big housefly. "I got urgent bizness with the Newnited States Gov'mint!"

"You ain't got bizness loose on a leash!" Mr. Ira yelled. "They oughta lock you up and throw away the key!" He shoved Mr. Rob. Mr. Rob shoved back. Then they grabbed each other and held on, rocking back and forth like two elderly billy goats.

Jay appeared at the top step with Miss Pauline right behind him. "Jay," Mr. Rob demanded, "come get your crazy neighbor so I can get on with urgent bizness." He shoved so hard, Mr. Ira took two steps back—clutching Mr. Rob's shirt and taking him with him.

Jay came down one step. Mr. Ira shook his free fist. "Don't you touch me!"

"Get him, Jay!" Mr. Rob ordered. "Pull him off me."

"Call the preacher! Lock up this maniac!" Mr. Ira hollered, still holding on.

Jay touched Mr. Rob's shoulder. "Mr. Lamont, the post office isn't open for important business on Saturdays. Why don't I walk you home, and you come back on Monday?"

Mr. Rob looked at him blearily. "Izzit Sattidy?"

"Sure is, sir. Let me walk you on home, now." Still holding the old man's shoulder, Jay gently steered him away from Ira.

Mr. Rob's arms dropped to his side and he slumped against Jay. "Glad of your comp'ny, boy. Little weak in the knees today." They moved together toward our path over the tracks. Jay gave me a little wave as they passed.

Mr. Ira spat near my shoes and trudged off up the road. I decided to go to Miss Pauline's house for a stamp later. If Mr. Ira had been in the post office, it would still stink.

I did want to warn Uncle Stephen, though, how crazy Mr. Rob was getting. I dashed over to the church where he went every Saturday morning to polish his sermon. I expected to find him busy with rags and a stack of paper. Instead, I found him preaching to an empty church. Looked like Uncle Stephen was getting almost as crazy as Mr. Rob.

"You need something?" he asked, peering down from the pulpit.

"Uh, yeah." I rubbed one ear. If Uncle Stephen *was* going crazy, it could be a delicate subject. "Mr. Rob is getting mighty—uh—sick. He and Mr. Ira got to shouting, then they started shoving. If Jay hadn't come along—well, I don't know what might of happened."

Something in my face or voice made Uncle Stephen come down and sit me down on the front pew. There, with Saturday light making the sanctuary dim and strange, he explained about the part alcohol played in Mr. Rob's peculiar sickness. I was both horrified and fascinated. "Back where I come from," I informed him, "white people don't get drunk."

I wasn't the only one worried. Wash Lamont came by that evening, and he and Uncle Stephen went up to the study to talk. When I went up to bed, I heard Wash through the closed study door. "How can I honor my father, Preacher, when he's fall-down drunk half the year?"

I hurried to my room and started undressing, but when I went to my closet to hang up my dress, I noticed a wide crack of light beneath my closet baseboard and heard Mr. Wash's voice as clear as if he was in the closet with me. "I might forgive him, Preacher, if he'd *ask*, but that old coot isn't the least bit sorry."

Quietly I pushed aside some shoes and sat down. I heard fumblings that meant Uncle Stephen was pausing to light his pipe. "I understand your father only drinks in winter?"

"Autumn till spring. They had four baby girls all died in the fall. People say he was a fine man before that—I wish I could have known him back then." His voice was anguished.

"He's a fine man half the year now. And I can see that not forgiving him is tearing you apart. Why don't you forgive him even if he doesn't ask, so *you* can be free?"

"Nope." I could almost see Wash shaking his thick black hair. "I can't forgive him until he mends his ways. Just for what he's done to my mama—Mama is a saint. If she hadn't tied herself to a drunk, she might be playing in Carnegie Hall by now."

"Carley"—I jumped, thinking Uncle Stephen had heard me, but he went on—"thinks the world of her and her music."

"Tell the truth, Nancy and I were real surprised Mama agreed to teach her, but it does her a world of good to have that little girl in her house. Speaking of little girls, how much longer will your children have their mama away from home?"

Uncle Stephen sucked his pipe real loud. "She's not away from home—except a few hours each day. Abby and John are doin' fine. And I'll try to talk to your daddy this next week and see if he's open to seeking help. Meantime, do think about forgiving him. Let God deal with Rob in his own way and time."

Mr. Wash didn't say he would and he didn't say he wouldn't, but his chair creaked like he was fixing to go. "Speaking of Carnegie Hall, you hear they're gonna build a headquarters for that communist U.N. in New York City? Givin' 'em a foothold in our country."

Uncle Stephen sucked loudly on his pipe again. "The U.N. won't be finished for years. We don't need to worry about it yet. But I'll tell you what worries me. Did you read the *Life* editorial claiming we're piling up national debts our grandchildren won't be able to pay?"

Wash snorted. "Now, there's something you *don't* have to worry about, Preacher. God wouldn't have made this country strong and rich if he didn't think we were smart enough—"

Just then Aunt Kate knocked at my door with laundry, so I had to worry about getting out of that closet without making a sound.

❋

Abby and I decided Mr. Rob's *damfool* was a perfectly splendid word. We were smart enough not to use it in front of grownups, but when Preston annoyed me, I loved to yell it and run.

One afternoon at Sue Mary's we three girls went to the bathroom together, as girls often do. Sue Mary climbed onto the commode and stuck her hand beneath her. Abby was scandalized. "What you doing dat for? You wetted all ober yourself!"

Sue Mary climbed down and went to the basin. "Mama said I have to do dat to remind me to wash my hands." She did so, with great thoroughness.

"She's a damfool mama." Abby climbed onto the throne and made sure her own hands were firmly clasped on her solid little stomach.

"You're a damfool!" Sue Mary said hotly. "Damfool, damfool, damfool!"

"What's that you're saying?" Miss Pauline filled the door.

Sue Mary stuck one clean finger in the corner of her mouth. "Abby said it first."

Miss Pauline rounded on Abby, perched helplessly on the

throne. "What kind of language is that from a preacher's daughter? When you get off that pot I'm gonna wash your mouth out with soap."

"Not dat soap!" Abby shrank back in horror. "It's got—!"

Without waiting for Abby to climb down, Miss Pauline advanced to the offensive soap, dampened it, and thrust her fat fingers into Abby's mouth. Anybody who knew Abby could have predicted what would happen. Miss Pauline had only herself to blame. Abby chomped down on those fingers like they were hot dogs.

"You obnoxious child!" Miss Pauline drew back one hand.

I grabbed her elbow. "If you hit her I'll tell Uncle Stephen, and he'll . . ." I didn't know what he might do. "Come on, Abby!" I dragged the gagging child off the toilet and out the door, still struggling to pull up her pants. We ran into the house and up to my room. Scooted under my bed. Huddled there trembling, wondering what would happen next.

What happened was a furious knock on the front door. Miss Pauline had arrived.

Nobody said a word to us before supper or during it. Abby and I waited in apprehension. Not until he finished eating did Uncle Stephen reach for his Bible, run his finger down a page, and read, "'And Jesus said, "Whosoever is angry with his brother—or her best friend—without a cause shall be in danger of the judgment, but whosoever shall say, Thou fool, shall be in danger of hell fire."' Do you know what that means, Abby?" She shook her red curls.

"It means God gets very angry if we call other people fools. God especially does not want you calling your best friend or her mother a fool. Because—"

Aunt Kate interrupted. "Do you know what a fool is, Abby?"

"No, ma'am." You'd have thought she was the most angelic child in North Carolina.

"A fool," Uncle Stephen explained, "is somebody who doesn't have any good sense, somebody who does things without a reason."

"Sue Mary's mama makes her wet on her hands and put wee-wee soap in my mouf!"

Uncle Stephen looked startled, but plowed on. "Whatever Sue Mary's mama does, you must not call her names. Don't ever call anybody a fool again. Do you hear me?"

"And don't say 'damn' again, either, honey," Aunt Kate said gently. "To damn somebody is to want to send them to hell. We don't want that for anybody, do we?"

Abby stuck out her lower lip and darted me a look. Clearly she wondered whether I knew that. I buttered another roll and pretended I was watching actors in a movie. Aunt Kate saw the look. "Where did you even hear that word?"

"From Carley," Abby said promptly.

"You never! It was Mr. Lamont!" I cried in protest.

"You said it," declared my treacherous little sidekick. "You called Preston a damfool and said Mr. Ira is a damfool for wetting on the railroad track where anybody could see."

"Ira comes close," Uncle Stephen said under his breath.

"Stephen!" Aunt Kate pulled down her eyebrows.

He recalled we were in the middle of a Serious Talk. "Just don't ever say it again. And Abby, you must apologize to Miss Pauline when we go for the mail tomorrow. Is that clear?"

Abby's lower lip crept out mutinously. "I'll 'pologize for calling Sue Mary a damfool, but I won't 'pologize for biting. Dat soap had wee-wee on it!" With that pronouncement she climbed down, stomped to her room, and slammed the door.

Chapter 20

Thanksgiving was terrible. Uncle Stephen made me sick to my stomach, smoking cigars and listening to Arthur Godfrey on the radio all the way to Big Mama's. When we got there, Aunt Sukie was living in Big Mama's back sitting room. Big Mama was sleeping in my single spindle bed *under my quilt*. Her four-poster was in Mama's room, and Mama's bed was in my room for Abby and me to share. Aunt Sukie kept turning away from me to talk to Big Mama's new dalmatian, Lucky, then forgetting what we'd been talking about. She'd also made pumpkin pies, which I hated, and forgotten to make chess pies, which I loved.

The grown-ups quarreled after I went to bed. I heard Uncle Stephen using his preacher voice, real loud. If Abby hadn't been snuggled so close, I could have climbed out and listened, but I didn't want to wake her.

The next morning I got up early and crept into Big Mama's room. Climbing onto the foot of her bed, I tucked my feet under my quilt. "Are you ready for me to come home yet?"

She pushed back her long, heavy hair. "Not yet, Carley."

With one finger I traced triangles sewn into Scotty dogs, using fabric from some of our favorite clothes. I touched pieces of Mama's pink flowered Sunday dress, the green plaid I wore to start first grade, Big Mama's yellow gingham house-dress, even triangles from Pop's old blue pants. "Remember when we made this? You said it would keep us together forever."

She put her big hand over mine, and her wedding ring

glinted in the light. "We are together. You, me, Lila, Pop. In the quilt and in our hearts."

"I want to be together for real."

"We can't right now." She used her "and we won't talk more about it" voice. Without another word she threw back the covers and put her gnarled feet on the floor. "Let me get dressed. Sukie's not as quick in the kitchen as she used to be."

During breakfast the grown-ups were very polite, pretending nothing was wrong. But when Big Mama told me after breakfast to take Abby and the kitchen slops down to Pearl's, I knew she wasn't through with whatever she had to say.

That's when I found the worst change of all: Pearl had a new black-and-white piglet. She had butchered Holly!

"We gave your granny some of the sausage." Geena stood just behind me, by the pen. My stomach clenched so bad I thought I'd lose my breakfast—probably returning a bit of Holly to where she'd come from.

"Whatsa matter, Carley?" Abby wanted to know. When I told her about Pop and me taking Holly down to Pearl and how Pearl had killed Holly, her face grew pink with indignation. "You are vewy, vewy bad for killing Pop's pig," she greeted Pearl.

"Sometimes, child," Pearl told her with a sigh, "you do what you has to do."

Pearl's sister Grace was living with her, sleeping on a bed in the living room. Grace was younger than Pearl, with a gold tooth she liked to show off when she smiled. She told Uncle Stephen when he came down to get us for dinner that she hoped to find a job and make money so she could study to be a teacher.

"Seems like every Negro we know's wanting to go to college all of a sudden," I remarked as he and I walked up the lane. Abby had skipped far ahead.

"Why not?" I expected a lecture, but he swished his walking stick at weeds beside the road and changed the subject. "You and Regina are about the same age, aren't you? Did you used to play together?"

"Regina? You mean Pearl's girl Geena? Geena used to be my very best friend." I was bragging to impress him, but as soon as I'd said it, I clearly remembered it was true. "When I was Abby's age, I used to go down to Pearl's lots of mornings. We'd make mud pies and dandelion stew out behind the wash pot, and Aunt Sukie would beat on the frying pan when dinner was ready. I felt real big getting to walk all this way alone."

"What happened?"

"Nothing *happened*, we just grew up and got busy."

"Nobody told you to stop playing together?"

My temper flared like a match. "Of course not. You act like Big Mama's the most prejudiced person in the world, but she's not." I stomped off to let him walk home by himself. "You'd better repent having such wicked thoughts," I called over my shoulder. But as I looked back toward Pearl's house . . .

It was the Saturday before I was to start first grade. Mama and I were walking down the rutted dirt road to Pearl's carrying our week's wash stuffed into pillowcases. Smoke rose from Pearl's yard, because Big Mama wanted, and got, her white clothes boiled. Before we got there, Mama said, "I want you to come home with me this morning. You need to get ready for school on Monday."

"I'm already ready. My satchel is packed and my clothes are laid out."

"Come home anyway. Big Mama's got things she wants you to do."

When we'd given Pearl the clothes, Mama said, "I'm taking Carley back up the road with me this morning. Mama's going to give her a few chores now that she's starting school."

Pearl looked at Mama and Mama looked back. Then Pearl nodded. "Geena needs to start helpin' more 'round here, too."

I'd never gotten that kind of picture in my head until Uncle Stephen. What was it about him that drew them out of me? I remembered that after that Saturday, Big Mama set me to dusting, vacuuming, and polishing silver on Saturdays. Mama carried our clothes down alone for a couple of years. She also drove me to the brick school downtown. Geena caught a bus before I got up and came home just before dark. We seldom played, seldom even met, except . . .

Another picture, a chilly, drizzly afternoon. I was sitting on our front porch wrapped in a quilt reading when Geena's bus stopped at our road. Aunt Sukie was cooking supper and Mama and Big Mama were shopping in Shelby. When I saw Geena, I threw off my quilt, dashed to the steps, and yelled, "Come read!"

She gave a happy little skip as she left the road for our wet grass. Drops collected like diamonds on her hair. I took off my sweater and gave it to her to dry her face, then we huddled together on the glider under the quilt to enjoy the marvel of our first grade readers. I scolded her for getting hers dirty and torn.

"I didn't," she said, indignant. "It was like that when I got it."

After a while we began to shiver in spite of the quilt. "Let's go to my room," I offered.

She shook her head. "Colored childrens doesn't go in white houses."

I was astonished. "Why not?"

"Mama says."

"That's not fair!"

"Lotsa things not fair."

"Yeah. Why do children have to go to bed at seven when grown-ups can stay up all night?"

"And grown-ups doesn't have to take a baf 'cept when they wants to."

"When we grow up, you can play in my house anytime you want to."

"You can play in my house anytime you want to, too."

Just then Aunt Sukie came to the hall door. When she saw us on the glider, she fussed at Geena. "What you doing here? Go on home. Your mama will be wondering what happened to you. 'Sides, Miss Carley's busy."

"I'm not busy," I protested. "We were doing our school-work."

"Well, you come on in, now. I got things for you to do."

Uncle Stephen's long legs soon caught up with me. "I'm sorry. I have no cause to criticize what I don't really know."

"Well," I reluctantly admitted, "maybe Mama and Big Mama sort of eased us out of being friends. But Pearl and Aunt Sukie helped, too." He didn't say another word.

By the time we got to Big Mama's, I realized why I always felt funny when Geena and I met. It was because my best friend Geena was now only Pearl's girl Geena. That's why she shuffled her feet and looked at the ground, why I talked too much and too fast. Why I noticed she had worn-out clothes and run-down shoes and didn't talk properly. What did she notice about me? Did she even remember we used to be friends? I grieved the loss of her, but couldn't think of a single way to turn things back to the way they were.

If I was quiet, nobody noticed. All during dinner, Big Mama kept looking at Uncle Stephen, tightening her lips, and shaking her head. He kept giving her the "I'm disappointed in you" look he gave Abby when she wouldn't behave. Driving back, Uncle Stephen and I rode up front so Aunt Kate and the children could sleep. I thought we'd talk or something, but he scarcely said a word.

About halfway home, I figured out what he and Big Mama must have been fighting about: he wanted her to take me back and she wouldn't.

That night I wrote in my diary: *It is tragic when nobody wants you.*

Part 4

Hark! The Herald Angels Sing

*I have sat nearly an hour without writing a word, remembering Geena,
Grace, Raifa, Maggie, and Abby—all the girls of my generation who
would finally grow up to question "the way things are." For the first time I
comprehend that racism is never natural; it has to be carefully taught. And
to those historians who would imply that racism derives from unjust
systems and red-faced white male bigots, I would say that it was kneaded
gently into me by good-hearted women of both races, repeating scenarios
they learned from their own mothers and grandmothers. I think they all
genuinely believed they were doing what had to be done.*

However, that's not the only reason I am not writing.

*Before me on the desk are Abby's detested photo of the two girls and the
boy, a shiny brown buckeye, a Christmas bulletin scribbled all over with
lopsided bunnies, and stencils cut from Uncle Stephen's shirt boards, white
with baby shoe polish. But before I can write about them, I have to face the
ugly beaded purse. How can I bear to begin?*

Chapter 21

Nobody really wants you.

I heard those words as I trudged to the bus, sat isolated in class, and practiced in the church basement until my fingers ached with cold. Uncle Stephen was tired of being nice to his wife's orphaned niece. I could tell, because I often caught him frowning at me.

One day I found *Daddy Longlegs* on Aunt Kate's shelf. It was the first book I'd ever read about an orphan, and it pointed me to what I must do. Saturday afternoon I mustered my courage and dignity and marched to the study. I opened the door without knocking, letting the squeak of its hinges announce me and break the silence. Uncle Stephen looked up from his Bible.

"Do you know of any good orphanages?" I asked without preamble.

He marked his place on the page with a finger and looked up at me. "Orphanages? There's Barium Springs, near Charlotte, and Thornwell down in South Carolina. Why?"

I took a deep breath to make my voice stop wobbling and settled my glasses more comfortably on my nose. "Maybe we ought to see if one of them would take me."

He shoved back his hair. "An orphanage? Whatever gave you that idea?"

"This book." I held it out. "I know you and Big Mama were fighting about me."

He took it, read the title, and dropped it on his Bible. "We need to talk. Sit down." I perched on the edge of his extra chair, legs dangling, shivering in spite of my sweater. His little heater hadn't taken the edge off the cold yet. He reached for his pipe and took a long time lighting it. Then he laid it on the ashtray and promptly forgot it. "Carley—" He stopped.

"Yes?"

He leaned forward, one fist gently pounding his leg, and muttered to himself, "Mrs. Marshall's gonna kill me, and Kate may, too, but I've got to do this. You deserve to be told, not left to find it out for yourself." Before I could ask, "Find out what?" he went on. "But first, we love you, and *like* having you live with us. I'm sorry you got any other idea."

I was bewildered. "You've been frowning at me all week."

"If I have, it's not because of you." He paused so long I wondered if he'd changed his mind. "Your grandmother's gonna kill me," he repeated. Then he took a deep breath and said a whole sentence as he exhaled. "Your daddy did not die before you were born."

My daddy wasn't on the list of things I expected to discuss. "He didn't?"

"No." He stopped again.

I felt a chill that had nothing to do with the frigid room. "When did he die?"

"He didn't."

My daddy was alive? I wasn't an orphan? My ears filled with a rushing sound I was certain was angels' wings. I nearly missed the fact that Uncle Stephen had stopped.

I realize now that the conversation was as hard on him as it was on me. At the time, I thought he wanted me to guess what happened. I *could* guess—one girl in our school didn't have a daddy because her mama never got married—but I found that hard to believe about my pretty, prim mother. I gulped—desperate, but excited. "Do you know where he is?"

"In jail. For killing somebody."

I gaped. The only person I ever knew who went to jail was Aunt Sukie's daughter's husband, who knifed a man. "Did he knife somebody?" My voice was a hoarse whisper.

"No, he hit someone so hard he died." He must have realized he'd been too blunt, because he added, quickly, "That was before you were born." As if that would take the edge off. But grief and shock are sharpest when we first feel them, whenever a dark deed occurs.

I wasn't halfway through dealing with that when he added,

"He gets out next year and keeps writing Mrs. Marshall that he wants you to live with him."

It wasn't angel wings in my ears, it was a hammer, pounding hard. "Live with him? I don't even know him! And he's a murderer!"

From the way Uncle Stephen shoved his hand through his hair, I knew he was almost as upset as I was. "Yes, although technically the courts called it manslaughter. That means he didn't go planning to kill the man ahead of time. But either way, he's not a fit father. We all know that. The problem is, sometimes a judge thinks a child belongs with her parent instead of with somebody else. That's why Mrs. Marshall wanted you to live with us. She wanted us to hide you. But you can't hide forever—not from him, nor from the truth. I don't believe in lying to children. But we'll all fight for you. Know that." He reached out and his hand rested on my shoulder like a benediction.

As upset as I felt about my daddy, my mind still whirled like an ecstatic dervish. Big Mama didn't want to send me away, she wanted to hide me. *She loved me!* My whole world, blurry and sad, refocused. What had been wobbling off-center clicked back into place. I was Carley Marshall of the Henry Marshalls, beloved granddaughter of Mrs. Henry Marshall. Uncle Stephen and Aunt Kate loved me, too. I was part of a team that could take on giants together—or a jailed daddy who wasn't dead.

Uncle Stephen shook me gently. "Carley, did you hear what I just said? Your daddy wants to see you."

One of those giants stirred in a distant corner. I tried to still it with logic. "How do you know? You told me that day we went walking that you'd never met him."

"I hadn't then. Later, I went to see him."

"In jail?" I knew what he was going to say as soon as he nodded.

"Last month. He's over in Raleigh. I thought maybe I could talk some sense into him if I went. I'm not sure I did, but at least he agreed he won't be able to take care of anybody but himself for a long time yet. Still, he said he'd like to see you, and I think he deserves that. Mrs. Marshall doesn't. You need to know that. We had some pretty strong words about it over Thanksgiving. But I think at least it ought to be your decision. I'm going to see him next week, and I've got permission for you to visit, too. You don't have to answer right now, but think about whether or not you want to go."

How could an eleven-year-old make a decision like that? I'd never made one more complicated than what I'd wear to school. I agreed simply because nodding was easier than shaking my head.

❄

Aunt Kate came into my room that night just after I'd turned out my light. "Carley? I forgot to give you this earlier. It came in the mail today." She laid something over me that was soft and warm as love. I didn't need the light to know what it was. Big Mama's quilt, made from our favorite dresses.

Chapter 22

We left when it was still dark, and it was dark again by the time we got home. In my memory, the whole day is gray.

On our trip, I think Uncle Stephen started getting cold feet. Big Mama had made one of her crisis-only phone calls the night before to fuss at him and tell me she didn't think going to see Roy was a good idea. Then at breakfast Aunt Kate had let us both know in no uncertain terms that he was wrong in taking me. To each of them he had said stubbornly, "Carley is going to have to face Roy out of jail soon enough. I think she ought to get some idea of what she's up against so she can get used to the idea."

But all the way over he tried to prepare me. He explained at least three times what we'd have to go through at the prison—"They lock every door behind you, and you may feel a little claustrophobic"—and must have said fifty times things like, "Now, Carley, you probably won't feel anything for Roy. He's a stranger to you." Finally he started asking if I was sure I wanted to go in. "You can change your mind, you know, and wait in the car. I won't be even an hour."

Of course I wanted to go in. I've always been able to rewrite a story to suit myself, so in the days between learning Daddy was alive and going to see him, I had convinced myself that he would never have hit anybody unless they deserved it. He was probably unjustly imprisoned. Picturing the imaginary Daddy I'd already shown around Job's Corner and talked to for months, I knew that while I couldn't live with him right away, we could become friends. I could write him letters until he got out of prison, then he could come see me at Aunt Kate's. And when Big Mama saw how good he was to me, she'd forgive him, too.

So when Uncle Stephen said, "You don't have to like him. He's not a particularly likeable cuss," I flounced in my seat and said impatiently, "You don't know. I might like him a lot."

He sighed. "Well, here we are, for good or ill."

Perhaps someone else would have noticed what the prison looked like, but I felt as scared as I had before my first piano competition. Once Uncle Stephen had parked the Chevy, the world got swallowed in a soft fog. He and I were the only solid substances in it. The ground felt spongy underfoot, and I flowed rather than walked toward a huge cloud with a door. I even remember the sky as overcast, but it can't have been. I saw sunlight glinting on barbed wire at the top of a high fence.

Inside, faces on cloud bodies stared curiously at us. Mainly at me. I knew that.

"We're here to see Roy Harburton," Uncle Stephen told them.

Harburton.

That was the first time I ever heard my own last name.

I wasn't given time to think about it. People thrust papers in front of us to sign. I signed Carley Marshall, then wondered if that was right. If it wasn't, could I go to jail, too?

Nobody even looked at my signature. A man was already motioning us to follow him and a woman into separate little rooms.

The woman who went with me had greasy brown hair and was chewing gum. She started to pat me all over.

I drew back in distaste. "What are you doing?"

"It's okay, honey. Just looking for weapons. You're clean."

I gaped at her in astonishment. In the world she lived in, did girls carry guns?

She motioned me back out to the big room where Uncle Stephen stood beside a man with a big ring of keys. As we walked down one long hall after another, I silently repeated over and over the name I'd just heard. "Harburton. Harburton. Harburton." It had nothing to do with me.

I remember sounds and smells better than sights. The jingle of keys fitted into locks. The slap, slap, slap of our feet on the bare floor. The smell of old grease, tomato soup, and coffee, mingled with a smell like Pearl's outhouse. The frightening clang of heavy doors slamming behind us. A thick, dull roar I could neither distinguish nor identify. Only years later would I know it was the concerted voice of confined men. They were particularly disturbed that week, because two days later three would be executed in the gas chamber.

I didn't know then about the executions, but I felt fear and rage oozing from every opening. I clutched Uncle Stephen's hand, the only reality in that world. I had seldom held his hand before. His palm was warm and damp—or was mine sweating into his? I know he felt strong and *there*. His red tie was the only color I saw in that gray cloud place, his eyes the only light. Indeed, I existed at all only because warmth from him flowed into me and gave me life.

At last we reached a break in the cloud, a room with a guard at the door, a long scratched table, and a man on the other side. My heart pounded so hard it made my knees wobble like willow switches. I turned my head into Uncle Stephen's sleeve rather than meet the eyes across the table, but Uncle Stephen prodded me, urging me to look. Whoever or whatever else he was, this man was my daddy.

Uncle Stephen held a chair for me and took one himself. "Hello, Roy." Even Uncle Stephen couldn't sound truly cheerful in that bare room. His trying made me even more nervous. "Carley, this is Roy Harburton. Roy, this is Carley."

Have you ever wanted something so bad you could taste it, only to get it and find it wasn't what you wanted at all? For months I'd wanted my daddy. I'd stared at his youthful picture and wondered how he would have aged. I'd listened to men's voices wondering which sounded like his used to. I'd gone to sleep at night wishing I could be tucked in by him.

But everything about this man repelled me. He scarcely resembled the man in my picture. He was not only older, but coarser and shadowy, as if his body had faded within those walls. His eyes, a light molasses brown, shifted from side to side, only occasionally darting to where Uncle Stephen and I sat in two straight chairs across the table. His hands were clasped so hard in front of him that the knuckles were white and bony. Worst of all, his hair was as mousy and limp as my own. *Oh, Mama, how could you ever love this man? How could you let him give me that ugly hair?*

"Car—car—Carley." His voice was as awkward with my first name as I was with his last. One hand moved tentatively toward me across the table. The guard at the door stepped forward to prevent him from touching me. "Hey," he said angrily to the guard, "I just wanted to give her what I made. Here. See?"

He thrust something at the guard, who took it, examined it, opened it, and handed it back. "Okay, you can give it to her."

"I made it for you," my daddy said, holding it out.

It was a small beaded coin purse of cheap yellow leather, inexpertly sewn with leather thongs and beaded crookedly. Hideous, a craft class idea of American Indian art. But what repelled me more was his hand. Long, thin, strong, a piano-playing hand. My own hand.

"Th–thank you." I managed a smile, but trembled as I reached for the purse. Carefully. I would not touch that thin rough hand.

"You don't like it." His light molasses brown eyes accused me of far worse crimes.

"Oh, yes, I do. I like it fine." I picked it up and pretended to admire it. "I've needed something to carry snack money in to school." That, at least, was true.

He leaned so close I could smell the last cigarette he'd smoked. "When you see your grandmother, you tell her she oughta got me out for Lila's burying. You tell her I said that, okay? Whatever she faults me for, I was married to her daughter. I deserved to get out that day for her burying. She shoulda got me out." His voice rose louder and louder. At the end he pounded the table. Again the guard moved closer. Seeing, he slumped back in his chair.

I felt like a punching bag being hit again and again. "I'll tell her," I said weakly.

"How are you feeling, Roy? Did you get over your cold?" Uncle Stephen talked in a false, cheery voice. The man and I exchanged quick, jabbing looks of identical misery.

Afterwards, what I would remember clearest about Roy Harburton was the hungry look in his eyes when he looked at me. That and a defiant anger I could not comprehend. What I remember clearest about me was the shame I felt at being connected in any way with him, and a hot writhing guilt at that shame.

I have never remembered much that I actually said—or that he said, either. I remember Uncle Stephen asked once if he thought I favored Mama, and instead of answering that, he burst out angrily again, "They should have let me out for Lila's burying. When you see Mrs. Marshall, you tell her I said that, you hear?"

And as we were going out the door he said, "Hey, Joe"—to the guard—"that's my girl!" And to us, "You all come back, now, you hear? I'll be glad to see you anytime."

I could hardly walk past the guard. Until that minute, some dishonorable thing within me hoped everybody in the prison thought I was Uncle Stephen's daughter, coming with him on a virtuous errand of mercy. To be found out was as humiliating as the way I felt about my daddy now that I'd met him.

"You'd think he was sitting on his own front porch or something," I muttered to Uncle Stephen as the door banged behind us, "inviting us back like that."

"I guess in a way this is his own front porch, right now."

We didn't say another word as we retraced our steps down the long halls. Our guide unlocked doors that clanged shut behind us. They rang the peals of my misery. I was chilled to the bone except for one warm shoulder where Uncle Stephen rested his hand.

One guard, whom I remember for his fat red nose, said jovially as we signed out, "Well, Missy, it won't be long now till you get your daddy back."

I was so startled the pen slipped. I went down forever in a North Carolina prison log as Carolina Rose Marsha—.

I waited until we were safe in the car with the heater on and the motor running before I asked the question that bothered me. "Why was he so mad at me? What did I ever do to him?"

"He's mad at everybody, Carley. Not you. You did fine in there. I was proud of you."

"That makes one of us," I told him sullenly. "Big Mama was right, as usual. I never should have gone."

I discovered in coming weeks, though, that I had needed to go. I'd find myself making up dialogues about things I wished I'd said, conversations in which I comforted him, made him laugh, and wound up in his arms as we both wept while an approving guard looked on. Then into my stories would float a very real picture of Roy's hard hungry face—a splash of cold water reality. So, as much as I hated to admit it, for once Big Mama had been wrong and Uncle Stephen right. I needed time to get used to the idea of Roy Harburton before I saw him again face-to-face.

Chapter 23

Every time I thought about Roy those next few days, I wanted to creep under a rock and hide. Having no daddy was better than having one you were ashamed of to the bone.

The December weather matched my mood: cold and miserable. Outdoors we talked in smoke signals. Indoors we huddled by space heaters. Aunt Kate finally missed something from West Virginia: cheap coal. We only bought enough to heat the dining room. Uncle Stephen had a kerosene heater for his study, which he moved to the upstairs bathroom a few evenings a week so Abby and I could bathe together in the big claw-foot tub. Miss Pauline complained, "Your house is so cold, Sue Mary gets sick playing over there." But she—and Velma—kept coming.

Our house smelled of wet wool, wet shoes, and—since Aunt Kate couldn't bear to leave Rowdy in the barn—wet dog. The halls were drafty, and a little heater Uncle Stephen lit in my room at night never did more than take the chill off the air. I climbed into bed clutching a hot water bottle and spent half the night trying to keep my feet tucked under my flannel gown.

Uncle Stephen and I were mostly quiet around each other. I didn't know what to say, and I suspect he was still wondering if he'd done the right thing. Aunt Kate was sure he hadn't. She never asked me one question, even in private, but the way she slammed plates on the table left us clear about her opinion.

Miss Rilla was also miserable. Mr. Rob was drinking steadily. When he shuffled down during my piano lesson to snooze on the couch, I could smell liquor all the way across the stuffy room. Miss Rilla whispered sadly, "He's having one of his spells today. He's not well, you know."

He certainly wasn't. Uncle Stephen came downstairs for a cup of coffee one morning to find Mr. Rob on our telephone with President Truman himself, personally inviting him to drop by for advice on the coal strike from the mayor of Job's Corner!

One Sunday the weather turned unexpectedly warm and sunny, so Uncle Stephen opened the two front sanctuary windows.

"Letting out some of the ecclesiastical stuffiness," he announced. A couple of young men actually laughed out loud.

Halfway through the sermon I heard somebody shuffling down the side aisle. "Howdy, Preacher," Rob called with a genial wave of one hand. "Saw you opened the windows."

"Howdy, Rob. Good to have you," Uncle Stephen replied.

"Go on talking. I'll just sit right here in front." Mr. Rob sat down on the other end of my pew, next to the window. Abby— who was sitting with me now that Aunt Kate was singing in the choir—pressed near me as liquor fumes wafted our way on the breeze. Mr. Rob slumped, folded his hands over his red plaid belly, dropped his chin on his chest, and gently snored.

Uncle Stephen preached on as if nothing had happened.

Mr. Rob must have left the back door open, for in a few minutes a gray cat leaped onto his lap and tested its claws on his old flannel shirt. Abby, entranced, slid away before I could catch her. "Kitty, here, kitty," she chirped softly.

Mr. Rob wakened and stared blearily at the child and cat. Then he gave Abby a broad smile, picked up the cat by its tail, and flung it out the window. Because Bethel's sanctuary was built above a daylight basement, the cat had a two-story drop. We heard a crash, then a diminishing yowl.

"You hurt it!" Abby pummeled him with her little fists.

"Did not. That cat loves to fly. Don't you know that, girlie?"

They were both talking right out loud, like we weren't in the middle of church.

"Honest engine?" Abby asked, eyes wide.

"Honest engine." Mr. Rob sank back into his seat, dropped his head, and began to puff gently. I slid over to grab Abby, but she shoved me away with her elbow and sat with him for the rest of the service, gently patting his arm.

Mr. Wash, of course, was incensed. As soon as church was over he bustled up front and hustled his daddy out the back way.

That afternoon, when they were supposed to be napping, I heard Uncle Stephen and Aunt Kate talking softly. I crept to their door to listen. "What on earth are we going to do about Rob?" Aunt Kate asked. "He gets worse every day."

"He only drinks to help him through the winter. Did you know they had four babies who died, and every one of them died in the autumn?"

"What on earth happened to them?"

"One died in its bed. Another was born dead, and two little girls died of flu the same year. When you look at Rob Lamont, you are looking at a man who's lost his dreams." I heard the bed creak as he turned over. "I just pray God will help him find them again."

As Uncle Stephen was fond of pointing out, God certainly answers some prayers in unexpected ways.

The next Tuesday was a cloudy, shivery day, and Aunt Kate had to stay late at school. I hurried home from piano, glad Mr. Rob hadn't come down and hoping Uncle Stephen would have hot chocolate waiting. Not too far away I heard the whistle of a train still out of sight up the track. Hugh Fred's business had been so good lately that trains were making several runs a day. I had plenty of time to cross the tracks and get home before the train came, but that sound still terrified me if I was near the tracks.

That day, as I put my foot on the second rail, I heard old Patch barking frantically down near Mrs. Cameron's. To my horror, I saw Mr. Rob on his hands and knees between the rails. "Mr. Lamont! There's a train coming!" I yelled in warning.

"Got to find my buckeye," he bellowed back. "Lost it, and it's my lucky buckeye."

"The train is coming!" I hollered. "Get off the tracks until it gets past."

"Got to find my buckeye, missy. Cain't do nothing without my buckeye."

The whistle wailed nearer. The train didn't move fast when it was loaded, but it would be there soon. I cast one quick, hopeless glance toward our house. By the time I could get Uncle Stephen, it would be too late.

Every fiber in my body rebelled against stepping toward

those tracks. A fist seized my heart, and then stopped my breath. Yet the next instant I had flung my music toward the road and was dashing along the cross ties, my yells and panting breaths keeping the beat. "Please, Mr. Lamont, get off the tracks. The train is coming. Get off the tracks! Please!"

Crouched between the rails, scrabbling around in the gravel, he didn't budge.

Just out of danger, Patch shivered and whined.

The whistle sounded for the upper crossing. "Get off the tracks, Mr. Rob. Jump! The train's coming!"

"Soon as I find my buckeye, missy." He was still down on all fours, scrabbling in the gravel. As I pounded up and towered over him, Patch growled low in this throat. Out of the corner of my eye I saw the old bulldog was trembling with fear, but he wasn't leaving.

Turning, I saw the train rounding the curve. It would arrive in approximately thirty seconds. Preston and I had counted it often enough. "Mr. Lamont—" I screamed.

I bent and heaved him with all my might. He tumbled off the train bed straight into a blackberry bush. I dove after him. My glasses flew off. Briars ripped my face and hands. Patch lunged for me and caught my right ankle between his teeth.

The three of us lay quivering as the train thundered by, two eternities long. I saw the engineer's face, white as a cemetery ghost. Hot air smothered us, briars stuck us, Patch held onto my ankle with a grip that pained me to the chest.

At last the train was gone, rumbling down the track. But being that close to a moving train had left me weak and shaking. Worse, Patch still held my ankle between his teeth. I didn't know what he might do if I tried to get loose. Beneath me, Rob Lamont wiggled and swore.

"Carley! Carley! Where are you? Are you all right?" I could hear Uncle Stephen on the road. "Carley! Oh, God!"

Patch growled. His teeth sank deeper into my ankle. Bile rushed up my throat. I had to spit before I could speak, and could only dredge up one weak word. "Help!"

Uncle Stephen's voice was on the road just beyond our blackberry bushes. "Where—?"

"In the dadblamed blackberry bushes," Rob bellowed. "Tell this girl to get off me!"

"The dog's got me, Uncle Stephen," I yelled, sobbing. "He won't let go."

"Rob, call off your dog. Are you all right?"

"I'm all right, 'cept this fool girl's laying all over me and she scared me so much I wet my pants." I knew. He'd wet the front of my skirt, too. "Let 'er go, Patch." Patch held on.

"He's still got me, Uncle Stephen!"

"Rob! Call off your dog."

"Patch, let 'er go. At ease!"

Patch ignored him.

"He won't let go," I whimpered. "It hurts so much—" The world was a whirling of heaviness, briars, and pain. I felt myself sinking, sinking . . .

Mr. Rob hunched his back once more and heaved me off. More briars ripped my face, clutched my coat, snagged my hair. One lodged itself in my left leg. Patch's teeth bit deeper. Flailing his arms and legs, Mr. Rob fought his way out, then dragged himself to his feet.

"Patch, let 'er go. Patch!" The beast opened his jaws and backed up, panting and glaring like he'd attack again any minute. As Uncle Stephen started parting briars to reach me, Patch growled low in his throat.

"If that bulldog bites me, I'll nail your hide to the church door," Uncle Stephen warned. "Are you all right, Carley?"

I burst into tears. "He was going to die, Uncle Stephen. He was going to get killed by the train!" I was shaking so hard the whole bush shook.

Gently he loosed each briar from my skin and clothes. When he helped me to my feet, he pulled me close. I smelled the starch of his shirt and the stench of fear. He brushed the hair back from my forehead like I was Abby. It was stuck to my forehead by sweat and tears.

"Where are your glasses? Oh, there they are." He reached into the briars, pulled them out, tried to settle them on my nose.

I took a long, shivery breath and settled them more comfortably. "I'm okay, Uncle Stephen. I was just so scared . . ." I looked down. My skirt had a long damp streak. Blood stained my sock. And I could not stand on my injured ankle. I felt myself sinking back into the blackberries. "Help!"

He put one arm under me and lifted, jerking his pants free of briars as he carried me to the road. "It was a scary thing to happen." He turned to Mr. Rob. "Has your dog been vaccinated?"

"Co'se he's vaccinated, Preacher. I take care of my animals." He gave me one quick, anxious glance. "Sorry to cause you trouble, missy. I hope you won't hold it against old Patch here that he thought you were attackin' me."

I shook my head, but couldn't speak for the pain. Uncle Stephen jerked his head. "Go on home, Rob, and get cleaned up. I'll take care of Carley."

He carried me across the road toward the house. I tugged his jacket. "My music's near the path. I threw it." I rubbed my streaming nose with one hand.

"I'll get it. Just let me get you inside first." He carried me into the dining room and laid me on the couch.

Miz Baines shuffled in. "What's happened to her?"

"Rob Lamont's bulldog," Uncle Stephen said shortly. "When Kate gets home, tell her I've taken Carley to the emergency room. And yes, Carley, I'm going to get your music first."

❊

By the time we got home it was dark. A light drizzle had begun to fall. Our headlights picked up a squat dejected figure standing beneath one of our maples, coatless and hatless, shoulders hunched against the rain.

Mr. Rob came to the car as soon as we stopped. "She all right, Preacher?" In the dim light I could see that his pants and shirt were fresh, but thin lines of blood had dried on his face and hands from the blackberry bush. For the life of me, I couldn't say a word.

"She's going to be fine," Uncle Stephen told him, coming around to lift me out, "but her ankle's gonna be mighty sore for a few days. What were you doing on those tracks?"

Mr. Rob looked down and shuffled his feet. "Looking for my lucky buckeye." Sheepishly he pulled one gnarled hand out of his pocket and opened it. On the palm lay a small brown nut. "Had the dang thing in my pocket all along." Tears coursed down the wrinkled gray cheeks between the scratches. "I don't know how to thank you, missy. I just don't. Here." He pressed it into my hand. Without thinking, I curved my fingers around it.

"Why don't you help by opening the front door?" Uncle Stephen suggested. Mr. Rob hurried to obey. Uncle Stephen carried me up the walk like I was Abby. At the door, he said, "Maybe Kate can scare us up a cup of coffee. Aren't you freezing?"

Mr. Rob started to shake his head, changed it to a nod. "This rain has a bitter edge on it. Winter's here, for sure."

Aunt Kate brought the men coffee and me hot chocolate and buttered brown-sugar toast, but we could all tell she wasn't feeling particularly hospitable to Mr. Rob. Me neither.

"Let's us men go upstairs," Uncle Stephen suggested. They were up there a long time. Mr. Rob left without telling anybody else goodbye.

Later that night as they washed and dried dishes, I heard Aunt Kate exclaim, "The child could have been killed! If not by the train, then by that vicious dog."

"Forgive him, Kate," Uncle Stephen pleaded. "Rob would break your heart if you really got to know him. Tonight, for the first time, he talked to me. All his life growing up, his mama told him he was no good and God would punish him. He said the only person who ever believed in him was Miss Rilla, and he let her down."

"By drinking?"

"No, he believes those babies died because he wasn't good enough to be their daddy. When he talked about those last two little girls—" Uncle Stephen's voice broke. When he next spoke his voice was all choky and muffled. "Kate, they were about the ages of Abby and John when they died. I couldn't stand hearing him talk about it. He said he'd have died for them if he could, and I knew just how he felt." He stopped. In a minute I heard him blow his nose. "When the boys came along afterwards, he was afraid to get close to them, because he feared if he did, God would take them, too. Can you imagine having that idea of God? He said he never picked them up or even hugged them, though it nearly killed him not to do it."

As mad as I was at Mr. Rob, I felt my own eyes sting.

Aunt Kate was made of sterner stuff. "I still think the dog ought to be put down."

"Think how you feel about Rowdy. If we put down Patch, we might as well put down Rob. He long ago gave up his dreams, his self-respect, and the love of his sons. By now he doesn't have much left except Miss Rilla and old Patch—except one thing." Uncle Stephen suddenly chuckled. "You know the last thing he said to me before he left?"

"He told you to come by the mayoral palace to discuss the Korea policy."

"No, he said he has a complete set of the Harvard classics. If

I want to read them, he'll let me borrow them one at a time. Imagine, Kate—we don't have a plain, ordinary drunk in Job's Corner. We have a drunk who reads the Harvard classics. Said he gets through them about once every five years. Neither of his sons is much in the reading line, he said, and it would be an honor to lend them to someone who'd appreciate them."

The next morning Uncle Stephen played dominoes with me, Abby, and Sue Mary. (Velma, we were told, just liked to watch.) Suddenly Abby crowed. "Here's Mister Rob!"

Sure enough, he stood in the doorway, holding a paper sack. Abby ran and flung herself at his legs like he was her long-lost grandpa.

Uncle Stephen rose to greet him. "Abby doesn't know what happened," I heard him murmur. "Let's keep it that way. But come on in, and see for yourself that Carley's on the mend." He pulled out a chair.

"Where's your flying cat?" Abby demanded, climbing up onto Mr. Rob's lap.

"Home practicing his broad jump." Mr. Rob held her awkwardly in the crook of his arm.

She rubbed her fingers against his cheek. "You got whiskers like a cat."

"Guess I do, missy," he said with an embarrassed grin. "Failed to shave."

He came every morning while I recovered. Abby sat in his lap and prattled on about her baby John and what she'd been doing all day. He never seemed to think she talked too much.

It was a good thing Abby talked to him. I never could think of much to say.

"To his credit," Uncle Stephen pointed out when I complained that I wished he'd just stay away, "he doesn't come drunk. And he's brought a different daily delicacy for your Highness."

That he had, thanks to Miss Rilla. One day it was lemon cakes. Another it was homemade cobbler from peaches she had frozen. The third day's offering, however, I refused to eat: homemade blackberry jam.

※

Our one spot of joy in that dreary December was a wedding. A beautiful wedding, complete with ushers in white coats and bridesmaids in green dresses with poinsettia bouquets. Mr.

Mayhew sang the Lord's Prayer, Aunt Kate and I sang a duet, and the groom's out-of-town aunt played instead of Freda, so there wasn't a single wrong note. At the reception they had wedding cake, and I got a piece with a whole rose of icing, which was my favorite part. Afterwards, the bride and groom went for a week at Myrtle Beach, and Miss Nancy made sure everybody knew they'd be coming back to live in an apartment she and Mr. Wash had fixed up in their upstairs.

Abby and Sue Mary played bride all week, wearing two old organdy curtains bobby-pinned to their hair. Up and down our chilly hall they marched, solemnly carrying wilted late chrysanthemums. Sue Mary even let go of Velma to carry her bouquet. They ordered me to hum for them, but when I sang, "Here comes the bride, big fat and wide," they ordered me to stop. They didn't mind that their wedding had two brides and no groom.

Jimmy Lamont, however, had been greatly impressed by the groom—as we found out when his mother came Thursday afternoon to talk to Uncle Stephen.

Miss Nancy came a lot lately to talk over her worries. She worried about her mother-in-law. She worried about her children. Most of all she worried that our nation was heading straight for disaster. Everything she read in the paper confirmed it. Uncle Stephen told Aunt Kate one night when they were doing dishes, "I keep telling her not to read the paper, if it upsets her so, but she won't give it up. Sometimes I think she likes getting upset."

Aunt Kate reached over and popped one of his suspenders. "I think she likes coming to see the preacher."

That particular Thursday while Miss Nancy was up in the study, Aunt Kate told me, "I'm grading papers, Carley. Please keep the children in the front room or the hall."

Jimmy sat down on the bottom step with Abby on one side, Sue Mary on the other. "Le's play wedding. I'm the goom. Kiss me." He puckered up and leaned toward Abby.

She drew back in disgust. "No!"

He turned to Sue Mary. "You kiss me, den."

She leaned over and gave him a quick peck on the cheek.

"No! Dis is de way dey dood it." He leaned over and kissed her full on the lips.

Sue Mary looked at him gravely for a moment, then said primly, "Do it again." She puckered up and leaned toward him. He obliged.

"Stop dat!" Abby ordered.

They ignored her. Jimmy kissed Sue Mary. Sue Mary kissed Jimmy. Jimmy kissed Sue Mary again. Abby was furious! I grabbed Aunt Kate's Brownie camera from her dresser and snapped a picture: Jimmy and Sue Mary face forward, hands folded in their laps but heads turned so their noses and puckered lips meet. Abby glowers at them from Jimmy's other side. On the back Aunt Kate wrote in brown ink, "Just mad? Or jealous?"

❋

On Saturday, Abby disappeared.

Aunt Kate and I were baking Toll House cookies for Christmas and assumed she was at Sue Mary's. But when I went to fetch her for supper, their house was dark. We checked our house, our yard, the barn, even Miss Pauline's hen house and in the post office. No Abby. It was getting icy outside, and Aunt Kate was frantic.

So was I. I couldn't bear to lose another person I loved.

Uncle Stephen rounded up Mr. Davy, Mr. Rob, Jay, and Mr. Wash to visit every house in the neighborhood. The only men they didn't ask were Mr. Ira and the groom—who had just gotten home. I insisted on going along. Aunt Kate would have come, too, except John had a cold and was fussy with new teeth. "Find her," she begged. Her face was white and she held John tightly, as if afraid he'd disappear, too.

I put on my heavy coat, mittens, a scarf, and a hat, but the wind whistled up my skirt. I almost wished I was little enough to wear leggings. Jay, Uncle Stephen, and I combed the churchyard. "Look behind every tombstone," Uncle Stephen told us. "She may have fallen and gotten hurt." There were a lot of tombstones, but no Abby.

Next we looked in every room in the church, although I told him Abby was afraid to go in when there was nobody there. Finally we walked up and down the tracks, our flashlights like little trains meeting in the night.

We saw another flashlight as Mr. Wash looked in every barn and henhouse and under the post office. We heard Mr. Davy calling in his pasture, and the *moos* of startled cows. He even went down along his creek. The last gray light disappeared and stars came out. It was a clear, beautiful night—but none of us felt like enjoying it. My stomach ached so bad I could hardly walk.

We met back at the house at seven-thirty. Nobody had found a trace of her.

"We'll have to call the police," Uncle Stephen said, drained and exhausted.

"You reckon that little girl needs her mama home?" Mr. Wash asked Aunt Kate. "Reckon she's run away to try and make a point?"

Aunt Kate stood up and walked calmly to where he stood. Above John's fuzzy head, her face had gone stark white, like Big Mama's did once when we came on a man beating a dog. But just as she opened her mouth, there was a knock at our door. She gave Mr. Wash a look that meant "I'll get back to you," and ran to open it. We all went right behind her.

There stood the bride and groom, with Abby.

"We brought her home in time for bed." They were rosy, happy, and all holding hands.

"Where have you been?" Aunt Kate cried, practically throwing John at me and grabbing Abby in a fierce hug. "We been looking everywhere for you!"

"I wents to see de bwide," Abby explained.

We all stared, speechless.

"We thought you knew where she was," the groom said, puzzled. "She said you did."

"She came about four," the bride told us. "I'd just washed my hair and set it in pin curls, when she knocked and asked to see the bride. I told her I was the bride, but she said, 'No. The bride is a beautiful princess.'" She laughed and blushed. "We'd picked up some of our wedding pictures as we came through town, so I showed them to her to prove it was me. She's been on the couch looking at them ever since—except during supper."

Aunt Kate's cheeks grew pink. "Supper? Oh, honey, why didn't you come home to eat?"

"She said would I like some fwied chicken, so I said, 'Yes, ma'am.' I never eated with a bwide before."

The groom kneeled and said gently, "But I asked if your folks knew where you were, and you told me they did." He had four little sisters of his own. "Why did you tell me a story?"

Abby glowered. "I did not tell a story. Dey do know where I am. I am in Job's Corner."

❀

Mr. Rob came over Sunday afternoon to talk to Uncle Stephen. We heard both of them go out, then Uncle Stephen bounded onto the porch half an hour later, whistling and happily slamming the door behind him.

"Why are you so happy?" Abby asked him glumly.

He picked her up and swung her around. "Mr. Rob makes the prettiest little models you ever saw. He's built the Statesville courthouse and the capitol in Raleigh, and half finished the White House. They are wonderful! I think he ought to show them downtown at the library."

She squeezed his neck. "Goody! Can we go see dem?"

He hugged her back, then set her down. "Nice try, little lady, but you are still grounded."

Later, I crept down to listen while he talked privately to Aunt Kate in their room. "It was like a miracle, Kate! Rob promised God if we found Abby, he'd stop drinking. You know I don't normally hold with bargains like that, but he came over today to ask me to help him make good on his promise. Together we poured every bit of his liquor down the drain, then we prayed together that God will give him strength to keep his resolve. Let's both keep praying that he will."

"Time will tell." Aunt Kate sounded like she didn't believe it yet. "But it makes me wish I hadn't switched Abby so hard."

"Me, too," Abby called from her bed in the adjoining room.

Chapter 24

Because Uncle Stephen had gotten to know their preacher, the Negro Presbyterian Church at Pleasantdale, Rock of Hope, invited our congregation to attend their Christmas pageant. The only people who went were Miss Hannah, Uncle Stephen, Abby, and I. I'd asked to stay home with John, but Aunt Kate and I flipped a nickel and I lost.

We got there early, of course—preachers get in the habit, and it's a hard one to break. I had plenty of time to notice how worn the pews and floor were, and that the piano was a battered upright like Big Mama used to have before I started taking lessons and we got a new one.

I reached for a pew Bible, thinking I would set a good example to people who were coming in talking. It fell open to Matthew 25 and one verse jumped out at me: "Inasmuch as ye have done it to the least of these my brethren, ye have done it unto me." I preened. There we were, attending church with some of Jesus' poorest brothers and sisters.

But just then a large woman sat down and started playing carols. That piano was so out of tune that although she did her best, it sounded dreadful. That's when I remembered what happened to our old piano: Big Mama gave it to Aunt Sukie's church. I slammed that Bible shut and stuck it back in the pew. God could at least credit a person for good deeds before calling attention to her family's failings.

The preacher fell all over himself making us welcome, but I could tell that the others wondered why we'd come. I wondered, too. I was glad Aunt Kate made Abby and me wear nice dresses. Maggie had on a red velvet dress with a matching hair-bow. All the women and girls wore Sunday clothes, and the building smelled so much like Aunt Sukie when she got dressed up that I got lumps in my throat. But I wished my skin wasn't so white. I kept tugging down my cuffs and skirt and pulling up my socks, so not much showed. Between clearing my lumpy throat and tugging down my sleeves, I spent the program in an agony of self-consciousness.

Abby, on the other hand, flounced happily in the pew waving to everybody she knew, then begged a pencil from Miss Hannah and settled down to show Maggie how Miss Pauline drew cats and rabbits. Drawing cats and rabbits was one of Miss Pauline's stellar accomplishments.

Negro Presbyterians seemed as reluctant as white ones to make noise in church. I could scarcely hear the woman who read the Scripture or the elder who prayed. But their choir was good, singing without the piano, and I tingled all over when Jay Anderson stood up in a red choir robe and sang "Oh Holy Night." He had the prettiest baritone I'd ever heard.

While he sang, children came down the aisle to form a manger scene so beautiful it made my eyes sting. I forgot I was white, sitting in a Negro church. As I told Aunt Kate later, "It didn't even seem funny to have a Negro Mary and Joseph."

But reality came back with the lights. At the back of the church, tables were covered with cakes, pies, and fudge. Everything looked delicious. However, Big Mama had told me *never* to eat or drink at colored houses, because the food might not be clean. I had to assume that rule went for churches, too. So there I stood, miserable and starving, holding a plate of two uneaten cookies to be polite while everyone else gorged themselves. When Janey Lou came up with a plate and urged, "Baby, try one of these chess pies, I made them special," I remembered that down at Pearl's I always made an exception when I got thirsty. I reasoned that a woman who spent her life in a washtub ought to be clean. Janey Lou was certainly clean, too. I ate her chess pies all the time at Miss Hannah's. So I gobbled down three. I wished I dared drink the punch.

It had started sleeting while we were inside. Abby fell asleep in the backseat on our way home and I was enjoying the swish of the wipers against falling ice and the crunch of our tires on the road when Uncle Stephen ruined it all. "I saw you weren't eating. Weren't you hungry?"

I considered telling a little lie, but since I was planning to eat cookies when I got home, I didn't. Besides, Uncle Stephen knew exactly why I hadn't been eating. He thought a minute, then asked a dumb question. "You eat ham, don't you?"

"You know ham is my favorite meat in the whole world."

"Did you know that in the Bible, God forbids Israel to eat pork because it's unclean?"

"Sure I know that. *Baptist* churches teach their children the *Bible.*"

"Sure they do. But if God says not to eat ham in the Bible, how come you eat it now?"

"Because in those days they didn't have Kelvinators, and pigs had diseases. We had a whole Sunday school lesson on that."

"Do you reckon maybe the rules about not eating in Negro homes could be kind of like that? Maybe they were started back when most Negroes had no plumbing or refrigeration. Maybe some food *wasn't* safe to eat—even for the people who lived there. But if people don't live like that now, do those rules still apply? And didn't Mrs. Marshall ever teach you that when you're a guest, you eat whatever you're served, because it's good manners?"

"I wish grown-ups would all get together and make the same rules before they start teaching them to children," I said crossly. "But until they do, I have to obey Big Mama. She's older and wiser than you." I had a little niggling worry, though, that maybe Big Mama hadn't thought about it that way. I'd ask her the next time I saw her.

Chapter 25

When we got home, we found Aunt Kate's Christmas present for Uncle Stephen: she'd invited his daddy for Christmas! Mr. Davy had picked him up at the bus station while we were at the pageant. He was to stay the whole week, while she took us children to Big Mama's.

Mr. Whitfield was almost as old as Mrs. Cameron, a shrunken man not much taller than I. He had a curved back, a thatch of long white hair, and a very long nose and chin—like gravity had pulled on them for eighty years and was winning. He also had twinkly eyes that changed color depending on what he wore. That night they were gray, the next morning green.

Uncle Stephen never suspected a thing, I wrote in my diary. *When he saw his daddy I'd have thought he had tears in his eyes, except men don't cry.*

The next day Mr. Davy brought up a tree from his pasture, and we all decorated it. Then Aunt Kate tied big red bows on the banisters and the front door while I cut stencils in old shirt boards. Abby carefully sponged canes, trees, and stars on our windows. We had the prettiest house in town.

Abby drove me crazy, though, bothering the manger scene. I spent a lot of time deciding where every single piece should go. But first she moved the wise men to the barbecue grill, "so's dey can come from a fire." She carried the cow, donkey, and sheep to the barn, because "dat's where dey belongs." And she put baby Jesus in her bed, because "it's *cold* in dat living room!" I spent the week before Christmas finding and remaking that scene. "Now you understand how frustrated God must have felt," Uncle Stephen told me, "trying to get the first one together."

Sue Mary arrived every morning of our Christmas vacation, with Velma. One day I asked, curious, "Where did you get Velma?"

She thought about it. "My daddy gived her to me de Christmas he goed away. Velma was my bestest present ever." A stranger would have thought she was hugging herself.

"Do you think Sue Mary is crazy?" I asked Aunt Kate while we heated tomato soup for lunch. "Because of Velma, I mean."

"No. Velma is just Sue Mary's way of coping with her daddy's death."

"Maybe I ought to get myself a Velma," I muttered. "I can't cope with my own daddy being *alive*." She didn't say another word.

Uncle Stephen made me send him a card and a poem I wrote, but I wouldn't sign "Love." The thought of him getting out nearly scared me to death. Every night I prayed, "Save me from fire and ghosts and don't make me go live with Daddy."

✳

Preston did his best to spoil everybody's Christmas by crossing the highway on Christmas Eve and getting hit by a car.

It was a glowering day, the low thick clouds a lot of colors, but all of them gray. Aunt Kate said it was a good day to sit inside drinking hot chocolate and reading books. Looking out once and spying Jay Anderson cleaning brush out of the old cemetery, I was glad I didn't have to work outside on that kind of day.

About three o'clock Jay thundered onto our front porch shouting, his breath making smoke in the cold air. "Mr. Whitfield! Mr. Whitfield! A car hit Preston and took off! He's hurt bad!"

"Go get Pauline," Uncle Stephen ordered me. "I'll call an ambulance and see if Emily's home." Even though Miss Emily hadn't worked as a nurse since before she got married, we still called her in emergencies.

"She and Freda were going to Charlotte," I called over my shoulder as I hurried out. I didn't even pause to grab my coat, so I was shivering by the time I got to Anderson's yard. My teeth were seriously chattering as Miss Pauline opened her door. "Preston got hit by a car," I gasped, holding a stitch in my side. "He's over by the churchyard, and Uncle Stephen—"

Suddenly a battered green pickup screeched to a stop across the highway. I turned to see two white men in thick jackets jump out and run toward Jay, who was bent over Preston. "Get away from him!" one of them yelled so loud I could hear him clearly. "Don't you hurt that boy!"

"Let him go! Let him go!" the other shouted, shoving Jay so hard that Jay sprawled backwards. He straddled Jay and bent down like he would hit him again.

I abandoned Miss Pauline and flew toward the churchyard, hardly bothering to look for cars on the highway. "Don't hit Jay!" I yelled as I ran, smoke signals rising before me. "He didn't hurt Preston. Preston got hit by a car! Don't hurt Jay!" The wind cut my windpipe like ice.

When I got close, I saw the men were Ken Williams, a farmer from up the road and a member of our church, and his oldest son, Tom. Tom played high school football, and they were both nice, normally. I couldn't understand why they were jumping all over Jay.

They didn't pay me one speck of attention. Mr. Ken bent down over Preston. "Hey, little buddy, you doin' okay? Let me help you up." He reached for Preston's arm.

"Don't move him," Jay shouted, rising to one elbow. He looked thin and small, lying where he'd fallen with Tom towering over him. He also looked cold. What had happened to his jacket? He and I would probably die of freezation before the ambulance came. Still, in spite of the cold and Tom above him, Jay shouted again, "Don't move him! The Red Cross manual says . . ."

"Who're you to talk 'bout Red Cross?" Tom demanded. "And what'd you do to Preston, there?"

"He didn't hurt him!" I grabbed Tom's big arm and shook it. "Jay saved Preston's life! He got him off the road and came for Uncle Stephen . . ." I had to stop. My chest hurt too much.

Mr. Ken stood erect and turned around. "Is that right? You sure?" I nodded, gasping for air and trying to keep my teeth from breaking each other apart. I waved weakly toward Miss Pauline, lumbering across the tracks. "Uncle Stephen's calling the ambulance, and I went to call his mama . . ." I had to stop again. As soon as I'd stopped running I'd started to shiver so hard I felt like I was doing a weird dance.

Mr. Ken took off his hat and scratched his head. Then he went to offer Jay his hand to help him up. "I'm real sorry about that, boy. It was a honest mistake, but I'm sorry."

His son turned to me, his face red from more than the wind. "Hey, Carley, where's your coat? Here, take mine." Quick as a wink he unzipped his jacket and peeled it off. He had on a flannel shirt and a sweater underneath, so I didn't mind taking the big football jacket one bit. I didn't even mind that the sleeves hung well past my hands. It was deliciously warm from his body.

While I was zipping it, Miss Pauline galloped across the road, red veins standing out on her cheeks, hair wild in the wind, and one large hand clutching her chest. She had, however, taken time to snatch her thick green coat off the hook as she came out the door. "Baby? Oh, baby!" She flung herself beside Preston in the frozen mud.

I hadn't even looked at Preston until then. He lay on his back, eyes open but looking like he couldn't quite see us. He was so white I could hardly see his freckles, but his face was blotched with blood like the freckles had suddenly spread. He'd lost a mitten, and that hand was bloody, too. One leg was bent all funny. And I saw what had happened to Jay's jacket. He'd put it under Preston's head. Jay was shivering so bad I wished I could share Tom's jacket, but wasn't sure Tom would like that.

Preston hadn't said a word until he saw his mother. Then he started hollering. "I'm dyin'! I'm dyin'!" The way he carried on, you'd have thought the car broke every part of him but his lungs. I decided he couldn't really be dying if he was that lively, but he looked like he might, all pale and bloody. I'm ashamed to confess that while I tried to feel sorry for him, I mostly was thinking, *What was he doing crossing that road?*

Miss Pauline scooped one arm under his shoulders and tried to lift him. Jay had backed away from the group, but he took two urgent steps forward, putting out one hand. "He ought to stay flat, Miss Pauline. That's what the Red Cross manual says."

She might not have paid attention to Jay any more than Mr. Ken had, but Uncle Stephen's voice rang across the road. "Don't move that child! The ambulance is on the way!" He and Aunt Kate had to wait for an oil tanker to pass. Aunt Kate was carrying blankets and a pillow I thought at first was John. Good thing it wasn't. Preston was no sight for a baby. He wasn't a sight for Abby or Sue Mary, either, but I saw them trailing Bonnie across the Anderson's yard. At least Bonnie had bundled them both up good. She'd even gotten Abby into her detested leggings.

Old Mrs. Cameron stood at the door to her store, and Wash and Nancy shielded their eyes on their front porch. Mr. Rob came out his front door with Patch, slamming it behind him. You'd have thought we were having a Save Preston Convention.

"Hey, Mr. Whitfield," the farmer greeted him over the roar of the approaching tanker. "We saw this boy hurt here and thought we ought to stop."

"Good for you," Uncle Stephen called back. "The ambulance is coming." The tanker slowed, decided everything was under control, and finally passed. Uncle Stephen and Aunt Kate hurried over. Mr. Rob got there about the same time, carrying two hot water bottles.

Miss Pauline scrabbled to her feet and flung her arms around Uncle Stephen's neck so hard he staggered back a step. "He's real bad, Stephen. My baby's hurt bad." Tears streamed down her pudgy face. Aunt Kate she wholly ignored.

He patted her arm and detached himself, looking real embarrassed. In those days, people didn't generally hug a preacher. "The ambulance is on the way. Luckily Jay was cleaning up the cemetery and saw it."

"I can't thank you both enough. I can't thank you—" Miss Pauline stopped mid-sentence to shout at Aunt Kate, "What you doin'?"

"Covering him with blankets and hot water bottles to prevent shock." I couldn't believe Aunt Kate was tucking good blankets around bloody Preston on the ground! Miss Pauline looked like she wanted to object, too, but wasn't sure if Aunt Kate might, just once, be right.

Uncle Stephen knelt beside Preston. "You okay, son? Help is coming. Hang in there." He gently put the pillow under Preston's red bristle and handed Jay back his jacket. Jay took it gratefully and quickly shivered into the sleeves.

Preston whimpered. "I hurt. I hurt bad."

"I know you do, but they'll be here as soon as they can. Lie still now." Uncle Stephen laid a hand on Preston's shoulder.

"Ow!" He winced. "That hurts my leg!"

With his free hand, Uncle Stephen motioned for Tom. "Tom, come over and tell Preston how you made that touchdown at the pre-Thanksgiving game. That was really something. I didn't think you'd get by that big fellow from the other team."

Preston's face lit up as Tom knelt on his other side. "Hey, Tom! I heard about your touchdown, but I didn't get to see the game."

"It was pretty exciting," Tom told him. "You see, the quarterback told me to go out wide to the right, but . . ." Until the ambulance came, Tom knelt right there talking about football.

Since I wasn't interested in football, I went over to where Jay was. He and I hung around, not wanting to leave but not knowing what to do, either. Mr. Ken and Mr. Rob joined us, looking like they felt the same. "Jay wants to be a doctor," I informed them.

"That right?" Mr. Ken eyed Jay uneasily. Jay looked at the ground.

Just then Bonnie and the little girls arrived. As soon as Sue Mary saw Preston, she started to scream. Abby thought that was such a good idea, she started screaming too. The only difference was, she was laughing and jumping up and down. Sue Mary wasn't.

Aunt Kate picked up Sue Mary and held her tight. "He's going to be fine," she said over and over in a soft voice. "Preston is going to be fine." She looked up at me. "You and Bonnie take the girls back home." But when she saw Bonnie's worried eyes, she changed that to, "Just take them somewhere and keep them quiet."

I had the idea to let them blow on tombstones to make frost. That kept them occupied for what seemed like a year, but really was probably more like half an hour until the ambulance wailed its way out of town. While the men were loading Preston in, Miss Pauline clutched Uncle Stephen's arm. "Don't desert me! Don't desert me!"

Seeing that it was she who was getting ready to desert us, riding with Preston, I thought that was silly, but Uncle Stephen offered, "Why don't Kate and I meet you at the hospital? Dad can watch all the children."

"Call Davy and Hannah to come, too," she commanded, climbing into the ambulance.

"We'll go down and tell them," Mr. Ken offered, motioning Tom to the truck.

"I don't need to go," Aunt Kate murmured to Uncle Stephen. "You, Davy, and Hannah will be plenty."

He bent real close. "Don't desert me. Don't desert me."

As Uncle Stephen and Aunt Kate drove away, Sue Mary started screaming again.

"It's because Daddy died at Christmas," Bonnie explained, trying to contain the octopus her little sister had become. "She's afraid Preston will die, too."

"Stop that! Preston's not going to die," I shouted. "He's too mean."

Mr. Whitfield bent down, wagged a finger at her, and said sternly, "You stop screaming right now, or you'll get no coffee for supper!"

Startled, Sue Mary stopped. "I doesn't get coffee for supper. Mama doesn't lets me."

"Fiddlesticks," he said. "I'm twice as old as your mama and three times smarter. A little coffee's good for a child. Let's go make it." She took his hand and trotted after him.

At supper he held one little girl on each knee and filled a cup with warm milk, sugar, and just enough coffee to turn it brown. They took turns drinking it. Aunt Kate told me once that with sixteen grandchildren, she never saw Mr. Whitfield sit down to a meal without a child on his lap. Abby claims to this day that she drinks coffee because her granddaddy taught her to.

He also asked Bonnie to look after John, which she loved, while he cooked supper: boiled eggs with cookies. Worried that we would die with no vitamins, I climbed to the top shelf of the pantry and brought down apples and tangerines I'd seen Aunt Kate put there.

When Uncle Stephen and Aunt Kate finally got home it was well past dark. They said Preston's leg and a couple of ribs were broken and he'd be in the hospital a week. Miss Pauline was sleeping there, so Uncle Stephen took Bonnie home to get their pajamas and toothbrushes, then Bonnie slept with me while Sue Mary slept with Abby.

"Will Santa know where to find dem?" Abby worried.

"We've already notified him," Uncle Stephen assured her.

Bonnie and I lay awake talking a while after we turned off the light. "Do you miss your daddy a lot since he died?" I asked.

I felt the bed wiggle as she nodded. "I miss him a little, but I miss Mama more."

"Your mama?" I was surprised. "I thought Miss Pauline was your mama."

"Oh, no, my mother's name was Catherine. Isn't that a pretty name? She died when I was born. I wish I'd been old enough to know her before she died."

I didn't say another word, because I didn't want her to suspect that big fat tears were running down my cheeks. I missed Mama so much. What if I'd never even known her at all?

✾

I woke Christmas morning while it was still dark. The whole world felt icy and clean, as if I were the only person alive. It was funny to have somebody in my bed, but warm.

At home, I always got up first on Christmas and crept into the living room to play with my Santa presents before Mama, Big Mama, and Pop got up. I had suspected for several years that Santa was really Mama or Pop, but we all pretended anyway. Last Christmas was our first without Pop, but Santa still came. This year, I didn't know what to expect.

Quietly I tiptoed down to the living room and peered in. The room was chilly and smelled like a forest. I flicked on the light and saw a wagon near the window labeled "For Abby and John, Love Granddaddy." Santa's piles of toys were labeled "Sue Mary," "Abby," and "John." My only presents were from the family, wrapped under the tree.

I turned off the light and the cold dark swallowed me. I didn't have a granddaddy. I didn't have Mama. I didn't have Santa. I didn't have anybody.

I collapsed to the chilly floor in sobs. I don't know how long I cried before I felt a touch on my shoulder. I looked up to see Aunt Kate kneeling beside me in the dimness. I could scarcely distinguish the green of her chenille robe, but could see the glint of tears in her eyes. "Oh, honey." She held out her arms and I fell forward, still sobbing. Only when I paused for a breath did I realize she was crying, too. "I miss Mama," I wailed. "And Pop, and Big Mama."

"Me, too." She sniffed and swallowed. "I wish I could have come when Lila died, but I was too pregnant with John. I never even got to say goodbye."

I stroked a wet strand of hair from her cheek. "She talked about you in the hospital. She said, 'I hope Kate doesn't remember what a brat I was when we were little.'"

Aunt Kate shook her head. "I was the brat. I did some dreadful things to her."

"Like what?" Distracted, I wiped my eyes on my flannel pajama sleeve.

Aunt Kate considered. "Like tell her butterflies were really fairies, but only very good people could see them, and she wasn't good enough."

I gasped. "You didn't!" I giggled in spite of myself.

Aunt Kate giggled too. "I did. When Mama found out, she spanked me good."

We laughed breathlessly together in the dimness. "I miss her a lot," I whispered.

"I do, too, Carley. I haven't talked about her because I didn't want to make you sadder. But I'd like to talk about her more. Okay?"

"Okay." I swallowed hard and felt much better, but there was something I wanted to get off my chest. "Aunt Kate? I took Abby and Sue Mary up to walk on the tracks one day last summer. A train came and it was scary. Jay Anderson saved us."

For a minute I thought she was going to be mad, then she bent and rubbed my cheek with hers. "Everybody's bad sometimes, aren't they, Carley? It's a wonder God puts up with us. But we're sure glad to have you around." She held out her hand. "How about if we go back to bed now and let the children think they're waking us?"

❧

Soon after we'd eaten breakfast and opened gifts, we heard a knock. Rob Lamont came in, wearing his old gray pants and a flannel shirt with several sweaters, but he was cold sober. "Merry Christmas, everybody! You ready, Preacher?"

"Sure am. You girls stay in the living room until I come get you. Okay?" Uncle Stephen was back in twenty minutes. "All right, girls. Come out."

In the backyard not far from our barbecue grill sat a lovely little house four feet tall. Even I could stand up in it if I stooped just a little. It had a yellow door, a front picture window, a back hinged window, and a sloping flat roof. Out-side it was covered with green roofing shingles. Inside it was papered with the same tiny pink rosebuds Miss Hannah had in one upstairs bedroom.

"This is your very own house," Mr. Rob told Abby.

"Yours, Carley's, Sue Mary's, and Ruthie's," Uncle Stephen added.

The two little girls approached on tiptoe, hands behind them, like they expected it to explode. At the door they peeped in. "It's got no furniture," Abby pointed out doubtfully.

"Not yet," Uncle Stephen agreed. "We'll have to work on that."

She frowned. "Does we has to sleep out here *all* de time, even when it's cold?"

He laughed. "You don't sleep out here at all, Abbikins. It's a *play*house."

"I made it just for you," Mr. Rob sounded anxious.

Abby flung herself at his knees. "I likes it! Thank you."

"I likes it, too," Sue Mary nodded. "Me 'n' Velma likes it a lot."

"Velma? Who's Velma?" Mr. Rob asked Uncle Stephen.

I left him to explain. My knees were freezing.

❦

Christmas Day was on Sunday that year, and the church was full. Ivy brought a new baby doll, and was as proud of it as Abby was of her new Sparkle Plenty. Uncle Stephen preached a wonderful sermon about how Christmas shows God's love for everybody, and managed to get through the whole sermon without directly mentioning civil rights, coal miners, or communists.

After church, Uncle Stephen went to visit Preston. He came back and reported Santa had been there and brought a Hopalong Cassidy hat, boots, and guns.

Mr. Davy and Miss Hannah came to eat dinner and meet Mr. Whitfield. Uncle Stephen had put a big turkey in the oven early that morning, and Aunt Kate had made dressing, mashed potatoes, green beans, and spiced peaches. Miss Hannah brought Janey Lou's homemade rolls and a big devil's food cake with white icing. She also brought my favorite present all day: a piano!

"We gave it to my sister when her son took lessons," she told Aunt Kate, "but nobody plays it since he died. Davy went yesterday to pick it up. We want you all to have it. This paper says it belongs to you all personally, not to the manse."

I couldn't believe it. "I can practice anytime I want without freezing fingers?"

Mr. Davy brought a present for the Anderson family, too— the first television I had ever touched. We took it over and plugged it in, but couldn't get a picture until Uncle Stephen and Mr. Davy could install an antenna on the roof. It was too icy that day.

Just before dinner, old Mr. Whitfield, Uncle Stephen, and I walked down to Mrs. Cameron's. "You are coming to dinner with us, and I don't want any back talk," Uncle Stephen told her in a voice that let her know he was joking.

"I need some adult conversation with all these young-uns," Mr. Whitfield added.

She grumbled, of course, but got on her coat and hobbled up the road with us. With four children, a baby, and a dog in the newly finished kitchen and seven grown-ups in the dining room, Christmas dinner was a noisy happy meal. Abby announced, "I won't eben fuss about eatin' in de kitchen, 'cause it's de mos' bee-you-tiful room in our house."

When I took in dessert to the grown-ups, I couldn't believe my eyes. "You are smiling!" I accused Mrs. Cameron.

She glared up at me. "Just stretching my lips, missy. Just stretching my lips."

Chapter 26

I realize that I said earlier that we were going "to Big Mama's" after Christmas, not that I was going home. That whole visit has blurred into other visits, leaving little memory of what we said or did, but I do remember one sharp pang of grief when I stood in Big Mama's kitchen and realized I now thought of Job's Corner as home. I felt swept by an undertow of homesickness that nearly drowned me in sorrow—and the whole time I knew I longed not for a place, but for a time when I belonged where I stood.

I remember one more thing. The first night after Aunt Kate and Abby were asleep, I crept from my bed to Big Mama's room. She was propped on pillows, reading her devotions. Lucky looked up from the foot of her bed and gave a low "woof."

I backed up. Since Patch bit me, I'd been terrified of all dogs except Rowdy. Big Mama shoved the dalmatian off and moved her feet to make space for me. Her bed smelled like it always did, of face powder, rose perfume, and a smell I could never define but would recognize as hers if I caught a whiff of it today.

She was using an old flowered quilt, one her own mama had made. I tucked my feet beneath it. The dog's tail beat a thump on the floor, and I stroked the quilt's flowers in time, not looking up. "I've been to see my daddy."

"So Stephen insisted on taking you, in spite of how I felt." She laid her devotion book on the nightstand and clasped her hands over the quilt.

I met her eyes and answered what she did not—would not—ask. "It was pretty awful."

"I told you it would be."

"You never told me one blessed thing! Not all those years."

"That's the way Lila wanted it. Lila and Pop."

"That's what you say, with neither of them here to dispute it."

Her eyes didn't waver under my glare.

I tried to settle my spine against the knobby footboard of the spindle bed. Big Mama pulled out one of her three pillows. "Here. This will help."

I wiggled to get halfway comfortable. "Will you tell me about him now?"

"What do you want to know?"

"Did Mama really love him? Were they happy? What finally happened?"

She thought a moment, her long dark braid over one shoulder, her face shaded except where the lamp shone full on one cheek. "They didn't have much time to be happy," she said finally. "Lila hadn't finished high school when they ran off to South Carolina to get married."

"You mean they didn't have a real wedding? Aunt Kate said she was in it."

"They had a real wedding after they told us what they'd done—and that you were well on the way. Pop gave your daddy a job in the store—he was a year older and had graduated. I helped Lila find a little place, but it wasn't much—not good enough for Roy. He liked fine things, lovely things. I think one reason he married Lila was because she was so pretty and he thought she was rich. Working on commission wasn't what he wanted. He wasn't willing to wait for nice things."

She stopped.

"So they were poor and he hated it?" I prodded.

Her voice grew harsh. "Roy didn't know how to be poor. First he borrowed money from his mother to buy a new car. Then he stole a suit, ties, several pairs of shoes."

"From *Marshall's*?" I couldn't believe my ears.

She nodded. "Pop found out and gave him a talking to, thinking he'd change, but he didn't. One day he found the combination to the safe in Pop's desk, copied it, and went back after closing. He had the door open when Jack, the watchman, found him."

She got up and padded to her dresser barefoot, took out a blue envelope, and held it as if in two minds about giving it to me. "All the newspaper clippings are there. I saved them for you from Lila's things—I figured you ought to have them one day. I just didn't reckon it would be so soon." She returned to the bed and spread them over the quilt. I saw Mama, looking very young and scared, and Roy looking defiant. But when I picked up one to read, she gave a little wave. "Don't read them now. I'll tell you what happened."

She climbed back into bed and pulled the covers over her knees. "Poor Jack was over seventy, and he'd worked at Marshall's since he retired from the sheriff's department. Roy said Jack startled him, and he pushed Jack just enough so he lost his balance, fell, and hit his head on a table. But the police said he hit Jack hard enough to kill him. The jury agreed."

I read the clippings later that night. The coroner testified that the old man was hit several times with fists, kicked in the belly so hard his spleen burst, and slammed against the edge of a table hard enough to crack his skull. Whoever and whatever I have become, there is a vicious streak in my ancestry.

"Why didn't the watchman just shoot?" I asked that night on the bed.

Her big shoulders rose and fell. "Who knows? Roy was family. Jack probably didn't know whether he had permission to be in the safe or not."

"Will Daddy go to hell?" That had been worrying me a good deal.

"That's up to God." From the look on her face, if she had a vote, he would. "He killed more than Jack that night. Lila was heartbroken—both at losing Roy and because she'd known Jack all her life. We all had. Then, before his sentencing, Roy and Lila both begged Pop to plead for leniency. Lila took it hard that Pop refused and Roy was given ten years."

"Ten years?" I interrupted. "He's served eleven-and-a-half."

"At first he got into a lot of fights. Pop hoped they'd keep him forever, but Roy eventually settled down."

"But he's stayed mad at you all." That wasn't a question. I'd seen the look in his eyes when he mentioned the Marshall family.

"Yes, Roy felt he could have gotten much less time if Pop had spoken up for him. Lila cried and pleaded with him to help Roy get a second chance—she swore he'd never go wrong again—but Pop wouldn't lift a finger. I never saw him so angry—or Lila. You came the night after Roy went to jail."

Her sigh seemed to come from the bottom of our well. "You were born at an angry, bitter time, sugar." She leaned forward and laid her big hand over mine. "But it wasn't your fault. Never think it was. You were the only ray of light we had in those dark, distressing days. And after a while, Lila moved back in here. She and Pop became close again. Almost like they used to be."

Almost. I remembered *how* they were close, hugs and pats and little treats for one another, but always something in their eyes—an uncertainty in hers, a sorrow in his. "What changed her mind?"

Big Mama hesitated. Then maybe she decided it was my burden and time I assumed it, or maybe she just needed to tell this part and I was handy. Maybe she even wanted me to suffer a bit. After all, Roy was my flesh and blood. "Roy wrote Lila cruel letters from jail, accusing her of going around with other men and influencing Pop against him. He even accused her of telling on him that night."

I felt a sharp hope rise within. "How *did* they find out it was him? Maybe it wasn't!"

Big Mama's fingers plucked at a loose thread on the quilt, then smoothed it back into the pattern. "It was him, all right. Pop saw him, and they found blood on his clothes."

"Pop saw him?"

"Yes. Pop had a feeling that night something was wrong. Roy had acted funny all afternoon—coming in and out of the office on one pretense and another. When Lila came to see us and said Roy had gone out, Pop thought he might be planning to steal the petty cash. He went down to the store about ten. When he got there, Roy was punching Jack. Roy saw him and ran. Pop called an ambulance at once, but Jack died on the way to the hospital."

"Why would Daddy think Mama told on him?"

"Because she'd come here that evening, and Roy had told her not to. He claimed she guessed where he was going, and came to tell Pop. But Pop put two and two together on his own. Lila never said a disloyal word against that man her whole life. She walked around stony-faced for weeks before the trial. Even after you were born she wouldn't speak to Pop. I had to leave little bits of money around her apartment and order groceries sent in to keep the two of you from starving. Then, when you were several months old, Roy's cruel letters started coming. I found her weeping one morning. She let me read the one she'd just gotten. I think by then she realized she'd made a mistake in marrying him, but she never once said so."

No, Mama would never say so. Our family doesn't admit we've made mistakes.

"Is that why she called me Marshall instead of Harburton?"

"No. Pop suggested she take back her maiden name after the divorce. The lawyer suggested she legally change your name to Marshall, too."

"Mama got a *divorce?*" My history was getting so rewritten I scarcely knew who I was.

"Yes, when you were a year old. Both Pop and the preacher suggested she move back in here and make a completely new start."

Poor Mama, it was a finish, never a start. Years of pallid living in her girlhood room, drifting from luncheons to visits to one good work after another, dressed in organdy and voile, her eyes eternally puzzled and a little hurt.

Did she ever long to break out and go? Where would she have gone? What could she have done, with me tied on behind?

Since that night in Big Mama's room, everything I have ever accomplished has been partially in atonement for the waste of my mother's life.

Chapter 27

If I hadn't kept a diary, I would never have believed three important things all happened on the last Saturday before school started again.

First, Preston got out of the hospital. Uncle Stephen insisted that we all—Bonnie, Sue Mary, Abby, and me—take balloons and presents and have a celebration. Preston sat there like a little potentate, bristly hair standing straight up and his face all pink under the freckles. You'd have thought it was an honor to have broken your leg. He even bragged, "The doctor says it's gonna be perfectly normal, and he thinks I'm just about ready to start my growth spurt."

We got home to see Aunt Kate on the porch, bent over something covered with a quilt. Uncle Stephen screeched to a stop and shouted for Preston to wait, then he raced up the walk and took the steps in one leap. All of us but Preston pounded after him.

Rowdy lay on one side, breathing hard. His eyes were glazed, and he had a big dent in one side. Tears streamed down Aunt Kate's face and onto the quilt. "He got hit!" Words poured through her sobs. ". . . napping . . . locked in the kitchen . . . couldn't get out by himself . . . heard brakes on the highway . . . man real upset . . . carried him here . . ."

"Let me carry Preston home, and we can think what to do." Uncle Stephen rested his hand on her shoulder for an instant and stroked her cheek with one finger.

"Miss Hannah has a first cousin who's a vet," I remembered. "Want me to call her?" Watching Rowdy suffer was making my stomach ache.

I called Miss Hannah and she called her cousin. He said he'd meet Uncle Stephen and Aunt Kate at his office, even if it was Saturday. Miss Hannah came and got me, Abby, and John and took us down to her house.

When they got back that evening, Uncle Stephen said the vet had wanted to put Rowdy to sleep, but Aunt Kate got so hysterical he agreed to keep him a few days to see how he did.

"How did he get out?" I wanted to know.

"Somebody probably came in to use the phone and let him out accidentally."

Aunt Kate's eyes blazed. "I don't for a minute believe it was an accident. Somebody deliberately let that dog out, and you know it!"

Preston would have been my suspect of choice if he'd been there. Aunt Kate suspected Nancy Lamont. Neither of them ever liked that poor dog.

Aunt Kate went to bed early with a sick headache. "She's had Rowdy longer than she's had me," Uncle Stephen explained as he fed us chicken noodle soup.

"Pwease, God," Abby prayed as I put her to bed, "don't let Rowdy die. He's been good."

Aunt Kate had to get up for a telephone call. "My principal says he will need me until at least the middle of February," she came to the dining room to report. "Thank goodness. I couldn't have stood to be in the house all day without Rowdy."

Abby stood in the doorway, tousled but wide awake. "I can't stands it neither. I needs to go to school."

Meanwhile, Uncle Stephen had remembered that we'd never gotten our mail. "Go ask Pauline for the key, please," he asked me.

Miss Pauline was so engrossed watching Gorgeous George wrestle on television, she scarcely looked around when I took the key from its nail. Terrified I'd step on a snake or get jumped by a ghost, I ran across the yard and had to try three times before I could unpadlock the door. By the light of a single bulb I grabbed our three letters and dashed back to the Anderson's porch with the key.

"Did you get your package from under the counter? Had your name on it," Miss Pauline said, eyes glued to Gorgeous George.

I was tempted to wait for daylight, but I didn't get enough parcels to pretend I didn't want to know what it was. It couldn't be from Big Mama—she hadn't had time to send one.

Down under the dark counter I found a small brown package addressed to me in large crooked letters. I returned the key again and hurried home.

Inside I found Mama's locket wrapped in a note: *I tuk it by mistak. Ples forgiv me. Yur frend, Raifa.*

What prompted its return? Aunt Kate thought it was Raifa's mother, an active member of a Pentecostal church. Uncle Stephen was certain the locket got among Raifa's things by honest mistake. I didn't care why she'd sent it back, so long as I had the locket.

In a burst of gratitude and compassion I wrote to thank her, and enclosed five dollars Mr. Whitfield left with Uncle Stephen for me—an impulse I regretted almost immediately.

Part 5

The Darkness Deepens

The circle of Remember Box artifacts on my front hall floor is getting as gapped as the original Stonehenge. I carefully choose five more items: a letter, a child's movie stub from a Winston-Salem theater (cost: nine cents), a wooden cube painted to look like Bethel Church, the molting green rabbit's foot key chain, and a program for the Bethel Church Bicentennial, printed downtown.

At the time, painting those wooden cubes consumed us. Who could have guessed that one day the movie ticket stub and the rabbit's foot would loom far more significant? Those days remind me now of Big Mama's favorite hymn: "Abide with me, Lord, fast falls the eventide. The darkness deepens. Lord, with me abide." That January the darkness was certainly deepening—in Job's Corner and in the world.

Chapter 28

This is the only letter from his dad that Uncle Stephen saved. The folds are so worn, I believe he must have read it often:

Dear Son,
So good to be with all of you. You have fine children, all three of them, and Kate is a jewel. I enjoyed our talks about light and darkness, but am still bothered that you seem to equate children of darkness with those who disagree with you. When we are most certain we're right, those who disagree may be God's balance. His ways are not always exactly our ways, remember. Generally truth is somewhere between where we think it is and where they think it is. If I were you, I would look for children of darkness among those who appear agreeable, but undermine things. Darkness is most fond of masquerading as light. Think it over.

Love, Your Dad

It was appropriate that he wrote about darkness, because that gloomy January our nation was consumed by dark things: the continuing coal miners' strike, civil rights, and communism. Terrified by Preston's predictions, Abby changed her nightly prayer from "If I dies before I wake" to "If I's bombed before I wake."

The only bright spot in those dreary days was that Rowdy

came back from the vet almost as good as new. He limped, and more slouched around than bustled importantly like he used to, but that just seemed to make Aunt Kate love him more. She gave him only warm soft food and sat on the couch with his heavy head in her lap, running her hands through his thick black curls. She even moved his bed from the barn into their bedroom. I asked Uncle Stephen if he minded sleeping with a dog. "I dare not complain. If Kate sent either of us to the barn, it would be me."

Our family was consumed by Baineses. Ivy had developed a medical condition on her legs that required weekly treatment at the Winston-Salem hospital, two hours away. Aunt Kate and I couldn't see why it was the preacher's job to drive her, but it seemed to make sense to everybody else. Mr. Hugh Fred said the Session appreciated his taking on that responsibility. Uncle Stephen said it was his job to serve people however they needed it. Miss Pauline told me it was good he was around, since he was the only man in Job's Corner who didn't have to work. (That was her excuse for sending Preston over most afternoons for help with arithmetic, too.)

Most weeks Abby went along and while they waited for Ivy, she and her daddy went to parks, museums, and movies. I wished I were four.

Abby came home the first week entranced with Ivy's treatments. "Dey painted her legs blue!" Aunt Kate made Uncle Stephen promise to put an old bedspread on the car seat so the blue wouldn't rub off. To me, she confided it was because she was afraid Ivy's skin condition might be contagious. I was careful not to sit in the front passenger seat after that.

Miz Baines continued to come each day to take care of Abby and John, until one day after school when Abby met us at the door to announce with glee and a happy hop, "Daddy fired Miz Baines 'cause she spanked me. See?" She turned and pulled down her pants. Two rosy palm prints covered her round white bottom.

Aunt Kate went straight up to the study. I headed for my closet.

She sounded close to tears. "But whatever possessed you to fire her? She wasn't wonderful, but she was all we've got."

"She wasn't all we've got. I can watch the children until you're done. It's only a few more weeks, isn't it?"

Her voice was a wail. "No. They asked today if I can stay the rest of the year. I went ahead and said yes, because I assumed it would be fine. They can't find somebody else right away."

He sucked on his pipe. "Tell them to start looking. I'll manage in the meantime."

"You can't watch children and run a church at the same time."

"I talked to Pauline. She says Abby can play with Sue Mary . every morning."

"Pauline doesn't watch those girls, and you know it."

"I'll be here if they need me. And Hannah says she'll gladly keep John until we find somebody else." His chair creaked, so he must be turning back to his desk.

"I can't farm my children out in the congregation! What will the Session say? Why did you have to fire her, Stephen? Couldn't you just work things out?"

"You saw Abby's bottom. I wonder sometimes if Gert's not a bit batty. They both are."

"I'll be batty, too, if I have to stay cooped up in this house with nothing to do but clean house and be the perfect preacher's wife." She gave a little gasp. "I didn't mean that. But I've liked teaching so much . . ." Her sentence ended in a sob, and I heard the door slam behind her.

I hauled Abby to my room. "What did you do to make your daddy fire Miz Baines?"

"Nuffin'."

"You must have done something."

"Nu-huh. He told her to go home cause she 'panked me. Hard." Abby's lower lip quivered with self-pity. Her parents often switched her, but they never hit her.

I was made of sterner stuff. "Why did she spank you?"

Abby hesitated, then stuck her chin in the air. "I 'pitted on her."

"*You spat on her?*" I backed away in disgust.

Abby wasn't the least bit sorry. "Yep. I looked up her skirt and she slapped me." One hand smacked her cheek in demonstration. "So I 'pitted on her. Den she 'panked me. Hard." Her gray eyes blinked in indignation.

"You looked up her *skirt?*" I was more appalled than ever. "Does your daddy know that?"

She gave an elaborate shrug she had to have learned from Sue Mary. "I dunno."

"You do too know. It's rude to look up skirts! He'd have switched you good."

Abby's lower lip stuck out so far a buzzard could roost on it. "She looked at me all the time in de baftub. I doesn't like being looked at. Dat's why I looked at her. But she 'panked me. So Daddy telled her to nebber come back, we don't need her any *more.*" She flounced out full of self-righteousness.

I went straight in to Uncle Stephen and told him the whole story. He marched Abby over to the Baines house and made her apologize for spitting and looking up the witch's skirt. However, he didn't hire Miz Baines back. "If she and Abby have reached that stage of warfare," he explained with resignation, "nobody knows how it might escalate."

Lots of people took sides in what Aunt Kate called the Baines Brawl. Some fussed at Uncle Stephen for firing "poor Gert." Others assured him, "Gert's mama left her that house and some money. They'll get by." One confided, "Gert's not been quite right since Ivy was born."

One night at supper Aunt Kate asked, "Have the Baineses multiplied? I seem to run into one everywhere I go."

I knew what she meant. When I'd gone over to Miss Pauline's to buy a stamp, Miz Baines was in the living room talking a mile a minute—until I got there. Then things got real quiet. While Miss Pauline found me a stamp, Miz Baines pulled herself heavily to her feet and reached for a cane as thick and black as Mrs. Cameron's.

"I didn't know you used a cane," I said, trying to sound sympathetic.

She limped heavily toward the door. "My knees hurt somethin' fierce, but I cain't afford a doctor right now." We all knew what "right now" meant: while she wasn't earning.

When I went down to Mrs. Cameron's store for notebook paper, Mr. Ira was lounging against the counter telling one of his interminable stories.

"I wuz burnin' stumps"—practically the only part of farming he ever did—"when I woke up, thinkin' I smelt bacon frying. You know whut it was? The soles of my own shoes. Might near burnt myself alive!" He stopped mid-cackle as I came in. "Got an extry dime, missy?" he wheedled. "So's I can git me a RC Cola and a packa saltines? Rationin's kindly slim down to our place these days."

"Sorry, I just have two cents to my name."

He shuffled out, clearly disbelieving me. At the door he turned. "Hear you had a little trouble with your dog a while back. Dogs need to be tied outdoors, not shut up in kitchens."

As he slammed the wooden door behind him, I knew, sure as anything, that he'd let Rowdy out. How else would he know Aunt Kate had shut Rowdy in the kitchen while she napped?

I was so angry I trembled as I fished a quarter out of my jacket pocket and laid it on the counter. "What I told him was the honest truth," I informed old Mrs. Cameron. "This is Aunt Kate's. She needs bread."

"You got no call to give that old beggar the time of day," Mrs. Cameron told me. "But don't let him catch you walkin' around after dark without that dog."

Chapter 29

The most important thing in our lives that January was Bethel Church's Bicentennial Celebration—which I shorted to "the BCBC" and Aunt Kate teasingly called "the BusyBusy."

Miss Rilla had given me a hard new sonata to learn, but I wasn't getting to practice on our new piano. Evenings our living room was full of the women's food and hospitality committees meeting to plan meals and sanctuary flowers, the high schoolers rehearsing a short play, or the Session meeting to plan the celebration. At least, the Session called them meetings. I called them fights. They argued way past my bedtime over things like whether anniversary bulletins ought to be mimeographed or printed downtown.

Afternoons, groups of women painted cubes of wood into little churches to decorate tables for the dinner, Nancy Lamont hand-addressed envelopes, or Bonnie made posters to put up in merchants' windows. Uncle Stephen said it didn't make sense to heat up the whole church every day and it was good to keep everything in one place. I just wished it wasn't being kept in my practice place.

Uncle Stephen drafted me to crank the handle of the old mimeograph machine in his study, churning out invitation letters to anybody who ever darkened the door of the church. After the letters dried, I folded them and stuffed envelopes. Abby and Sue Mary licked envelopes and stamps until they couldn't stand the taste of glue. When I caught them making Rowdy lick some, I got a rag and saucer of water and finished them. Velma was no help whatsoever.

Practically the only people in the entire church—not just Job's Corner—who weren't working in our living room that month were Miss Rilla, Mr. Rob, and Mr. Ira. The Lamonts at least stayed home. Mr. Ira showed up at our house at least twice a week, stinking to high heaven and telling long-winded stories that distracted other people while they worked.

Mr. Rob worried us all sick. After Christmas he'd disappeared into his house and never come out. He didn't even come down to listen to my music lessons. I heard Uncle Stephen and Aunt Kate talking in their room one night. They were afraid he was drinking again. Uncle Stephen went to see him a couple of times, but Miss Rilla always said he didn't want to be disturbed.

It was bitterly cold and constantly raining. Uncle Stephen—who seldom complained about anything—grumbled to Aunt Kate one day that if he'd known Job's Corner got so much rain, he'd have moved to Seattle, where it was drier.

Aunt Kate said he was grouchy because he was working too hard. In addition to helping everybody else, he was working on the program. He located three Grant sons who agreed to come and say a few words. He found four missionaries who received support from or were sent out by the congregation, who would come say a few words. He had promises from Presbytery and Synod executives to come say a few words. He secured two dignitaries from Iredell County to come say a few words. It was going to be a lot of words.

"What?" Aunt Kate joked. "Nothing from the mayor of Job's Corner?" But it wasn't words that worried her. It was music. "We simply cannot permit Freda to play."

Uncle Stephen shoved his hand through his hair. "Could Carley?"

"Freda plays better than me," I objected, horrified.

"I'm not sure she does." Aunt Kate's nonchalance was higher praise than she'd normally give to my face. "But," she added practically, "we can't dethrone Freda and put in Carley. Of course, I don't know what difference it will make, given our choir. I wish Pop was still alive. He could come and do a solo."

"Too bad you can't use Jay Anderson," I said carelessly. "He's got a beautiful voice."

Thus do we unleash monsters that come back to haunt us.

Uncle Stephen took me seriously. In fact, he thought we needed to invite the entire Rock of Hope choir to join ours for the celebration. That led to the idea of inviting the whole Rock of Hope congregation, since the two churches used to be one.

"It was Carley's idea," he told the stony-faced Session.

"Carley suggested . . ." he told the uneasy choir members.

You'd have thought I was running for Miss Get the Races Together USA. Yet I had a niggling suspicion he'd had that in mind all along. Remember our first day's walk in Job's Corner? "Maybe one day we'll all worship together again," he had said. He was bound and determined it would happen at the two hundredth anniversary of Bethel Presbyterian Church in Job's Corner, North Carolina, in the Year of Our Lord nineteen hundred and fifty.

That solved one problem: Hugh Fred explained privately to Uncle Stephen that he couldn't let Freda play for the service. I heard them talking up in Uncle Stephen's office.

"It's not that I'm prejudiced." Hugh Fred's voice came clearly through the wall. "I have a lot of respect for Negroes— have a Negro foreman, in fact. He keeps the others in line, and I pay him well for that. But I don't believe in mixing the races. I believe God made us different so we can each have our own sphere."

"It's hard to disagree with a man like that," Uncle Stephen told Aunt Kate in the kitchen later that night while we all three cleaned up after supper. "Especially when both Preacher Gates up at Rock of Hope and Meek, who's clerk of their Session, say his name with reverence. Preacher Gates says Hugh Fred pays part of his salary every month and gave the building a new roof last year. He even shuts down the factory when they have a funeral."

"Maybe Hugh Fred's right," Aunt Kate suggested. "Maybe you're trying to push something that neither race wants."

"God wants it," Uncle Stephen insisted.

Her hand moved in a quick slash of disgust. "Oh, well, then. If Stephen Whitfield and God want it—"

"Everybody is going to want music at the celebration." He shoved back his hair with one hand and popped his suspenders with the other. "Think of something, Kate, can't you?"

Since I was getting credit for inviting Rock of Hope, I decided to put forth an idea I thought a whole lot better. "Ask Miss Rilla to play piano and have Aunt Kate play her cello."

"She never comes out," Aunt Kate said dubiously, drying the last pot.

Uncle Stephen wrinkled his forehead in the frown that meant he was thinking. "Maybe she would for this. I could at least ask her. What do you think, Kate? Is it worth a try?"

She shrugged. "You could ask. Hugh Fred couldn't object if Miss Rilla came out of hibernation to play. After all, as Carley said, she's his aunt—"

"—and Freda's teacher," I added.

In the perverse way of grown-ups, nobody ever remembered afterwards that I suggested asking Miss Rilla to play. Nobody ever forgot I suggested asking Rock of Hope.

And nobody ever forgot what brought Miss Rilla out of hibernation.

❧

Since I could never practice at home, I started going back over to the church, taking Rowdy. For heat, Uncle Stephen carried over a kerosene heater he'd found in the Grants' barn and taught me to light. It was a smelly thing. I hoped Rowdy and I wouldn't die of fumes.

At that time of year, twilights were gloomy. By the time I finished practicing it was often dark, so I took a flashlight to see my way home. Did I like practicing in an empty, clammy church surrounded by a cemetery? I liked it better than not being able to practice at all.

One evening I came out to find it was drizzling, a sneaky rain that worked its way down my neck as I sprinted toward the highway. I was hanging onto Rowdy's leash and busy watching for Mr. Ira, so I was seriously annoyed when the Greyhound bus squished to a stop on the other side, blocking my way. As the bus splashed away into darkness, I crossed the road and flashed my light toward the alighting passenger, expecting maybe Bonnie coming back from the dentist.

The white face and scarcely familiar voice came as a shock. "Carolina Rose!"

"Daddy?" Nobody had told me he was getting out. And what was he doing in Job's Corner? He had no umbrella, no boots, and no raincoat—just a light jacket.

"Carolina Rose!" he said again, as if getting used to it. Picking up his suitcase, he came along the verge toward me through the gloom. "Baby, it's so good to see you."

Rowdy growled and pulled on the leash as he got closer. A car whizzed past too fast and too close for comfort. I waved toward the path with my light. "We need to get off the highway."

I led the way over the tracks and onto the muddy road, then stopped. I didn't want to take steps that would show him which house was ours. But Rowdy strained the leash and barked, giving it away. Reluctantly I followed the determined dog toward our yard.

I felt a heavy hand on my shoulder from behind. "Honey. Baby doll. My very own little Carolina!" A cloud of stale cigarette fumes and onions surrounded us both.

I pulled away. Rowdy turned, barking furiously. The man backed off and held up one hand. "Steady, fella. I'm not gonna hurt her. I just came to see my little girl. Got out this morning and took the first bus here." When he smiled, stained uneven teeth gleamed in the porch light. "We're the only family we have now, honey, since your mama passed."

"Carley?" Aunt Kate had heard Rowdy. She came onto the front porch and peered through the rain. "Supper's ready." As the light from the hall silhouetted her and lit up her hair, I heard the man beside me take an appreciative breath.

"Kate! It's me, Roy!" He bounded through the puddles on the walk and gave her a hug like he'd been doing it every day for ten years. She stepped back so the porch light fell on her. I saw that her face was white, her eyes enormous.

"Roy?" she said doubtfully. "What are you doing here?"

"Came to see Carolina Rose—and you and Stephen. That's a fine man you've got, Kate. Yessir. A fine man. I thought maybe he could help me make a fresh start." At the end a little uncertainty crept into his voice. It was more attractive than his earlier brashness.

"I—uh—I don't know." Aunt Kate motioned toward the door. No Southern woman turns away somebody when she's already announced supper is on the table. "Come on in and eat. You can talk to Stephen afterwards."

Supper was an awkward meal. Abby couldn't understand why I had another daddy than Uncle Stephen, especially one not named Marshall or Whitfield, and she pouted when Uncle Stephen told her to stop asking questions and eat. Uncle Stephen was rushed because the Session was coming at seven-thirty. Aunt Kate was trying to be hospitable without being nice.

I sat there swamped in guilt. It was my fault the meal was

so awful. It was my daddy who was a killer and ex-convict, unfit for Abby to know. My being there had drawn him like a drop of honey draws a fly. God was not fair. All those years of longing for a daddy, and then to get this one! He was even less attractive out of jail than he'd been in it. His hair was newly cut but greasy, and he had whiskers in spots where he'd been too careless to shave right. I decided that from then on, I'd call him Roy.

Roy ate like a man who, if he'd ever had manners, forgot them years ago. Aunt Kate apologized that we just had fried Spam, turnip greens, home-canned peaches, and grits, but he ate like it was steak. He must have eaten half the Spam. I didn't take any. I knew that anything more solid than grits would come right back up.

"I sure do like home cooking," he said, reaching for another canned peach and drowning a new helping of greens in vinegar. "It's been a while since I ate anything this fine, Kate. It sure has. And you got two beautiful younguns."

"Thank you." She toyed with a forkful of grits and put them back on her plate. I saw her give Uncle Stephen a quick pleading look, then lean down to feed Rowdy her Spam.

Uncle Stephen pushed back his chair. "Roy, I've got a meeting in less than an hour. Why don't you and I go up to my study while the women clear away?"

Aunt Kate and I didn't move while their footsteps clumped up the stairs.

Abby jutted her lower lip. "How come Carley gets two daddies and I just gets one?"

"You can have mine," I said, shoving back my own chair. "I don't want him. Aunt Kate, why on earth would he come here?"

She shook her head. "I wish I knew, honey. I surely wish I knew."

She had John to put to bed and more ironing to do, and I had dishes. "I'll take them from the rinch water," Abby volunteered. She dragged over a chair and climbed up beside me, pestering me with questions I could not or would not answer.

We heard the dining room door open. "Stephen said I should sit here while he has his meeting. Hope that's all right, Kate."

"Sure, Roy. Does your mother know you're coming home?"

"I haven't rightly decided about going back to Shelby. Have to think a bit about what I want to do with the rest of my life."

Aunt Kate and Roy circled conversational topics like two wary dogs, avoiding me, Mama, and Big Mama. Since that was all they had in common, there were long pauses. Then I heard the strike of a match and Aunt Kate say sharply, "Please don't smoke that cigar inside. Go out on the back porch!"

He came through the kitchen and stopped to shake his head. "I sure hate to see Kate ironing and you washing dishes, Carolina. You all weren't raised to that kind of work."

"It's honest work," I said shortly, giving the grits pot an extra hard rub.

Abby turned on her chair and frowned. He chucked her under the chin, infuriating her, then ambled out the back door in a cloud of stinking smoke. His cigar glowed and ebbed like a little lighthouse at the edge of the porch. I feared, however, that we would all get shipwrecked on the shoals.

He moved off into the yard. I watched his cigar pass the window headed around to the side of the house. After a while he came back in, rubbing his hands. I was wiping the last counter while soapy water swirled down the drain.

"You'll freeze out there and get real wet in that jacket," I scolded. "Don't you have a raincoat?" As soon as I said it, I flushed. Why would people in jail need raincoats?

"Rain's stopped for the time being, Carolina." He seemed real pleased about something.

"Don't call her Carolina." Hands on hips, Abby glared at him. "Her name is Carley. Carley Marshall Whitfield."

"Marshall Whitfield?" he repeated, puzzled.

"Yes. I am Abigail Marshall Whitfield. Mama is Kate Marshall Whitfield. Daddy is Stephen Marshall Whitfield. Carley is Carley Marshall Whitfield. Tell him, Carley." Her words might be comical, but nobody could laugh at the solid mass of hostility Abby had become. I had never seen her react that way to another human being. If she'd been a dog, she'd have had her hackles raised and her teeth bared.

"Carley." Roy tried the name and shook his head. "Sounds like a boy to me. Carolina Rose, now, that sounds like your mama. Pretty and sweet." His smile chilled my bones.

"Then you'd better call me Carley. I'm not pretty or sweet." I groped overhead to pull the light chain before I remembered they'd put in a switch by the door when they remodeled. "We're done in here and I've got homework. Come on, Abby."

Aunt Kate was finishing up one of Uncle Stephen's shirts.

"Abby, honey, go hang this on our closet doorknob and get your pajamas. It's time for bed."

"I doesn't want to go to bed until Carley's daddy leaves." Abby wiggled onto the couch and sat with her legs straight out, a determined sentinel.

Aunt Kate looked at Roy. "Are you going on tonight, Roy?"

He gave her what he may have considered a charming smile. "I asked Stephen if I could stay the night. He said you have an extra bed upstairs."

I threw her a pleading look. Upstairs meant he'd be close to me.

"There's no heat in that room," she said, as if she were considering it. "You'd do better to sleep down here on the couch."

"Anywhere, Kate. This couch will be fine." He settled into Uncle Stephen's chair.

Abby sat on the couch until she literally toppled over asleep. Aunt Kate carried her to bed. Rowdy padded away with them. I sat at the table with my spelling book open, pretending my daddy wasn't there. Which was odd, when you think about how many times I'd sat there wishing he was.

Somebody in the Session must have said something funny, because we heard them all laugh. Roy stood up and dropped one hand to my shoulder in a rough caress. "Come outside with me a minute."

Outside was total blackness. I could hear little flecks of rain hitting the glass. "It's raining again. I don't want to." I bent back to my book.

His hand tightened. "I said, come with me. I want to take a little trip."

"Where do you want to go?" I was both annoyed and puzzled.

"I was thinking of Mrs. Marshall's. I haven't seen her for a very long time."

"You'll have to wait for tomorrow, then. There aren't any buses at night, and you have to call for them to stop. Uncle Stephen might even take you to the station."

His hand tightened on my shoulder. "I can't wait that long. And you're going with me. Come on, get up."

"I don't want to go." Uneasy, I pulled away. "I have school tomorrow."

He shook me roughly. "You can miss a little school. Come on. I'm your daddy. You have to come."

"No, I don't. Uncle Stephen says you can't take me without a court order." I tried to pull away again, but his grip tightened. I took a deep breath to call out, but his other hand shut off my mouth. His thumb and forefinger pinched my nose so I couldn't breathe.

"If you yell, I'll break your neck. So help me I will. We are going, and we're going now. I've put up with enough from you Marshalls. It's time I got what's comin' to me. Come on!"

He released my nose, but kept one hand over my mouth as he steered me down the hall, pausing long enough to let me disentangle my coat from the others on the hall rack. I heard Uncle Stephen's voice right on the other side of the door. I thought about stumbling to make a noise, but didn't know what Roy might do. The best thing, I decided, was to go on to Big Mama's and let her talk sense into him. Big Mama was the best sense talker I knew.

But as we went out the screened door, I banged it shut as hard as I could with one foot.

As we crossed the soggy grass I heard the jingle of keys. He must have taken Uncle Stephen's rabbit's foot key chain—the hideous green one Abby bought him for Christmas with her very own money—from its nail by the door. That's when I realized what was really happening. "You can't steal Uncle Stephen's car!"

"We're just borrowing it." He opened the passenger door. "Get in."

"No! I won't go!" I squirmed beneath his hand. He shoved me in so hard I fell across the seat. Before I could get up, he'd locked my door, hurried around, and slid beneath the wheel. As the engine caught he backed quickly. Not until we were on the road did he fumble around to turn on headlights.

I looked nervously at him, hunched over the wheel. "Do you still remember how to drive?"

"Sure, but all the buttons are in the wrong places. Where's the blasted heater? Find the heater, will you?" His teeth were chattering and his shoulders shook with cold and damp. My own teeth chattered in spite of my coat. I pulled mittens from my pocket and put them on, then leaned forward and turned the right buttons. "It takes a while to warm up," I warned, hugging myself and huddling into the corner near the door. The car stunk of his last cigar, onions, and the acrid sweat of fear. I cuddled my nose into my collar and breathed my own warmth.

As the wipers swished back and forth, my eyes stared into blackness. Not one other car was on the road. I couldn't think of a thing to say for what seemed like hours. "That's my school," I blurted without thinking, then felt dumb. I wasn't giving him a tour, for heaven's sake!

The school looked foreign and mysterious in the wetness. Other familiar landmarks slid past on the way into Statesville: our grocery store, the Farmer's Cooperative Exchange, a Baptist church that was nothing more than a basement with a roof until they could raise more money. Usually the red brick fronts looked friendly. Tonight they stood dark and aloof.

Downtown he stopped at Broad Street and looked both ways. "Which way?"

I shrugged, mystified that he was asking me. "I don't know."

"Whaddya mean you don't know? You all drove here, didn't you?"

"We drove from West Virginia. Big Mama sent me there first. When we've gone back to her house, we've always gone up the road the other way from Job's Corner."

He swore, using words I had never heard before. I cringed against my corner, feeling their lash even if I had no clue to their meaning, afraid he'd use his hands when he ran out of words. Instead, he made an illegal U-turn in the middle of the street and headed back the way we'd come. By now the heater was smelling hot. Uncle Stephen always turned it off a while when it smelled like that. Roy seemed not to notice.

We passed a solitary streetlight. His face looked yellow, set and mean. In spite of myself, I started to cry and beg. "Take me home, Roy. Please. I don't know the way to Big Mama's. We're going to get lost in the dark. Please take me home. You can go tomorrow. I don't want to go to Big Mama's tonight."

"Shut up!" he ordered, "Mrs. High-and-Mighty Marshall owes me, and you're going to make her pay."

"Pay what?" I was furious with myself for sniveling, but unable to stop.

"Plenty." The word was short and brutal. "Half the store, for one thing. Lila's half. It belongs to us." He gloated at my expression. "She hasn't told you that, has she? They don't part with their money, those Marshalls. We'll have to take what's ours."

I didn't like the way that "we" and "our" cut me out of the

Marshalls. "It's not my store, it's Big Mama's. Pop left every bit to her."

"Half would have been your mama's, if she'd lived. That half belongs to you and me, and I don't aim to wait until the old buzzard dies to get it."

That turned off my tears. "Big Mama is not a buzzard! And that store is no more mine and yours than it is—Aunt Sukie's. Now take me home this minute!"

"I'm going to take you home all right," he said grimly. "Our home. From this day on, you are Carolina Harburton. You belong to me."

My stomach ached with fear, and I needed to go to the bathroom. "Daddy." I used the word deliberately, tried to make it sound loving. "Let's go home. I'll tell Uncle Stephen you needed something from the drugstore and I went to show you the way. Please!"

He shook his head. "I'm not going anywhere but to get what is rightfully ours. You are Lila's legal heir. We deserve half of that store, and we're going to get it."

"Then let's go tomorrow. We can call Big Mama and go for lunch. Let's don't try to go tonight. We'll probably run out of gas. No filling stations are open this late."

He seemed to be considering that, but just then we crested the hill near Keene's. Down in Job's Corner, I saw the manse blazing with light. The yard was full of cars. People milled around on the porch. Two police cars flashed their lights.

Roy saw them the same time I did. Then we both saw a third police car heading back our way. He swore between clenched teeth and hunched farther over the wheel, peering from side to side. Without warning he twisted the wheel and skidded left in front of the oncoming police car, onto the road that ran past Keene's. It was a county road, dirt covered with gravel, with drainage ditches on each side. Our tires screeched as he fought the wheel and got the car steady.

"Where are you going?" My teeth felt like they'd break from being jounced around.

"Wherever this road goes, baby. Where does it come out?"

I could scarcely speak, we were bouncing so. "I-I-I've no i-i-idea. I-I-I've never been p-p-past that h-h-house over y-y-yonder."

Up the muddy red hill we slithered and raced, rounding curves so fast I thought for sure we'd end up in the ditch. Roy always recovered just in time. "Yahoo! Your daddy can drive!" he crowed as we crested the hill and started down. "Lordy, it feels good to have a car again!"

"It's n-n-not your c-c-car," I reminded him angrily. "D-d-don't you wr-r-reck it."

His sentences were deteriorating to mostly swear words, but in jubilation he spoke without them. "I'm not going to wreck it, baby. I'm just getting us out of this county. A map I looked at to get here showed Job's Corner sittin' nearly on the county line. They can't chase us past that, and it ought to be around here somewhere."

A tree loomed ahead as if planted smack-dab in the middle of the road. "Watch out!"

He veered just in time. "I told you, your daddy can drive."

His high-pitched laugh blended with the wail of a siren, faint but getting louder.

He heard it too, and swore again. "How much further to the line?"

"I told you, I don't know." All that swearing was making me jittery. Nobody I knew talked that way—not even Mr. Rob at his worst.

I peered anxiously behind. The road curved too much to see headlights, but a red flasher pulsed against the sky. If only they came fast enough!

Roy saw them too, and picked up speed again. Faster and faster we sped through that terrifying night on a road made for pickups and tractors. The poor Chevy splashed through puddles and jarred like it would fall apart any minute. I expected I might, too. If we didn't all burn up from the heater catching fire.

I stole another look behind. The red light was getting closer. Another minute or two—

Then I saw it, up ahead. A small white sign with black letters: *Alexander County.*

Roy laughed, a wild exuberant sound. "We made it, Baby! Home free in one minute!" He pressed the pedal to the floor.

Would the police be able to chase us across a county line? I didn't know. But if Roy was right, once we crossed that line, I belonged to him.

I grabbed the wheel and pulled with all my might. The car swerved, fishtailed, slid back and forth across the road, then nose-dived into a two-foot drainage ditch.

Without seat belts, we kept moving after the car stopped. Because I was holding onto the wheel, the side of my head hit the dashboard. I saw stars, heard Roy's nose hit the steering wheel. Roy swore and slammed into reverse. Wheels spun. The engine stalled. As my vision cleared I yanked the rabbit's foot and jerked the keys from the ignition. They came right out. There were no safety ignition switches in those days. Without looking first or caring what was there, I shoved open my door and leaped into icy knee-deep water.

Chapter 30

I heard his door open.

Ordinarily, could I have climbed that slippery clay bank with a throbbing head and sodden shoes? I did it without a thought. When I ran smack into a barbed wire fence, I slid under slicker than Sue Mary's Velma. Still clutching the rabbit's foot and shivering from a lot more than wet shoes and socks, I started to run.

The moon was hidden behind thick gray clouds. I could scarcely see. Wet grass caught my ankles and my feet slithered on mud. My own blood roared in my ears and my head felt light as a balloon. My side ached. My bladder burned. But I ran like an Olympic star—until I hit a solid softness and sprawled on the sodden ground.

"Mooo?" Through the drizzle, the moon slid for an instant from behind a cloud. I saw light reflected in large brown eyes. This was no field. It was a pasture. I had plunged into the back end of a sleeping cow! She smelled of warm milk with foam and sweet fresh manure, but all I could think of were horns.

Petrified, I started to my feet. Then Roy bawled behind me, "Carolina, where are you? Carolina, you come back here!"

I paused on hands and knees, biting my lips against the cut of a sharp rock under one palm, hoping the cow wouldn't gore me before I could get up and run. There was enough light for me to see the silhouette of Roy climbing over the barbed wire fence. I could hear the police car engine droning far away, but getting closer. Would they come in time?

Roy untangled his pants from the barbs and moved into the

pasture. He cupped his hands around his mouth. "Carolina! Where are you, honey? Don't run from me."

The cow shifted slightly, as if making room. Her bulk was warm and high. I crept around behind her and peered over her neck. Far across the pasture I could just distinguish Roy's shape moving cautiously nearer. I could also distinguish large mounds of other cows beneath the winter sky. There must be twenty in that field.

Most farmers had gathered their animals into the barn that drizzly, frosty night. Later we would learn that this farmer's wife had gone into labor prematurely just after noon, and he'd rushed her to the hospital. He hadn't gotten back yet, and the hired man who normally would have brought in the cows for him was away visiting his mother.

"The hand of God," Aunt Kate would maintain.

At the time, I thought it was the wrath of God for some dreadful, unnamed sin. Even as most of my mind concentrated on Roy and his movements, part remembered all the people Big Mama knew who'd been gored, trampled, kicked, or otherwise fatally injured by cows.

Temporarily, though, this cow was less terrifying than my daddy. Her back was like a big hard pillow. And warm. Crouched close to the ground, I pressed myself against her while icy rain drizzled down my neck and through my hair, spotting my glasses so I could hardly see.

Their lenses could reflect light! I snatched them off and jammed them in my pocket. Roy became a terrifying blur, my real-live movie monster.

He crept nearer, bending to lower his silhouette against the sky. "Carolina? Where are you, honey? Carolina!" You'd have thought he was the sweetest daddy in the world, out looking for his little girl in the rain.

Across the pasture another cow mooed. He must have thought I'd disturbed her, because he headed that way. Relieved, I inched lower, pressed against that soft-hard back and as close to the soggy ground as a person can get without becoming one with the grass. My cow still didn't make a sound.

"Carolina? Carolina!" His voice was getting an angry edge. "Where are you? Bring back those keys right now, you hear me?" He wove across the pasture through the cows, eventually turning back toward me and coming ever nearer.

I prayed to God and all the saints I knew. *God, please let him think I'm part of this cow. Mama, help me! Pop, please!*

"Carolina Rose! If you know what's good for you . . ." I could see him clearer now, his pants a dark softness, his jacket lighter above them. He was peering all around. If I could see him, it was just a matter of time before he saw me. I crouched lower, then dared one peep over the cow's broad back. He was coming my way!

Somewhere nearby a cow lifted her tail and sprayed. He turned quickly toward the sound, his voice crooning. "I won't hurt you, baby. Daddy was just playing with you. Come on back and we'll go to your Uncle Stephen's for the night. We can go home tomorrow. Come on out, wherever you are." He sang the last sentence like a boy playing hide-and-seek. I held my breath and prayed my cow wouldn't take it into her mind to stand up and draw his attention. She lay solid as a mountain. Whence cometh my help.

"Carolina Rose, this is your father speaking. You come here right now if you know what's good for you. You hear me? You come here right now, or I'll—"

I heard slamming doors. He heard them too, and froze.

Somewhere across the pasture a night bird called. Lucky night bird, having a normal evening prowl. With feathers to keep it warm and dry, and wings to lift it above danger and cows.

Far across the pasture, voices yelled, "Harburton? Where are you? Let her go, Harburton. You don't want her to get hurt." I could tell from the way the voices moved here and there that they had no idea where either Roy or I were—even what side of the road we were on. Roy and a million cows were between me and them. I stayed where I was, not daring to call out.

Roy bent lower as soon as he heard the voices, but still he inched along, peering here and there. He was so close I could hear the soft sliding of his feet on the grass. I held my breath so he couldn't hear me, but felt shameful hot urine flowing beneath me.

"Harburton? Harburton!" The policemen's voices went up each time they called his name. The cows started to bawl. Roy crouched not ten feet away.

PleaseGodpleaseGodpleaseGod. It was one desperate word in my mind.

Suddenly a cow heaved herself to her feet and ambled toward him. Another followed, then another. One by one a pasture full of cows humped to their feet and sidled in his direction.

"Mooo? Mooo?" They obviously hoped he'd lead them home.

"Shoo!" Roy whispered, flapping his hands. They mistook that for a signal. Their *moos* grew more urgent and excited. More and more large liquid blobs streamed toward him. I had thought there were twenty cows in the pasture. There were closer to fifty.

He swore. "Get away! Go on! Get!" His whisper was louder, and high. The cows nudged him, nosed him, shifted him this way and that. Of all the animals in the field, only mine lay silent and still.

"Harburton, where are you?"

Roy's curses rang across the pasture. "I'm being eaten alive by cows. Save me! Shoo, blast you! Shoo!" He backed away. The cows followed. He backed again. They followed again. It was all I could do not to giggle. They looked like partners in a huge odd dance. When he raised his arms, they nudged his chest and armpits with their broad wet noses. "Mooo! Mooo!"

"Stop that!" He lunged among them, and they lowered their heads. "Mooo! Mooo!" Instead of him leading them, they butted him toward the fence by the road.

My own cow turned her head. Maybe it was my imagination, but I swear I saw her wink.

One of the policemen pushed his way competently among the milling herd, slapping rumps and shoulders. "Whoa, Bossy. Whoa, Bossy." I heard a click. Had Roy been bitten by a cow?

A second car skidded to a stop. A door slammed and Uncle Stephen shouted. "Carley? Carley!" His voice floated across a distance greater than one pasture. It came from a place of safety and warmth I could scarcely remember. "Where's Carley?" I heard him ask. My teeth were chattering and I shivered in a sudden gust of rain, but I still dared not make a sound.

"Haven't seen her," the policeman on the road replied. "But we got him."

I took a deep breath and listened. Sure enough, I heard Roy snarl something to Uncle Stephen, heard Uncle Stephen demand, "But where is Carley?"

"I'm here," I called, climbing shakily to my feet and putting on my glasses. The words came out like a squeak. I coughed and tried again. "I'm over here." I stood and waved both arms like a semaphore. "Over here."

The cows started moving in my direction.

I don't know to this day how I got past all those cows to Uncle Stephen. I don't remember running. What I remember is floating about a foot off the ground. Nothing seemed very real. The only thing I do remember clearly is, before I left, I gave my cow a pat. Her wet skin quivered under my hand as if I'd been nothing more to her than a fly.

I tried to jump the ditch, but I landed short, slid down the far bank, and sat waist deep in water. Everything was so unreal that my immediate thought was, "Good, nobody will know I wet my pants."

Then Uncle Stephen reached down and jerked me out in one strong motion. To this day, that's how I define salvation: strong arms reaching down and lifting me from desperation to safety.

He skinned off his jacket and wrapped me in it. Pulled me to him and cradled my head against his starched white shirt. He smelled of pipe tobacco and home. "You all right?"

My hair was plastered to my cheeks. My clothes were sopping wet. My head ached so, I couldn't even cry. I nodded, rubbing my face against his starchy front. "I'm fine." He pressed my head to him so hard I heard his heart beating. *Tha-whump. Tha-whump.*

After a while I felt like I could stand alone, so I pulled away, heaving for air.

"You want to talk about it?" He gently touched the bump where I'd hit my head.

I felt too numb to talk, but he seemed to need to hear my voice. I looked over at his coupe, its round rump high in the air. In the flashing police light, raindrops glittered red on its upended back window. "We wrecked your Chevy," I said miserably.

He shrugged. "It'll fix. It's been in ditches before."

"I have your keys." I handed them to him like a marathon runner who'd carried her torch a hundred miles.

He took them and dangled them from the rabbit's foot, their jingle a merry discord in the grim night. "Thanks." For once, he didn't seem to know what to say.

Mr. Hugh Fred stood beside his gray Hudson. Just beyond sat the police cruiser. By its back door Roy slumped between two officers, looking at the ground. In the glow from the car dome light I saw handcuffs glint on one wrist, and a black blot on his chest from his nosebleed.

One of the policemen sloshed through the mud toward us. "We'll need to get a statement from her." He sounded apologetic.

Uncle Stephen rested one hand on my shoulder. "Could we take her home and get her dry and warmed up a little first? She fell in a ditch of water; she's soaking wet."

The policeman hesitated. "If she could just give us a quick idea of what happened, she can make a full statement to the men at your house while we run this fellow in and book him."

His voice carried through the night. Roy's head jerked up, and he looked straight at me. He tugged desperately to free his arms, but he was cuffed to the other officer. "Steady!" the policeman told him angrily.

The terror on Roy's pinched face was more than I could bear. I couldn't send him back to those doors clanging like the sound of death. "No!" I said.

Roy might be a terrible person, but he was my daddy. Whether I liked it or not, it seemed I owed him something. Not what he claimed—not half of Marshall's store—but something. The fifth commandment calls it honor. Uncle Stephen would call it a second chance. I didn't call it anything. I just knew I couldn't sleep at night if I sent Roy back to jail.

"No!" I started to babble desperately. "We were going to the drugstore to get him some toothpaste, but I didn't know the way, and I got us lost, so we started back, but we saw all the police at the house and he got scared. That's all." I had to keep looking at Roy. I couldn't look at either a policeman or Uncle Stephen and tell a flat-out lie.

A little flicker of hope crossed Roy's face, but Uncle Stephen's hand tightened on my shoulder. "Are you sure?"

I hesitated, looking straight at Roy, to *be* sure. He looked back. I could tell he was holding his breath. I nodded. "Yeah." I turned and stumbled toward Mr. Hugh Fred's backseat.

"Nobody's going to believe that cockeyed story!" Mr. Hugh Fred's voice was sharp and angry across the top of his car. "And if they do, you're going to look like a fool for rousing the county."

Uncle Stephen leaned in and looked at me. I looked back. I wished God would open the sky and say, "Carley, here's what you do . . ." But I'd had my miracle for that night. I laid my head against the back of the seat and closed my eyes so I wouldn't have to look at him.

I heard Uncle Stephen say, "We need to get her home." But nobody got in. I could hear Mr. Hugh Fred drumming his fingers on the top of the car, but I didn't hear Uncle Stephen. I peeked through my lashes and saw he'd gone over to talk to the policemen. He pulled out his wallet and handed Roy some bills. He spoke, Roy nodded, then Roy got into the backseat of the police car and both policemen climbed in front.

"What happens now?" Mr. Hugh Fred asked as he and Uncle Stephen got in and slammed their doors.

"They're going to take him to the bus station and get him a ticket to Shelby. And we're taking this wet child home."

I sat on Uncle Stephen's jacket, trying not to get the Hudson's soft plush seat any wetter than I had to. I dearly hoped I wouldn't leave any stink of mud or worse for Freda to smell the next time she got in. Nobody said a word the whole way home.

When we got there, the porch and house were still full of people, although by now the police had called on their car radio to tell them I was safe. Aunt Kate came running down the porch steps. I fell into her arms and burst into tears.

"You poor baby. If I'd even imagined—" she started.

I wanted to tell her everything—how awful it had been. I wanted to sit in her lap wrapped in a blanket and cry until all the terror was gone. But Uncle Stephen was right there, so I'd have to tell her we'd just gone to the drugstore. I opened my mouth, wondering how I'd muster the strength to lie again. But he put a hand on my shoulder, like he had the day we'd walked out of the jail. "She's soaking wet, Kate. She can talk later."

Aunt Kate opened her mouth, then looked at my face. "Come on upstairs and let's get you some dry clothes." Her voice wobbled, but she pulled me briskly through a crowd of people on the steps. "She needs a good hot bath," she explained as we passed.

"I fell in a ditch," I offered. My teeth were chattering like John's favorite rattle.

As we went through the front door I heard Uncle Stephen explaining that his car was still in a ditch. Davy Anderson offered to take him back in the pickup to tow it out.

Aunt Kate helped me upstairs to my room. I collapsed on the side of my bed. My knees seemed made of macaroni. "I'll run you a bath," she said and hurried out. In just a few minutes she came and led me to a steaming tub full of her own special bubble bath. She pointed to one of her nicest, save-for-company pink towels and her best Elizabeth Arden bath powder and asked anxiously, "Can you bathe yourself, or do you want help?"

"I can do it." I couldn't wait to scrub myself inch by inch.

If I'd hoped to remove the memory, I was doomed to disappointment. But at least I got warm and clean. Pink as the towel and warm in flannel pajamas and my robe, I came out to find Aunt Kate sitting on a straight chair in the dark hall. "Before you go to bed, you have to talk to the police. And there's somebody else downstairs you need to see, too."

I cringed. Had Roy come back? "It's a nice surprise," she assured me, smiling.

The fire Uncle Stephen had made for the Session was still going. In front of it, reflecting its glow like a fluttery dove, sat Miss Rilla!

"Oh, you really are all right," she cried, rising and hurrying toward me with hands extended. "They told me, but I had to be sure." It seemed utterly natural to hold her close. I felt her heart like a frightened sparrow beating against mine.

I gave her one last hug. "I'm fine," I said, and was surprised to find I almost was. "Weren't you terrified to come out?"

She started to shake her head, but we both knew that wouldn't be true. "Some things are so important, honey," she told me in her whispery voice, "you have to ignore your fears and just go ahead and do them." But her eyes were beginning to dart here and there, seeking safety.

In a far corner a small black shape rose and croaked. "I'll take myself off, too. Lotsa excitement for one night."

I turned, took a step toward her, then stopped. Mrs. Cameron and I were not hugging friends. "Thank you for coming," I told her. "As you can see, I'm not dead yet."

"Didn't think you would be." She stopped in the door to add, "You're too ornery to die."

❦

Uncle Stephen made me tell him, Aunt Kate, and the policeman the truth. "I know you didn't go voluntarily, honey. We won't press charges if you don't want to, but we have to file a report in case Roy ever tries to get custody."

I shuddered. "I thought if I let him go, I'd never have to see him again."

"You won't if I have anything to do with it," Aunt Kate said grimly.

I told the policeman about Roy making me go with him, and trying to escape on Mr. Hugh Fred's road. But I only told Aunt Kate about the cow. Nobody who wasn't raised by Big Mama could understand how terrifying that was.

The next afternoon Uncle Stephen, Aunt Kate, and I went over to formally ask Miss Rilla to play for the Bethel Church Bicentennial Celebration. Uncle Stephen started by telling her that Freda wasn't going to. She twittered and fluttered and indicated that she wasn't quite sure Freda was up to that kind of program either.

"It's not whether she can or not," he said bluntly, "it's that Hugh Fred won't let her. We've invited Rock of Hope to share our service—Janey Lou, Jay, our friends and neighbors. I feel that since both races were in the church at its founding, it's appropriate to celebrate the two hundredth anniversary together. But Hugh Fred won't let Freda play under those circumstances."

She pressed one hand to her gray bosom. "You want me to speak to him?"

"He's not going to change his mind, I'm afraid. What I really want is for you to play. My wife, Kate, here, plays cello, and she'd like to work up a program with you—"

She shrank back, forestalled him with one raised hand. "Oh, I couldn't. I simply couldn't."

His voice was gentle, but his words sharp. "You know that old hymn, 'Once to Every Man and Nation Comes the Moment to Decide'? This is your moment, Miss Rilla. A chance to strike a blow for justice and truth. Some do it with a hammer. Some with sermons. Your chance has come through piano keys. Won't you do it—for God and Carley?"

I squirmed, being lumped with God like that. Miss Rilla darted me a look like she wondered if I'd grown a halo. Her nose grew pink and she pressed her lips together, but I could see her struggle most clearly in her eyes. They darted in fear from one side of the room to the other, looking for a way out. Then they came to rest again on me. She clasped her hands in front of her and lifted her chin. "Yes, Mr. Whitfield. I will be honored to play for your celebration."

Chapter 31

The Bethel Church Bicentennial Celebration began at four o'clock in the afternoon on the last Sunday in January. That same day Russians started putting up blockades and inspecting all trucks into East Berlin. Thank goodness Mr. Mayhew didn't know. He might have tried to cancel our proceedings. God gave us a stamp of approval: after a week of freezing drizzle, we had a brilliant sunny afternoon.

All the ladies wore new hats. All the gentlemen came in suits and ties. All the little girls, black and white, wore starched dresses and hairbows. Aunt Kate didn't have time to get a haircut or hem up the new dress Big Mama sent, but she wore a huge smile, because Uncle Stephen had called and invited Big Mama to the celebration, and she'd come! Her black crepe and fur boa were easily as fine as Miss Emily's, but Mr. Hugh outshone all the men. He looked like a movie star in his black suit. Freda stayed home with a cold she hadn't had that morning.

Miss Hannah, in her own best black crepe, brought Mrs. Cameron in her usual black skirt and sweater, protesting and grumbling. I noticed she stayed for dinner afterwards, though.

Sue Mary came without Velma. Both arms were wrapped around her baby doll in its blue blanket. Even Miss Pauline and Preston looked presentable. She'd brushed her bushy brown hair, and he limped in on crutches wearing a blue suit and red tie. I nearly fainted.

The Baineses arrived as we did. "Howdy, Ladies," Mr. Ira said around a wad of chewing tobacco. Miz Baines's bulging look toward the head table where Uncle Stephen and Aunt Kate sat with Grant sons, Iredell County dignitaries, and Presbytery and Synod executives. Uncle Stephen was looking at those empty seats, too. He shoved back his hair and his eyes roamed the room. When they met mine, I knew what he expected.

I took a deep breath. "Big Mama, we need to sit with our guests."

She surprised me. "We certainly do." She led the way toward the empty seats at the Rock of Hope table. Feeling very self-conscious and more than a little gracious, I followed her. "May we sit here?"

"Sure thing. Sure thing." They shifted their chairs a little, as if one stout elderly white woman and a skinny eleven-year-old white girl needed more room than five middle-aged Negroes. I didn't know a soul. The burden of being a good hostess had never felt so heavy. "Your music was beautiful," I told them.

"Thank you, Miss. Thank you." They nodded and smiled, then looked down.

They were as embarrassed as I. There we sat, human beings at the same table, and couldn't think of a thing to say.

Big Mama tried. I have to give her credit. But the way she tried was by doing too much talking. She told them she was Aunt Kate's mother come from the Piedmont area. She told them about the store. She told them about raising me. She told them Mama had died. She practically told them how many fillings she had in her teeth.

Just about the time I was taking a breath to interrupt, a familiar deep voice said, "Miss Carley, may I sit with you all? Emily is busy in the kitchen, and Freda couldn't come today. She has a bad cold." My face grew red with embarrassment. I'd been avoiding Mr. Hugh Fred since the night with Roy. But either he'd forgiven me or Uncle Stephen had talked privately to him, because he acted just as friendly as he used to.

"Sure, Mr. Hugh Fred. Big Mama, this is Mr. Hugh Fred Keene. I'm sorry," I said to the others, "but I don't remember your names. I have a dreadful memory," I added, hoping their feelings wouldn't be hurt.

"I know everybody." He nodded to the three men and two women. "How you doin', Ben? Life treatin' you all right, Carrie? Good to have you with us, Cope. Wasn't that a fine program?"

He was as at ease as he was in our living room, shaking the men's hands with an affable smile. He reached for his glass of tea. "I been countin' the offering. That's thirsty work." Everybody chuckled.

Once he'd asked about each of their families, though, he didn't seem to think he needed to say anything else to them. He turned to Big Mama and they started talking about the church, Job's Corner, and Marshall's. The Rock of Hope folks spoke in low tones to one another. Stuck between the two groups, I couldn't think of a single thing to say—which anybody who knows me will probably not believe. Our meal was not what I would call a triumph of racial reconciliation. Still, we ate at the same table and had embarrassment in common, if little else.

When we got to dessert, I felt a tug on my skirt. "Carley, Carley!" Maggie stood behind my chair. I pushed back and she held out her arms. Without thinking, I picked her up just as I did when I baby-sat her. She sat facing me, one leg down each side of my skirt, holding up a chess pie. "Look, Carley, your fav'rite!" She took a bite, then held it out to me. "You can have one bite."

That tart was held in a hand I had already seen crawling all over the floor of the church. This was one Negro hand I *knew* was dirty. And Big Mama was sitting right there.

"One bite," Maggie repeated, holding it out, then drawing it back. She nibbled it, then thrust it at me, beaming.

Maybe Big Mama would disown me. Maybe I would come down with some awful disease. Maybe I'd even die. But I could not hurt Maggie's feelings. I swallowed hard and took a bite.

"Yumm!" She grinned, took another bite, and held out the chess pie again.

"Yumm!" I agreed. Bite by bite, we finished the tart between us. Then she wiggled around facing the table and leaned back so my chin rested on her scratchy little braids.

"In closing," Uncle Stephen announced, "Jay Anderson will give us a solo of a hymn that may not be familiar to most of us, but is one of my wife's favorites. Jay?"

Aunt Kate's cello played a haunting introduction, then Jay's baritone filled the basement room.

Immortal, invisible, God only wise,
  in light inaccessible, hid from our eyes . . .

Jay sang from memory, lifting his face toward the ceiling as if in prayer. I could almost see God up there, hidden behind the light. Light as bright as Miss Rilla's face seeing Mr. Rob in church. As shining as Miss Hannah when she touched her dead nephew's picture. As loving as Aunt Kate smiling at Uncle Stephen at the North Carolina line. As blinding as the moment when I realized Big Mama only sent me away because she loved me. As soft and safe as the glimmer of a cow's eyes in the dark.

Through four verses Jay's voice rose like liquid honey over the congregation while Aunt Kate's cello shaped the melody. Finally he sang, in a hushed voice,

All laud we would render, O help us to see
'tis only the splendor of light hideth thee.

We sat in a deep and reverent stillness. I felt tears sting my eyes, saw them running down the cheeks of Miss Hannah, Jay's mother, and Janey Lou.

At last a small voice broke the silence. "Are we *ebber* goin' home," Abby demanded loudly, "or are we gonna be in dis church de whole rest of our lives?"

Mortal Ills Prevailing

As I get to this place in the story, I realize that that year in Job's Corner
was a lot like my first merry-go-round ride with
Mama when I was three.

At first we circled so slowly that I saw clearly the red flower on Big
Mama's hat and Pop's chocolate ice cream cone as they waited for us by the
rail. In two leisurely revolutions I watched a woman with bright blue hair
sell a girl in a green dress a puff of pink cotton candy.

Gradually we moved faster. I had to snatch glimpses of Big Mama's
flower, Pop's ice cream cone, and the woman's bright blue hair.

Suddenly, after an unexpected jerk, we went flying. Everything became one
terrifying blur. When I think back to Job's Corner, February and early
March were that unexpected jerk before the terrifying blur.

Perhaps it is not surprising that the Remember Box contained little to
memorialize those days: a thank-you letter from a coal miner's family in
West Virginia and the label from a can of Hi-C Orange Drink.

Chapter 32

I wish I could say that after the BCBC, everybody in Job's Corner became a saint and lived happily ever after. But nobody can be good and holy in February. It's a naturally ornery month. Even Uncle Stephen changed his tune. On dreary mornings as he banged pots around, he sang,

A mighty fortress is our God, a bulwark never failing,
Our helper he amid the flood of mortal ills prevailing.

As usual, he was off-key, but the song was appropriate. We had a lot of mortal ills those days, and it was all we could do to keep them from prevailing.

For one thing, the Russians could be coming. Thanks to Mr. Mayhew, our whole school worried right along with President Truman that Russia had more bombs than we had thought. I went through my stuff and made a list of what I would take if we had to evacuate. We had bomb drills three and four times a week.

Uncle Stephen said Mr. Mayhew was ridiculous. "The biggest threat to our country right now is poverty and Senator McCarthy." He and Aunt Kate talked a lot about Senator McCarthy. I stayed in the corner of the dining room, pretending to read while really listening.

"He's crazy," Uncle Stephen raged, "but once he convinces people we've got Russian spies everywhere in the country, nobody will be safe. It'll be the Salem witch trials all over."

I lifted my head and said boldly, "If Russians want a spy

here, they ought to use Miss Pauline. She knows what's in everybody's mail, and everybody goes over there to gossip."

They totally ignored me. But I kept my eye on Miss Pauline. I discovered I could crawl under the post office and hear through cracks in the floor. I listened there most Saturday mornings, hunched up and cold, but didn't hear anything worth calling President Truman about.

The coal miners' strike was getting nasty, too. Uncle Stephen was called to come conduct the funeral of one of his former elders after somebody dynamited an engine room at a mine. He came home from West Virginia exhausted and disheartened. "John L. Lewis himself ordered the miners back to work, but they won't go. He's lost touch with his men."

One night at supper he put down his fork. "I swear, Kate, this roast is delicious, but I can't eat it for thinking how hungry some of our people are."

She set down her own fork and nodded. "I know. Maybe we ought to send them the money I make until the strike is over. We'd planned to live on your salary anyway."

"I gots four nickels dey can have," Abby offered.

"I can send them a dime a week," I added. Big Mama sent me a quarter each week. I usually put a nickel in church and spent the rest on candy.

Uncle Stephen's eyes got pink. He reached over and ruffled John's fluffy hair. "Well, Son? You got something to send?" John waved his spoon and banged it on the high chair. "Motion passes," Uncle Stephen said happily. "I cannot tell you how good this makes me feel. But do not mention this outside this room. Promise me, Abby? Carley?"

I got by without my dime each week, but when Preston talked about how rich we were with two people working, it was all I could do not to break my promise—and his head.

The next Sunday Uncle Stephen asked people to give a special offering to help coal miners' families. He collected six dollars. Mr. Wash said he wasn't giving, because the miners were being influenced by communists. Uncle Stephen was very discouraged that night. "Honey," Aunt Kate consoled him, "to them it's just a cause. To us it's people."

The following Sunday he told about a little boy named Kitt. "His daddy worked in the mines until he lost his leg and couldn't work anymore. After that, Kitt's big brother's wages were all they had to live on. That wasn't enough for them to have anything saved to get them through this hard time." He also told about Kitt's uncle Willie, who had two children just the ages of Ruth and Jimmy Lamont. "They are eating bread with cream gravy because that's all they've got." He sent the plate out again and collected nearly a hundred dollars. Mr. Wash gave twenty. "Children oughtn't to go hungry just 'cause their parents are deceived," he declared.

❧

As if Uncle Stephen didn't have enough on his plate already, Billy Graham came to Columbia, South Carolina, and split our church.

Three elders took their families one Sunday night, and Uncle Stephen said that's all they talked about at Session on Monday. They wanted to get up a special trip from Bethel to hear him. The other elders—and Uncle Stephen—couldn't see why Presbyterians needed to go hear a Baptist evangelist. Seemed to me Presbyterians and Baptists mistrusted each other without much reason. They weren't either one as bad as the other thought they were. But you wouldn't catch me saying that around Bethel—or to Big Mama, either.

❧

The second week of February, Miss Hannah got a bad cold and couldn't keep John. Uncle Stephen said he'd just keep him upstairs with him while he studied, but Aunt Kate was in tears. "You can't take him hospital visiting with you, and I will not leave him with Pauline. I'll call my principal and say I have to quit. That's the only option." She headed toward the phone.

Uncle Stephen closed his eyes. I didn't know if he was praying or just couldn't stand to think about it. Then suddenly he exclaimed, "Wait, Kate. Grace!"

Aunt Kate turned at the door. "Have you just come up with a sermon topic, or am I supposed to guess the next word?"

He spoke in short bursts. "No, *Grace*. Pearl's sister. Down behind your mother's. She was looking for a job. Maybe she'd come take care of the children!"

Aunt Kate nodded slowly, like she was thinking it over. "She might."

"If you call Mrs. Marshall tonight, she can go down and ask her. If Grace is willing, she could come in a day or two. Go call your mother!"

Grace arrived by bus on Saturday, bringing a surprise from Big Mama: a big can of a new kind of orange drink that tasted sweet as Kool-Aid and didn't have to be mixed. It was called Hi-C. We drank the whole thing that afternoon to celebrate Grace's coming, then Aunt Kate, Grace, and I had a contest to see if any of us could sing a high C. We couldn't.

Grace, unlike Raifa, was pleasantness itself. She came straight into the house, took an apron from one of several paper bags she'd brought her clothes in, and asked simply, "What you want me to do first?" For the next three years, she was a gentle smiling presence in our drafty old manse. Abby and John loved her. Aunt Kate liked talking to her about home. Uncle Stephen liked teaching her—said she was smart as a whip. And Rowdy padded after her like she was Aunt Kate.

Uncle Stephen refused to put her where Raifa used to stay, so Mr. Hugh Fred arranged for her to stay with Miss Emily's cook Miranda, who had an extra bedroom. When we took Grace that first night, Uncle Stephen said you could tell Miranda worked for the Keenes. She had heat, all the panes in her windows, and no cracks in the floor. Grace's room wasn't big, but it was all hers.

Grace hadn't been with us a week, however, when Uncle Stephen and Aunt Kate started the Clothes Washing Fight. Miranda didn't have a washing machine, so Uncle Stephen told Grace to bring her clothes to our house and wash them. Aunt Kate and Uncle Stephen fought about that every evening for two weeks, with days of icy politeness between.

I agreed with Aunt Kate. At that time, remember, only whites tried on clothes in department stores. Negroes had separate drinking fountains and rest rooms. Those weren't "new" laws to me—they were the way things had been all my life. I'd learned separation of the races right along with "stand up straight" and "be sweet, now." While the memory makes me squirm, the idea of sharing a washing machine with a Negro was about as attractive as eating from a cat's bowl. I figured Negroes felt the same.

One night while Aunt Kate was at Circle meeting, I tried tactfully to explain. "Uncle Stephen, I don't think Negroes like having to share things."

He put down one of Mr. Rob's Harvard classics. "Share what?"

"You know, things. Like washing machines."

"Oh?" He cocked one eyebrow.

"Yeah. When Aunt Sukie used to stay with me each year while Big Mama and Mama went to visit cousins in Atlanta, she brought her own sheets. I don't think she liked to sleep on ours. And she kept her dirty clothes in a pillowcase beside her bed. She took the pillowcase and her dirty sheets home with her when her nephew came to fetch her at the end of the week."

"Maybe that's because Mrs. Marshall didn't have a washing machine."

That hadn't occurred to me.

"And where did Grace wash her clothes before she came here?"

I stared at him, appalled. It hadn't occurred to me, either, that Pearl might have washed her family's clothes in the same pot she used for ours.

Late that night, Aunt Kate brought out the family cannon: "What will people think, seeing Grace carting clothes up and down the road? They'll know she's using the church's machine."

Uncle Stephen slammed his magazine down on the foot-stool. "Then I'll buy another machine and put them side by side! I will not ask anybody to wash clothes in a bathroom sink when there's a washing machine in my kitchen."

After that, Grace brought a sack of clothes down each week and washed them, but she always did it while Aunt Kate was at school.

Another thing Aunt Kate wasn't happy about was study hall. Since his accident, Preston had been coming over every day for Uncle Stephen to help him with arithmetic while I did homework. One day we got to the dining room and found two brown faces at the table. "We're going to have a study hall," Uncle Stephen informed us. "I'm still going to help you with arithmetic, Preston, but I'm also going to help Jay and Grace prepare for college."

Preston turned toward the door. "I gotta help Mama today. Can't study." He hobbled out, crutches and cast clattering against the hall floor.

I followed him and grabbed one arm. "You get right back in there and be nice!"

"I ain't gonna study with—"

"If you say that word in this house, Uncle Stephen will wash your mouth out with soap. And you can't be Christian unless you believe God loves everybody the same."

I couldn't believe it was me saying that. A year before, I'd have been heading out the door in front of Preston. It just went to show how much Uncle Stephen had gotten under my skin, whether I liked it or not.

Preston's face screwed up so tight with indignation, his pig eyes nearly disappeared. "Mama'll have a fit."

"It won't be the first time. Now you get back in that room, you hear me?"

He went, reluctantly. Jay and Grace pretended they didn't know where we'd gone, but I was miserably aware they had to have heard every word.

Every afternoon after that we had study hall.

"But what if the Session finds out?" Aunt Kate worried one night when she thought I'd gone upstairs. "You aren't paid to tutor Grace and Jay. I'm surprised Pauline lets Preston come."

"I'm paid to do the work of the Lord. He was, above all things, a teacher."

"Yes, but what if people don't understand?"

"If I limit my ministry to things people already understand, I can hang up my hat. Part of a preacher's job, Kate, is to expand people's understanding."

As if to prove his point, the next morning on the bus Preston surprised me. "Jay and Grace are all right. But don't tell Mama we study together. I told her Jay comes over to see Grace."

I didn't let on to him, but I hadn't told Big Mama, either. I suspected she might get almost as upset as Miss Pauline.

❦

On the first Sunday in March a surprise storm swooped down from the North Pole after an almost balmy winter. Most people stayed home. The rest sat chilled to the bone, clutching coats around us and wishing our old furnace put out more heat. The only thing any of us had to be glad of was that the coal miners had finally gone back to work, so coal was cheaper.

Aunt Kate said that anybody who came to church that day should have been rewarded with a sermon about how wonderful they were just to be there. Instead, Uncle Stephen preached on "Judge not that ye be not judged," illustrating his text by talking about Senator McCarthy attacking somebody named Lattimore.

"Senator McCarthy does not *know* Lattimore is guilty."

Uncle Stephen got so excited he actually pounded the pulpit. "But he's declared him as guilty as if he'd already had a trial! What if we were judged like that? Thank God we have a Judge on high who knows our every weakness and still loves us."

Mr. Mayhew got up and walked out, right in front of everybody.

"I don't like politics in a sermon," Mr. Wash said bluntly at the door afterwards.

"You oughta talk more about Jesus and less about government," Mrs. Cameron agreed.

"Hard to find a proof text for that one, wasn't it?" Mr. Hugh Fred joked, pulling his collar higher as he got ready to go out into the cold.

Aunt Kate was as mad at Uncle Stephen as he was at Senator McCarthy. In their room after dinner, I heard her warn him, "You'd better be careful. It's not just Negroes they lynch. It's preachers, too."

While I washed the dinner dishes and Grace dried (we got no invitations that Sunday), I told her about the sermon, then muttered, "Uncle Stephen better watch out, or he's gonna get in trouble."

Grace's laugh was pleasant as music. "Your uncle is a living saint. But saints sometimes forget God's love is too hot for folks to tolerate when they're frozen in their opinions."

"That is true," I agreed, dumping the silver into the dishwater. "And Uncle Stephen doesn't understand how some people think, either. People like Big Mama, for instance. I mean, I know she's a little prejudiced, but—"

Grace whirled on me, dishtowel flying. "Don't you say one word against Mrs. Marshall! She's been kinder to Pearl than any living soul, colored or white." She looked around to be sure we were alone, then lowered her voice. "Pearl owes her very life to Mrs. Marshall."

I stood like a statue, supporting my arms in the dishpan. "She does? Why?"

"Don't you be tellin' Pearl I told you this, mind, but Pearl got married when she was just fourteen. Her man was over forty, and he beat her something awful—even when she was carryin' Geena. Our folks worked one of your granddaddy's farms, and Mama was so upset, she told your granddaddy about Pearl. He told Mrs. Marshall, and she got in her car and drove right to where they were livin'. She told Pearl if she wanted a place of her own, they'd build her a house behind them and find her enough work to support her and that baby. Mrs. Marshall paid the doctor when Geena was born, and all these years Pearl's had that house rent free. Don't you say one word against her in my presence, you hear me? And look how she's taken in Aunt Sukie!"

That made no sense. "Aunt Sukie works for her," I pointed out, wanting to be fair. "She's the one doing Big Mama a favor by living there."

"Don't you believe it. Sukie's gettin' past it. And now that she can't hardly remember her own name, her kinfolks won't have a thing to do with her. If Mrs. Marshall hadn't taken her in, she'd have had to go to the county home. Mrs. Marshall is another living saint."

I wrote in my diary that night: *Growing up is supposed to make you wiser, but the more I learn about people, the more confused I get.*

We had a bright moon that night. I sat a long time that night looking out my windows at the cemeteries across the road. I wondered if all those people got wise before they became skeletons.

But Job's Corner had skeletons in other places besides the cemetery, and one of them was fixing to come out real soon.

Part 6

On the Wings of the Storm

It is late at night. So few things remain in the sacred circle that it is mostly a memory, like Job's Corner. Seeing my hall floor, a stranger would think I've just grown untidy.

I pick up the tiny organdy gloves and the two manila envelopes that shocked Abby, then I return one envelope to the floor. Carrying the other, I wander into my living room, turn on a light, and begin to read.

But the clippings don't tell the whole story, and that's what Uncle Stephen has asked me to do. With great reluctance I go back to my desk. Now I must face the beginning of the time I have tried so hard to forget.

Chapter 33

One day in the middle of March while I was practicing piano, Abby came in, sprawled on the living room floor, and drew a whole page of small tan circles.

"What are those?" I asked when I noticed.

She pulled her tongue in from one corner of her mouth. "God's Cheerios."

"His what?" I must not have heard her right.

"His Cheerios. You know—" She took a breath and sang in a deep little voice, "His Cheerios of wraf de deep tunderclouds form, and dark is his paf on de wings of de storm."

When years later a revised Presbyterian hymnal rendered those lines "The chariots of heaven" and "bright is his path," Uncle Stephen shook his head in dismay. "Sweetness and light religion, that won't face either God's wrath or life's storms. If they'd ever experienced a real storm they'd know it's through the darkness God comes, not in brightness." I didn't reply, but I knew what storm he was talking about. I'd spent a lifetime trying to forget it.

Its wings were beginning to beat around Job's Corner that March morning of 1950. In only a few days they would sweep us all into the maelstrom. And when God came—if God came—it would have to be on a very dark path.

Unable to hear approaching wings, I stared at Abby in astonishment—not because she'd confused chariots with Cheerios, but because I had never realized how well she could sing.

"Come here a minute." I pulled her up onto my lap. "Sing 'la' on that note." I touched middle C.

"La," she obliged on pitch.

"Now sing this one." I touched an F. Again her pitch was perfect.

"You're a real singer!" I told her, just like Pop used to tell me. "Let's do a scale together."

One by one I took her through all his exercises. She leaned her head against my chest, just like I used to lean mine against his.

I don't know how long we'd have sat there if Ira Baines hadn't pounded up the porch steps screeching breathlessly, "Call a nambulance! Call a nambulance! Ivy's took bad!"

Aunt Kate hurried to the telephone. "I'll call Emily, too."

Uncle Stephen was already on his way out the door. Mr. Ira followed him, rocking from side to side. His upheld arms looked like windshield wipers searching for a car.

I ran, too, Abby at my heels. But remembering the day Preston got hurt, at least I stopped to grab our jackets. By the time we got to the porch, Uncle Stephen's long legs had carried him halfway across the tracks and Mr. Ira was at the road. Neither noticed us following them.

"Where you goin'? What's happenin'?" Preston hobbled across the tracks just behind us. His cast was off, but he still limped.

"Ivy's took bad," Abby told him verbatim. "Mama's callin' a nambulance."

Uncle Stephen and Mr. Ira went right in the front door. I stopped at the edge of the lot. The big black dog lunged on his chain, begging for a chance to be allowed to eat us alive.

"Come on," Preston waved one warty hand imperiously. "'Round back. We can see from there." He led us around the house and pushed through some bushes. Under one window was a wooden Coca-Cola box. In those days, you bought Cokes in a red wooden tray with sections for twenty-four small bottles. Those trays had wonderful uses. Uncle Stephen kept sorted nails in one in the barn. Aunt Kate kept cleaning supplies in another under the sink. This one made a step wide enough for three if we all crowded, and we had a good view of Ivy's bedroom.

"What is it? What is it?" Abby kept asking, jumping up to see better.

"Hush," I warned her. "If you keep making that racket, your daddy will send us home."

Ivy was doubled over on the bed, clutching her stomach and

He stepped back and lit a cigarette, blew smoke across the yard. "She's buying bonds for you to go to college."

"How on earth do you know a thing like that?"

He laughed, a secretive little sound like we shared a dirty secret. "I got a friend in the bank. She tells me things."

"Well, nobody's told me. And even if it's true, they're for college. That's years away."

"He—heck, baby, I can double or triple them before you're ready for college. You call and ask her, okay? Tell her to send you those bonds, you need them real bad."

Pop used to say fools light their way by the gleam of somebody else's money. For the first time, I understood what he meant.

Roy tossed his cigarette into the grass without even bothering to stamp it, then leaned down with both hands on his thighs, peering into the playhouse like a coiled snake. "I need that money by Thursday afternoon, Carolina Rose. I got someplace to go right now, but I'll be back. If you call her tonight, she can mail the bonds and you'll have them by then. See you Thursday." He turned and strode toward a rusty green Ford parked up by the cotton field.

I could hardly wait to talk to Uncle Stephen, but he came home from the hospital very late. As soon as Aunt Kate heard his car she said, "Abby, run tell Daddy dinner's on the table. He's got Session in twenty minutes."

"I'll go," I offered. I could at least tell him we needed to talk. But one look at his face and I changed my mind. "Is Ivy worse?"

"No, she's coming home tomorrow morning." He spoke so shortly, I knew he didn't want to talk right then. I'd have to wait until after Session, if I could stay awake that long.

While Aunt Kate was putting the children to bed, I crept to the telephone three different times, but I didn't have the courage to call Big Mama. Besides, I didn't know how.

When Uncle Stephen finally came home, I started downstairs, but he called in the hall, "Kate, come to our room. We need to talk."

I missed the first part. By the time I got to the door, their voices sounded real worried.

"Who does the doctor think it could it be?" Aunt Kate asked.

"God only knows," Uncle Stephen replied.

"Gert must know."

Uncle Stephen grunted. "She's the most transparently malevolent woman I've ever met."

Aunt Kate's voice was muffled, as if she were pulling her sweater over her head. "Evil incarnate. Years ago she'd have burned at the stake."

It took me ages to look up all those words. It turned out they were just saying what I'd known all along: Miz Baines was a witch.

❋

Ivy got home Tuesday morning. After my piano lesson, I went to the old cemetery, determined to curse Miz Baines in the name of the Lord. We'd been studying Elisha in Sunday school, and I'd been impressed with what happened when he cursed jeering little boys in the name of the Lord: two she-bears came at once and tore them up.

Mr. Mayhew talked about how the bear stood for Russia and God was about to tear it up for laughing at the United States. I didn't pay much attention. I was wondering what would happen if I cursed Preston in the name of the Lord. But if even Aunt Kate admitted Miz Baines was evil, this seemed far more urgent. If I succeeded with Miz Baines, I'd move on to Preston. I pictured myself as a Wonder Woman for Jesus, wiping out evil on every hand.

I was delighted to see Miz Baines chopping kindling while Ivy rocked in her chair. The old witch had her back to me but was so close I could see a rim of dingy slip and purple veins behind her knees. Good. I should be able to curse her thoroughly.

Squatting behind the cemetery's drystone wall, breathing the very dirt that might have been there two hundred years, I pointed a finger through a crack, closed my eyes, and said in a low, fierce murmur, "Wrath of God, fall upon yon sinner! Smite this wickedness from off the land. In Jesus' name, Amen."

I opened my eyes to disappointment. The only change of scenery was Mr. Ira, shuffling between us off to his field with a can of kerosene clutched to his chest like he was Moses carrying the commandments.

I crouched for several minutes, scarcely breathing, but nothing happened. Miz Baines just kept swinging that axe as powerfully as any man, her old black shoes rolling to each side like she straddled a steep roof.

When she stood erect I held my breath, expecting a bolt of lighting to ignite the sagging black cardigan she wore against the mild March wind. Instead, she pressed one hand to her back, straightened up a bit, shoved back a wisp of long white hair that had escaped her bun, and called, "You doin' all right, Ivy?"

"Doin' all right," Ivy said in her flat voice.

"That's good."

I knelt until my knees were numb, but not one thing happened. Finally I left, disgusted. Being a prophet of the Lord was harder than I'd realized.

I was crossing the front lawn of the church on my way home when I saw Preston take our path, then turn up along the tracks—where he was definitely not supposed to be. I darted behind the thick trunk of the church magnolia and watched. He laid one of Sue Mary's favorite baby dolls on the rail! Then he rubbed his warty hands together, snickered, and hobbled on across the highway and up toward Baines's. He must be carrying a message or mail from his mama.

The idea of going down those tracks away from the path made my stomach ache, but I listened carefully. Hearing neither a whistle nor a hum of track, I dashed along the cross ties.

As I snatched up the doll and headed to return her, I told her sourly, "I should have started with Preston after all."

Chapter 34

The next morning—Wednesday—I opened my eyes in confusion. My clock said I didn't have to get up for more than an hour, but down on the porch below my windows somebody was pounding on the door and calling in a voice too blown and hoarse to recognize. "Mr. Stephen? Mr. Stephen!"

I flung off my covers and flew downstairs, the floor chilly under my warm feet. By the time I reached the front door, Uncle Stephen was opening it. Jay Anderson fell over the threshold and stood gasping for breath. "Sorry to wake you up—"

His long thin face was no longer mahogany, but a dull, ashy gray. And he didn't need to take off his green corduroy cap. He wasn't wearing it. That was practically the first time I'd known him to go outdoors without it. The smells of spring came in with him—moist earth and new growing things pushing up through damp rotting leaves. Uncle Stephen shut them out as he closed the door.

"You didn't wake me. I've been for a walk and made coffee. What's wrong?"

Jay panted and trembled, trying to get it out. "It's Mr. Baines. He's—he's—" He shot me a quick, uneasy look. "Dead! Lyin' in the woods up behind his house!"

"Steady, man. Steady." Uncle Stephen gripped his shoulder and spoke low and calm. "Take a few deep breaths. Carley, go get him some water." While he was talking he led Jay into the dining room and pushed him down into a chair.

Rowdy was finishing his breakfast as I filled a glass. Jay

drained it in one gulp and handed it back. "Thanks." He took a deep, shuddering breath, then seemed to be waiting for something. When Uncle Stephen looked at me, I knew what.

I stood like a hat rack. "Go on back to bed," he commanded with a jerk of his head. "This has nothing to do with you."

Nothing to do with me? I trembled to think how wrong he was—and what he'd say when he found out. I knew exactly what had happened. When I'd called down the wrath of God on Miz Baines, Mr. Ira had walked between us. Whatever angel was in charge of those things had misunderstood who I meant. But how could I explain? And if I didn't get a move up the stairs, the wrath of Uncle Stephen was fixing to fall on *me*.

I edged toward the stairs and climbed as slowly as I dared. Before I got to the top Jay was pouring out his story. I rounded the newel post, sat down, and scrunched close to the rails, tugging my nightgown over my shins and curling up my toes as I strained to hear.

"I was runnin' to catch my ride and saw somethin' lyin' in the woods by his field, just at the edge. I thought it was a log or somethin', but when I got closer, I saw it was him."

"Did you touch him? Was he stiff?"

"Yeah, stiff. Cold too. Cold as—as a frog. He's dead, no doubt about it."

I heard Uncle Stephen hurry to the hall, then the clicks as the dial circled to 0 and back. In just a few seconds he started talking real low. I only caught a few words. "Whitfield . . . pastor of Bethel Church . . . Job's Corner . . . dead man . . . field behind the church. Thank you." He hung up with a click and returned to Jay. "Before they get here, come show me where he is. Just let me get something to cover him with."

Nobody else in the house seemed to have heard a thing. I went back to my room feeling very alone, and sat shivering on the side of my bed. Golden fingers of sunlight reached through my windows and inched across my pink chenille spread, but they didn't warm me. My soul and body were slowly freezing from the outer edges in. I hadn't liked Mr. Ira, but I hadn't intended for him to die. What would God do to somebody who called down his wrath if it landed on the wrong person? Was I guilty of murder? Shivering and terrified, I waited in dread for fire from heaven.

Uncle Stephen preached once about fire from heaven. He said it came to burn, destroy, and purify. He'd tried to make us think it was a good thing, that it would leave us better than before. I had no such illusions. I knew it would pulverize me.

When I heard them come back, I hurried back to the railing. I wanted to run down and ask, "How did he look? Was he burned to a crisp?" But if I did, Uncle Stephen would just send me back to bed again. I sat down and leaned hard against the banisters with my hands clasped around my knees.

They went to the dining room and closed the door. I heard noises that meant Uncle Stephen was bringing coffee. I waited until he was back in the dining room before I crept down and pressed my ear to the door.

Jay sounded impatient. "I told you, I was goin' to catch my ride, and it's a lot closer through the woods and along the edge of Baines's field than around by the road. I was a little late for my ride—omigosh!" I heard the soft smack of his palm against some part of his body. "They won't know what's happened to me. I gotta let 'em know so they'll go on and not *all* be late." He dashed toward the door. I fled to the bathroom, my heart pounding.

Uncle Stephen caught him as he opened the door. "They've probably gone by now. I'll call Mr. Keene and explain." I hid in the bathroom, heart pounding that he'd find me there.

He didn't tell Mr. Hugh Fred about the body, just said, "Jay's had an emergency and isn't going to be able to come in today. All right? And would you tell the men he usually rides with? Thanks." He turned back and draped one arm over Jay's shoulder. "Now let's have another cup of coffee while we wait for the ambulance and the police." He shut the dining room door behind them.

"Police?" I heard Jay's voice rise an octave on the last syllable. "Why do we need police?" I hurried back out to listen.

"I'm pretty sure they come for any unexplained death."

"I don't want to talk to any *po*-lice." That time Jay gave it the usual Negro accent on the first syllable. "You tell 'em what they need to know. You saw him. He's just lying there. Probably fell asleep and died without ever waking up."

"But you found him. You'll have to tell them about that."

Jay's voice rose in fear. "Please, Mr. Whitfield, you talk to 'em. Pretend you found him on your walk. Please! A dead white man and a black man right there? They're gonna think I killed him!"

"Shhh!" Uncle Stephen warned. But our house was as silent as if everybody was dead.

Uncle Stephen sighed. "I don't think anybody would be big-oted enough to accuse you just because of that, Jay. But I'll stay right with you. And before they come, let's practice a few times so you can tell them without being nervous. All right? Tell me the whole story again. You were running to catch your ride . . ."

I hurried to my room and pulled on the first clothes I came to. I didn't care that I was wearing a green sweater, red plaid skirt, and blue socks. I dragged my comb through my hair and tiptoed downstairs, carrying my saddle oxfords. When I smelled coffee, my stomach growled, but I just hugged my middle and hoped I wouldn't starve before I got back. I simply had to go. Like Nancy Drew, I needed to look for clues, and this might be my only chance to see what I and the wrath of God had done.

I paused on the porch only long enough to put on my shoes, then hurried over the path to the church. We'd been having a spell of fine weather, but that morning was crisp with a sharp wind. Once I crossed the road, I was careful not to place a foot before I'd examined the ground for clues. But I didn't see a thing except rocks, leaves, and red dirt.

I shivered as I cut through the old cemetery, making a bee-line for the Baines's field behind their house. Not that it was much of a field—the only cultivating Mr. Ira ever did, as I said once before, was burn stumps. His "field" looked more like a war zone than a growing place, a desert of weeds growing around blackened stumps that once had been trees shading a pasture.

As I climbed the drystone wall into the edge of their yard, I scraped the skin off one of my knees. It stung so badly that I stopped to lick it, my own blood salty to my lips. The Baines's man-eating dog bayed in frustration that I was out of biting range. I hoped Miz Baines wouldn't come out to see who was riling him. My knee hurt too bad to run.

A little stand of trees separated their yard from the field, and the trees smelled fine that morning, all piney and cold. The kind of air you want to swallow whole. But I didn't have time to linger.

Just at the edge of the trees I saw Jay's hat. He must have dropped it when he ran. Picking it up, I slapped it against my leg as I walked. Then I came to a dead halt.

Mr. Ira was easy to spot. He was halfway across the field, a long lump under Aunt Kate's best sheet, looking like a covered log among all the burnt-out stumps. Aunt Kate would kill Uncle Stephen when she found out he'd taken that sheet.

Before I approached the body, I circled that edge of the field, carefully looking for clues. But I couldn't see any sign of angels. All I found was a short red strip of caps Preston had dropped sometime (not too long ago, they hadn't been rained on) and the top from a bottle of RC Cola. I suspected that had been Jay's. Jay was partial to RC. Finally I had to admit I was just putting off what I had to do.

Nancy Drew was braver than I. My stomach cramped at the thought of lifting that sheet. I took a couple of steps back, thinking maybe I'd just go on back home. But if I did, I knew I'd regret all my life that I'd not taken at least one peep. Slowly I waded through the weeds. Burrs caught my socks as if to pull me back. A crow circled overhead, cawing a warning.

I shaded my hand to watch him, flying around without any worries. What did he care if Russians were building bombs and angels of the Lord were smiting people right and left?

Then I looked more closely and saw it wasn't a crow, it was a buzzard making wide lazy circles, waiting for me to leave so he could land. In the distance I saw a black speck I knew was another. How did they know to come?

"Shoo! Shoo!" I shouted, waving my arms. The first buzzard circled upwards, but would not go.

My stomach was aching so bad I could hardly stand it. Holding one hand to my midriff to lessen the pain, I bent and lifted one corner of the sheet. Saw manure-spotted shoes. Dropped the sheet and moved to the other end where his head must be. I had to stiffen my spine and all my resolve to lift that sheet again.

Mr. Ira looked like he'd just lain down and not gotten up. Nothing looked singed. I sniffed and couldn't smell anything burnt—just Mr. Ira's regular stink with a few other nasty smells besides. He hadn't bathed since I'd seen him the day before, or shaved or combed his hair, either. His chin was covered with a white stubble, and his sparse hair stood out around his head like a white ruffle.

Then I noticed his eyes. They were all milky, and they looked straight at me!

I took a quick, horrified step back. My foot slipped on a damp leaf. I fell sideways onto my sore knee, and as I flung out one hand to break my fall, I hit Mr. Ira's shoulder.

Stiff as a baby doll, his whole body turned slightly to one side. Now I could see black dried blood matting his hair in the back.

What I had to do next revolted me, but I had to see. I had to know before anybody else. I had to turn him right over and see how bad it looked.

Angels of the wrath of God didn't always use bolts of lightning or tongues of flame. This one had just given Mr. Ira a good hard whack on the head.

A fierce green taste boiled up my throat. I jumped up, staggered back, and let it pour out. Then I stood wiping my lips on my sleeve and feeling like I ought to apologize to somebody. "I'm sorry!" I whispered, looking beyond the buzzard to the low gray clouds. "I am almighty sorry."

Mr. Ira looked pitiful, lying there all stiff on his side with a dent in his head and his hair all black and bloody. When I noticed Jay's hat lying where I'd dropped it when I fell, I fetched it and laid it on the ground, then—holding my breath and hoping I wouldn't pass out beside him—I turned Mr. Ira back over so the cap cushioned his wound. Even if *he* couldn't feel anything, I felt better knowing he wasn't lying on the bare ground.

I stood looking down at him feeling like I ought to do something more. "Rest in peace," I finally said. That's what the preacher said at Mama's graveside.

I tugged the sheet back over him and smoothed it as best I could. At that minute I was so numb I didn't feel a thing, but as I was going back through the woods I started trembling so bad, I had to hold onto a pine tree to keep from falling. Tears streamed down my face. "I didn't mean to," I sobbed to the rough bark. "I didn't mean it to be this bad." In that black minute, I thought of Judas weeping on Good Friday. "I'll be good forever," I promised that pine tree. For the first time, I saw that consequences can be so much more terrible than we intend.

I crept back to the house, feeling soggy and limp and hoping nobody had seen me. I didn't want to ever detect anything again. Nancy Drew books never mentioned how it took all the starch out of you. I had to lean against the hall wall before I had enough strength to climb the stairs to my room. Behind the closed dining room door, Jay sounded like he was getting tired of telling the story. ". . . edge of the woods, like you saw him! Like I said, I thought he was drunk."

"Has he slept out before when he was drunk?"

"Lots of times. Miss Gert always goes lookin' for him when it's really cold, but I guess last night she didn't bother."

"Maybe you'd better tell them that."

I heard a chink that meant somebody had put a cup back in its saucer.

Uncle Stephen prodded. "So you saw him. What happened next?"

"I went over and saw his eyes were wide open, staring at the sky. I didn't think too much about that, because Mr. Baines can be a bit peculiar."

"They won't like you saying that. Just tell them what you did."

"I said, 'Mornin', Mr. Baines,'—but unless they know how peculiar Mr. Baines is, they'll think I was nuts, talking to the man like I thought nothin' of him lyin' there looking at the sky when he ought to be home in bed."

Uncle Stephen sounded like his patience was wearing thin. "Just tell them what happened, Jay."

"*Nothing* happened! He didn't move, not even flick his eyes, so that made me go closer. That's when I saw his eyes were all milky, like—you saw them. You know."

"I know," Uncle Stephen agreed. "So what did you do then?"

"I bent down and shook his shoulder, but it didn't feel right. It was like shaking a . . . a block of wood or something. His whole body moved, all one piece. My auntie was like that after her stroke, so I thought maybe he'd had one, too. I knelt down close and touched his cheek. That's when I knew he was dead." His voice rose again. "So help me God, Mr. Stephen, anybody who'd touched him would know he was dead."

"And you came straight here, right?"

"Yessir."

"But you did touch him?"

"Yessir. I shook him once, then touched his cheek just that once. But the po-lice aren't going to believe me. They're gonna think I killed him. You know they will!"

"Nobody killed him, Jay. Like you said, he probably just lay down drunk and never got up again."

"But what if he didn't? What if somebody hit him or something? We never thought to turn him over. What if . . ."

The dining room grew so still I felt like time had stopped. Then a chair shoved back. I poised to bolt, but Uncle Stephen just took a couple of turns around the room. I knew it was him because he walked heavier than Jay. At last he said, "I hate to admit it, but you could be right. We can't go back over there again, but I wish we'd looked more carefully. Just for the record, you didn't kill him, did you?"

"No, I did." The words were out of my mouth before I knew they were coming, but so soft only I heard them. I knew what I had to do, though. I put my hand on the knob.

Before I opened the knob Jay said, "On my honor, Mr. Stephen, I never touched him. What cause would I have to hurt Mr. Ira?"

If I hadn't known how serious this was, I'd have thought Uncle Stephen laughed. "Almost everybody around here has wanted to throttle Ira a time or two. I still think he just lay down and died, but if he didn't, the police will find out who did it. You don't need to worry." I took my hand from the knob. I didn't know how the police detected the work of the angel of the Lord, but there was absolutely nothing to connect me to the angel.

I heard a chair scrape as if Uncle Stephen was resettling the room, the way people do when they are finished with a talk and getting ready to leave. "But let me ask Davy Anderson to run you up to work, and I'll talk to the police. If they still want to talk to you, they can come back tonight."

"I can't go to the fact'ry! I'd be seeing Mr. Baines's face all day long. I'd saw my hand off or something!"

"If you stay here, you're going to spend the day talking with the police. Do you want to do that?" Jay didn't answer. "Go on to work. I'll explain how you came across him on your way to work and came straight here to report it."

Before I could get away, Uncle Stephen had opened the door. But he came out so fast he didn't notice me until he started dialing. When he turned around and his eyes met mine, he couldn't have looked more startled if I'd been Mr. Ira's ghost.

I turned and hared up the stairs.

❊

Uncle Stephen wasn't home when I got back from school. I was frantic to talk to him about Roy, who would be arriving in twenty-four hours looking to collect a fortune I didn't have. Grace said Uncle Stephen was over at the church, but when I crossed the highway, I saw wisps of blue smoke floating in the old cemetery. I found him smoking his pipe, one knee propped on the old stone wall at the back corner. I moseyed over to join him. Between the trees of the woods I could make out pieces of Mr. Ira's field.

"What you doin'?" I asked cautiously, wondering if any whispers of my curse lingered to reach him.

He nodded towards the field. "Watching the police do their job."

For the first time I noticed two officers. One was crawling around in the weeds. Another was at the edge of the woods, carefully examining every trunk. "What're they looking for?"

Uncle Stephen wasn't as bad about keeping things from children as Big Mama and Aunt Kate. "They've discovered that Mr. Baines was murdered. Somebody hit him hard with a stick of wood. Now they are looking for clues."

I pictured huge angel footprints in the weeds. "What kind of clues?" I asked cautiously.

"Oh, threads from a sweater, maybe, or footprints."

I stared at the woods, terrified. Had I left a thread from my sweater when I hugged that tree? Would they be able to tell it was mine? For the moment, getting rid of that sweater seemed more urgent than talking about Roy.

I whirled around. "I gotta do homework. Bye."

"Wait!" I turned back at his shout. "We don't want children running around alone until this thing is cleared up. I'll walk you back."

"It's okay. I'll run fast. You can see me all the way home." I could feel Uncle Stephen's puzzled gaze as I hurried as fast as you can run through a humpy cemetery full of tombstones.

In my room, I examined the sweater I'd pulled on that morning. Sure enough, on one sleeve I saw where rough bark had pulled the yarn. Had I left some telltale threads? Quickly I thrust the sweater between my mattress and springs and smoothed the pink chenille spread. If the police came, I would pretend I was sick and couldn't get out of bed.

As I gave the spread one last pat, something fell through the springs: Raifa's letter, from our first day in Job's Corner. The police might examine wastebaskets. I didn't want them asking Aunt Kate or Uncle Stephen whose letter it was. Quickly, while Aunt Kate was pouring Hi-C in the kitchen for herself and Abby, I slid into her room, opened the lid of the Remember Box, and shoved the letter inside. I didn't think Aunt Kate would permit the police to look inside her private box.

Uncle Stephen came home at dusk, his hair standing on end. "They've taken Jay downtown for questioning," he told Aunt Kate without even kissing her hello.

"Why?" My voice was just a scared squeak across the dining room.

He popped one of his suspenders. "Heaven only knows. I explained until I was blue in the face that Jay just found the body and came straight here, but the police said they have a few unanswered questions."

He turned away.

"Wait—" I still needed to tell him about Roy.

"Not now, Carley. I need to go upstairs and work on my Easter sermon until dinner."

I went out to the twilit front porch and sat in the swing in spite of the chill. In a perverse way I even enjoyed feeling my bones turn to ice. If I told the police I killed Mr. Ira by unleashing the angel of the Lord, did that make me a murderer? I wasn't any better than Roy.

Roy. I suddenly remembered how he'd grabbed Mr. Ira by the neck and threatened him. What if he'd stayed around the neighborhood and killed him, to protect me? He'd already killed one man.

Swinging slowly on the darkening porch, I first faced the dilemma that would haunt me for days to come. Either I'd killed somebody by calling down the wrath of God, or my daddy had killed him and I'd have to dishonor him by turning him in. In one case I might have to go to jail. In the other, I'd be breaking a commandment and surely go to hell.

I went inside with the worst stomachache I'd ever had. All evening I stayed in the kitchen with Grace, who walked around like somebody in a trance, not singing a note. I went to bed knowing that Thursday would be even worse than Wednesday.

Thursday, Roy would come.

❧

I didn't hear a word my teacher said all day. I couldn't swallow a bite of my lunch. Coming home on the bus, I decided I'd lock myself in my room. When Roy came, he'd have to talk to Uncle Stephen. But Uncle Stephen wasn't there.

I didn't want to put Aunt Kate, Abby, and John in any danger, so I took a book out to the swing. It was the kind of warm spring day that generally made me glad to be alive, but I'd gladly have traded it for a raging blizzard blocking all roads west. Instead of reading, I sat there practicing things I would say to Roy about why I didn't have the money, and steeling myself to scream down Job's Corner if he tried to make me go with him. I felt like a tethered goat waiting for the lion.

Roy didn't come.

That evening we had a communion service at the church to remember Maundy Thursday, the night they arrested Jesus. When we got home, Grace was standing at the screened door waiting for us. In the dim porch light, she looked like a gray ghost.

"Mr. Stephen, you gotta do something. They've taken Jay to jail!"

Chapter 35

The next day was Good Friday, so we didn't have school. At breakfast, Uncle Stephen sat with his head hanging over his cereal bowl. "I feel like Judas." He picked up his spoon and laid it right back down without eating a bite. "If I just knew why they kept asking me about going over there—if I knew what evidence they think they have—if they'd just talk to me—"

"Talking doesn't always work, Stephen," Aunt Kate reminded him. "And you can't go jumping in on things that don't concern you, either. You had no business carrying one of my best sheets over there in the first place." She spoke sharply, and that's when I first knew Aunt Kate was worried, too. As much as she liked that sheet, she'd never care more about a sheet than a person.

Grace came in and started collecting our bowls, even though the rule was, we carried our own dishes to the sink or ate out of them at the next meal. She gathered up all the dishes until she got to Uncle Stephen, then held them out to him like an offering. "You gotta do something."

I think we were all glad when the phone rang.

Uncle Stephen came back smiling. "Hugh Fred has found Jay a lawyer and will even pay him. We're going down to meet with him right now."

If you think after he left we all sat around talking about Jay and Mr. Ira, you can think again. It was Easter weekend in a preacher's family. As he went out the door, he asked Aunt Kate to please cut the stencil for Sunday's bulletin, since he might not get time. When she finished, I had to mimeograph the bulletins and fold them. Normally Abby folded, but she was dreadfully crabby that morning. Besides, Aunt Kate said we wanted these to look especially nice for all the people who didn't usually come to church. I doubted they were coming to look at bulletins, but took special pains to get the folds straight just in case. I would have hated to think I drove someone away from church with a crooked bulletin.

After she finished cutting the stencils, Aunt Kate had to go help Miss Hannah decorate the sanctuary with lilies. On the way to the church she carried Miz Baines a chicken she'd asked Grace to fry while we worked on bulletins. While Aunt Kate was at church, Grace and I had to dye a million eggs for the hunt the women were having Saturday. In the middle of that, Abby whined until I helped her try on the Easter outfit Big Mama had sent her, complete with new shoes, straw hat, and her first gloves.

John joined the ruckus by finally learning to crawl. His palms and knees were a rainbow palette from dye spills on the floor, and Grace and I wore ourselves out dashing to keep him from heading down the back steps to explore the world. "It's time we got us a latch on that back screen," Grace said, laying a chair on the floor sideways as a gate.

"Why don't we just close the back door?" I pulled it to and locked it. Still expecting Roy any minute, I'd locked the front door behind Aunt Kate already.

Grace flapped her hands in front of her face. "You open that door immediately! We could die from all these vinegar fumes!"

"No, John!" Abby shouted as he tried to scale the new chair-gate. "Le's put Rowdy's collar on him and tie de leash to de table leg."

Grace looked from John to the table as if thinking it over, but shook her head. "I think Miss Kate would have a fit. Why don't we take a break and make some Kool-Aid? Oh, we can't. The sugar canister is empty. Run over to the store for some, Carley?"

I moved back to the counter like turning over purple eggs was the most important job in the world. "I'm not setting foot outside today."

"Nobody's gonna get you between here and next door," she scoffed.

"I'm not going," I said firmly. "You and Abby go. I'll dye the eggs."

I locked both front and back doors and kept one eye cocked

on the kitchen window for Roy's rusty green car. I worried until they got back. What if Roy decided to kidnap Abby? Could Grace fight him off?

"What you got this door locked for?" Grace demanded when she'd had to ring the front doorbell to be let in. "Ain't no murderer gonna come up these front steps in broad daylight."

"I just felt safer." I didn't want to confess I was terrified of my own daddy coming, not a murderer. I also didn't want to have to confess that Mr. Ira's death probably hadn't been murder, but the misguided action of an angel of the Lord.

Abby dragged home with a pink face and climbed up onto a chair. "I's perfectly 'zausted," she announced. She laid her head on the table and fell fast asleep.

Grace gathered her up to carry her to bed. As Abby's face brushed her cheek, she exclaimed, "She's real warm. You think she could be sick?"

"I think she's like the rest of us," I replied. "Weighed down by the cares of the world."

We'd barely finished dying all those eggs when Uncle Stephen returned. Grace lifted dark worried eyes to his face. "Did you see the lawyer? Did you get Jay out?"

Uncle Stephen sprawled in a kitchen chair and stretched his legs in front of him, grateful for the glass of tea she put before him. "He's scum," he said flatly. "A direct descendent of a carpetbagger. He thinks Jay is guilty, but says he *thinks* he can get the judge to reduce the charge so Jay'll just go to jail for life instead of to the gas chamber."

Grace's hand flew to her mouth. "What you gonna do?"

Uncle Stephen heaved a huge sigh. "Get Jay a better lawyer—if I have to pay the fee myself."

He also wanted to pay Jay's bail, but Aunt Kate put her foot down. "We don't have that kind of money. Besides, people are going to think you know more than you do."

Even Mr. Davy said mildly, when he came by to bring us some of Janey Lou's little chess pies, "Jay'll be safer where he is for the time being."

All afternoon people came in and out of our house, bringing us gifts of food for Easter and talking about murder. Seemed to me they were divided half and half. Some thought Jay killed Mr. Ira by accident. Others thought Mr. Ira had finally provoked him beyond endurance. Nobody even suggested he might be innocent.

Between visitors I mostly cowered in our grim gray living room, sitting by the window staring at a perfectly beautiful day I was too terrified to go out and enjoy. I wanted to run onto the porch and shout, "It wasn't murder, it was the angel of the Lord!" but I didn't dare. I didn't even dare tell Uncle Stephen. If he didn't laugh, if he happened to believe me, he might feel honor-bound to turn me in. If you called down the angel of the Lord and it killed somebody, were you arrested for murder? I didn't think I could stand living in prison with all those men.

That, plus worrying about Roy coming any minute, made me the most miserable person in Job's corner that afternoon—next to Jay's mama, of course.

I refused to consider that Miz Baines and Ivy might be miserable. In fact, I refused to think about them at all. Whenever the thought of one of them crept into my head, I tried to shove it out before it could grow into more guilt than I could bear. But I did wonder once if I'd feel so bad if the angel had smitten Miz Baines, as I'd requested. I concluded that I would. I didn't know how Elisha looked himself in the mirror after he'd had those two boys torn up by the she-bear. I went upstairs and wrote in my diary: *Being a prophet of the Lord entails fortitude I do not have.*

Uncle Stephen knocked on my door, jingling his keys. "Want to come to town? Abby's napping, and I want somebody to ride with me to take Mrs. Baines to the undertaker."

Startled, I dashed to open the door. "Has she died, too?"

He laughed for the first time that day. "No, she's got to take him Ira's suit and pick out a casket. Don't we have library books due? I can drop you off there and pick you up."

I didn't want to go, but if I stayed home, Aunt Kate was sure to find something for me to do. Besides, I wouldn't mind being gone if Roy came. I collected all our books and climbed in the backseat. I figured I could tell Uncle Stephen about Roy on the way to Miz Baines's.

Instead, I found Miss Nancy already in our front seat. "I'm gonna sit with Ivy while Gert's gone," she explained. On her lap she held a plate of peanut butter and jelly sandwiches, covered with waxed paper. "Gert says this is all Ivy will eat right now," she said, as if apologizing.

Miz Baines stumped out to the car carrying a paper sack. Without even greeting Uncle Stephen or me, she said to Miss Nancy, "Give her the pink medicine at four o'clock, with plenty of water." She climbed into the front seat and smoothed her black skirt over her knees. "I shorely do 'preciate you bein' with me for this sad event, Preacher. I shorely do." She still ignored me entirely. Given her poor eyesight, I figured maybe she hadn't seen me in the backseat.

She gave her sack a couple of pokes with one finger. "Need to run this suit by the cleaners before we go to the undertakin' place. Needs a good cleanin' and pressin'."

"I don't think the suit has to be real clean," Uncle Stephen said, turning onto the highway.

"Co'se it does! Cain't be buryin' somebody in a dirty suit for all eternity. I wanna leave his shirt, too, to git it starched 'n' ironed. Ira never had a shirt done up by the cleaner in his life, but he's gonna git one now."

"But the undertaker wants the clothes this afternoon."

"They can clean 'em in one hour if you pay extry. You wouldn't begrudge poor Ira that little bit, would you? And the man can wait one more hour. Ain't no cause to be hurryin' somebody into the ground. He's gonna lie there long enough as it is, contemplatin' eternity."

She settled the sack more comfortably on her broad lap. While she talked, she kneaded the paper. The crinkly sound matched her crackly voice. "I've been thinkin' 'bout them casket liners, and I've 'bout decided on rose velvet. Ira mighta liked blue better, but he ain't gonna see it. I will, and I'm partial to pink. I'd like to picture him in it when he's gone. What do you think?"

When I met Uncle Stephen's eyes in the rearview mirror, his ears turned red and I had to press my mouth hard not to giggle. I could tell he was thinking the same thing I was: Mr. Ira would be a whole lot prettier and cleaner in death than in life.

I knew, though, that Uncle Stephen would try to discourage such extravagance. He always believed a plain pine box was good enough to dispose of a body once the soul was done with it. Sure enough—"I think you ought to pick the least expensive thing he's got, Gert."

"Well, now, Preacher, you may not know it, but Ira 'n' me took out policies to assure our lives some years back. I'm gittin' paid five hunnert dollars for Ira dyin', and it seems fittin' to spend it ever' bit on him. They 'uz askin' if I'd like a vault extry, to keep out the cold and rain."

Uncle Stephen made a sharp, impatient sound. "For heaven's sake, Gert—"

"It comes with a lifetime guarantee." Her voice was wheedling, as if she was begging him to pay for it.

"Whose lifetime?"

She sat silent while four telephone poles went by, then spoke like she was talking to herself. "I swan, I never thought of that. And how'd I know if it was workin', lest we dug him up now 'n' then to check?"

Uncle Stephen said shortly, "It would seem a more fitting memorial to Ira if you used that money to feed yourself and Ivy."

"Oh, me 'n' Ivy'll get by. We always do. Co'se if I was workin', things 'ud be a mite easier." She turned her witch's profile and gave him a waiting sort of look.

Uncle Stephen turned, too. "Carley, you still back there? You're mighty quiet."

"I'm contemplating eternity," I told him.

Saturday morning, Miss Nancy dropped her bombshell.

Abby generally went for the mail, proud as punch of the job, but she still wasn't feeling good. Before the egg hunt, I ran over.

Inside the post office I found Miss Nancy and Miss Pauline leaning so close together over the counter their hair merged into one enormous head. Miss Nancy was so short, she had to stand on the tips of her toes.

Before they saw me, Miss Pauline said, "Looks like Gert would've seen something."

"It could have been while Gert was working over at the manse. Ira'd never have noticed a thing." Miss Nancy's head darted like a robin's, looking for danger. She saw me and flicked one hand. Miss Pauline's mouth shut like a mouse-trap.

She handed me our mail with a cheerful booming voice as false as her teeth—although I will say that she was never mean to me like she was to Aunt Kate. Some days I still thought Miss Pauline wasn't so bad. This wasn't one of them, however. Especially when she said, "Tell your aunt I've got a dozen eggs dyed." Bonnie had dyed the eggs. I knew that as well as she did.

I didn't let on, though. "Yes, ma'am." I bobbed my head and scampered down the steps.

I headed toward our house, then doubled back and crept underneath the post office. I heard Miss Pauline ask, breathlessly, ". . . in trouble?"

"Didn't sound like it. The doctor didn't talk to me, of

course. He came while Gert was gone and said he'd come to see Ivy. Gert got back while he was still there, and he took her into the kitchen to talk. The only part I heard was, 'You're going to have to watch her, now. We don't want any little accidents.'"

"It *had* to be Jay. He was over there all the time doin' little things for 'em—carryin' in wood and all. Who else was ever over at their house?"

I could think of several people. Miss Pauline ran over a lot of afternoons to gossip. Miss Hannah took them food sometimes. Mr. Hugh Fred rode that way most Saturday mornings. Mr. Wash had put on a new roof for them in March. Seemed to me like Miss Nancy ought to at least remember that. Maybe she did, because she replied, real positive, "It *had* to be Jay. Ira must have found out."

I was trying to figure out what they thought Jay had done besides murder when Preston hollered from his porch, "Hey, Carley, what you doin' sneakin' 'round under there?"

I scrabbled out and ran.

Miss Pauline leaned out the door and yelled something I didn't catch.

I careened down the road, up our porch steps, through the front door, and straight into Uncle Stephen, wearing his second-best gray suit and gray straw hat. "Whoa—what's the hurry?" He caught me to keep me from falling.

Gasping for breath, I blurted, "Miss Nancy and Miss Pauline—they're saying Jay killed Mr. Ira—because he—because Ivy—" I came to a dead stop. I realized I had no idea what Miss Nancy thought Jay had done.

Uncle Stephen looked down at me and I looked up at him. When his eyes flickered, I knew he already knew whatever Miss Nancy found out. He was also wondering how much I knew. If you think you can't tell that much from one eye flicker, you never grew up in a house where you had to learn to read people good, because they never told you a blessed thing.

"How'd they find out about Ivy?" he asked sharply.

I was still trying to catch my breath. "While Miss Nancy was over there yesterday, the doctor came. She heard him tell Miz Baines she has to be extra careful so Ivy won't have any accidents."

"What's all the shoutin' about?" Grace came from the kitchen, John crawling after her. Abby clutched at her skirt like she was two, not four.

Uncle Stephen waved them back into the dining room. "Nothing. Carley just got an earful of gossip over at the post office and needs to let off steam."

"I doesn't see any steam," Abby objected, looking me up and down.

"To let off steam means to shout when you need to, so you feel better," he explained.

"I needs to right now." She opened her mouth and let out a roar they could have heard in Statesville. "I still doesn't feel better," she complained.

She looked pretty bad, actually. Her face was flushed, her eyes bright. But we were all too busy thinking about other things to notice.

"Is it about Jay?" Grace looked anxiously from me to Uncle Stephen.

He nodded. "The Job's Corner biddies have come up with the one thing the police lacked: a motive. They think he's been"—he gave me a swift look—"courtin' Ivy, and Ira found out."

"Jay wouldn't!" Grace sounded as scandalized as I felt. Miss Nancy hadn't said one word about courting. Besides, Jay was a Negro, and Ivy white.

I opened my mouth to ask a whole lot of questions, but Uncle Stephen wasn't paying attention to me, he was saying to Grace, "Of course he wouldn't, but that won't stop 'em saying so. I think I'd better go over there and put out this fire before it spreads."

He started toward the door, then looked at his watch. "No, I'm due in Statesville to talk with a lawyer who may take Jay's case. I'll talk to Pauline and Nancy when I get back."

❋

Poor Abby couldn't go to the egg hunt. Just as we were about to start, she whined, "Scratch my back, Mama. It itches!"

Aunt Kate pulled up her dress and groaned. "Chicken pox! I never should have taken her to school with me a couple of weeks ago."

Abby's whole back was a mess of little red bumps. She protested she still felt good enough to go, but Aunt Kate refused to let her. "I can't risk you breathing on somebody and giving them your germs."

"I won't breeve," Abby pled. Aunt Kate just shook her head and left her home with Grace.

I could see her from where I hunted eggs, sitting forlorn on our front steps. Once she left the steps and came to the tracks to yell, "Carley, you better find me some eggs!"

I took her a basketful, but the ungrateful wretch cried because they were hard boiled and couldn't be scrambled.

Chapter 36

Two days after Easter we had Mr. Ira's funeral. That's when Abby embarrassed us by saying how bad he smelled. She shouldn't have been there at all, since she still had chicken pox, but Uncle Stephen asked me to take her up to the balcony. He thought children ought to see what a funeral was like before they had to attend one for somebody they loved. "Abby will at least know how to behave." As somebody whose first funeral was my own mama's, I thought he had a point: I'd been nervous the whole time I would do something wrong. But I wasn't sure Abby was learning good funeral behavior at Mr. Ira's. Miz Baines sat there sniffing and moaning the whole time, while Ivy never stopped playing with her doll.

I went around in a fog the next few days, wondering whether Mr. Ira had been smitten by the angel of the Lord or murdered by Roy. As days passed and Roy still didn't come, I became more and more convinced that he must have killed Mr. Ira and was afraid to come back. I kept wondering whether to tell Uncle Stephen he'd been around. Everywhere I went I looked over my shoulder, expecting to see his old rusty car.

The only two places I felt truly safe were in my room and under the post office. So the next Saturday morning I sneaked next door and quickly wriggled between the wild onions to get underneath. As I settled myself, though, I noticed how much the weeds around the post office had grown since winter, and how green they were. I shifted uneasily. Any one of them could harbor a snake. I was just about to crawl out and go home when heavy feet clumped up the steps.

"Well, look who's here!" Miss Pauline boomed in that jolly way she had with people she liked. If it had been Aunt Kate, she would have made the very same words sound like an accusation. "Long time, no see, Stephen."

"Abby enjoys coming so much, I hate to usurp her prerogatives." He thumped his box on the counter, jarring the whole little building. "But these books are too heavy for her to carry. If they're too much for you to throw on, I'll take it downtown."

"I'm strong as an ox." I heard her weighing the box, getting out the metal stamp box, and rustling through the stamps. Then her voice got softer. "Lonely as one, too. I miss seeing your smiling face over here."

She must have kicked off her shoes, because the smell of hot feet filtered through the cracks in the floorboards, making me want to sneeze. I grabbed my nose as Uncle Stephen replied, "Don't feel much like smiling lately, between Ira getting murdered and Jay going to jail."

"You got to get over Jay." From the way the counter above me creaked, I knew she was leaning her elbows on it. If she wasn't careful, Uncle Stephen would see down her dress. She'd bought several lately that looked too small to me.

Above me, Uncle Stephen shifted his feet. "Jay's not likely to get over it any time soon. I hear the county jail isn't exactly a ritzy hotel."

I shifted again and a sharp rock bit into my right knee. I clapped my hand over my mouth to keep from yelping in pain, and got a mouthful of dirt. I was so busy wiping my tongue on my shoulders that I completely missed what Miss Pauline said next. I was also scanning the perimeter of my hideout for slithering bodies or forked tongues.

What finally got my attention was when I heard Miss Pauline say, "I hate to see you wearin' yourself down like this, Stephen. You're practically skin and bones." As if she had the right to worry about him!

Uncle Stephen gave a funny laugh, like he was embarrassed. "I'm not that skinny yet."

Her voice dropped so low I had to strain to hear her. "Why don't you come over and watch television with me some evenin'? My kids go to bed by eight, and I see Kate turnin' her light out soon after nine. You must get lonesome over there in that big house all by yourself. If you come, I won't tell a soul."

Uncle Stephen's voice was plenty loud and firm. "You know

I can't do that. It wouldn't be right. And besides, I'm glad of the peace and quiet. That's when I do my best studying."

He jiggled coins in his pocket. "How much do I owe you?"

She sighed. "You owe the government a dollar and five cents. You don't owe me a thing, but I sure wish you'd come over sometime. It's lonely being a widow at my age. I get so hungry to talk to a grown-up. I'd never tell a soul," she repeated.

"Have you considered joining the Women's Circle? They get together once a month and have a great time." I heard him putting his money back in his pocket.

"I don't wanna sit around with a bunch of women." If she'd been Abby, I'd have thought she was pouting. "Do you like the new color I've put on my hair?"

She'd rinsed it with red, which I thought made her look a lot like one of Mr. Davy's cows. Uncle Stephen merely said, "I'm glad to see you taking an interest in yourself. You really do need to get out more."

Her voice got soft and slow, like Aunt Kate's in their room at night. "I'm a homebody, Stephen. You wouldn't catch *me* goin' out to work every day if my man was at home. He'd get plenty of attention." The counter creaked as if she were leaning farther over it.

"Pauline!" He sounded so shocked, I wondered what she had done.

"Oh, Stephen, can't you see how it is with me? Can't you *see?*"

Was she *crying?* And why had the building given that little lurch?

"Stop it!" I heard him walk quickly to the door. "Let's pretend this never happened, shall we?" From the way he clattered down those stairs, you'd have thought the murderer was after him.

Above me nothing moved for a long minute. Then, from the way she slammed the stamp box closed and onto the counter shelf, you'd have thought she was planning to commit murder herself.

I looked carefully for snakes, then started to slither out between the weeds. As I was half-out and half-still-under, my arm touched something that moved quickly away. I bolted, which was amazing when you consider that my heart had stopped. It was a miracle I didn't die and lie beneath that post office forever. I never went back under there again.

❦

As we moved through May, I felt like a person leaning forward with her feet nailed to the floor. I couldn't wait for the end of school, but didn't want time to take a single step toward the time when Jay would go on trial for his life. Uncle Stephen was nearly frantic trying to help Jay's new lawyer find evidence to get him freed. "There's got to be something they don't have," he must have said a million times. "There just has to be."

Aunt Kate was tired of the whole thing. "Let Jay's lawyer do the worrying," I heard her beg one night after they'd gone to their room. I'd gone downstairs for a drink of water, and when I heard them talking, I stopped and pressed my ear to the door. "You've got a church and a family to worry about." I heard his shoe hit the floor, but couldn't hear what he said. Her voice went up a notch. "If you won't do it for me, do it for the children."

He sighed so loud I heard it clearly. "I'm doing *this* for the children, Kate. Do you want them to have the kind of daddy who'd turn his back while an innocent man goes to jail?"

Their bed creaked, then the sliver of light under their door went out. In the dark I heard Aunt Kate say in a soft, worried voice, "Principles are well and good, but they won't feed us if you get put out in the street."

Uncle Stephen was also trying to help Miz Baines and Ivy. "I wouldn't recommend her to look after children, but she's got to have help," he told Aunt Kate one suppertime. "They are destitute." He talked to Presbytery and Synod to see if funds could be found. Aunt Kate went over there several times a week to take food, and called other church women to take food, too. Uncle Stephen went over every day for a pastoral visit. Often when I climbed off the school bus I saw him sitting on a chair under the tree with Ivy.

Grace drooped around with her eyes big and sad, but at least she stayed pleasant. Aunt Kate was getting mean as a snake. Grace explained softly one evening, "She's plumb worn out, between gettin' ready for the end of school and workin' with that ornery choir director. Besides, she's worried sick about Jay and your uncle. He can't keep on like this."

By "like this" she meant going to the jail three or four times a week, meeting with Jay's lawyer at least once a week, visiting Ivy and Miz Baines every day on top of his usual hospital visiting, church visiting, studying, counseling, preaching three times a week, leading the men's Bible study every Sunday, tutoring Preston in arithmetic, going every time somebody called with a crisis, and helping Grace prepare for college. He was so tired that his shoulders drooped, so thin that his clothes hung on his lanky frame. Abby complained, "You nebber play wif us anymore." John whined and put his arms up when Uncle Stephen came into the room. Uncle Stephen would pick him up for a second, but had to give him to somebody else pretty soon and hurry on to his next thing to do.

He was preaching a lot about newspaper stories in those days, too. One Sunday when I told Aunt Kate that particular sermon sounded more like a review of the week's news than the Gospel, she said sadly, "He can't preach his heart right now, Carley. It's so fragile that if he opened it, it would break."

Another Sunday when I was collecting bulletins after church I heard Mr. Mayhew talking loud behind the sanctuary. I went up into the choir loft and put my ear to the door to the back hall in time to hear him say angrily, "I've had all I can take of these sermons saying we have to love our enemies and do good to those who spitefully use us. That's not what people need to hear these days. We need messages spurring us to stand up for truth and liberty!"

"Seems like Stephen just can't understand what a threat those Russians are," Mr. Wash agreed. "I don't know what it would take to convince him."

"He's got so much on his mind," said a voice so soft I didn't immediately recognize it. "He's real worried about Jay."

"Jay's not a member of this church," Mr. Wash declared.

"Besides—" I knew Mr. Mayhew was puffing out his round cheeks and pursing his pouty lips. "I'm not going to keep coming here and listening to un-American sermons. I need to find another church."

"I hate to see you do that," the soft voice replied. "You've been in Bethel all your life. Why don't you weather this out? We'd have a hard time finding somebody of your caliber to lead the music and teach our children. And you'd miss us, too."

"There comes a time," Mr. Mayhew said grimly, "when you

have to do what you have to do. I feel God is leading me away from this church."

I reported that to Uncle Stephen after dinner. He gave a short, unfunny laugh. "Have you ever heard anybody say God was leading them to do something harder, nastier, or less pleasant than what they were already doing? When God called Abraham it was to a long lonely journey. When God called Moses it was into danger. When God called Jesus, it was to a cross. When you hear somebody saying God's calling them, Carley, listen real good. If it's away from their personal inclinations and into something more difficult, that person might actually be hearing the voice of God."

Mr. Hugh Fred came by that afternoon. "Can I talk to you a minute, Stephen?"

Aunt Kate, Grace, and I were making taffy in the kitchen while Abby and John napped. I asked to be excused and hurried upstairs to the bathroom. Quickly I scrubbed my sticky hands, then tiptoed to my closet in time to hear Mr. Hugh Fred say, ". . . know how worried you are about Jay. I am, too. He's one of my best workers. But you mustn't neglect the needs of the congregation." Now I knew who the soft voice had been with Mr. Wash and Mr. Mayhew.

"Name me one need I've neglected." Uncle Stephen's voice was high and sharp. "Who is saying these things?"

"I can't name names. That wouldn't be right. But I can tell you that Gilbert Mayhew handed me his letter of resignation after church today."

I heard a sharp little movement, and was scared Uncle Stephen would say, "Carley already told me." He didn't say a word.

Mr. Hugh Fred went on, "He's going to be sorely missed. He's been part of the church all his life. Like I told you when you first came, you don't want to get these people's backs up. And in Job's Corner we not only love God, we love this country. Some of your sermons lately have sounded like you think God loves Negroes and Russians more than white Americans. Now I know that's not what you mean to imply, but that's how some people are hearing you. And you can't do them any good if they stop believing in what you have to say."

Uncle Stephen was quiet for so long I was beginning to think I'd have to go back downstairs or Aunt Kate would come looking for me. Finally he said, "I need to think and pray through all this. Thanks for coming. In the meantime, do you have any suggestions for what we do about a choir director and Sunday school teacher?"

"I had one idea about the choir. Wash's brother Clay is coming back from the Air Force in a couple of months. He's very musical. Do you think Kate would hold the choir together until then? We can ask Nancy to recruit somebody for the Sunday school."

They pushed back their chairs and left the study. I waited until I heard Mr. Hugh Fred's Hudson drive off before I went back to the kitchen, stopping by the bathroom to flush.

I found Uncle Stephen scrubbing his hands. "Give me some of that taffy," he demanded. "If I don't pull taffy, I'm going to wring somebody's neck."

The next Sunday, Mr. Hugh Fred announced Mr. Mayhew's resignation as choir director and Sunday school teacher. I could tell from the way several people rustled in their seats that it was a complete surprise to them. I could also tell from the way some others sat very straight and still that for them, it wasn't.

Miss Hannah came up that afternoon with a big coconut cake. "Thought you might need some cheering up, old dears. Once that trial is over, all this will blow over. You wait and see." For once in her life, Miss Hannah was wrong.

Chapter 37

"Jay's trial is scheduled to start Monday," Uncle Stephen informed me on Friday before the last week of school.

I hurried up to my room, stood in front of my mirror, and practiced what I would say to the judge. "Your Honorship, Jay did not kill this man. I called down the wrath of God upon him. He was smited by an angel of the Lord."

I could say that seven different ways to a mirror, but with an honest self-appraisal that made my stomach ache, I knew I could not say it to a judge. It is one of life's bitterest ironies that the most dreadful consequences may come not from the wicked things we do but from the silly ones. And foolishness is so much harder to confess than wickedness.

I also practiced saying, "Uncle Stephen, maybe it wasn't Jay, but Roy who killed Mr. Ira. Roy was hanging around here that week, and he got real mad because Mr. Ira was bothering me. Maybe he killed him in child-defense." But then I thought how angry both God and Roy would be at me if I turned him in, and I knew I never could.

So, I was too embarrassed to confess about the angel of the Lord and too frightened to turn in Roy. However, it seemed to me if Jay went to jail for life—or even to the gas chamber—because I was a coward, the least I could do was be there.

Aunt Kate didn't want me to go to the trial, but Uncle Stephen said it would be "an educational experience." He also said he could use the family support, since she wouldn't take time off school. She gave him a sharp frown and told me privately, "Don't be quite as sure of Jay's innocence as your Uncle Stephen. He wears blinders on some issues, as you well know."

Uncle Stephen also offered to find somebody to keep Abby and John if Grace wanted to come, but she shrank back against the sink. "I couldn't bear it. I just couldn't."

We didn't talk in the car on the way to court. I was wishing I were braver, and Uncle Stephen was nervous about testifying. As we got out at the courthouse, he said, "Please don't let me make a mistake that can cost Jay his freedom." I knew he wasn't talking to me.

He had to wait outside the courtroom, so I sat with Miss Hannah and Mr. Davy with Mr. Hugh Fred behind us. We were the only Bethel people there. Not even Miz Baines had come. "Where's Jay's mama?" I asked, peering around.

"In the back." Miss Hannah pointed. I saw a Negro section full of dark unhappy faces. Meek's silver hair gleamed in the dimness, and he gave me a little salute with one hand. Miss Hannah put her big hand over mine in my lap, and it felt like an anchor holding me in my seat. Otherwise, between my fear and the heat, I could have risen like a balloon. My blue gingham dress stuck damply to my back. The only thing lazier than the ceiling fans were the flies buzzing against the windows, too hot to do more than hover near the sill.

Jay came in wearing tan slacks, a white shirt, and a green tie I recognized as Uncle Stephen's. He gave me a quick, trembly smile, then sat with his back to us facing the judge.

A tall man with brown hair and a blue suit sat beside him. All I could see of him was his back.

"That's his lawyer, Vance McGrew," Miss Hannah whispered, "and the man on the other side is Prosecutor Red Lamar." I stretched high in my chair to look. The way Uncle Stephen had talked about "the prosecutor," he was the bad cowboy in this movie. He was tall, burly, and redheaded. Sweat already beaded his forehead.

We all had to stand up for the judge to come in, but I was a little disappointed. I'd expected somebody who looked a bit like God. Judge Pye was a roly-poly man with glasses who looked like he'd be happier with grandchildren on his lap than sitting in a stifling courtroom listening to lawyers.

Uncle Stephen was called at the end of the morning. When they asked his name, his voice was so husky he had to cough and start over. He threw Jay an apologetic look.

Prosecutor Lamar walked heavily toward where Uncle Stephen sat behind the rail, pulled out a handkerchief, and wiped his dripping forehead. "Let's wrap this up quick, Preacher, and go home for a glass of tea." People tittered.

"He's a real card," Miss Hannah whispered fondly. "I've known him for years." She knew everybody in Statesville.

"Good," I whispered back. "Maybe he'll be nicer than Uncle Stephen expects."

Sure enough, he leaned his elbow on the rail and continued pleasantly. "Mr. Whitfield, would you tell us in your own words about finding the body, please?"

Uncle Stephen explained how Jay came for him and they'd gone to view the body, how he'd covered it with a sheet—"My wife's best one, as I learned to my regret when she found out." People laughed at that. I figured there must be a goodly number of Baptists among them.

He went on to tell how he'd returned to the house with Jay, and even explained why he'd sent Jay on to work. "I was afraid the police might not listen to a Negro man and hoped they would listen to me."

Prosecutor Lamar tapped his cheekbone with one forefinger. "Now let me get this straight. You all did not touch the body when you went over to look at it?"

"No, sir."

"And what was the defendant wearing, do you remember?"

Uncle Stephen looked puzzled. "Pants and a shirt—I don't remember the color."

"And a hat or cap of any sort?"

He thought a minute. "No, sir, he wasn't."

Prosecutor Lamar's laugh rumbled deep in his belly. "I was testing your memory, sir. At that early hour, my own would not be half so reliable. Now tell the court how long you have known the defendant, Mr. Whitfield."

Uncle Stephen took a deep breath and gave him a little smile. "Nine months—he helped us move in last August."

"Have you had other contacts with him since then?"

"Yes, sir. He helped me build a barbecue grill behind our home, and that day he mentioned he hopes to attend college, but needed tutoring. In the spring I tutored him several afternoons a week after work. He also started going out with the young woman who takes care of our children, so he came by on weekends to pick her up for church or a date."

"Hmmm. You say you've known Jay Anderson for nine months. Exactly how well have you known him?"

Uncle Stephen was puzzled. "Like I said, I've tutored him, he dates Grace who looks after our children—" He looked my way. I gave him what I hoped was an encouraging smile. "—and we built a barbecue grill together."

Mr. Lamar leaned one elbow on the bench like they were old cronies. Perspiration rolled down his thick neck and curled his red hair. "A barbecue grill, eh?" He looked down and patted his enormous paunch. "I love barbecue, as you can see."

"Come on out some Saturday, sir, and we'll cook you some."

Mr. Lamar's belly laugh rasped contagiously through the stuffy room. "Cook a lot, Preacher." He wiped his head with the handkerchief again, carefully folded it, and returned it to his pocket. "So the defendant has often been inside your house. Is that what you said?"

Uncle Stephen nodded. "Yes, he has."

"Has he ever eaten a meal at your house?"

Still puzzled, Uncle Stephen nodded again. "Supper, occasionally."

"And where were these meals eaten?"

"In the dining room, where we always eat."

Mr. Lamar smiled affably. "Who else was present when he ate these suppers? Present at the table, I mean."

Uncle Stephen shrugged. "The family. My wife and myself, our children, a niece who lives with us, and Grace. We had no other guests, if that's what you mean."

"But Jay, there, he was a guest?"

"Yes. That is, he was both a guest and a pupil. The times I remember him eating with us, we'd run so late with our studying that I just invited him to stay."

Mr. Lamar looked toward the jury, then at the defendant. Finally he leaned so close that Uncle Stephen shifted back in his seat. He lowered his voice and spoke with an elaborate pretense at confidentiality. "I've heard you described as a nigger lover."

A vein pumped in Uncle Stephen's forehead, but before he could speak Mr. McGrew leapt to his feet. "Objection, your honor! Language offensive to my client."

Judge Pye nodded. "Sustained. Rephrase your question, Counselor."

Mr. Lamar smiled affably. "No offense meant, your honor. I was just trying to establish how well the preacher, here, knows the defendant. Mr. Whitfield, would you call Jay over there your friend?"

Anger still pounded in Uncle Stephen's temples and he clenched his teeth, but his voice was level. "I certainly would. Jay's a fine young man. But even if he weren't, as a Christian, I am called to love all men, including both Jay Anderson and you, sir."

His words rang out preacherish in the sweltering courtroom, and I knew he was lying. Nobody could love that ruddy mountain of hot flesh that crowded and smothered him. I could smell the prosecutor's sweat from where I sat. If Mr. Lamar didn't move away soon, Uncle Stephen might suffocate.

"And you invited this *Nee-gro* to your home for dinner?"

"Yes, sir."

Mr. Lamar smiled and leaned over the rail again. Uncle Stephen arched back slightly. "Mr. Whitfield," the lawyer crooned, "is it possible that you love this *Nee-gro*—" The emphasis sounded worse than if he'd gone ahead and said the more offensive word.

I burned with anger for Jay, who sat with his head bowed, shoulders tense, and sweat staining the back of his clean white shirt. I could picture his fingers—delicate fingers that could carve a doll's head or write a beautiful script—clenched and straining before him.

"—*Nee-gro* a little bit more than you love some white men? Me, for instance? You've never invited me to dinner."

Uncle Stephen leaned forward. "I just did, sir, if you recall." Chuckles rippled again through the courtroom. I nudged Miss Hannah happily. Uncle Stephen had told *him*!

"How about the members of your congregation. Have you invited all of them to dinner?"

"Sure. They were all invited to a barbecue the weekend before Halloween."

"I don't mean en masse." The big prosecutor spread his huge hands, and I could see they were covered with soft red hair. "I mean for a cozy dinner, such as Jay Anderson had. Have you invited each member of your congregation to a family dinner, Mr. Whitfield?"

"Objection!" cried Mr. McGrew. "Stephen Whitfield is not on trial here."

The prosecutor turned to Judge Pye and said, in the tone of one being very patient, "I am seeking to establish that this witness may be prejudiced in favor of the defendant."

"I'm not prejudiced!" Uncle Stephen said indignantly. But when Jay's lawyer shook his head slightly, he flushed. He'd told me in the car, "The hardest part's going to be not speaking except to answer the questions they ask."

"Overruled," the judge said. "Answer the question, Mr. Whitfield. Has your family entertained members of your congregation?"

"All the members," Mr. Lamar added.

Uncle Stephen hesitated, then shook his head. "We've entertained some, but not all."

Mr. Lamar leaned forward confidentially. "But I know you've done a lot of good at that church. You look like a fine man. A man so fine, in fact, that you'd do almost anything for a friend. Am I correct?"

Uncle Stephen hesitated. "I try, sir. I try."

"Do or say almost anything for a friend," Mr. Lamar purred, his huge head nodding in satisfaction. "Especially if he's a Nee-gro. Right, Mr. Whitfield? Even if he's a Nee-gro who murdered a poor old white man in cold blood and left his body there for animals to eat."

"No!" Uncle Stephen exclaimed. "That's not true! I wouldn't—Jay—"

Mr. Lamar flapped his ham hand at Judge Pye and spoke through Uncle Stephen's sputterings. "No more questions, your honor." He flapped one hand at the jury and lumbered back to his seat.

Uncle Stephen opened his mouth to continue his protest, but Mr. McGrew had hurried toward the judge. They talked softly for a minute, but the judge shook his head. Mr. McGrew turned toward Uncle Stephen, looking disappointed. Now I could see his face. It was long, and the skin hung in wrinkles like a hound dog's. But his eyes were very large, gray, and gentle.

"Mr. Whitfield, would you please tell the jury your personal opinion of the defendant, any opinion you've formed of his character while tutoring him these past months?"

Uncle Stephen had been sitting with his head bowed. Now he looked up, but his shoulders were slumped. "Jay Anderson is a fine young man and an asset to this community. He attends church every Sunday. He's courteous to adults and beloved by children. And he's kind. In the dead of winter he chopped wood to keep an elderly neighbor supplied with firewood, and refused to accept a penny for it." I knew all those things were true, but nobody else did. After Mr. Lamar, I was pretty sure most people were convinced Uncle Stephen would say nice things about Jay just because he was a Negro.

"No more questions at this time," Mr. McGrew said.

An impersonal voice said, "The witness may stand down."

I couldn't believe his time in court was up. He'd said nothing to save Jay. The jurors were all frowning. He threw Mr. McGrew a look like Rowdy's when he got caught killing a bird, and stumbled down to a seat just in front of me. The back of his best brown coat was wet with sweat.

Mr. Davy leaned forward and patted his shoulder. "Everything's going to be all right," he whispered. "Don't you worry one bit."

But from the way Miss Hannah clutched my hand, I knew she was as worried as I.

When court recessed for lunch, Mr. Lamar came back through the crowd with a jovial grin. "How you doin', Miss Hannah?" He pumped her hand. "Mama sure would love to see you if you have time to run over before you go back out to Job's Corner."

"Not today, Red. But I'll get in to see her soon. I want you to meet Carley Marshall, Mr. Whitfield's niece."

He gave me a wide grin and a thick damp hand covered with fine red hair. "Glad to meet you, Miss Carley. Gettin' a little field trip today? Or should I be callin' a truant officer?"

"Jay's a friend of mine," I wanted to say boldly. "And he didn't do it." But he moved off before I had a chance to say a word.

Lunch was a dismal affair—soggy sandwiches and milk that could have used more refrigeration. Even Miss Hannah and I couldn't think of much to say. We hurried back to the courtroom to get our seats before somebody else did. Vance McGrew came over to put his hand on Uncle Stephen's shoulder. "I never imagined he'd get that virulent."

Uncle Stephen clenched one fist. "I never imagined I'd *feel* that virulent."

Mr. McGrew squeezed his shoulder and went back to Jay. He smiled while they talked, but his eyes kept crinkling at the edges like he was worried.

The police started testifying about all the things they found and did not find at the scene of the crime. The courtroom got hotter. The flies buzzed louder. Words seemed to get fuzzier and fuzzier. After a while I leaned against Miss Hannah's arm and slept.

"Thank God for the bee," Aunt Kate would say later. One had flown in through the open unscreened windows. Next thing I knew, I was being stung.

"Ow!" I shouted, waking up to fiery pain.

Every eye in the room turned my way. My face got hot. "Sorry," I mumbled. "I got stung by a bee." My face felt as fiery as the bump.

"Continue," Judge Pye said to Mr. Lamar.

I straightened my glasses, which had gotten crooked while I slept, and rubbed a small red bump that was rising on my arm. Mr. Lamar said to the witness, "So when you lifted the body, please tell the court what you found there."

"A green corduroy cap," said the officer. "We later established it belonged to the defendant."

"The defendant who, based on Mr. Whitfield's testimony, was not wearing a cap when he first reported the body?" said Mr. Lamar. If he'd been a cat, he'd have purred.

"That's right, sir. And Mr. Whitfield told us they didn't touch the body when he returned with the defendant to view it."

"What did you conclude from this?" asked Mr. Lamar.

"Objection!" cried Vance McGrew, but the officer had already said, "That it fell beneath the body when he fell."

"No, it didn't," I said indignantly, still too sleepy to think clearly. "I put it there."

Again all heads swiveled my way. Judge Pye pushed his glasses up his nose and peered down. "What did you say, little lady?"

My whole body was melting in humiliation. In a minute or two I would puddle on the floor beside Miss Hannah's sensible black lace-up square-heeled shoes. Meanwhile, the judge was still waiting, peering down his short, fat nose at me.

He flapped one hand my way. "Approach the bench, please."

Puzzled, I looked around for a bench. Miss Hannah nudged me. "Go up to the judge, honey. He won't hurt you."

Slowly I got up and walked up the aisle, through a wooden gate somebody held for me, to the tall desk where he sat. "What was that you said a second ago?" repeated the judge.

"I, uh—" I had to stop and clear my throat. "I put that hat under Mr. Baines's head. I didn't like for him to lie right on the ground, you see."

"Objection!" "Move for dismissal!" Both lawyers shouted at the same time.

"Where did you get the hat?" The judge leaned over and looked at me over the top of his glasses. He still looked like somebody's granddaddy. If he hadn't, I'd have been terrified. But he looked so friendly, I answered in a normal voice.

"I found it in the woods near Mr. Ira's field. I figured Jay had dropped it, and I was going to take it back to him. But I couldn't just let Mr. Ira lie on the ground—" I gave Jay a stricken look. "I ruined your hat."

Judge Pye nodded to a man to one side. "Swear her in."

The man who had been testifying got down, and I had to climb up in that little box where Uncle Stephen had had such a rough time. My heart was beginning to gallop like it was going to leave whether I did or not.

The bailiff said a whole lot of words I could scarcely hear over my heartbeat, but I raised my hand and said what he told me to.

The judge, Mr. McGrew, and Mr. Lamar talked a minute, too low for me to hear. Mr. Lamar was breathing so hard I thought fire might come out his nostrils any minute. Finally the lawyers sat down, and the judge leaned over to me. "Tell the court when this happened—the thing with the hat."

"After Uncle Stephen and Jay went over and came back, while they were drinking coffee and talking about what Jay ought to say."

"Coaching the killer!" Mr. Lamar crowed, smacking his palm on the rail right in front of my face so hard it made me jump.

"He was not!" I said angrily. "Jay was scared people would think he killed Mr. Ira because he'd found him. Uncle Stephen said surely nobody would be bigoted enough to accuse him just because he's colored, but—"

Mr. Lamar turned pink and coughed. My own face flamed. How could I have used that word right there in public? "Negro, I mean."

Judge Pye nodded encouragingly. "So you went to see the body yourself? Why?"

I swallowed hard. If I lied to a judge, I might go to jail, too.

So, looking at the floor, I muttered, "I put a curse on Mr. Baines by mistake the day before. I meant it for his wife, but he got in the way." Tears filled my throat. I had to fight through them to finish. "I think he was probably struck down by the angel of the Lord, so I went to see what that looked like."

As the courtroom roared with laughter, I felt myself shriveling to three inches tall. Judge Pye banged his gavel. "Order in the court. Order, or I'll clear the room!" Everyone grew still. "What did you see?"

"Mr. Baines lying under Aunt Kate's very best sheet. I lifted the sheet, and his eyes were all milky."

"And you felt so sorry for him you put the hat under his head?"

I was sorely tempted to say "Yes" and leave it at that, but I had taken an oath to tell the whole truth. I swallowed the big lump in my throat and said in a voice hardly more than a whisper, "No, sir. When I started to go, I slipped and fell. I knocked him over a little, and saw he had a hole in his head. I turned him over to look better. Then I couldn't leave him lying on his face, so I turned him back over. And it was because he had that hole in his head that I put the hat under him. I couldn't bear to have germs get in."

A titter ran around the courtroom. My face felt like it would burst into flames any second and increase my misery.

The judge looked down at me, very stern. "Never touch anything at the scene of a crime again. Do you understand me?"

"No, sir. Yes, sir. I mean, I won't." My head bobbed until I felt dizzy. "I don't aim to ever *be* at the scene of a crime again. Once was plenty for—"

Mr. McGrew rose and interrupted. "Based on this testimony, I move that the case be dismissed."

The judge peered at Mr. Lamar. "Do you have any other evidence that definitely points to Jay Anderson as a suspect in this slaying?"

Mr. Lamar hesitated, then shook his head. "Not directly, your honor. Only that he was the one to find the body."

"We can't try everybody who finds a body. Nothing else?" When the big man shook his red head, the judge banged his gavel again. "Case dismissed."

Jay's head lay on his crossed arms on the table before him. Mr. McGrew rested a hand on his back. "It's over, Jay."

Jay looked up, and I saw tears in his eyes. "I can't thank you enough for what you did, sir. You, too, Carley. I just can't thank you enough."

"I didn't do anything," I mumbled, embarrassed. I was embarrassed for two reasons. First, if I hadn't stuck his hat under Mr. Ira, he wouldn't have had to go to jail. And second, what I wanted to do was hug his neck and cry right there with him. But I couldn't hug a Negro. They might lock us both up. So when I looked up and saw his mama and his relatives all hanging back like they'd like to come up but didn't dare, I just said, "I think your mama's waiting for you."

He looked over his shoulder, and his face lit with a smile like God's the first time he saw the world he'd made. "That's gonna be one happy woman tonight, for sure."

Uncle Stephen wasn't happy, though. Even after almost everybody else had streamed out, he sat with his head bowed and hands clasped between his bony knees, looking like he'd been washed, wrung out, and hung to dry.

I went over and spoke to the top of his head. "You ready to go?"

He looked up at me in exhaustion and disbelief. "Why didn't you tell somebody about that cap before now? With all the talking you do about everything else, why didn't you at least mention that cap?"

I stepped back, feeling like he'd slapped me. He'd never spoken so unkindly before. "I—I thought you'd be mad. About me going over, I mean. Besides—"

"If you'd stayed home like you were supposed to—"

One long thin hand fell on each of our shoulders. "Shhhh." I looked up into the face of Mr. McGrew. The wrinkles in his face all seemed to point to his eyes and his lips, and both were smiling. "This has been a lesson to us all of the griefs that could be averted if people would talk and listen to children." I felt him squeeze my shoulder and saw his fingers tighten on Uncle Stephen's. "Don't keep replaying it in your mind, Mr. Whitfield. It's over and couldn't be better."

Miss Hannah spoke up behind him. I was surprised, because I thought they had gone. "How about if we all go by the Sealtest dairy bar to celebrate? You, too, Vance, our treat."

Mr. McGrew said he'd like to, but he had other cases to prepare. Uncle Stephen shook his head. "I think I'd like to just go on home."

"Then can we take Carley and you go on?"

He left like a convict escaping.

He was in his study with his door closed when I got home, and wouldn't come out for supper. Abby called him. I called him. Aunt Kate went up and went inside, but she came down sighing and shaking her head. "He says he isn't hungry."

All evening she and Grace peered at the ceiling as if expecting a hole to open up and let him down. Abby got crotchety and wouldn't go to bed. Even John was fussy. Finally I went up to bed. It was more like a funeral downstairs than a celebration.

I was still undressing when the doorbell rang. Next thing I knew I heard heavy footsteps coming upstairs and somebody knocking at Uncle Stephen's door. "Brother Whitfield? May I come in?"

It took me a minute to recognize the voice of Meek, Janey Lou's husband and Jay's uncle. His deep voice rumbled while I was finishing putting on my pajamas, then I curled up on my closet floor to listen.

"You have no cause to punish yourself, sir. We won! Jay is a free man."

Uncle Stephen's voice sounded like he had a very bad cold. "I didn't win. I was an utter failure. It was my testimony that got Jay arrested, I did horribly on the witness stand—"

"That was just because Mr. Lamar kept trying to trick you. He didn't want you to tell the truth."

"No, he didn't. But Scripture tells us we are to be as wise as serpents and as harmless as doves. I plumb forgot that first part. In my own pride, I thought if I just marched in there and told the simple truth, Jay would walk out free. Instead, that lawyer made a fool out of me. I wasn't wise, I was the worst kind of fool."

"We do have to walk right careful through this world, sir. They's always folks ready to twist the truth. But put it behind you! It's over now."

"I can't, Meek. Because—you want to know the worst part? I hated him. I'd have throttled him, if I could. How can I be a preacher when I harbor such hate in my heart?"

Outside my west window the moon sailed toward the mountains—from whence cometh my help. "Uncle Stephen sure could use some help," I begged them silently.

I heard a creak, like Meek was shifting in his chair. For a long time he didn't say anything, then he spoke hesitantly. "It's not my place to speak, maybe, but it seems to me a preacher has to understand everything in a human heart before he can help others. As long as you've never felt hate, how can you help somebody else who has? Maybe today isn't one you'll be proud of, but I 'spect it'll be one that will be important in years to come." His chair creaked again. "And I'd be willing to wager, if I was a bettin' man, that it wasn't really Mr. Lamar you hated. Truth is, he's not a bad man. I've run across him down at Miss Hannah's from time to time, and he's a lot of fun when he wants to be. But there's something in him—a mean, dark streak—"

"Racism." I heard Uncle Stephen blow his nose. "It was his racism I hated, his confounded certainty that Jay killed Ira simply because Jay's Negro." He shoved back his chair. "You're right—even I liked the fellow a time or two." His voice was beginning to sound normal again.

Meek chuckled and slapped something—probably his leg with his palm. "But wasn't his face a study when little Carley said you told Jay nobody would accuse him just because he was a Negro? I thought he'd have a heart attack. And when Miss Carley said she'd put a curse on poor Mr. Ira—" His bass chuckle rumbled again.

Uncle Stephen chuckled, too, but he added, "I'll have to talk with Carley about that. We can't have her unleashing her powers all over town." I heard him scratch a match against his desk. "But you came up here for a purpose, didn't you? Not just because you heard I was locked in my room licking my wounds?"

"I came to thank you, from the bottom of our hearts. We're proud to know you, Mr. Whitfield, and that's the truth. And if there's ever anything we can do—anything at all—"

"You already did, Meek. Just now. Thank you." I heard shuffles like both of them were getting to their feet. At the door, Uncle Stephen said, "God sure works in mysterious ways, doesn't he? Who'd have thought he'd use a bee and a little girl to not only win a law case, but teach me something I needed to know?"

"And for us, it's over." Meek sounded as happy as I felt. "It's all over, sir."

That's what we all thought. That was before Miss Pauline opened her mouth to spew out fire and brimstone.

Part 7

The Splendor of Light

On my hall floor four things remain: a small brown bag full of fuzzy bees, one last envelope of clippings, a green pillbox hat with a little spotted veil, and a silver dollar that glitters in the light. I will need to send that dollar to John. It's the only thing in this box he might appreciate. I have decided somewhere along the way that I will give the box to Abby. But whatever will I do with these clippings?

As I open them, a bitterness rises on my tongue. I know right away what it is: the taste of betrayal, unforgiveness, and heartbreak. All my life I have wrestled with questions that rose that next month in Job's Corner. Must we forgive people who deliberately wrong us and have no remorse? Are those who are merely misguided and yet do evil any better than those who deliberately do wrong? Why is it easier to forgive someone for hurting me than for hurting someone I love? How could people to whom we'd given our hearts and lives do this to us?

It was that month of June when I first realized my own heart and life now belonged to Aunt Kate, Uncle Stephen, and Job's Corner, for I took personally acts of betrayal against them. The rest of my life I have struggled to put together the genuine liking I had for some people with a cringing that they could do what they did.

Abby and John were never tainted by those days. Should I tell them what really happened, or skim lightly past this part? No, I must tell the story as best I can. In fully entering the darkness, maybe I will finally discover what Uncle Stephen called "the bottom," that splendor of light Jay sang about. Maybe in the telling, I will find my own liberation.

Chapter 38

The morning after Jay's trial, while she was pouring his second cup of coffee, Aunt Kate suggested, "Stephen, why don't you take the bus over to your daddy's Thursday for a couple of nights? You haven't had a day off in—I can't remember when."

His eyes brightened. "You'd be all right here?"

"We'll be fine. We're going to Mama's Friday afternoon anyway, to take Carley back." She bent down and kissed the top of his head.

Gratefully he drew her toward him and rested his cheek against her waist. "What did I ever do to deserve you?"

He left on Thursday, and we left Friday as soon as school ended. None of us imagined what would happen the day I got home.

I stayed with Big Mama a week. I wouldn't bother to tell you about that, except a couple of important things happened. Mostly it was unsettling. I didn't feel like I belonged anymore. My school friends acted happy to see me, but I didn't understand half the stuff they talked about. Aunt Sukie was getting as forgetful as Grace had said: sometimes she called me Carley and sometimes she called me Kate. Once she even called me Lila. Big Mama was at the store all day. I went with her once and put things on shelves, but the only good part of that was, I earned enough to buy Aunt Kate a book for her birthday, Elizabeth Barrett Browning's *Sonnets from the Portuguese*. The clerk recommended it when I asked for something romantic. Except for that one time in the kitchen when she kissed his head, it had been a long time since Aunt Kate and Uncle Stephen had held hands or kissed. I thought maybe poetry might help.

On the second day I was there, I walked down to Geena's. She came out and we sat on the edge of her saggy porch, trying not to let the jagged edges of the boards get splinters behind our knees. Geena had grown tall that year, and very stout. Her thigh would have made two of mine as we sat there side-by-side in shorts, one pale and thin, one solid and brown as melted chocolate.

"Do you remember how we used to play house out behind the wash pot?" I asked boldly, bending down to pick a grass weed to chew.

Geena slewed her eyes sideways as if uncertain what to say.

"And how we pulled chickweed and called it greens?"

Suddenly she grinned. "I 'member you made me eat wild onions, tellin' me they was good for me."

"You told me spiders would bite my bottom in the out-house," I reminded her.

Her chuckle was deep and round. "You believed me, too."

"Remember when we put pokeberries in your mama's wash pot because we thought Big Mama would like purple sheets?"

She hooted in derision. "What you mean 'we'? It was you said she'd like her sheets purple. My mama like to have killed me for that."

"Big Mama whipped me good, too."

Once started, our tongues couldn't go fast enough. We got to laughing at some of the things we used to do until we lay back and rolled on the porch, clutching our sides.

When we caught our breath, she asked hesitantly, "You want a RC Cola? Mama bought some this week." We both went to her kitchen, opened RC Colas, and stood by the sink drinking them like we'd never stopped being friends.

I decided I'd ask Aunt Kate if Geena could come for a week later in the summer, to visit me and Grace. I didn't care what anybody thought about it.

The last day before I left, I made Big Mama take me to visit my other grandmother. "You won't like what you see," Big Mama warned.

"She's my own flesh and blood," I replied. "I think I ought to at least recognize her if I meet her on the street." I didn't tell

Big Mama what else I wanted: to ask her casually if she'd seen Roy lately. I wanted to know if he'd gone to California without my college money, and I could finally breathe easy.

We called ahead so she'd know to expect us, but we had to call a neighbor to take the message because she didn't have a phone. We also couldn't go until after Big Mama got off work at six. The shadows were growing long as we drove through poorer and poorer streets.

Several times on the way Big Mama acted like she was about to tell me something, then she'd stop. Finally she said, "The reason you never knew her is, she drinks. I hope she'll be sober this evening, but you never can tell. She used to show up on our porch any hour of the day or night, crying and begging for money to pay the rent. We knew good and well she'd spend it on liquor. Finally Pop started paying her rent directly to the landlord, but he made her promise not to bother Lila."

Maybe she felt she'd said too much, because she added, "She's not evil, just weak. Her second husband started her drinking, and she never conquered it." She stopped the Buick before a tiny white house just like all the other houses on both sides of the street. None of them had any front yards to speak of, and they all looked exactly alike. Seeing my puzzlement, Big Mama explained, "These are mill houses, built for people who work in the thread factory. She worked there all her life—as long as she could."

She came to the screened door even before we knocked, a skinny woman in a cotton housedress, twisting her hands in front of her waist. She had sagging shoulders, gray hair pulled back in a roll at her neck, and a lot of wrinkles. She looked a little like Roy, except she had faded blue eyes that looked like they'd seen a lot of life and none of it worth remembering.

"Won't you all sit down?" she asked politely, coming out onto the porch and pointing to three chairs. Two of the chairs were weathered rockers that looked like they stayed out all the time. I chose the third, a white straight chair that looked like she'd put it out special for us.

She didn't look drunk, but whiffs coming through her open door smelled like Mr. Rob on his bad days. She bent forward in her rocker to look closely at me. "I swan, you're the spittin' image of my precious Roy!" She put out one claw hand and clutched mine.

I cringed at the description, but let her hold onto me. I even squeezed her hand a little. Whoever and whatever else she was, she was my flesh and blood.

A drop of water formed at the tip of her nose and her eyes reddened. "You're all I've got of him now. We are all God's spared, you and me."

"What's happened to Roy?" Big Mama asked before I could.

She turned in surprise. "Didn't you hear? He was killed in a wreck." She swiped her eyes with one hand. "Week before Easter it was, that Monday evenin'. He'd been off somewhere and was headin' home when a truck hit his car. They said he was on the wrong side of the road passin' on a curve, but you know how people are. They'll say anything." She brushed her nose with the back of one hand, then reached that hand out to pat mine. "It was in the papers, but they got his name wrong. Apparently he'd borried somebody else's driver's license." She drew herself up in indignation. "It took them two days to notify me."

I kept my face solemn and said, "I am so sorry," like we were talking about a stranger.

Meanwhile, Relief jumped up inside my head and danced a jig, saying, "You need never be scared of him again." Good Breeding admonished sternly, "You just heard that your daddy died. You ought to be sad." A third voice said piously, "Poor Roy. I hope he got right with God before he died." I recognized that one for the imposter it was: What I Ought to Be Thinking. What I really was thinking was, "Roy was lucky he died in a car wreck, and not in the gas chamber for killing Mr. Ira."

I can't be proud Roy was my daddy, but I try to remember that he saved me from Mr. Ira when I needed it. That may have been the finest thing he ever did. Maybe, even, the last.

We sat on that front porch less than half an hour. When I think back on it, I can appreciate the fact that three people with absolutely nothing in common except the blood in my veins could sustain the fiction of fellowship that long. Roy's mother—for that was how I thought of her now—kept looking back at her front door like she'd enjoy a drink if we'd just get up and go. Big Mama kept shifting her bulk in the inadequate rocker to remind me not to stay too long. And me? I did what I always do when I get nervous: chattered too much about nothing. I told Roy's poor mother about my teacher, my grades, my piano lessons, Bethel Church, Mrs. Cameron—when I got to

Mrs. Cameron I finally noticed the glazed look in her eyes, and realized I was doing exactly what Big Mama had done at the Bethel Church Bicentennial Celebration. It was time to leave.

"Glad to meet you," I said, standing and sticking out my hand.

"Come again," she said weakly.

I would go again, each time I visited Big Mama for longer than a couple of days. When I got old enough to drive I visited more often than the Marshall side of the family knew. I felt sorry for that faded old woman who had lost everyone she loved and her own self-respect. Gradually we began to have enough history together to enjoy one another's company to a limited degree. When she was sober, she sometimes told me stories about Roy as a child that made me pity and almost love him. When she died while I was in college, I actually grieved. But I never could bring myself to think of her as my grandmother. Each of us has places our pride will not go.

❀

Uncle Stephen insisted that I ride the bus back to Job's Corner. "Carley's plenty big enough to ride eighty miles on a bus by herself," he told Aunt Kate when she protested. "Haven't you noticed how she's growing up?"

I was glad he thought so, but I rode the whole way rigid in my seat, hoping none of those people around me were murderers or kidnappers.

You can't tell by looking at them, you know. As Big Mama often said, a lot of evil can hide behind good manners and a thin layer of skin.

Take Miss Pauline, for instance . . .

I got home on Saturday, the day Miss Pauline entertained Job's Corner with confidences that would shake our world. That's the afternoon when Preston came over to inform me, "You don't know anything, smarty pants. If you knew everything there *is* to know—what old Stevie boy's *really* been doin'?—well, all I gotta say is, when we get through with him, he'll be lucky if he don't get tarred, feathered, and run out of town. Just you wait!" That's when I decided I'd rather go to hell than have to forgive Preston for what he was saying—and when I finally gave him the licking he so frequently deserved.

But I didn't tell Uncle Stephen what we'd been fighting about, and he didn't ask. As a result, the first he suspected anything was wrong was Sunday morning. Very few people came to church. There was no Freda and no choir.

Uncle Stephen looked around puzzled, then joked, "In most churches, Low Sunday is the week after Easter. As usual, Bethel has its own unique style."

Only a few people smiled nervously. Nobody laughed out loud.

In spite of the small congregation, he delivered his sermon about how God can use unexpected things—even bees—to bring about justice. He'd been excited to find some little fuzzy bees that florists put on flowers to make arrangements more interesting. He'd bought enough to give everybody one, but he plumb forgot to hand them out. I guess Aunt Kate must have thrust them to the bottom of the Remember Box that very afternoon. He also delivered the shortest pastoral prayer in the history of Bethel. Just before he was about to pronounce the benediction, Mr. Hugh Fred stood up.

"Before you dismiss us, Stephen, I want to request all the elders to stay for a called meeting of Session. You, too, please."

"You all come down to our house for dinner," Miss Hannah told Aunt Kate at the door. "Janey Lou is frying a chicken. You can ride with me, and Mr. Whitfield can bring Davy later."

We climbed into her big Oldsmobile and rattled along with a cloud of orange dust that sprayed out behind us like a fox's tail. Uncle Stephen said Miss Hannah always drove like Jehu, furiously. That day she drove more furiously than ever. She also talked a blue streak all the way down there and right up till the two men arrived.

"My ears is tired of listenin'," Abby confided to me as we went to wash our hands.

Miss Hannah had set all the places in the dining room, but when the two men got there, she took one look at Uncle Stephen and quickly moved my place and Abby's to the kitchen. Anybody could tell that he was angry. He was as white as the sheet he'd used to cover Mr. Ira, and his hair looked like it had been attacked by an eggbeater.

"I wants to eat in de dinin' room," Abby objected, her lower lip quivering.

Miss Hannah heard her from the back room, where she'd gone to fetch John's high chair. All her life Hannah Anderson kept a high chair for her smallest guests. "You all eat in with Janey Lou today, old dears," she called, rattling something to get the high chair out, "and when you are through, go out in the yard to play. I think the grown-ups need to talk a little."

When she'd bustled out and closed the swinging door behind her, Abby looked at me, her eyes large and worried. "What's de grown-ups talkin' 'bout?" she demanded suspiciously. "Is we gonna get a whippin'?"

Janey Lou came from the sink and put one hand on Abby's red-gold curls. "They ain't studying you at all, honey chile. Dis is grown-up business. Now you eat up that chicken leg, and when you're through, I'll show you how to suck the bone."

The grown-ups talked for a very long time. Janey Lou carried one of Miss Hannah's quilts outside and spread it on the grass a long way from the house. I carried John out, and Abby and I played with him until they both fell asleep. Then I sat there smelling the fresh summer air and enjoying the view of the mountains across the pasture. They no longer seemed too far away. Job's Corner was home. But I did wonder what was going on now.

When Aunt Kate called us to get in the car to go home, she was pale, but nobody told us children a thing. That whole evening and the next day, Uncle Stephen stayed in his study. Finally he came down to supper, still white and quiet. "Eat, Stephen," Aunt Kate urged, passing him the meat loaf. "You have to eat."

He shook his head like he'd gone deaf and blind. "I don't even know what to preach about next week—if they let me preach. Love—grace—people will twist anything I say."

"Some won't," Grace reminded him. "Folks who come to hear the Word of God hear that, and folks who come with their ears full of hate hear that. You preach what you're given to preach, Mr. Whitfield. Don't let anybody change your mind about that."

"Thanks." He reached out to cover her hand with his own.

At the last minute, though, he drew his hand back like he'd been burned. He and Aunt Kate exchanged a stricken look. He got up and left the table without another word.

Chapter 39

A clipping from the *Statesville Daily Record:*

Retarded Girl Molested, Preacher Charged

Local pastor Stephen A. Whitfield has been charged with the molestation of Ivy Baines, 18, a retarded member of his congregation. Earlier this year, Mr. Whitfield drove the girl to Winston-Salem for weekly medical appointments, and recently he has been "consoling her" for the loss of her father. Charges were brought after a routine medical examination revealed Miss Baines had been molested and a church member found written statements in her handwriting saying, "I luv Stevn, Stevn luvs me." Her tearful mother declares, "We trusted him, and look what he did."

Mr. Whitfield denies all allegations. Presbytery has instigated proceedings. A church court trial will be held in the sanctuary of Bethel Church, Job's Corner, on June 21 at 9 A.M.

The father of the young woman was brutally murdered in March. Jay Anderson, Negro, was acquitted in that case, which is still under investigation. Mr. Whitfield appeared in that trial as a witness for the defense. His niece, Carolyn Marshall, led to dismissal of charges by admitting she had tampered with crucial evidence.

That was the first time my name ever appeared in a news-paper, and they got it wrong. They didn't use a very good pic-ture of Uncle Stephen, either, which I thought was awful since it was right on the front page. But at least I finally found out what was going on. That day's paper had disappeared from our house, so I went over and read Miss Pauline's, because at that time I still had no idea she had spread the story.

I went home and got out my dictionary. It took forever to look up all the words, and I still couldn't understand the impor-tant one: "Molestation." It meant: *to annoy, disturb, or perse-cute somebody, to injure them, to make annoying sexual advances.* I looked up that last, confusing term and found a lot of big words that all seemed to go round and round. Nobody ever really got educated by reading a dictionary. I still couldn't understand what everybody was so upset about.

As best as I could figure it, Uncle Stephen had been pester-ing Ivy to advance her to become a woman. Anybody could look at Ivy and her baby doll and see she wouldn't ever be one, but it seemed like they'd all be proud of Uncle Stephen for trying to help.

Preston's ideas about what they were talking about were as ignorant as mine. When he saw me the next morning, he sang, "Stephen loves Ivy. Ivy loves Stephen."

"So what?" I demanded. "Uncle Stephen loves every-body—even you. And Ivy ought to love him. He traipsed all the way to Winston-Salem for weeks to get her legs painted."

"But he can't marry her," Preston insisted, sidling so close I could smell his dirty boy smell. "He's already married. But you could marry me, Carley. When we grow up, I mean."

I shoved him away. "I wouldn't marry you if you were the last man on earth. And Uncle Stephen wouldn't marry Ivy, either. You're crazy to think such a thing."

But in the next weeks, that craziness seeped into the pores of Job's Corner. People we'd known nearly a year were just hes-itant enough to let us know they hadn't quite made up their minds what to believe. All except Miss Pauline, Miss Nancy, and Miz Baines, of course. They treated us like we had leprosy. When I read *MacBeth* in tenth grade, I immediately visualized their faces circling the cauldron.

To make matters worse, Miss Pauline was extra nice to Abby and even pretty nice to me. One night Abby got furious with her mother and roared, "Don't you say mean fings about my fend Miss Pauline! She's de nicest wummin in Job's Corner!"

The craziness invaded our house. Aunt Kate and Uncle Stephen fought late at night, their voices rising like echoes of doom from the kitchen.

"Why would I need a filthy, retarded girl when I've got you? Answer me that."

"Somebody did, Stephen."

"Well, it wasn't me."

"Can you prove it?"

"I don't have to prove I didn't, they have to prove I did."

"Why didn't you always take Abby? How could you drive her over there alone?"

"Do you think I haven't asked myself that a thousand times? But Abby wanted to stay home some weeks. I didn't want to force her to go. It was supposed to be fun for her."

"Yeah, fun and games."

"Kate, it wasn't like that and you know it!"

"I know you've been too tired and busy for me for a long time."

"I have not. But with Easter and the trial—oh, honey, if *you* don't believe me . . ."

"I don't know what I believe anymore. I am so tired! Tired of this place, tired of the people. Tired of trying to please everybody. Tired of becoming somebody I don't even know. I'm dowdy, my clothes are ugly—"

"Buy yourself some new ones."

"We don't have the money! Besides, if I dress nice, somebody will criticize me for spending too much."

"Let them. We can't base our whole lives on what other people think."

"What people think is *important!* Why can't you ever see that? You've got to fight this, Stephen, you've just got to! Prove you didn't do it!"

"How do you prove you didn't do something when nobody was there to see?"

"Ivy was there. She says you love her."

"I was *nice* to her. Probably the only person who ever was."

"But how nice? That's what people want to know. How nice *were* you to Ivy?"

From what I could pick up listening around corners and through cracks in doors, it was Mr. Wash who insisted that the

Session ask Presbytery to try Uncle Stephen for molesting Ivy, and Davy Anderson who tried to convince the elders it was merely the work of women with meddling tongues. Mr. Hugh Fred said it might be better to let somebody from outside resolve the matter. Uncle Stephen said he couldn't blame him for feeling that way. But he sounded tired enough to die.

When I asked why they'd have the trial at church instead of in the courthouse, Uncle Stephen explained that Presbyterian church government is what the United States government is based on, but it's separate. "A preacher, like the president, can't be tried by a regular court or even his Session for things relating to church discipline. He has to come before a council of Presbytery—preachers and elders from other churches—for them to hear his case."

"What happens if they decide you are guilty. I mean, I know you aren't," I added hastily, "but what if they make a mistake?"

"Then they defrock me, and don't let me preach, serve communion, or baptize people."

"Not even in a white suit?"

"Not even in a white suit."

Uncle Stephen got very calm after the letter came saying Presbytery's council would meet in ten days at Bethel Church. He said it was now in the hands of God.

Aunt Kate got mean as a snake. She snapped at me, jerked Abby's hair when she brushed it, even screamed one night at John when he wouldn't stop crying and go to sleep.

For Uncle Stephen, that was the last straw. "You've got to get out of here, Kate. You aren't doing any of us any good. Go see your mother for a few days."

"If I go, I don't know if I'll ever come back," she threatened.

He flinched, but said softly, "That's a decision you'll have to make."

My decision was already made. I didn't want to go with her. Isn't that odd, when you consider that less than a year before I couldn't wait to get away? But it seemed to me that in some ways I belonged as much to Uncle Stephen as Aunt Kate, and I thought she was wrong. Besides, I'd just gotten back from Big Mama's. I didn't want to go back so soon.

I went for a long walk to think how to explain clearly what wasn't exactly clear to me, and wound up all the way down at Miss Hannah's. I'd never walked that far alone before. She was in her kitchen icing a chocolate cake. She always claimed Mr.

Davy had a hollow sweet tooth, but everybody knew she ate as many sweets as he did.

When she saw me, she brought two plates down from the cabinet. "Hello, old dear. Want to help me test this cake?" While she cut the cake, I went to another cabinet and got down the rose pink and robin's egg blue aluminum glasses like I was right at home. I poured us each iced tea and put in lots of lemon the way we both liked it. Miss Hannah never suggested a child drink milk when she was having tea.

We carried our snack out to the side porch and rocked gently as we ate.

"My violets are doing well," she said, looking with satisfaction at twenty-four fuzzy-leafed African violets blooming in every known shade of pink and purple. When Miss Hannah talked about her plants she used the same proud and happy tone Aunt Kate used when she said things like "Abby's smart as a whip" or "John's going to walk early."

"They sure are," I agreed, relishing the extra chocolate icing she'd put on the side of my plate because "it's a shame to throw this away."

She licked chocolate off her upper lip. "Everything going all right with you?"

"No. Aunt Kate's going to Big Mama's for a visit and I don't want to go." I didn't mean to blurt it right out, but my tongue always did have a mind of its own. I tried to backpedal. "I mean, I like going and all, but I've just been there, and . . ." I stopped. Even to Miss Hannah I couldn't say, "I just can't bear for Uncle Stephen to be alone right before his trial."

Her forehead puckered in disappointment. "Oh, dear. I'd been counting on asking you to come down and help me clear out a bit. I've been meaning to clean out my upstairs storeroom and the room at the back, but I'll need somebody to climb up to get things off top shelves, and to run up and down the stairs. I'm not as young as I used to be. If you can't—" She stopped as if struck by a sudden thought. "Perhaps Mrs. Whitfield would let you stay down here with me while she's gone. Could we ask her?"

The next morning Aunt Kate piled Abby, John, Rowdy, and Grace into the Chevy and drove away. I went down to sleep at Miss Hannah's.

At first I'd begged to sleep at our house, saying I didn't want to have to move all my stuff. Actually I didn't want Uncle Stephen to rattle around that big house alone every night. I even worried that Miss Pauline might come calling after her children were in bed.

"It wouldn't be proper for you to be here alone with Uncle Stephen," Aunt Kate told me. "Especially right now."

I thought that was dumb, until I went for the mail the afternoon she left.

"I see your aunt's left town," Miss Pauline wheezed. Her face was pinker than usual and her little pig eyes glittered blue, like Preston's.

"My grandmother got sick," I lied. "Aunt Kate had to go take care of her."

"I don't blame her one bit." Miss Pauline handed me a stack of letters. "I wouldn't stay with that man, either, after what he done. I bolt my bedroom door at night." She leaned over the counter and put her ruddy face close to mine, although there wasn't another soul around. "You by yourself over there with him, or do you have that colored girl, too?"

"Grace went home to see her folks, and I'm down at Miss Hannah's," I was glad to inform her. "Uncle Stephen's alone, but he's not worried. None of us are. He hasn't done a thing." I put my nose in the air and headed down the road.

Miss Hannah gave me her prettiest upstairs bedroom. It had creamy wide plank walls, sloping ceilings, a rose and green carpet on the floor, and a bed so high I needed a stool to get in. But as pretty as it was, the room didn't help me sleep very well. I kept thinking that this was the most spread-out my family had ever been, sleeping in three houses. At night, the distances between us seemed enormous and dark.

Each morning Miss Hannah and I got up and talked about cleaning out her storeroom, but somehow we never did. We played canasta, talked, fed the hens, talked some more, made our lunch, played more canasta, took a nap (she napped, I read), and by then it was time to start what she always called "Davy's supper."

In the evening we talked some more. We talked about school, flowers, funny things Abby said, and Mr. Davy's sweet tooth. We talked about everything in the world except Uncle Stephen and the upcoming trial.

One evening when we were finishing up a bowl of ice cream

before bed, she reached out her heavy hand and put it over mine. "Carley, would you mind calling us Aunt Hannah and Uncle Davy? It would mean a lot to us."

"Sure, A–Aunt Hannah." It felt so good I said it again, with a grin. She squeezed my hand. Even her glasses beamed.

Uncle Stephen came down to supper several nights, but he just picked at his food. He said he was getting a lot of studying done, had a garden planted, and had been to see some folks in the hospital. "Gettin' a lot of prayin' done, too," he admitted. "I've gotten to the place Moses finally came to at the edge of the Red Sea, when God said, 'Hey, Boy, get out of the way and watch what I'm going to do.' I just wish I had a clue what that might be."

Uncle Davy put his hand on his arm. "We'll be right there with you."

"But I hope it doesn't involve a Red Sea," Aunt Hannah joked. "Davy doesn't swim."

I'd figured I'd be there two or three nights at the most, but by Sunday, Aunt Kate still wasn't home. The church was full of people, although some went out the back door so they didn't need to shake Uncle Stephen's hand. Lots asked about Aunt Kate.

That afternoon after Janey Lou left, while Aunt Hannah and Uncle Davy stretched out for their Sunday nap, I tiptoed into the kitchen, dialed the operator, and asked her how to place my first long-distance call.

I kept my voice soft. "Big Mama, it's Carley. "

"What's the matter, honey? I can scarcely hear you. Are you sick?"

"No, ma'am, but Aunt Kate needs to come on home. Let me talk to her, please."

Neither one of us noticed I'd called Job's Corner home. Matters were too deep for that. "Kate's resting right now. I don't like to bother her."

Tears choked my voice. "Somebody's gotta bother her! Do you know what people think about her being gone right now? Half the folks at church today asked me where she was, and the other half kept giving me funny looks. You tell her to come on back. We *need* her!"

Big Mama sighed. "She has to do whatever she feels is right, honey."

"It's not what we feel, it's what we do. That's what you

always told *me*. Tell her this is a time when that really is true."

"I'll tell her, but whether she'll listen or not is another story. How's Stephen?"

"Bearing up, I guess, but he needs his family. You talk some sense in her. You hear me?"

"I'll try."

I hung up weeping, but hopeful. "If anybody could talk sense into her," I assured myself, "it's Big Mama."

Chapter 40

I wanted to get to the church and hide before anybody else arrived. I'd picked my hiding place: the "slaves' gallery" or balcony. Its rising pews were old, with high backs. I could scrunch down behind one and never be seen. I might even be able to bob up and see occasionally.

I told Miss Hannah I needed to go home to practice the piano, and left very early. Nobody was at the church yet when I arrived. I hurried around back and went in that way, so nobody could see me from across the highway. I don't know if I was more worried about being seen by Miss Pauline or Uncle Stephen.

I had sneaked into the manse kitchen and taken an apple, four slices of bread, the jar of peanut butter, and a knife. I didn't know how long the trial might last, and I didn't want to starve. I carried them all up to the balcony and went over to the side away from the stairs, carefully listening for the first warning that I needed to duck. Absently I started eating the apple.

The church was still and warm. The air had that stale holy smell all churches get when they've been shut up. Sunlight streamed through the east windows and turned the cream and mahogany pews pink and gold. One ray came through the window, hit the cross up front, and reflected over the whole big room. I wished I could pray something big and important that would make a difference, but all I could say was what I'd begged in the pasture with Roy: *pleaseGodpleaseGodpleaseGod!* My stomach ached so bad I finally put down the apple half-eaten.

The sound of tires on gravel warned me that people were

beginning to arrive. Regretfully I slid to the floor and scrunched up. It was dusty, and a tight fit. I'd grown more than I'd realized.

"Whatja doin'?"

I looked up to see Preston ducked over, heading toward me. "Why aren't you in summer school?" I hissed. He was *supposed* to be learning arithmetic.

"Why ain't you down at Aunt Hannah's?" he countered.

"I have a right to be here. It's my uncle."

"It's my preacher, and Mama's gonna testify. But she'd skin me if she knew I was here."

"Uncle Stephen, too," I admitted.

"If we shove that pew up a little, we'll have more room. They ain't screwed down up here." He put his shoulder against it and pushed. Before the adults arrived we had made a wide, comfortable nest. Preston stuck his legs out under the front pew and leaned against the seat of the one behind. "Ain't bad up here," he said. He ate the rest of my apple, spread a piece of my bread with peanut butter, and crammed it into his mouth whole.

"At least you don't smell," I told him.

"Took a bath to come to church," he said thickly. "Even if it ain't Sunday."

Four strangers in dark suits—three gray and one navy— came in. At first I figured they were janitors dressed nice, because two of them carried the communion table down to the floor near the front pews and brought down four choir chairs to set behind it and one to set beside it. The others went around opening windows and talking about baseball. But then they sat down behind the table and started setting out papers. I wondered if they were the lawyers, judge, or jury.

After a while Uncle Stephen came in. He shook hands with each of them. One of them acted like he thought Uncle Stephen had leprosy, but I heard the one in the navy suit say in a low voice, "This is a hard thing, Stephen."

"'I'm glad you came, sir."

"Wouldn't have missed it. Just hang on tight and pray, you hear me? Now why don't you wait out back until we call you?"

Uncle Stephen went out through the back door about the time some of our members started coming in. Everybody wore Sunday clothes, which looked odd on Wednesday.

The way people chose to sit on the right or the left reminded me of a wedding. Miss Pauline and Miss Nancy marched to the next-to-the-front pew on the left, like good Baptists. I'd have bet they never sat that close to the front of a church in their lives. Mr. Wash looked like he wasn't sure where he wanted to sit, exactly, but finally he sat beside his wife.

Aunt Hannah and Uncle Davy came in, both dressed for Sunday. She even wore her hat and gloves. They took the pew across from Mr. Wash and Miss Nancy, and Aunt Hannah gave them a little wave. Mr. Wash waved back and half-stood, as if he'd like to join them, but Miss Nancy tugged his arm to sit back down.

In just a minute some more people came in and went down beside Aunt Hannah. They looked around, then the woman leaned over and whispered something. Aunt Hannah shook her head. I knew what they were asking. The same thing everybody was going to ask: *Where on earth was Aunt Kate?*

In a minute, Mr. Mayhew came down the side aisle and sat beside Miss Pauline. "Uncle Gil!" Preston smacked a fist into his palm.

I hadn't seen Mr. Mayhew since school got out. He was dressed in the brown suit he always used to wear to conduct the choir. I saw him look up at the empty chairs, and wondered if he missed Bethel.

Other people straggled in—the young bride and groom among them. They came halfway down the aisle, stopped, and looked—obviously trying to decide where to sit. He was about to slide in on the left behind Mr. Wash when she tugged his elbow and made him go to the right about five pews behind Aunt Hannah. I could tell, though, that he wasn't sure that was where they belonged. That made me sad.

Mr. Hugh Fred and Miss Emily came in and did the same thing—sort of waltzed around in the aisle a minute trying to decide where to sit. Finally he left her and went up to shake hands with the four men. They motioned for him to sit on a front pew. He looked around, and took the one in front of Mr. Wash. Miss Emily slid in behind Uncle Davy. Mr. Hugh Fred frowned, but she ignored him.

About that time Mr. Rob and Miss Rilla came in. When they saw where Wash was sitting, Mr. Rob shook his head like he was disgusted. He and Miss Rilla marched right up and sat with Miss Emily.

The rest of the people who came in sort of evenly divided between the right and the left. I didn't hear anybody speak above a murmur. You'd have thought it was a funeral.

In a way it was. The death of our honeymoon at Bethel Church.

When I heard somebody coming up the balcony stairs, it scared me to death. I scrunched way down and tried to see who it was by their feet. I recognized those worn loafers. Bonnie Anderson. "Oh, no!" Preston slid further down behind the pew. Bonnie never saw us. She went straight to the front row of the balcony and rested her arms on the railing.

I wondered who was keeping children like Jimmy Lamont and Sue Mary (and Velma). Later I heard that Aunt Hannah had asked Jay's sister Cecile to keep children in the nursery. She'd even brought up juice and cookies for them to have for refreshments.

When everybody was seated, one of the four men behind the table took out a stack of clean paper and a pen. A second said something to Hugh Fred. He went down the aisle and came back leading Ivy Baines by the elbow. Her mother trudged along just behind, leaning heavily on her cane with her head thrust forward like an avenging turtle. He motioned them to the front pew on the left.

Meanwhile the man in navy had gone out and brought Uncle Stephen back. Uncle Stephen looked odd in a coat and tie instead of his robe. I hoped if they defrocked him, they took him out back to do it. Some of his underwear had holes.

He sat on the right front pew.

Mr. Hugh Fred was still standing there, sort of in the middle of the aisle. He looked from Uncle Stephen to Miz Baines, at Uncle Stephen again, and then back at the congregation. There were a few more people on the side for Miz Baines. Mr. Hugh Fred looked like he might be counting, then he hitched up his pants to save the creases and sat down beside Miz Baines.

Uncle Stephen gave him a look like Jesus must have given Judas—sad, but understanding. Then he looked down at his hands. At that moment, I almost gave up.

The shortest of the four men stood up and cleared his throat. "Before we begin, the moderator of our Presbytery will open with prayer."

One of the men stood and prayed longer than I could listen. Sometimes it's a good thing God has patience.

Next, the short man put on his reading glasses and picked up a book. "I want to read from the Presbyterian *Book of Church Order* concerning the rules of discipline." I didn't understand it all, but I did understand the part about "the aims of discipline are that God may be honored, that the purity and welfare of the Church may be maintained, and that those under the Church's discipline may be brought to repentance and restoration." I wondered what it would take to bring Miss Pauline and Miss Nancy to repentance. More than four men in dark suits, I suspected.

The third man said, "A written charge has been laid before Presbytery against Stephen Allen Whitfield, pastor of Bethel congregation. Mr. Whitfield, are you aware of the charges against you?"

Uncle Stephen half-stood and nodded. "I am, sir."

"And how do you plead?"

"Not guilty." Uncle Stephen said it without a tremor and sat back down. I wanted to clap. Preston made a short grunt of disbelief. I elbowed him to be quiet.

"Who is the first witness against this man?"

Mr. Hugh Fred stood. I wondered if, as Clerk of Session, he'd be prosecutor like Mr. Lamar, but all he said was, "The first witness, sir, is Mrs. Ira Baines."

She hauled herself to her feet and took the witness chair, a crow of a woman all in black. She made a fuss of arranging her skirt and propping her cane in front of her for everybody to see.

The man in the navy suit leaned forward. "Do I understand, Mrs. Baines, that you lost your husband recently?"

"Yessir, I did." Her witch's voice took on a pitiful timbre.

"Our condolences are with you."

From where I sat, through the open window I could see the granite tombstone with Baines carved across it. Miz Baines hadn't lost Mr. Ira, just relocated him—in a clean suit.

The man who had read earlier asked, "Do you solemnly promise, in the presence of God, that you will declare the truth, the whole truth, and nothing but the truth, according to the best of your knowledge in the matter in which you are called witness, as you shall answer it to the great Judge of the living and the dead?"

"Yessir, I do," she quavered.

"Would you tell this court in your own words what exactly it is that you charge Mr. Whitfield with?"

"Yessir. I charge that he has took the affections of my girl Ivy from her mama and made her love him instead. I charge that he's done things he oughtn't have done with her. That's what."

"And do you have proof of this?"

"I know what I know. Ivy thinks the sun rises and sets in Mr. Whitfield. I can't do nothin' with her anymore." She gave Uncle Stephen a look of pure spite. "And the doctor says she's been messed with."

The man looked at Hugh Fred. "Do you have medical records to substantiate that?"

"We have, sir," Hugh Fred handed him a piece of paper. While the four of them looked at it, he added, "Dr. Wilkes from Iredell Memorial Hospital has promised to be here by ten."

"Then call your other witnesses until he gets here."

Miss Pauline took her oath and told about finding pieces of paper where Ivy had written "I luv Stevn." That wasn't a surprise to anybody. She and the newspaper had already told the whole state of North Carolina.

Miss Nancy testified about what she'd overheard the doctor say. She also told them that as Sunday school superintendent she felt Uncle Stephen had been distracted of late with "outside activities" and didn't seem to have his mind on "being a proper preacher to this congregation," and that he spent "way more time than he should sittin' under a tree talkin' with Ivy."

I couldn't believe it when Mr. Mayhew took the witness chair next. "Do you know Mr. Whitfield?" Hugh Fred asked.

"*Very* well." Mr. Mayhew's poochy little red lips quivered with importance. "Not only did I used to direct this church choir, but I also teach music up at Mount Vernon Elementary, and Whitfield's niece, Carley Marshall"—Preston elbowed me in the ribs and snickered softly—"was my assistant all last year. She was forever quoting him as an authority."

"And what did Carley say about Mr. Whitfield?"

"That he took Ivy to Winston-Salem all the time. Carley said she wished she could go, but Mr. Whitfield wouldn't permit it. She also said he doesn't think Russians are a threat to this nation, that they are people like anybody else and would like to be our friends. She says he prefers Negroes to white people—"

"I never!" I exclaimed softly. Preston poked me harder.

"Mr. Whitfield's political views are not the issue here," the man in the navy suit objected sharply.

"No, sir, but any man who would corrupt a child living in his own home—who knows what he would do to a young woman who can't defend herself? And I don't know if you know about a trial we had here recently, when a Negro was accused of murdering Mr. Baines? Well—"

"We know about that. Thank you, sir. You may stand down."

"He oughta let Uncle Gil say what he had to say," Preston whispered. "He shouldn'ta cut him off."

"He'd already said enough," I retorted angrily. I couldn't believe Mr. Mayhew had used me against Uncle Stephen. "He knew good and well I couldn't go to Winston-Salem because I had to go to school! He made it sound dirty." I might have said more, except I heard the creak of boards that meant somebody else was coming quietly up the stairs. I jerked Preston and we ducked just in time. Tan pants and brown shoes came right up to our row.

Jay sat down at the far end of our pew, neat and clean in a white shirt. A new tan cap dangled from one hand. He looked startled to see us on the floor, but just gave a little wave and hunched forward to listen to what was going on.

It wasn't much. By then the doctor had gotten there and was mumbling to the men. I couldn't hear a thing until one of them said, "So you are absolutely certain."

"Absolutely." The doctor backed away and sat with Uncle Stephen. That was the nearest seat.

"Mr. Whitfield?" the man in the navy suit asked, "do you have any witnesses?"

Uncle Stephen stood. "Only two people in the world know the truth about this: myself and Ivy Baines. I'd like permission to question Ivy, please."

A buzz of conversation rose from the congregation. I felt my heart sink to my toes. Ivy never said more than one or two words, and usually just repeated whatever people told her to say. If that was the best Uncle Stephen and God could do—

The four men put their heads together. Three kept shaking their heads, and the man in navy kept talking. Finally the short man nodded. "Very well. Ask her to take the chair, please."

Uncle Stephen walked over to where Ivy sat. "Ivy, would you sit up in that chair, please?"

"Okeydokey, Stephen." She was all dressed up in her pink Bicentennial Celebration dress. Her limp brown hair had been curled and stuck out in funny places. Miz Baines had even dabbed lipstick and rouge on her, but she carried her worn-out baby doll.

A ripple of excitement below made me get up on my knees and peer down. Coming down the right side aisle was the most beautiful woman I'd ever seen. Her suit was emerald green linen, with a tiny waist and straight skirt. Her hat was a matching green pillbox, and as she turned into Aunt Hannah's pew, I saw that a short veil with black spots covered the top half of her face, making you want to search through the holes for her eyes. I would never have recognized her except for the baby in her arms.

I was as shocked as if I'd caught Aunt Kate parading in her bathing suit down the street. I'd never known she was so gorgeous. Pretty, yes. But this woman belonged on the cover of a magazine. With a proud tilt to her chin, she ignored the whispers and slid in beside Uncle Davy. Aunt Hannah leaned over and reached for John. Aunt Kate handed him over. Then she gave Uncle Stephen a blinding smile.

He stood five inches taller.

"Ivy, do you know who I am?"

"You Stephen. My friend. I love you, Stephen."

Several people leaned together and whispered, but Uncle Stephen just looked at Ivy. "Tell me, Ivy, where did we go together?"

"Get my legs painted. Blue." She stuck one out and raised her skirt to her knee. "Make me well."

"That's right, they did make you well. What else did we do?"

"Eat ice cream with Abby. I like chocolate."

"And what else?"

She clapped her hands and laughed out loud. "Write. Ivy write!"

He nodded and turned to the men. "I have been teaching Ivy to write a little—Ivy and my daughter Abby. "

Ivy put out a hand and patted Uncle Stephen's arm. "I love you, Stephen."

"I know, Ivy. But tell me, do we do anything else together?"

She looked puzzled, then nodded. "Talk."

"What do we talk about?"

She struggled to remember. "Flowers. I like flowers. Clouds. Pictures in clouds. God. God loves Ivy." She looked up and smiled. "I love you, Stephen."

Uncle Stephen bent over and said gently, "I love you, too, and God loves you. Who else loves you?"

"Mama. Daddy . . . Daddy went away." Her voice trembled.

"He still loves you," Uncle Stephen said gently. "You just can't see him. Now Ivy, have I ever touched you?"

She held out her elbow. "Put me in a car."

"That's right. I help you into the car. Have I ever touched you any other place?"

She reached over and patted her shoulder. "Good girl."

He smiled. "I'd forgotten that. I patted you after you got a shot and didn't cry."

"Good girl," she repeated, nodding and patting herself. She caught her dolly up to her neck and hugged it. "I love you, Stephen."

"I love you, too, Ivy. But have I ever touched you anywhere except on the elbow and the shoulder?"

"I love you, Stephen." She got up, shambled back to her mother and sat down, rubbing her cheek against Miz Baines's bony black shoulder. She took one of her mother's hands and began to play with it in her lap.

Uncle Stephen let out a deep breath as if it was the end of hope, then turned to the table. "If any of you want to ask further questions . . ."

The men put their heads together. They looked as sick as I felt. Ivy hadn't been any sort of witness at all.

The short one spoke for them all. "Let's take a fifteen minute break."

Preston scrunched over and rubbed his head against my shoulder like Ivy was doing to her mother. I pulled away in disgust.

"I seen her get touched," he said slyly.

"You did not!" I didn't mind talking out loud now. The noise downstairs was enough to cover our voices. But I wasn't about to listen to any more insinuations about Uncle Stephen. Now that Aunt Kate was there, I was even considering going down to sit with her, to give Uncle Stephen more moral support.

"Did, too." Preston wiggled his bottom and covered his mouth to snicker. "She was nekkid, and I seen it mor'n once. Last time was t' day before Mr. Ira got his brains knocked out."

"You did not!" I repeated. "Uncle Stephen was at Presbytery all that day."

"It warn't Stevie."

"Don't call him Ste—" I began automatically, then stopped. "Who was it?"

"Ain't gonna tell you."

"You've got to tell!"

"Do not."

"Do too!" I grabbed his hand. I flinched as I touched his warts, but I did not let go. "You've got to go tell the men."

He pulled away. "Do not. I'll get in trouble."

I grabbed him by the shoulders with both my hands and felt the power of Elisha rising within me. Not anger, not vengeance, but a soaring sense of truth. So *that* was how a prophet felt when filled with the Word of the Lord. I put my face close to his and let my eyes blaze deep into the black holes of his pupils. "If you do not tell, the wrath of God will smite you. Bears will eat you, and you will never be able to escape."

He cringed. "I don't wanna!"

"I don't care what you want. Come on!"

I jerked him up and dragged him behind me. Jay moved his knees to let us past, but I didn't even pause to say hello.

Down the stairs we clumped and along the empty left side aisle. Two of the men in dark suits had gone out. The short one was standing looking out a window at the cemetery, like he'd rather be out with the dead than inside with the living. I didn't blame him.

The man in the navy suit was rearranging papers on the table. Thank heavens Miss Pauline and Mr. Mayhew had also gone out. That made it easier to drag Preston right up to the table and thrust him forward. "He's got something to tell you. Something important. He saw somebody touching Ivy."

Startled, the man looked from one of us to the other over the top of his glasses. His eyes were as black as Rowdy's had been. "Is that true, son? Did you see Ivy with a man?"

"I—" Preston sort of choked up and stopped. He clasped his pudgy hands behind him.

I grabbed one thumb and bent it back as far as I could.

"Ow! Stop it, Carley! I'm tellin'! But I ain't gonna say it right out loud in front of everybody. Mama'd kill me."

"Wait, son." The man in the navy suit motioned for the short one to come back to the table. They put their heads together and thumbed through the little book.

The short man read aloud, softly, "All persons of proper age and intelligence are competent witnesses, except such as do not believe in the existence of God or a future state of rewards and punishments." He peered at Preston over his glasses. "Son, do you believe in God?"

"Oh, yessir."

"Do you believe God rewards good behavior and punishes bad?"

Preston threw me a frightened look. I glared back. "Yessir," he squeaked.

They forgot the most important question: whether Preston had proper intelligence.

By then, of course, everybody else inside had seen us. Uncle Stephen and Aunt Kate were standing real close together over near the far side aisle, but they'd stopped talking and were looking right at us. Mr. Hugh Fred had stopped talking to Miss Rilla and was frowning, asking with his eyes what we were doing there. Miss Nancy had her lips all primmed like she wanted everybody to know *her* daughter had gone wherever children were supposed to go. Mr. Wash looked like he wished he was on a roof somewhere.

People started easing our way like those cows in the pasture moving near Roy. The man in navy went right on, speaking very softly. "You saw something related to this case? You actually saw the girl with Mr. Whitfield?" His eyes looked very sad.

"No, sir. But I seen her with *somebody*." Preston was so pink you could scarcely see his freckles. "I can't tell you who, though. Mama'd whup me."

"When was this? Where were you?"

Preston backed up. I knew he didn't want to answer. I grabbed his thumb again and pulled it back. "Ow! Okay, Carley. Stop it. I'll tell." He bent over the table and mumbled, "I was peekin' in the window, over to her house."

"On the Coca-Cola box?" I hazarded. I'd always wondered why Miz Baines had it there.

Preston nodded reluctantly.

The man in navy ignored me. "And you saw her with a man?"

"Yessir. And Ivy was—nekkid."

He'd meant to say it soft, but it's a sharp word, and at that very instant the whole church had gone still. His words reached at least the front pew.

In a blur of black, Miz Baines jumped up and hobbled over on her cane. "What's he sayin'? What's he sayin'?"

The man in navy got up, leaned over, and began, "He saw Ivy in a state of undress—"

"Nekkid." Preston's head bobbed like a cork on water.

Miz Baines grabbed the back of his collar. "Where'd you see a thing like that?"

"In your window."

"Peepin' Tom! Peepin' Tom!" She shook him so hard I thought his head would fall off. "What call you got to be lookin' in my winders at my baby takin' her bath?"

Preston squirmed, trying to get away. "She weren't taking no bath. She was—"

"Maybe we'd better . . ." the man in navy pointed one thumb toward the door, aiming to take Preston into the back hall.

But Miz Baines was still hanging on. She twisted Preston's collar. His face turned puce and his eyes bulged. "Stop it!" he gasped. "Let me go."

"Let him go," the short man ordered, pulling at Miz Baine's clenched hand.

She loosened her grip, but didn't let go. "You got no call to be sayin' things about my Ivy!" She shook him hard. "She ain't done nothin'!"

"She lay there nekkid and let her daddy touch her," Preston roared right out loud. "I saw him. Lotsa times!"

I gasped.

The short man tugged the knot of his tie.

The sanctuary broke out in a buzz of voices. Above them all, Miz Baines screeched, "It's a lie. It's a lie! You got no cause to say that about Ira, 'n' him gone to his eternal reward!"

Preston jerked away from her finally. His face was so red I thought he'd explode like that coal miner, and his voice was hoarse. "Reward nothin'! He ain't gone to heaven for what he was doin'. I seen him. I seen him!" He jumped up and down, pointing his finger at her and shouting.

She raised her cane. "I'll kill you, boy, sayin' things like that!"

"Mama!" Preston shouted. He dashed behind the table. "Don't let her get me!"

Miz Baines rushed toward the table. Preston backed up and

pointed a finger at her like a little prophet Elisha. "She chased Mr. Ira out the door, 'n' she grabbed a stick of firewood . . ." She raised her cane again and tears of terror poured down his flushed cheeks. "Don't let her hit me! Don't let her hit me!"

By now the sanctuary was in uproar. Miss Pauline came thundering down the aisle like a bull after red. The man in navy bravely stepped between the scared fat boy and the heaving witch with her thick black cane. "Now, now—" he began.

He didn't get to finish. Miz Baines started screeching like a banshee and pounding the table with her cane. "Old goat. Rotten old goat. Touchin' and pettin' my baby. I fixed him, 'n' I'll fix you, too, if you talk nasty about my Ivy. I killt that goat and I'm not one speck sorry. Not one speck, no sirree bobtail. So there!"

She left deep ridges in that table that may be there today. Then she threw back her head with its sparse white bun and she started to laugh. It made the back of my neck prickle. I wanted to run, but I was afraid if I moved she'd notice and come after me.

Uncle Stephen hurried toward her. "Gert? Gert! Calm down. Calm down."

She whirled on him and raised her cane again. "You can't take Ivy from me! I done killt Ira when he tried and I'll kill you, too!" She raised her cane to bring it down on his head.

Mr. Wash took two leaps and grabbed the cane from behind. Between them, he and Uncle Stephen held her—barely.

I stood rooted in terror. Miz Baines might get loose any second and kill us all. Her mouth foamed at the corners. Her white hair was streaming down in her eyes. Her face was bright red. Her eyes looked like gray fire. She breathed like a horse who's been running miles. Mr. Wash and Uncle Stephen were hard put to hold her, strong as they were. Uncle Davy went to help.

The small man turned to the man in navy, waving his hands like a washing machine agitator. "What should we do? What should we do?" He was shaking all over, and his high voice sounded like a coop of hens when a cat's around.

"Where's the doctor?" the man in navy demanded loudly.

"Outside getting some fresh air," somebody volunteered from the back. "I'll get him."

The man in navy looked toward Uncle Stephen and asked, "Do you have a telephone in the church?" Seemed to me like Uncle Stephen had his hands too full to be bothered. Miz Baines was twisting and turning like a wild thing.

"There's one in the manse." My words came out more air than sound, but the man in navy heard me.

He nodded toward the short man. "Go call an ambulance—and the police."

We passed the doctor in the crowded aisle, fish swimming through heavy water in opposite directions. I more dragged than led the little man across the tracks. He panted and gasped all the way, but he kept up.

Abby and Rowdy sat on the top porch step. "Hey, Carley. We's home!"

"I see you are, honey, but I can't talk now. We gotta use the phone."

I pointed to it, then collapsed in a dining room chair. The way I was breathing, you'd have thought we'd run all the way from Statesville.

Grace came to the door. "What's goin' on? Is it over?" Her eyes were anxious.

I shook my head. "It's just heated up. Preston saw Miz Baines kill Ira, because he—"

Suddenly I was aware of Abby, standing right by my knee. For the first time in my life, I was the grown-up who didn't want to talk in front of children.

"I can't tell you right now. But can I have a glass of water, please? Better make it two. We got company."

The man came back to say he'd called both the ambulance and the police. We drank our water, then hurried back over the tracks. Abby roared to go too, but I ignored her. By the time we got back, the doctor had given Miz Baines a shot and she was resting in a Sunday school room. At least, that's what Aunt Hannah told me. Softly, because she was sitting beside Ivy with her big hand over Ivy's like she'd sat with me at Jay's trial.

Ivy looked like she could use an anchor. Her eyes were lost like a hurt puppy's. "You seen Mama?" she asked me.

"Your mama is talking to the men," Aunt Hannah reminded her.

"Oh, yeah." Ivy sadly leaned her head against Aunt Hannah's broad shoulder.

I didn't see Miss Pauline or Mr. Mayhew—or Preston, either. It was funny, but I was kind of disappointed. I wanted to make sure Preston was okay. I even hoped I hadn't hurt him when I jerked back his thumb.

People were milling around filling up the aisles and the

front of the church. I wandered around until I got to where the man in navy was asking Uncle Stephen, "Is this gorgeous woman your wife? What'd you do to get her to marry you, hog-tie her?" He sounded relaxed and genial, like he had crazy women and terrified boys jumping around him every day of his life. Uncle Stephen told me later that's called poise.

Uncle Stephen looked at Aunt Kate like he'd just been given a date with Miss America. "Honey, this is John MacClelland, the executive presbyter. He was my preacher when I was called to the ministry."

Aunt Kate gave him her hand. "I feel like I already know you, Stephen has talked so much about you. He even named our son for you." The man held out his arms and John went to him like he'd known him all his life, reaching for his glasses and gurgling happily.

Mr. MacClelland beamed all over. He reached into his pocket and brought out a silver dollar. "John, my granddaddy blessed this and gave it to me new the year I was born. I want you to have it, with my prayer that you'll be a blessing to your family as you grow up."

Uncle Stephen showed it to me later. It was dated 1888.

When they all noticed me, Uncle Stephen pulled me to him in a bear hug. "This is Carley, our niece, whom we couldn't do without." I felt myself turning all shades of red, but I was too worn out to say a word. Besides, I felt all weak and teary.

Under my shoulder, I felt Uncle Stephen trembling, too. We stood there and sort of propped each other up waiting for the people to leave. I wanted to shout, "Why don't you all go home? You've had all the excitement we have to offer this morning."

"Why don't you go back to the door and shake hands with folks?" Mr. MacClelland suggested to Uncle Stephen. "I think people need to speak to you before they go."

He was right. As soon as Uncle Stephen got to the door, people streamed by to shake hands like it was his first Sunday all over again. They kept saying the same things, over and over:

"I never doubted you for a second. Not a second!"

"I'm real glad the way things had turned out—except it's a pity about poor Gert, isn't it?"

"We look forward to seeing you in church next Sunday, Preacher. Had a touch of flu these past few weeks." You'd have thought Job's Corner was the flu capital of the nation.

Preston strutted by like a hero, but Uncle Stephen bent

down and said real soft, "If I ever hear about you peeking in somebody's window again, I personally will wear out your britches. You hear me, boy?"

Preston gulped. "Yessir." It was all I could do not to giggle. But somehow, after that, Preston and I made a truce. Seemed to me he wasn't quite as obnoxious as he'd been in the past. He had to cross the road by himself again, though. Miss Pauline and Mr. Mayhew had gone out before we got to the door. I didn't see her until the next day at the post office, and after that she just pretended nothing had happened.

Wash Lamont came by with Miss Nancy held firmly by one elbow. "Thanks for helping me hold Gert," Uncle Stephen told him. "I owe you one."

"It was a sad situation, Preacher. Hope there's no hard feelings for my motion at Session. I felt we needed bigger guns than us working on this."

"You were right, and you've always been upfront with me. I appreciate that in a man."

Miss Nancy looked miserable. She kept opening and closing her mouth without saying a word, until Uncle Stephen bent to ask, "Did you ever get a chance to go over those Vacation Bible School materials?"

Her head bobbed like a bird pulling a worm. "I sure did, Mr. Whitfield. They look great." She sounded as relieved as the bird looks when the worm finally pops out.

"Let me know when you want to get together to plan."

"I sure will." She reached out and took his hand in both of hers. "I'm so sorry," she said in a little choked voice.

He patted her shoulder. "Hey, God's in the forgiving business. Isn't that great?"

She smiled, her eyes a bit watery. "Sure is, Mr. Whitfield. Sure is."

Uncle Stephen stayed to tell all the Presbytery men good-bye. Last I saw of him he was down at the front of the sanctuary with Mr. Hugh Fred, who said warmly, "Now that that's over, we can get back to business as usual."

I listened, but I didn't hear Uncle Stephen reply.

Aunt Kate was talking to Miss Emily. I heard Miss Emily saying, "I have a lace tablecloth I'd like to give you for when you have Circle meetings at your house. It was my mama's, and I'd be honored if you'd accept it."

Leaving them still talking, I went home alone. I found Abby

standing at the end of our walk scared to death. "De police comed to de church! Did dey take away my daddy?" She pointed.

I whirled to look. Sure enough, a police car was pulled up to the back side door. "Heavens no. Your daddy didn't do a thing wrong. In fact he did something very right. Shall I go help you unpack?"

She bobbed happily beside me up the steps and across the porch. "Know what, Carley? Big Mama iddn't just your Big Mama. She's my Big Mama too. I nebber knowed dat before. My mama was her little girl."

Mama's face seemed to shimmer before me in the dim hall. "So was mine."

Abby put one hand into mine. "Big Mama told me your bad daddy died. Do you want to share my daddy?"

I bent down and gave her a hug. "I'd like that very much. Thank you."

※

"That sure turned out too big for Presbytery to handle," Uncle Stephen said that evening when Abby and John were in bed. He, Aunt Kate, and I were all sitting around the dining room table. They were drinking coffee and I was having hot chocolate—feeling real proud to be there.

He turned to me. "And Kate and I have decided on a new policy around here. Children will be told what's going on, not left to find out by themselves. So what do you want to know?"

I stirred my chocolate to cool it a little. I wanted to know how the world got into such a mess that daddies could hurt their daughters and black people could be denied their Constitutional rights. I wanted to know if the Russians were coming and if we'd be prepared before they got there. I wanted to know what made Mr. Mayhew think he could use me like he did that morning. I wanted to know why I'd had to have a daddy like Roy. But at the moment I was so sleepy, I just had one question. "What's going to happen to Miz Baines and Ivy?"

"I expect both of them will be sent to the state mental hospital over in Raleigh. Hopefully they'll let them share a room." He chuckled. "Now I have a question. Are you going to bed before you fall asleep, or do I have to carry you?"

I stumbled to my feet. "I'm going. Good night."

I did want to know one more thing, though, and I knew I'd

have to find it out for myself: why Aunt Kate came back. When I'd asked earlier, she'd said, "I decided it was time."

So I waited in my room until they went to bed, then I crept downstairs for the last time in my life to listen at their door. I heard her say, "It was partly Mama, talking sense into me. She said, 'Katherine Elaine, just because you're a preacher's wife doesn't mean you have to be a frump. The good Lord made you beautiful for other people to enjoy. Let them. Let Stephen enjoy you, for heaven's sake. He's got enough on his plate without having to look at an unhappy ugly wife.' Then she took me out and blew a month's rent from Pop's farms on enough clothes to last me a lifetime. I can't remember when I enjoyed anything so much." I heard her give a soft chuckle. "Well, yes, I can, but that didn't involve clothes."

He murmured something I couldn't hear, and she laughed again. "But it was really John. I'd look at his eyes, and see yours. I'd wash his feet and see your dear funny toes. I'd try to brush his little bits of hair, and they'd be as unruly as yours. He needs you, Stephen. I need you. And no matter how far I tried to go away from you, if I took John, you'd be there. I love him because I love you. So here I am, if you'll have me back."

That was the first time I ever heard a man sob. It didn't sound a bit sissy.

Is Now and Ever Shall Be

It is almost dawn, and I have finished the last chapter. I creep downstairs and out on the deck in pearly grayness, so caught up in the past that for a moment I am surprised to see my own yard instead of Job's Corner. I sit in my swing and push off with one bare foot. While I swing, I think about all that happened.

Why did Pauline, Nancy, and even Hugh Fred try so hard to get rid of Uncle Stephen? Was it really about Ivy, or was it about Grace and Jay? Did they think if we left, things could go back to the way they'd been? Things would never be the same after 1950—for anybody in the U.S.A. That was the year a lot of people lost not their innocence, but their blinders. Four years later, a Supreme Court decision would merely confirm it.

As I think about those people, now long dead, I remember that moonlit evening when I looked across the road and wondered if people ever got wise before they ended up in the cemetery. I still don't have an answer. But I do see that each of us is a blend of good and bad. And I think old Mr. Whitfield was right: darkness masquerades as light because even evil knows that good is more powerful.

While I watch, light slides toward me from wherever it has spent the night. The morning after Uncle Stephen's trial I got up early, too, and watched this same old sun rise in the east and circle the spire of Bethel Church like a halo. The light shines from the darkness and darkness melts.

This morning's dawn is fiery red, the birds louder than any I have ever heard.

I stop the swing and sit, savoring the moment. Uncle Stephen was right. Nature may fool us into thinking we've subdued her, but it's an act. Every dawn she comes out and roars.

And right down at the core of things there is a goodness, a deep-down splendor, that evil cannot destroy.

But Uncle Stephen was right, too, about our only getting glimpses now and then. As another poet once said, "The world is too much with us, late and soon." When the phone rings, the peace is shattered. Reluctantly I rise and hurry to answer it before it wakes my poor husband, who has endured much from me already these past few weeks.

"When are you going to finish that book?" Abby demands without preamble. "I've been waiting and waiting, and Daddy and John will be home soon and wanting it, too."

I have an impulse to lie, say that it isn't finished. Run upstairs and burn it before it can taint her love for Job's Corner and all its people. But that's not the way life is. Ultimately, we all deserve the truth. And we all must make the journey alone.

"I'll send it out today," I promise. "You'll have it tomorrow. But I wrote it the way it happened. Okay?"

"Of course." She pauses, then demands suspiciously, "You didn't make me talk funny, did you?"

"Me make you talk funny? Why should you think that? Happy reading."

The last sound I hear is an Abby Roar.

Also by Patricia Sprinkle

When Did We Lose Harriet?
Patricia Sprinkle

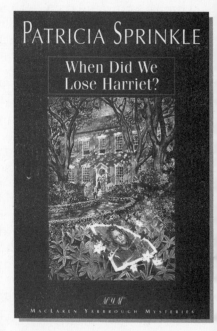

A teenage girl has been missing from her Montgomery, Alabama, home for six weeks. She may be a runaway, a crime victim, or both. What's amazing is other people's lack of concern. Just one person cares she's gone: a spunky amateur sleuth on the sunset end of sixty.

Armed with razor-sharp insight, a salty wit, and tenacious faith, MacLaren Yarbrough follows a trail of mysterious clues in search of answers to questions that come hot and fast and that grow increasingly alarming. How did a fifteen-year-old girl come across a large sum of money? Why did she hide it instead of taking it with her? Where is she now? And who is willing to kill to keep MacLaren from probing too far?

Masked by Dixie charm and the scent of honeysuckle, a deadly secret lies coiled . . . one that holds the ultimate answer to the question, When did we lose Harriet?

Softcover 0-310-21194-4

Pick up a copy today at your local bookstore!

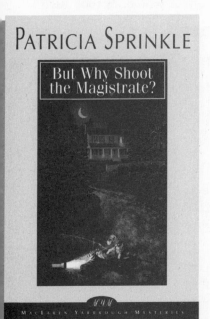

Women Who Do Too Much
How to Stop Doing It All and Start Enjoying Your Life

Are you tired of being all things to all people? Do busyness, guilt, and stress overwhelm you? In *Women Who Do Too Much*, Patricia Sprinkle shows the woman who does too much how to do less. By tackling the larger issues of goals and commitments first, she helps you determine what God created you to do—and helps you to focus on doing just that. In addition she gives tips to help you handle the demands of everyday life—plus exercises at the end of every chapter to help you apply what you learn.

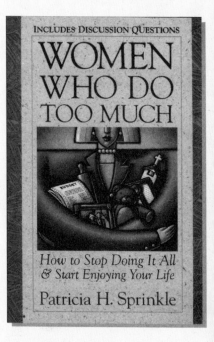

"Who doesn't need help taming the tiger of time? With a warm mixture of practicality and humor, Patricia Sprinkle creatively offers hope for all of us who need to capture, conquer, and control the ever-running hours on the clock. When finished, we see time not as a ferocious animal, but rather as a friend—a precious gift from God."

—June Hunt, Author of
Seeing Yourself Through God's Eyes
Softcover 0-310-53771-1

Pick up a copy today at your local bookstore!

Children Who Do Too Little

Why Your Kids Need to Work Around the House (and How to Get Them to Do It)

Many parents, rather than fighting their children over chores, would rather do the chores themselves. But Patricia Sprinkle argues convincingly and entertainingly that kids need to do chores. They need to develop basic life skills such as cooking and cleaning. They need to learn responsibility and the value of hard work. In short, they need to learn how to become dependable, capable adults.

In *Children Who Do Too Little,* Sprinkle shows why and how parents should teach their children household skills and gives suggestions for making teaching easier.

She discusses:
- ❖ Why we do it all for our children
- ❖ How to handle the child's own room
- ❖ Guidelines for good family meetings
- ❖ Cleaning games to make work fun
- ❖ How to get kids to work
- ❖ The pay-for-work vs. allowance debate
- ❖ Cleaning tips that make life easier

Complete with discussion guide, *Children Who Do Too Little* is a book every parent will benefit from—and every child as well!

Softcover 0-310-21146-8

Pick up a copy today at your local bookstore!